# A Storm Summoned

## BOOK THREE

## J.C. WADE

J.C. WADE ORIGINALS

For Tayt, Jayce and Rhys, my little warriors. Do what is right and let the consequences follow.

# Chapter One

*Perthshire, Scotland*

*Ruthven Keep*

*Early March 1297*

Ewan didn't enjoy lifting a blade against his wife. Nor did he relish in her sore muscles or bruised pride whenever he overpowered her. Indeed, he hated the way her muscles now shook from fatigue and her hands clearly ached from gripping her weapon so tightly. But Ewan also wanted her *alive*, and the best possible way to ensure such an outcome, was for him to train her. Hard. Or as hard as his principles would allow.

The women's solar, where they practiced at swordplay was private enough, with just enough room once the furniture was pushed to the walls. Edyth rarely used the room otherwise, disliking the typical womanly arts that were practiced therein. And with his mother and sisters gone, it was the best place to practice at war out of sight.

Not that he cared whether people saw that he was training his wife. He didn't. In fact, it seemed to him that the more people that knew she could handle a blade, the better her chances of avoiding conflict. The fact of the matter was that it was damned miserable outside and she was four months pregnant. The lists were deep in mud. He would not put her out in the cold in her current condition.

Tired yet determined, she replanted her feet and squared her shoulders. He should end this here and now. He *should* tell her that she was only being stubborn now that her arm shook and her breath came short. But Ewan knew his wife well enough to know that she counted obstinacy as virtue rather than vice. Nor was she prone to stillness. Telling her she should rest was like telling a bird not to fly.

With some effort he ignored her gritted teeth, disregarded the way she shook and flexed her hands after some of the hard blows he'd given her. If he'd been sparring with one of his men, he might encourage them through callous banter. He might comment on how quickly they fatigued, at their weaknesses, and they would rally, redoubling their efforts.

But this was his *wife*. Ewan could only feel concern and a modicum of self-loathing mingled with unabashed pride at her efforts.

Auburn hair clung to her sweaty neck, the color high in her cheeks. Her chemise was nearly wet through with her efforts, the softer places of her body shining pinkly through the fabric. His eyes fell to the small curve of her womb, hidden in billowing fabric, to where their child grew.

"Again," she demanded rather breathlessly, though her eyes shone with determination.

Ewan relented. The memory of recent events was still fresh enough that he could ignore any reservations he felt.

Only three short months had passed since he'd returned home from the highlands, where he'd deposited one Andrew Moray, an escaped prisoner of war, into the capable hands of his brother-in-law, where he could convalesce and gather followers.

Ewan, a sworn vassal to the English King, had secreted Moray away, only to return home to find his world further invaded. He'd learned two startling realities upon his return: one, the appointed sheriff that had plagued their lives since the English fealty pledging ceremony was gone. Dead. Killed by none other than his newly pregnant wife. Every day he thanked God for giving him the foresight to give Edyth that dagger.

The second startling reality was that an English garrison was being built upon their lands. A garrison that would house nigh on three hundred of His Majesty's soldiers. The thought made Ewan's belly turn sour. That sodding, dog-hearted tormentor who called himself their king never ceased to invent new ways to disrupt their lives.

The foundation stones were still being gathered and trees felled even now as a late winter storm bore down on them from the high places. It bit and clawed through wool and fur-lined cloaks to the very meat on a man's bones.

His trees. His land. And there was nothing he could do about it. *At least not openly.*

The only silver lining to the rather dismal storm cloud that was King Edward, was that Ewan was not wholly at the mercy of the English. There were already whispers of rebellion. Already, there were some loyal Scots who resisted the English sheriffs, those who opposed the increased taxes for a war that was not of their own making.

They did not openly fight, of course. Not as yet. They could not do so and live, for no one man could stand against such a foe in open combat and survive. But there were other ways of resisting. And Ewan eagerly awaited his turn.

Not a month past, an English fort had been attacked at night far to the south, leaving naught but a hollow, charred husk behind. Other tales reached him of men that had refused to give up their sons to fight in Flanders. They were dragged to the tower, of course, to rot away even as their sons boarded the ship to the continent, but their refusal was as sweet as any melody to his ears.

There were other whispers. Rumors of a man called Wallace that had openly killed the Sheriff of Lanark and had escaped the King's justice. He hoped it was true, for with each whispered tale of defiance, Ewan's hope grew. He knew that with each fire, each sword buried in the chest of the enemy, the flame of insurrection would spread to other noble houses. They were not alone. *They could fight back.*

He would rather see his own house turned to ash than in the hands of that greedy bastard, Longshanks. Already there were nigh on forty men at arms and craftsmen living in *his* garrison with *his* men. Already there were fights amongst them. Already the tenuous truce between the previous sheriff's men, his own vassals, and newly appointed soldiers and craftsmen threatened to break.

But he would have to do his part in the fight for independence carefully. If he planned on rebelling with Moray and his uncle—and he did—he would be putting his entire household in further danger. Increasing Edyth's ability to defend herself was paramount. Especially now that she was carrying their child.

"Again, Ewan," panted Edyth. "Do not go easy on me; treat me as you would a vassal." Wiping clinging hair from her eyes with her forearm, Edyth reset her feet and readied her blunted short sword, her green eyes intent on him, alive with a fire of which he was sure he would never tire.

Edyth struck quickly, feinting with her sword in an effort to plunge her dirk into his ribs with a quick, upward thrust. Ewan avoided them both, jumping backward and deflecting her sword with a jerking swipe that cost Edyth dearly. Her sword skittered across the floor, the clang of metal overloud in the quiet of the room. It could not be made more plain that her muscles were too fatigued to continue with any of her usual skill, despite her desire to remain.

Edyth's pink mouth was pressed into a thin line. Her eyes danced to the fallen sword, which had come to rest against a wooden chest near the window, then back at Ewan, quick as a flash. He could see her mind working, could sense her desperation. She readjusted her feet and her hold on the knife, her eyes narrowing as she considered her options.

"Yield, Edie."

Edyth shook her head, once, her eyes hard upon him. "I still have my dirk," she said needlessly, moving it to her dominate hand.

"Aye, and I've my sword, with a much better reach. You'd 'ave tae get verra close, indeed, tae harm me with yon wee knife."

Edyth exhaled through her nose distastefully. "What do you recommend I do, then, in a situation such as this?"

"Ye yield. Drop yer dirk and wait til the enemy is close enough afore jabbing him in the kidney with yer sock knife."

She seemed to think about this for a breath then nodded. "Alright. Then by all means, come closer."

Ewan could not help his answering smile, however small. "Drop yer dirk, temptress, and I might."

Edyth canted her head to the side, frowning. A furrow appeared between her eyes. "I am but a small woman. Surely you can take this *wee knife* away from me."

Ewan shook his head, his smile growing. "Ye forget that I'm no' a fool; I ken my adversary far too well. Drop it. Yield tae me." Such a thing did not come easily to her, he knew. He'd be lying if he said he didn't enjoy watching her struggle with the notion.

She shrugged slightly; one shoulder raised in supposed indifference. "If you're afraid of me, then you need only say so."

Ewan laughed. He could not help it. Saints above, but she was lovely. He was just about to open his mouth to retort when the door opened. He moved quickly to stand in front of his wife, whose back was to the door. It mattered little to him that someone discovered them, but he would not expose her as she was, underdressed and slick with sweat.

It was Iain, his younger brother, poking his head through the opened door. "There ye are," he said rather grouchily. "I've been lookin' for ye all o'er the keep. Oh, hello, Edie," he said upon moving fully into the room.

Edyth, for her part, was now covered by her arisaid, her fiery hair spilling from the loosened plait that had held it out of the way of her eyes. She turned to greet him, looking tired despite her insistence to the contrary.

"How goes it," asked Iain. "Have ye bested him yet?"

Edyth sighed in mock despair and pushed at the hair clinging to her cheek. "Almost I had him." She could not quite hide her smile, however, which sullied the effect.

Ewan scoffed. "*Almost*? Almost I had your surrender."

Poking a long finger into Ewan's side, she said, "Never has such a word escaped my lips."

Iain sat on the edge of a table and folded his arms across his chest, a look of consideration on his face. "Mmph. I cannae see Edyth surrendering, even were yer blade pressed against her throat. No, dear sister, the problem is that ye're fighting fair." Iain glanced at his brother briefly, appraising him. "You should let me teach ye some things tae help even the odds a bit more. I've a few secrets yet, that Ewan would no' expect. At least not from the likes of you."

Ewan wanted to say fighting his wife while she wore next to nothing wasn't exactly fighting fair but held his tongue. "What do ye want, Iain?"

His brother's grey eyes swiveled to him, his dark, wavy hair partially obscuring his face. He held up a piece of folded parchment as answer. "A letter has arrived for ye. From the Stewarts. I thought as ye might wish tae read it. The messenger is in the hall, awaiting a response."

Ewan set down his weapons and retrieved the proffered note, the red wax seal as bright as spilled blood. Edyth's and Iain's voices fell away as he read. Alexander Stewart was an ally and had sought for an alliance through marriage with the Ruthvens for years.

First with Ewan and their daughter, Alice. When that failed, they then wished to pair his youngest sister, Cait, to the Stewart widower. But Robert Stewart was far too old for her and had children half grown.

When that intention also failed, they then set their sights on the last unwed Ruthven: Iain. A betrothal Iain was not eager to see put into place. Alice was older than even Ewan and, while not undesirable as a bride, she was quiet and meek and not the sort of lass Iain usually gravitated toward.

Iain's quick tongue and ready smile had drawn lassies the whole of his adolescent life. He had a broken nose as proof of his determination to woo unwilling lassies. No, that wasn't true. Unwilling *fathers*. Iain was not a bad catch, though. He was a noble son, educated and desirable, but Ewan knew of no father who encouraged loose behavior.

Alice Stewart had a large dowry to be sure, but her quiet demeanor and meek attitude toward Iain at the fall festival had his brother dismissing the potential suit. He couldn't blame Iain. Ewan could well remember the monumental effort it had taken to get the lass to speak at dinner when she'd last come.

Ewan frowned slightly as he gazed at the letter in his hand. The Stewart was not inquiring about the potential betrothal. No, it was far, far more serious. He forced his fingers to relax their grip on the edges of the missive and reread the letter again, his eyes darting across the page, his breath arrested.

"What is it?" asked Edyth, coming to stand near his shoulder. He handed her the missive so she could read it herself, his good mood deflated.

"King Edward has sent out convoys gathering men for his war in Flanders. Sir Cressingham has so far taken fifteen lads from clan Livingstone, nine from Bruce, and twenty from Alexander's own lands. The convoy is expected to leave on the morrow and move toward Murray. Alexander writes tae say we will no doubt see them in Perthshire within the month. He offers his home as sanctuary to those we do no' wish tae have taken for King Edward's war in France."

Quiet filled the large space. Color drained from Edyth's face, leaving her wan to the lips. "He means to let us hide our men in Doune? But how could we possibly choose who would go and who would stay?"

Iain swore softly and ran a hand through his shoulder length hair. "King Edward is not content with only taking Wales and Scotland. He would still try to wrest France from Phillipe."

Ewan knew this. He'd fought in France for two long years before coming home upon his father's death. "Of course," said Ewan, not quite hiding his contempt. "Why send English sons tae die when he now has the whole of Scotland at his disposal? Better we die than sassenachs."

Edyth clutched his arm, her worry evident in the lines on her face. "Are you in danger of being taken? Or Iain?"

Ewan shook his head. "No. We are landowners and protectors of the realm. It will be our soldiers and our green lads they'll have an eye for."

Edyth's grip on his arm tightened marginally. "You will send them away to Doune, won't you, Ewan?"

Ewan looked to Iain, who knew what this choice would cost. The Stewart would want the marriage contract of Alice and Iain to be fulfilled after such a gesture. He would not do it for nothing.

"The choice is yours," said Ewan softly to his brother, and he meant it. He would come up with another way...send the young lads into the high places, even in such weather, instead of to the Stewart lands.

"It's one thing to conscript soldiers," continued Edyth, "and quite another to take young boys into war who have no hope of survival."

Ewan patted her hand that was still wrapped like a vice around his bicep as he studied Iain. "Aye, and Cressingham willnae care which he takes, sae long as he has warm bodies tae present to the King. Hiding the younger lads of clan Ruthven with the Stewarts would be ideal." He sent his wife a look of regret. "Still, we must consider all our options."

Iain, looking grim, said, "Aye, taking them awa' would be ideal if it came at no cost. But we both ken Alexander Stewart tae be as canny and as ruthless as any other son of Scotland. He seeks my agreement of marriage tae his mute, stodgy daughter." He scowled. "I dinnae trust anything that man says or does."

Ewan ignored Edyth's disapproving look at Iain's hasty remarks regarding the lady. "Aye," he acknowledged wryly. "He willnae do such a thing for nothing, but as I say, the choice is yers. Ye needn't agree to this marriage."

Iain's scoff could have parted the red sea. "Och aye, and drive a wedge between our clans as wide as the Firth?" He shook his head. "Da would no' give me such a choice." He pressed his lips together briefly, his eyes dark with thought. "No, Ewan," he said after some inward deliberation, "tis only fitting I shoulder this burden. Besides, our Cait would n'er let me live in peace, should I escape what she couldnae."

While it was true that Ewan had married his unwilling sister, Cait, off to the Thane of Nairn, it was different with Iain.

Yes, Cait had contested. Yes, she'd begged him to hold off, but he'd wanted her away from the mounting trouble in Midlothian. He wanted her safe, far from Edward's reach. Not that he'd succeeded. She now housed the convicted traitor, Andrew Moray, within her walls. If the English found out about Moray, Cait would most certainly lose much.

Iain was different. He was born into the role of a soldier. A second son; a man hewn into a fleshy weapon. He *should* be here to help Ewan prepare for the coming storm. Ewan had plans for Iain. It was he who would play the role of loyal English vassal once Ewan's treason was known.

It was Iain who would denounce Ewan's actions and, God willing, claim the title of Earl of Perthshire to keep their family's lands intact. And, if Ewan ended up in the tower or dead, it was Iain who would then care for Edyth. And their child, he reminded himself.

"You will take them yourself?" Edyth asked Iain, yanking Ewan's attention back to the present.

"Aye." Iain's usually jovial, sparkling eyes turned dark and serious. "And with our signatures upon the contract of marriage." He forced a smile that did not reach his eyes. "I might as well not make two trips, aye?"

Edyth squeezed Ewan's arm, a soft sound of surprise escaping her. "You will marry her when you find such fault with her?"

"What does it matter?" asked Iain, though Ewan could see the discontent in the lines of his body, in the set of his mouth. "I will do it if it means saving sons of Perthshire. We cannae leave our lads tae that bastart, Cressingham. I must go. It's no' all bad," he added differentially. "Ye ken what they say, it's better tae bed with the de'il ye ken than with one ye dinnae. It wouldn't surprise me if faither wished tae keep the alliance between our clans just sae he would be privy tae what that scunner, Alexander was up to."

"But," sputtered Edyth, her eyes full of regret. "It hardly seems fair. For either of you."

"What is fairness, sister, in such circumstances? Would that King Edward had the heart o' a woman, for we would live in peace all our days."

# Chapter Two

Edyth sighed as her maid, Gelis, poured hot water into the basin. Her shared chamber with Ewan was large and while comfortably appointed, was drafty. The brazier was not quite large enough to warm the whole of the space, and with the chill of winter still clinging resolutely to them, it was almost unbearable, but she sorely needed bathing.

Her stomach growled as she washed herself. She was past the sickness and the aversions to food that had plagued her for weeks. Now it seemed as if she couldn't get enough to eat. She smiled softly as she recalled eating an entire crock of preserved plums with bannocks at the nooning meal yesterday. Ewan had not said a word, only given her his share of bread and refilled her cup each time she'd emptied it.

Gelis mumbled under her breath at the state of Edyth's chemise, pulling her thoughts to the present, which was wet through with sweat. She, herself, was no longer red faced from her sparing session with Ewan and a chill had started to settle in her bones, making her shiver uncontrollably. "...unfit... should be resting instead of gallivanting about. I'm of a mind tae say sommat to him, I am."

Edyth smiled as she dipped the rag into the basin. "Your master means well, Gelis," she said, glancing at her maid. Gelis was older, stooped in such a way that spoke of a lifetime of labor, but she was sturdy and gruffly kind, reminding Edyth of her childhood maid, Mira. "He only means to teach me how to protect myself more fully."

Gelis' lips fell into a flat line, showing her displeasure. "And ye with child. It's no' my place tae say, but if Himself's mother were here, she would put a stop tae such goings on, and no mistake."

No, it wasn't her place to say, but Edyth took the maid's griping in stride. "I wish for him to teach me, Gelis. With child or not, I will not be at the mercy of cruelty." *Never again.* Edyth was not a violent person. She did not have vast experience with fighting, but her father had no sons and so she'd been taught *some* things.

It was fortunate, indeed, that he'd sought such an education for her, for thrice now she'd killed men. Each time she'd saved her own or another's life. And each time she'd been lucky. But luck would not hold out forever. Besides, Edyth could feel that something was coming. She knew it in her bones. Violence would come on swift wings and, this time, she would to be ready.

As Edyth wiped down her chilled body with the cloth, Gelis readied her new clothes, laying them out upon the bed. "Will it be the red or the blue hose, milady?"

Edyth scrubbed her face then her neck, canting her head to see what Gelis held aloft. "The red, I think."

Gelis hummed softly to herself as she worked, gathering soiled clothing for the laundresses. Edyth's mind caught hold of the woman's family, which all lived together in one of the larger crofts at the edge of the river. "Gelis," asked Edyth rather tentatively, "how old are your grandsons now?"

Gelis did not pause as she unrolled the red hose and laid them next to the clean chemise and green gown. "Arran is six and ten, Bran no' yet four and ten. Why?"

Edyth re-dipped the rag into the basin, the steaming water warming her chilled fingers instantly. "Hugh Cressingham has recently left Stewart lands."

"More taxes for King Edward," said Gelis with a shake of her head. "He won't be too far off from Perthshire, then. Himself best tighten his purses, I say."

Edyth, feeling unaccountably anxious, quit her bathing and faced her maid. Should she say something? Haps she should leave such news to her husband, but she'd just recently found a place here, amongst the clan's people. Only now was she starting to be accepted. She counted Gelis as a friend. Could she keep such a thing from her?

Deciding quickly she said, "Yes, Gelis, taxes. But that is not all. Cressingham seeks more than coin. He conscripts Scotland's sons to fight in Flanders."

Gelis paused in her ministrations, the slippers she was holding clutched in venous hands. "Conscription." The word was a mere whisper, a breath of apprehension, a terror for all.

Edyth nodded and ignored the cold; the dripping rag held tightly in her aching hands pattered water onto the floor. "Ewan is sending men of such an age to the Stewarts, to avoid such an outcome. He would send your grandsons away, I am sure. They are not warriors, trained to fight."

Gelis seemed to sway on her feet slightly, her eyes unfocused. "A—aye, milady. That is good o' Himself. Aye. That is good. I thank ye, mistress, for tellin' me. I'll warn my son."

Edyth watched as Gelis crossed herself, feeling better for telling her. She, herself, would want to know. She would want time to prepare the boys. Time to say goodbye. With so much uncertainty in the world, time with loved ones was all that mattered.

"Yes, we must be ready, Gelis. We must look for Cressingham and his solders on the roads and keep our young ones safe."

Gelis swallowed heavily and nodded. "Aye, mistress. Now, let's get ye intae sommat warm. Ye shouldnae be shiverin' as ye are."

*Nairn, Scotland*

  *Cawdor Keep*

Mistress Caitronia Ruthven, now Cawdor, stared out the lancet
window into the dark night. The wind coming off the sea was as the roar
of a great beast. It beat upon the shutters and doors, whistled through the
cracks of their stone keep, to seep and settle into her bones. The torches
sputtered, faltering in the gust, making shadows dance and writhe.

She could not see the waves, but she could hear them just under the
gusting gale. A relentless pounding that aggravated her restlessness. It
had been weeks since she'd been out of doors or felt the sun on her face.

The men behind her, seated around one of the tables in the great hall
did not seem to notice the cold. She didn't know how. Stubbornness,
perhaps. Or maybe it was as William had said: her blood would thicken
in time. It would not seem so bitter cold then. How long would that
take? Winter seemed never ending here, in the far north of their island,
and it was only March. Winter would linger for weeks still.

Nairn was boldly set upon the rocky outcroppings that met the North
Sea, with no forests of trees to block the incessant wind. It seemed
impossible the keep did not crumble and decay from the salty air that
clung to its surface.

William had told her that his people were resilient. When she'd asked
him why he'd chosen her as a wife, he'd said that he'd needed a woman
grown. One that knew her mind; a wife that did not balk at life's
difficulties.

At the time, she took it as a complement that he viewed her in such a
light, for that is how she wished to view herself. Now, though, she wasn't
so sure of herself. Was she the woman she'd thought she'd been, back
in the safety of her uncle's castle, surrounded by trees and embraced in

the safety the hills provided? Here she could only feel exposed, cold and afraid.

She was not afraid of her husband or his people. They were as he'd said: kind and hard working. They'd accepted her as their mistress with the upmost felicity. But no matter how kind, she still missed her own people and her own land. Mountains and rivers and forests seemed a very far way off here, in Nairn.

William had warned her that Nairn was a hard living and she'd believed him. But nothing had prepared her for the actual effort required. Enduring the darkest of nights with the wind's ceaseless howling. And the cold. She could not describe it, so pervasive and lasting it was.

Here, there was only sand and oatgrass, beautiful but stark, and a weak protection against the ocean's onslaught. Some days she did not know herself. Today was one such day. She felt awash in the political dangers that lived within the walls of her new home. What could possibly hide them here, out in the open?

This home was filled with warring men. Free men who would not be ruled. Plotting men that expected much from her new household. She might laugh at the circumstances were they not so serious. She, as a lass, had been forever listening at doors and begging her brothers for news. Begging to be included in the politics of the day. Now she was awash in treasonous plots and held traitors in her hall. Now she longed for days of ignorance.

Of course her own people did not wish to be ruled by a foreign king no more than these presently debating when and where to strike out. But here, now, it was different, for she knew that soon enough, talk would turn to action. Were any of them ready?

Cait closed the wooden shutters tightly, her fingers slipping on the dewy surface of the latch, her mind lingering on home. She missed the orchard that overlooked the keep and the winding river. Those trees that had held her all her life, grown up around her, and watched as she'd turned her back to them in leaving.

Cait mentally shook herself. It would not do, this ceaseless longing for something she could not have. This was her home now. It had its own beauties. The people were strong, just as William had said. No matter how the wind and rain beat upon them, they did not bend to it. Hers was a life filled with intrigue and sedition, a life she had thought would feel adventurous.

"Now is the time to strike!" one man insisted, his hand pounding on the table. "William Wallace has killed Lanark's sheriff. He gathers followers in Selkirk day by day. We would do well to show our alliance to his cause and follow suit."

Another man snorted "Follow his cause, ye say? You'd have the burgesses follow a lowlander? They willnae do it. It must be a highlander that calls for action, or they willnae have any part o' it."

"It matters little tae me who this Wallace is, so long as he continues his fight against England," intoned her husband. "We cannae win against the English and only the burgesses are behind us. We need all the swords we can muster."

"Aye," agreed Andrew Moray, his dark, introspective eyes roving over the huddle of men. He was still thin after his imprisonment in Chester Castle, but the sallowness of his skin had turned to pink. His voice was strong now, without a waver, nor were his eyes glassy with fever. Upon their meeting, Cait had worried her brother's effort in helping his escape would be for naught. She would wake each morning with the expectation of finding him lifeless in his bed, but he'd proved her wrong.

"Let us regard this Wallace as a friend," continued Moray. "Dinnae discount him so readily, MacDuff. Anyone who openly wages war against King Edward should be counted as a friend."

MacDuff, a balding ox of a man nodded in a way that reminded Cait of her horse whenever she greeted her. "Aye, a friend, but no' our leader. Most lowlanders are sae embroiled in English politics, they cannae even see the bars o' the cage Edward holds them in. Should we set them free, they would damn us for it. The burgesses willnae follow such a man."

There were several introspective noises at this comment mingled with a few grunts of disagreement. Cait went to the table and retrieved the empty tray the maid had brought in earlier, wishing to be free from such talk. "Can I get ye aught else from the kitchens?" she asked.

William's soft smile lifted her melancholy heart slightly. She did like her husband. Very much. He was her sun in this endless winter. "No' just the now, *mo ghaol*," he said, his blue eyes speculative. He stared at her as though he were trying to read her very thoughts, his arms crossed over his jerkined chest. "MacDuff thinks few lowlanders will follow this Wallace rebel. He fears that most will side with Longshanks. I would hear your thoughts on the matter, having grown up sae close to the borderlands. Yer family is allied with several lowlanders, are they no'?"

Cait, uncomfortable, studied the occupants at the table briefly before placing an empty horn cup on the tray. Being asked such a question in front of such important men made her vastly uneasy. Did William truly wish her to speak in front of all these men? What did they care what she thought on the matter? Still, she would not shrink from them.

"I think it would be a foolish man indeed who would make enemies out of potential friends. What does it matter where he lives? He is a Scot, is he no'?"

A few of the men pounded the table, grumbling their agreement. "Smart lass," said one rather large man closest to her. His beard was so thick, she could not discern a mouth at all.

"As far as lowlanders choosing England," continued, Cait, "I cannae say. With so many o' the great men imprisoned in the Tower, those left in power might well choose safety over freedom." She licked her dry lips, thinking of her uncle and her brothers, of her sister Aldythe, married to a man in the Lindsay clan. "But not all will choose England. There are still some noblemen left who would rather fight and die, than to live under such a king. And there are others who simply dinnae ken which way tae turn. They only lack the courage tae stand alone. These would follow Wallace if they saw that he had numbers behind him."

"Ye've got one with brains, I see, William," said another man, nodding his agreement. "If we show our support, more will follow. It's the number o' men that matter tae these sort o' men, no' the leader."

"Mmph," grunted another man. "Even the lassie can see the benefit o' aligning with Wallace." He pinned a gimlet eye on MacDuff, who looked rather red in the face.

The heavily bearded man at her elbow sat back in his chair, openly appraising her. "What manner of war would ye wage against England, Lady?"

Here Cait faltered. She did not relish in the idea of war, nor did she have the slightest notion of strategy, but she had the experience of being misjudged and discounted. She was a woman, after all. A second-class citizen with few privileges and even fewer rights. England no doubt viewed Scotland in much the same way. Something to own and repress. A nation unshielded and too weak to fight back against the stronger foe.

Pursing her lips slightly in thought, Cait considered her words carefully before speaking. "I cannae speak o' war, sir. I only ken that it must happen, or we will be bound forever tae a king not of our making. We will be Scotsmen no longer, but Englishmen." She paused to curtsey her goodbye, but stopped herself, recalling a memory from her childhood.

She looked over the men, biting her lip. "Do ye mind how fish congregate in the shallow, warm pools o' a river, away from the current tae bathe in the sun? I spent many an hour down in these same pools and I noticed something about how they lived. A small fish might attack a larger fish resting in these pools by easing their way in the shadows until they were close enough tae strike.

"When the smaller fish was close it enough, it would dart forward and strike the delicate, vital parts of the larger fish. The gills or the fins, mostly. But these wee, aggressive fish wouldnae linger and risk being eaten. Instead, they would dart away and hide in wait until the larger fish grew comfortable again. This would happen over and over, until the larger fish's fins were torn beyond use or until they gave up their place and left the shallows for deeper parts of the river."

Cait's words were met with a ringing silence that made her feel as if she'd shared too much. In an effort to hide her embarrassment, she quickly gathered the remaining cups nearest her. She felt a fool. She shouldn't have spoken so openly about a subject she had no real understanding of.

William ran a hand over his beard, the color of dark honey in the low light. "Aye, I take yer meaning, but isn't that just what's been happening all over the lowlands? English forts 'ave been sacked, routed and burned and the English havenae caught anyone. At least no' yet. Still, England has not quit her place here amongst us."

Cait inclined her head, acknowledging his words, wishing the earth would swallow her whole. But William and the other men were still looking at her expectantly, appraising her. She took a deep breath, clenching the tray tightly. She would not show them her insecurities, so with courage she did not really feel, she said, "Aye, that's what has been done. But with sae few of us striking, it will take a long time indeed, for any real, lasting damage tae take place. King Edward is a mighty fish, indeed. He must feel the pain of it afore we can gain any ground."

One man grunted, a frown of introspection written on his face, while other men's eyes roved around the circle, each speaking a secret language Cait could not decipher. She ignored these men and looked to her husband.

"My wife is as wise as she is beautiful, is she no'? It's as she says, the wee fish must congregate, or we'll be eaten by the beast that lingers in our shores."

The Moray leaned forward, his eyes sparking with purpose. "Abhainn, get ye word tae this Wallace and let him ken we wish tae align ourselves with him, should he accept us. Ranald, call a meeting with the burgesses o' the north. We must strategize together and coordinate our next move."

"It's too early," warned a man at the far side of the table. "We mun speak tae the burgesses afore we announce ourselves untied with Wallace. We cannae raise the standard until we ken their minds."

"The burgesses will come tae us, once Moray makes his intentions known," argued another man.

"Aye, they will," agreed Moray, a stubborn set to his whiskered chin. "Now it is up tae us tae help the cause along. Let us plan where we will strike first. We cannae let Wallace do all the work. We have much we can do here, in the north country."

Next came a volley of ideas, disagreements and dissentions that made Cait's head spin.

Finally, having heard quite enough, Moray shouted over the din: "We cannae attack as the English do, with ranks o' soldiers and war engines." The room quieted immediately. He lowered his voice, looking to each face as if explaining himself to a small child. "We mun strike fast and hard in the dead of night. Take castles that the English have stolen awa' and burn them tae the ground. It would better that no one hold them o'er the English. We cannae let them have a hole in which tae hide."

Cait did not linger. Her wame unsettled, she took the tray of cups and left, unheeded by all. How was she to prepare for what was to come? When William had shown up with a dying Moray, the way forward had been obvious and morally necessary to her mind. How could she turn him away, even had she wished to?

And even now, despite her deep desire to be free from the English thumb that was now so painfully suffocating her family, it was quite another thing to plan for and participate in the violence that would free them. At some point talk would turn to action and William would leave. She would wait, her heart in her throat, until his return. And it would not just be one occasion, but many, until he died or they were free.

And not only would she have need to worry over her husband, but also her brothers. The thought of any of them suffering or dying by the sword sent a lance through her heart. How was she to go forward? How could she sit and wait? She was not strong enough. She could not do what was expected of her. Tears stung the back of her throat but she hastily swallowed them away. Tears were useless things; she would not fall prey to self-pity.

They had to fight lest their country be stolen away by a ruthless king. And with that violence would come the eventual freedom they craved, or their own deaths through treason. Either way, the cost was dear. She could not say if any of them were ready.

# Chapter Three

E wan walked the length of the forest where his timber was being harvested. Rory, his captain, was with him. Ewan glanced at Rory's injured right hand—his sword hand—now curled in a woolen glove, weak and mostly impotent. The sight of it stirred Ewan's ire, making him wish, yet again, that he could have been the one to kill the malicious sheriff, Bladwin de Biggar. Rory had sustained the injury from the sheriff whilst Ewan was away helping Andrew Moray escape into the highlands. A punishment for Rory's insolence. Torture for his loyalty to Ewan.

Dozens upon dozens of his trees had been felled, pulled by oxen to the foundation site. An ugly scar gouged into the once pastoral hillside, bisecting it, to where the timber had been dragged. The frozen mud was covered in icy snow, pitting the earth in dangerous, ankle-turning ruts. The timber sat in piles in the middle of one of his hay fields, waiting for the foundation stones to be laid. Amid the churned turf, broken twigs and scraps of bark made the walk all the more difficult.

"Ye may have no forest left after they're through," said Rory gruffly, kicking at a frozen pile of ox dung in their path. "Not even the weather has slowed them much."

Ewan tamped down his anger. The shape of his entire world was changing, landscape included. He let out a breath, swallowing bitter words. They billowed out on a breath and hung in the air between them. The wind had died down well enough to leave the gutted forest eerily noiseless. "Did the first set o' lads leave today tae Stewart as we discussed?"

"Aye" Rory quipped. "All without tears, save from some o' the mothers." At Ewan's inquisitive look, he continued, "Their tears were for the lads that were left behind. They dinnae wish tae have their own sons taken tae die in the name o' Edward. And there is the risk, always, of danger upon the roads."

Ewan could not blame them. "Aye. When Cressingham comes, he will take what he will, mother's tears be damned." He could only pray now that Cressingham did not encounter his people on their way to Doune.

They'd had to go canny here, as well, as the previous sheriff, de Biggar, still had loyal men in Perthshire who might take notice of any garrison beds suddenly being free. They'd chosen mostly younger lads, whose absence would likely go unnoticed, but they had also chosen three of their favored knights to go with them. It would not do to lose some of their best fighting men to King Edward.

"The others await your word on when they should leave."

Ewan nodded. They'd chosen to send them in two separate groups, so as to not call attention to themselves. A large party, travelling together, would require explanation. It was best for all if their absence wasn't noticed by anyone, of course, but if they *were* seen, they were to say they had gone on a hunt, which could take weeks. Plenty of time, he hoped, to be reasonably excused by Cressingham.

"When d'ye expect 'im? Cressingham, I mean."

Ewan rotated his injured shoulder, which always bothered him more in the cold and shook his head. "I cannae say. Soon. Within a fortnight, I'd wager."

"Mmph," grunted the captain. "Any news o' Graham?"

"None," said Ewan, stepping over a stump. Months ago, when he and two of his loyal retainers, Fingal and Graham, had ventured into England to help Andrew Moray escape Chester Castle, they'd come upon some bad luck. Moray's escape had not gone unnoticed, and in an effort to lead the guardsmen away from the escapee, Fingal and Graham had scattered to draw them away, leaving Ewan with the task of bringing the prisoner to the docks, where they had eventually boarded a ship.

Ewan had waited, his heart in his throat, for the sun to fully rise and for the ship to be readied. Fingal had made it back just in time, but the captain of the ship had waited as long as he was willing; in the end, they'd had to leave Graham behind, with no idea of what had happened to him.

"I've written tae my uncle, tae see if his contacts have heard o' what might have happened." Ewan had hope, though. If Graham had been captured, he would most likely have been imprisoned there at Chester and, if such a thing had transpired, Ewan would have heard of it by now. "My uncle willnae waste time in telling me should he gather any intelligence."

Rory grunted in reply, bending over to inspect a satchel that had been left out in the forest by one of the workers. They were all in the keep now, enjoying a midday meal. The sack jangled when he lifted it, ringing through the clearing. "Only chisels," muttered Rory, letting it fall back to the forest floor with a clatter. A bird erupted from a holly nearby, the noise jarring it into flight.

Ewan followed the bird's path with his eyes through the forest until he caught hold of something suspicious nestled between two craggy granite boulders a fair distance away. From where they stood, it appeared to be a rather lumpy mass hidden by a sizable stretch of greying canvas. It was tucked into the base of the rocks, where he knew a small cavity naturally formed. A good hiding spot for something one wished left unnoticed and untouched.

The object, whatever it was, was large enough to warrant his attention. Such a thing would be expected, perhaps, out in this forest. Supplies. Tools. But Rory and Ewan had not ventured out into his ruined wood to merely stretch their legs. No, they were looking for something in particular. Something that had been taken from the household in secret.

Edyth, who had tasked some servants in the kitchens with inventory, reported that some goods were missing. A hogshead of ale, a crate full of bottled cider, and, more troubling, several bolts of delicate wool fabric, spun and woven to Edyth's specifications by some talented women in the village. The latter was by far the most expensive of the items that had disappeared. They'd hoped to sell them in Edinburgh where they could garner a hefty sum.

Haps some wandering soul had decided to take what didn't belong to them with the same hope? "Do ye see that?" asked Ewan, not waiting for a response. He moved forward with purpose, his suspicions growing with each step. It was the right size and shape. "Cut the ropes on that side," directed Ewan. He did not want to ask if Rory could, seeing as how the man was already sensitive about his hand being injured. It would be best if he simply allowed Rory to believe it was expected of him. Haps, with time, he would expect more from himself as well.

Ewan watched surreptitiously as Rory fumbled with his dirk, his stiff hand struggling to grasp the handle of his weapon with any strength. Ewan took his own time, not wishing to make Rory feel hurried, and was rewarded when his captain sliced through the stiff rope holding the canvas down with a small gasp of pain. Ewan repressed the desire to ask after him, not wishing shame him.

Together they pulled the covering away to reveal crates and bundles aplenty. "There's a sight more than tools here," observed Rory gruffly, lifting the lid of a crate to reveal the missing bottles of cider.

"And here is some of the household silver," groused Ewan, lifting a tureen and a platter. "I didn't even ken it was missing."

Rory lifted another crate's lid to reveal the bolts of fabric nestled within. "Looks as if yer ladyship was right about inventorying the stores. Shall I get some lads from the keep tae cart all this back?"

Ewan shook his head, calculating the potential cost of selling these stolen goods. "No," he answered with finality. "We leave it here. It willnae do us any good to take it back and not know who it is that's been lifting from our stores."

"Ye mean tae hide and watch?"

"Aye," Ewan answered. "Though I think I have a good idea who it is that's been stealing from me. De Biggar's boys," finished Ewan at Rory's lifted brow. "They werenae so keen on leaving the alehouse for the garrison. And with no new sheriff here as yet tae mind them, they would be eager to get back at me for past slights. Can ye think of another who would steal from me?"

"Mmph," grunted Rory noncommittedly, pulling his corner of canvas back over the stolen property. "Ye could be right. De Biggar wouldnae have minded a bit o' theft; haps his men feel the same."

Ewan knew they didn't. They'd caught the sheriff thieving from his people not long before his death right alongside his men. "He was a slippery wee eel, Sheriff de Biggar. I'm no' sorry he's dead."

"Aye. We can agree on that."

"Let's get another man or two and set up for the night over there," motioned Ewan. There was a thicket of evergreen bushes, mostly holly and juniper just over the rise, where they could easily view the scene without being seen themselves. "Haps we can put someone else in the trees further down the path. That way they can signal tae us when someone comes."

Rory grunted, looking at his injured hand briefly. "As ye say."

Ewan hoped it *was* de Biggar's faithful foot soldiers that had been stealing from him. There were only six of them left and they were the ones who caused the brunt of the discord within the garrison. How satisfying it would be to run them all through. He'd wanted to do it months ago but had feared retribution from de Warenne.

"Let's make haste, lest they return tonight."

Unfortunately for Ewan and his chosen guards set to keep watch, the thieves had not made their appearance for an entire fortnight. He had his men and been taking it in turns to sit in the cold through the night, waiting for their chance to catch them in the act to no avail.

He was growing weary with the sleepless nights and the ever-present concern of Cressingham's inevitable appearance, so it was with some relief that Ewan's scout had come back with news, his bonnet dusted heavily with snow.

Cressingham's men were coming with wagons, sturdily fortified to keep men detained and a host of heavily armored men and horses. Two of the barred wagons were full of shivering men, many not yet even old enough to shave. They huddled together, covered in plaids and cloaks, their lips chapped from wind and cold.

"They've split off in twa groups," explained his scout. "Cressingham is with the larger of the parties, somewhere south of the Caimbel lands by now. It seems that the smaller of the company is making their way toward us."

Per his scout, some were not constrained into the wagons, but walked behind in a long line. These were the best dressed of the lot, with heavy, fur-lined boots and winter cloaks to keep them warm. They did not look any happier to be prodded along by their taskmasters than those bound in a cage, but at least they had the freedom of movement given to them. None had weapons of their own, of course. It would not do to have a revolt break out on the road to Edinburgh.

Ewan thanked his scout and sent his squire, Alec, to fetch Iain and his captain. Cressingham was not yet near Perthshire, thankfully, but their time was running short. It was time to send the next group of lads to the Stewart lands.

Ewan stifled a yawn. Himself, Iain, Rory and Fingal had been taking it in turns to hide in wait each night for the thieves to make themselves known to them. Nothing as yet had happened, aside from a few more items being added to the cache, all without their witnessing it happen. How were they doing it unseen and undetected? It irritated him to no end.

Iain was the first to arrive, alive with animation. His heavy winter cloak was wet on the shoulders, his cheeks and nose pink from the bracing wind. "Brother, I've good news. Inan and Johnne have learned some valuable information about your little problem."

"Of which problem do ye speak, Iain, for I'm tormented by several at the moment."

Iain removed his grey cloak with a flourish and sat upon the edge of Ewan's desk, reaching for Ewan's cup of ale. "Why o' the thieves in the wood, o'course."

"Thank God," sighed Ewan. "I'm growing tired of hiding in the holly for naught."

"It will be tonight," said Iain cheerfully, then frowned into the empty cup set upon Ewan's desk. "The lads caught wind o' it whilst gambling at the alehouse last night. They were discrete," promised Iain at Ewan's unspoken question. "They paid one o' the maids within the alehouse tae listen outside of their private room. They will move the items tonight."

"You're sure?" asked Ewan, not quite able to quash the bubble of hope that sprang to life within him. His feelings toward the thieves had only grown in the past weeks as he'd waited in the bitter cold. Especially since another of his retainers complained of de Biggar's men causing discord amongst his ranks.

Iain shrugged in his usual amicable fashion and looked about the room. "Does it matter if it's true? One of us will have to be out there in the cold regardless. Have ye aught else to eat or drink, Ewan? I missed the nooning meal."

Ewan shook his head. "Why did ye no' eat?" But Iain only grinned in a wicked way. "Never ye mind, Iain. I dinnae wish tae know." Then thinking better of it, Ewan added, "Will I be hearing from an angry father regarding his daughter's loose behavior come tomorrow? God's teeth, Iain. Cannae ye see I've got enough tae get on with?"

But Iain did not get a chance to reply, for Rory entered then, pulling their attention. "What news?"

Ewan spared no time in telling them both of what his scout had reported. "Cressingham will be here in Perth verra soon. Three or four days at the least. We need to move the next group of lads out today."

Ewan saw Iain's good mood deflate instantly; his time in Perth had come to an end. Iain would have to escort the group of lads to Stewart himself.

"Take some o' the hounds to lend credence to our hunting lie, should any of the king's men question your leaving," commanded Ewan. Iain nodded, but looked rather pale, and dutifully shared his own news with Rory regarding the thieves, though with much less cheer.

"Let's plan our attack then," said Ewan, motioning for Rory to come closer. He laid a ledger upon the desk as well as an empty scroll of parchment. "Here is a list of the missing stores Lady Edyth has provided." Ewan scrounged around for a quill and ink, muttering orders to Rory.

"Get ye word tae Inan and Johnne. I want them tae be lookouts when we do this. I'd hate tae be caught unaware." Ewan unrolled the parchment, which had a rough-drawn map of his lands. Iain stepped closer, following the lines of forest, field, and river in relation to the keep with his eyes.

"Shouldn't you be getting ready?" asked Ewan, pausing in his instructions to Rory about placement of men.

Iain met his brother's expectant eyes. "I can help," he said, his voice gruff.

"Aye ye can," Ewan said with feeling, "but I need ye tae take the wee lads beyond our borders. I want ye gone within the hour."

"Within the hour?" Iain asked, indignant. The brothers stared at each other for a long moment, Ewan lifting a sardonic brow that made Iain grumble. Iain's shoulders slumped before pushing away from the desk and gathering his cloak about his solid frame. "Aye, as ye say," he said, sounding unhappy about the entire business.

Ewan opened the small chest on his desk and pulled out a prepared letter and a bag of jangling coins. "Take these. Ye may have need of the silver and...and Alexander will be wanting the signed marriage contract." When Iain reached for them, his face carefully blank, Ewan softened his tone, holding one end of the rolled parchment. "There's no one I trust more with their safety than you, Iain. I'll remind ye that this is the course of action ye chose. If ye wish tae change yer mind, speak now."

Iain's lips thinned slightly as he considered. After a brief pause, he pulled the contract from Ewan's fingers and said, "Nay, brother. I'll do my duty by the lads. It's just that I cannae help but notice that, once again, ye keep all the entertaining tasks for yerself."

Ewan could not help his sad smile, knowing Iain's trepidation in leaving had everything to do with marrying the Stewart lass. "How is taking ten lads through the mountain pass no' entertaining?"

Iain scoffed and safely stowed Ewan's offerings away in his cloak. "There's aways the hope that we meet trouble on the road. Haps I could still make use o' my sword after all."

"Be well, Iain," said Ewan, searching his brother's face. "Send me word once ye've arrived."

Iain nodded once, his jaw clenched tight. And then he was gone, the door thudding softly closed in his wake.

# Chapter Four

That night, in the blustery cold that was early spring, Ewan waited patiently beside Fingal and Rory. It reminded him of when they'd waited outside of Chester Castle for any hint that the Moray had successfully escaped. He might have remarked at how he and Fingal were making a habit out of such pursuits, but refrained, mostly because he was too busy shivering.

Ignoring the need to stamp life into his feet, Ewan stared through the thick brambles. It was very late, indeed. The moon was high and the sky cloudless, casting the clearing in sharp relief. While such a moon was useful to them, watching and hiding in wait as they were, it could prove just as useful to the thieves. Moving at the wrong time in such a light could easily announce their presence, no matter how well hid they endeavored to be.

Rory cocked his head slightly as if trying to strain his ears. Ewan thought he'd heard it too...voices carried on the wind. Sure enough, in the next few seconds where he held his breath, Ewan heard the designated signal from another of his men, who were hiding up in the trees that skirted the fields, indicating someone was coming. Two mournful hoots, as from an owl, drifted to where they were huddled.

Immediately the air grew tense as Rory and Fingal shifted silently, Fingal's hand reaching automatically for an arrow. All their waiting in the cold was about to pay off.

Fingal was the best archer he'd ever seen, able to hit a target even at the deep range of one hundred yards. Rory, who was an excellent swordsman—or had been before his right hand had been tortuously burnt—pulled his short sword from its scabbard with his left hand. He'd been training with it for over a month now, but he was still clumsy and unsure.

Ewan had seen the worry in the man's eyes during their training sessions and could sense his fear of failure now, but such feelings were exactly why Ewan wished him here. He needed Rory to be challenged out of his self-imposed inadequacies. Surely such a confrontation would give the man the courage to continue as his captain in arms.

Yes, he was changed, but that did not mean he could not fight and win. Besides, Edyth said that, with time and practice, he could regain full use of his right hand. What better way to practice, than to impale a thief on the end of his weapon? And with Fingal behind them, ever watchful, there was no chance of Rory being defeated. Fingal would fill any opponent full of arrows before the blade ever had chance to fall.

Ewan nodded once to his men, in his eyes an unspoken command. Tonight they would win back a piece of what had been lost to them as soon as King Edward had imposed his rule upon them. They had the right to defend themselves and defend themselves they would.

Twigs snapped, punctuating the silence like a crier's bell, followed by whispered commands for quiet. "No one is out 'ere," wheedled one man, sotto voce. "An' no one saw us leave. I made sure o' that, I did. We can march right out o' the front gate and none would be roused tae stop us."

Ewan felt Rory stiffen, no doubt sharing Ewan's righteous anger. What had they done to the posted guards atop the wall and at the gate? They would be sure to get answers from them before they exacted their revenge. Ewan held up a hand, indicating that they needed to wait, and strained his ears, his other hand grasping the hilt of his drawn sword so tightly his knuckles ached.

Another man was speaking, bits and pieces reaching them in intervals as the wind shifted. "...All here...bringing a horse and the cart." It sounded as though there were only two men, who expected more to meet them and, no doubt, transport the stolen goods.

There were more indeterminable words and the sound of the canvas being pulled back. Ewan squinted through the leaves. There were three men, one of which had been hidden in the shadow of the boulders. He could now see them all because one of the wretches brazenly lit a lantern. He held it aloft, surveying the stolen goods.

One of the men was silent and watchful, his hand on the pommel of his sheathed sword. This man Ewan recognized. A surge of triumph lanced through him. He'd been right. It was one of de Biggar's men.

The man holding the lantern issued a low whistle, as if he were impressed by what he saw. "These will fetch a good price." He set the lantern atop a crate and rummaged around, unconcerned with the noise he was producing. The sound of stone bottles being jostled came next, followed by a greedy snigger. "I dinnae think Richard will mind if we take one for ourselves. What else do you think we could lift off the Scottish bastard?"

Ewan could not see this man's face well, but he knew the name Richard well enough. Another of de Biggar's men. Richard was not present, however. He must be the one coming to collect the stolen articles. The third man, the one who spoke about the gate being unguarded, was not a soldier. At least Ewan did not recognize him. He was older and did not carry himself as a trained guard might, his shuffling stride being far too unbalanced for a man of the sword.

"Pass one of those tae me, laddie," commanded the man Ewan did not recognize.

Unwilling to wait for more men to arrive, Ewan nodded to Fingal, who quickly and efficiently drew back his bow. The old archer aimed through a clear space within the copse hiding them, then let loose. The woosh of the arrow through the air had barely sounded when there was a dull thud followed by a tight scream.

Fingal had shot the man who'd asked for a bottle of spirit just as he took hold of it, the arrow piercing through his hand. The bottle fell to the ground with a wet clatter. The other men, both soldiers, drew their swords, one of which hissed indeterminable commands at his companions.

The man with the arrow through his hand was holding the injured appendage in front of his face, howling, while one of the other men walked in a tight circle, his head on a swivel, his weapon held at the ready. "Show yerself!" he barked.

The remaining man who'd lit the lantern and was rooting through the crates, apparently felt that the situation was not in his favor. He moved to flee, darting this way and that, jumping from shrub to fallen log.

"What's the scunner doing?" whispered Rory, bemused, his words swallowed up by the injured man's cries of pain.

"I think he means to evade us," murmured Ewan, one eye still on the other man, who stood warily, sword drawn, eyes darting around the small clearing.

Fingal let out a soft scoff and took aim once again. He let the arrow fly with practiced ease and watched as it embedded effortlessly into the fleeing man's back. Immediately dropping like a stone, he laid quite still.

"Show yerself!" shouted the last man standing. He did not look worried in the least, only angry. "Do not hide as a coward! Come and fight!" His shout was loud enough to drown out the sniveling of the man shot through the hand. He knelt in the snow, cradling his arm, gasping and sobbing. He was seemingly uninterested in who might be lurking in the wood and only quivered.

Surprisingly, the man who'd been shot in the back with Fingal's well-placed arrow was not, in fact, dead. With a groan and slow, painful motions, he pulled himself forward, or attempted to. Hands scrabbling in the crusted snow, the man failed to pull himself out of the clearing, his legs unable to cooperate.

Ewan looked to Rory, communicating silently that Rory was to make sure that the injured men did not suddenly sprout wings and escape. He would need his full attention on the uninjured man.

Rory's greying beard twitched slightly in the wind. "Better we just kill the bastard and be done with it."

Ewan acquiesced. It was over in seconds. The crawling man's arms gave way and he fell like a marionette whose strings had been severed, nothing but a dark scab on the snowy forest floor. The man with the injured hand howled all the louder, begging for mercy. "Please dinnae kill me! We weren't going tae hurt nobody. Have mercy!"

"Shut *up*, you mammering milk sop, else I'll kill you myself," growled the swordsman. He was wild eyed, his lip curled in defiant hostility. His lank, dark hair blew in the wind, half concealing his face, but Ewan would recognize him anywhere. He'd been present when de Biggar had threatened his wife.

At the time, Ewan had been too preoccupied with the sheriff to deal with this rat. He'd failed to kill him, unsure of what he could do under King Edward's suffocating rule and still keep his own head. But he would not make the same mistake again. He would kill him tonight, but not before he got some answers.

Ewan gave Fingal a whispered command to keep the man alive. With as long as it took to draw breath, the arrow had found its home in the man's left thigh. Haps it wasn't sporting, to injure him in this way, but he rather liked the idea of making the man suffer. So, too, he wished to ensure Rory's safety.

To the man's credit, he did not scream or wail as his companion did. He only staggered in place, grunting and cursing, stumbling as he fought to stay upright. "You craven, gutless, coward! Come out and fight me like a man!"

Ewan held up a hand, staying Fingal. Ewan exchanged a brief look with his men and pushed his way through the brush, his sword shining like a beacon in the low light. Rory, who was close behind, moved to the sobbing man still kneeling in the snow, sword drawn. Ewan doubted

Rory would have need to harm the man. From the looks of it, he'd already pissed himself.

"Never have I seen such conviction from a thief," said Ewan. "This is no' the first time ye've stolen since coming here, I think. We meet once more, but this time, I willnae spare yer life. What have ye tae say?"

Blood darkened the soldier's hose and dribbled onto the ground, turning the icy snow a gruesome shade of black. Ewan did not think he would speak, but he waited, watching the man's narrowed eyes, the plumes of his breath billowing from him in quick bursts.

He was right; the man did not wish to speak with words, for he lifted his sword, welcoming Ewan's wrath. He could well understand the man's choice for action. He, too, would wish to die as a warrior: cleanly, under a canopy of trees, instead of in the dank stench of a dungeon.

"What is yer name?" asked Ewan as he set his feet. "I would know it before I feed you tae the pigs."

The man snarled and lurched forward clumsily, his left leg dragging. "You incriminate yourself," he said snidely, his sword stroke falling heavily against Ewan's counter swing. The hilts of their weapons locked together as Ewan struggled against the weight of the man, who was surprisingly stronger than he looked. "A repeat offence will not go unnoticed." His breath was hot against Ewan's cheek, his sneer flashing as bright as steel. "One body found in the forest in such a state can be ignored, but not two."

Ewan grew as cold and as still as a statue. Could he know what Edyth had done? How she had killed the sheriff and how his men had left the body to the beasts of the forest? No. There was no proof and those that *did* know would never betray him. Never. Still, the man's words were like a thorn to his heart. Talk was dangerous and when it came to Edyth, Ewan would take no chances.

Lurching backward, Ewan freed his sword and swung his blade in a tight circle, his wrist flexing, before he took up his stance once more, and invited the man to attack. "Yer sheriff was a thief, just as you are. I'll gladly send ye tae greet him in hell."

The man laughed breathily and spat on the ground, limping heavily as he reset his feet. "Where is your bitch you call a wife? Isn't she the one who does your dirty work for you?"

Ewan felt all color drain from his face. His grip on his weapon tightened involuntarily, his breath arrested. "Ye'll no' speak o' my wife," warned Ewan, his voice deadly.

The man laughed hollowly and spread his arms wide. "She leads you about by your bollocks. When the new sheriff comes, he will know of her sins."

Ewan slid the dirk at his hip from its sheath with his left hand, a familiar, cool weight that calmed him. Grounded him. He would carve the man's tongue from his head. Then feed it to him. "Overly concerned with my bawbag, are ye no'?" quipped Ewan, bouncing the dirk slightly until his hand found his favored grip.

He moved forward purposefully and when the man lifted his weapon to meet Ewan's sword, his eyes holding fast to the connection that their swords made, Ewan thrust the tip of his dagger through the soft spot just under the man's chin. Blood poured from his mouth and jaw in great rivulets, spattering Ewan's face when he coughed involuntarily.

"Never again, will ye speak o' my wife," snarled Ewan. He shoved the dirk deeper, eliciting a choking, wet sound from the man. "When ye meet the sheriff, tell him she sends her regards." Ewan let him drop to the ground in a lifeless heap, blood freely pooling in the ruined snow. Ewan's breathing was coming fast, his heart hammering with unspent emotion. He'd killed him far too quickly.

Turning from the grisly scene, he met Rory's eyes, which were dark and emotionless. His sword was held to the weeping man's neck, but he stepped away, an invitation for Ewan to exact the fullness of his wrath.

Ewan wiped the blade of his dirk onto the fallen man's sleeve and walked slowly to the cringing man at Rory's feet. "Sing for me, little bird," said Ewan softly, "else I'll put another hole in you. What have ye done with my guards at the gate and atop the wall?" His voice was calm, but inside, he felt as though he might burst with unspent rage.

The man held up his good hand in supplication, begging silently for Ewan to spare him further injury, his watery eyes pleading. He was shaking so badly, Ewan rather thought he'd rattle all the teeth from his head. "I only plied them with strong drink," blubbered the man. "I swear! T'was only wine we gave them, steeped with some herbs. *Please don't kill me. Mercy, my lord. Mercy.*"

Ewan frowned sharply. "What sort of herbs?"

"I—I dunno," he said, shaking his head frantically. "It was what the witch gave me. I t—told 'er as I was ailing and had trouble sleeping through the night. Sh—she gave me a packet o' herbs."

Ewan suppressed the urge to wrap his hands around his wiry neck. It was thinly corded with muscle, easy to break. And haps seeing the life leave his eyes would ease some of the rancor living in his breast. The bastard had used his wife against his own men. Against *him.*

Ewan would make sure he paid for his treachery. Dearly. But he forcibly dampened the surging wrath within him. It would not do to kill the man too quickly. He must get answers first. Only then, he could kill him. And he would delight in it.

With forced calm, Ewan replaced his sword and crouched before the bleeding man. He'd been right. The man wasn't a soldier. He blubbered far too much, for one. His clothes were those of a craftsman, his hands large and strong from his labors, his knuckles bruised and scraped raw. A carpenter or a stone mason, perhaps? It would be easy to pull answers from him, a man who lived by his hands.

"Who took these goods from my stores?" asked Ewan. One might think he was asking about the weather, for how indifferent he sounded. The man was not fooled, for Ewan's hand hovered an inch from the arrow shaft sticking out of the back of his hand.

He licked his lips, his watery eyes darting around the circle of trees. "I...dinnae be hasty now," wheedled the man. "I dinnae ken aught, milord. I'm just—" What the man was about to say, Ewan did not wait to hear. Hand striking as quick as a snake, his fingers grasped the bloodied shaft protruding from flesh.

The man cried out, as expected, grasping onto Ewan's wrist with his good hand. "*Please*," he begged. "Mercy! Agh! Dinnae...please!" he begged.

"Answer me," instructed Ewan calmly. "Tell me true. Who took these stores from my house?"

The man gasped and gulped air, his mouth moving like a dying fish. "W--we bribed a k—kitchen boy tae leave the door open fer us. We went in a—after the house was asleep and hid them in the tool carts and unloaded them in the morning, once the work began."

"Do not tell me lies," Ewan growled. He could think of no one in his service that would fall for such a thing.

"I s—swear it's the truth!" whined the man. Ewan applied torque to the arrow shaft, his patience growing thin. "Agh! I swear! Please! No' my hand!"

"Ye'll understand our hesitation in believin' a thief and a cheat," intoned Rory, who brought the tip of his sword to the man's neck. This action was enough to empty the man's face of all blood. He looked as white as the snow.

"I swear!" the man sobbed. The scene was quite macabre, with one hand shot through with an arrow, blood coloring his wrist and forearm and the other besmirched with the same from where he'd cradled his injury. In this light, the blood looked almost black, glistening like moonlight on the loch, dotting the pristine snow on the ground. "I swear on my mother's grave," said the man. "Pl—please spare me."

"Who are you?" Ewan demanded.

"H—Henry, sir. I'm a laborer from Prestonpans, intent on the build of His Majesty's garrison."

"And how did ye get involved with this lot?" he asked, indicating the lumpy mass a few feet away. Henry glanced at his dead companion and shut his eyes against the gory sight, his throat bobbing. "Th—they wished me tae build them a false bottom to a cart, so we could smuggle the goods more easily out o' the gate. They said as they'd give me a fair share o' the profits."

Ewan lifted his brows. A false bottom in a cart would have come in handy when stealing away Moray. "Where is this cart o' which ye speak?"

The man shook his head, tears falling freely. "One o' the men...a guardsmen. His name is R—Richard. He's meant tae meet us and help load the goods."

"When?" demanded Rory, his keen eyes darting around the darkened forest. They hadn't heard the call from the other men in the trees as yet, but they might have missed it for all the noise they'd created. "T—tonight. He must go slowly lest the wagon be heard."

It made sense. A wheeled cart pulled by a horse in the dark of the night would be seen from far off. Even with the guardsmen atop the wall and at the gate drugged, there would be others who might hear the squeak and creak of a wagon and go to investigate.

Ewan frowned, wondering what else the man might know or be hiding, if anything. It was obvious that he was not the brains behind the operation. "What more have ye tae say before I run you through?"

The man shook his head, frantic. "Please. Dinnae kill me. My wife and bairns...let me go. I will leave and ne'r return. Ye have my word."

Rory scoffed. "The word o' a thief. Laird, he has heard much," he said pointedly, his eyes darting to the dead man a few feet away. The man who seemed to know far too much about Edyth. But Ewan had no intention of leaving the man alive. He'd learned his lesson last fall, when he'd spared the lives of de Biggar and his lackeys.

But Rory was right. The man *had* heard much. Ewan drew his dirk, eliciting a cry of alarm from the man. "I cannae forget that ye've used my wife against me. That, I cannae forgive."

The man's tear-stained face crumpled. He hung his head in his good hand, sobbing. Rory sneered in disgust at his shameful behavior. There was little glory to be found in taking a man's life when he wept like a child, but still Ewan did not back down.

Ewan offered his blade to his captain, but he shook his head. "No Laird," said Rory. "It's you that should do it."

Ewan did not hesitate. His dirk was swift and sure as it found its home in the man's neck. He let him fall to the ground, the sudden silence ringing in his ears.

# Chapter Five

They had little time to act. Indeed, they had scarcely moved the first man behind the thicket of evergreens before they heard the distant signal from the men in the trees. All three of them stopped, frozen for desperate seconds, then sprang into furious action. They needed to move the bodies so that their coming companion would not see the dead bodies and flee before they could apprehend him. Rory took one man under the arms and dragged him through the snow, his teeth set, while Ewan pulled the other.

Fingal nocked another arrow and crouched with the dead bodies behind the screen of juniper and holly bushes. They could hear the distant squeak and rumble of a cart coming slowly down the logging road. They had only a moment, perhaps, before the cart reached the crest of the little hill before they would be seen.

Ewan was quicker with his burden. He deposited another of the dead men atop the craftsman then hastened to help Rory, whose stiff and clumsy hands struggled to hold the last felled soldier. Ewan, unwilling to speak, motioned with a stiff jerk of his chin to allow him to take over Rory's burden. Rory, flushed and grim-faced, left him to it and did his best to disturb the ruts in the snow from the dead men's feet. There was little they could do about the spilled blood. Hopefully the newcomers would not notice right away.

Just as they all hid themselves behind the thicket, the cart came into view at the crest of the hill, driven by the supposed Richard. Their breaths were sharp and fast from their efforts, their eyes squinting through the thick branches.

Fingal held up one finger, indicating that he only saw one man. But then, as the cart came further down the slope and the bed of the wagon was more easily seen, it was clear that there were more men. As the light from the moon fell upon the conveyance, two dark shapes sat huddled behind the driver. More of de Biggar's men? Or traitors?

As the cart came to a stop and the two men sprang from the back, Ewan's heart thundered in his ears. He knew the driver. He recognized him as one of de Biggar's men that had dared threaten Edyth in the fall at the festival. Richard. Yes, it was plainly him. Ewan registered the fact and dismissed him immediately.

It was one of the two men from the back that caused his breath to catch in the throat and his wame to curdle. *We bribed a kitchen boy tae leave the door open fer us.* The kitchen boy, Elias. Ewan knew him well, as his wife tutored him, had spent months teaching the lad to read and write in the great hall after the nooning meal so that he could help with the inventorying of their stores. Stores he was readily stealing from them.

Fingal hesitated, his tight hold on the bowstring slackening. His eyes darted to Ewan then back to the clearing. "Kill the soldiers. Spare the lad," whispered Ewan, his lips numb, for it was becoming quite plain that the soldiers realized something was amiss.

Fingal nodded and pulled the bowstring back, his wrinkled face looking quite pale in the moonlight. The first solider, who was inspecting the cut rope on the canvas died first, an arrow through his throat. He fell with a wet sputter. The second, Richard, fell just as quickly, an arrow through his heart.

Elias, dark eyes wide, turned to run, but Ewan had anticipated such and sprang from their hiding spot the second Fingal's fingers had left the bowstring. "Halt," he shouted! "Elias, *stop!*"

The boy looked over his shoulder, the fear in his face evident. He hesitated and stumbled over an exposed root, plowing a deep rut through icy snow as the force of his body collided with the earth. Ewan was upon him in seconds, his chest heaving and his mind reeling. "Why, Elias," gasped Ewan, turning the lad over onto his back forcefully. Overcome, Ewan balled the lad's tunic in a gauntleted fist and pulled him to his feet, shaking him for good measure. Ewan could not help himself, so full of rage as he was.

Elias was at the age where sparse whisps of hair had started to grow more heavily above his upper lip. They gleamed silver-white, caught in the low light as a cloud drifted over the moon. Ewan shook him again when he did not answer. "*Why?*" he demanded, all but growling. It was a blow to him, seeing this young lad betray him. It was like a knife to his heart, causing it to stutter in shock. "Answer me, damn you!"

Elias did not fight his laird. He only shook his head, his eyes screwed shut. "Forgive me," he gasped, his fingers closing around Ewan's wrists as he held him aloft. Ewan hadn't wanted to believe what the craftsman had said. Hadn't wanted to hear that one of his own would betray him, but it was true. He'd been deceived. What a trusting fool he'd been. His wame soured, bitterness infusing him.

Elias' grip on Ewan's wrists was tight. "I couldnae...they...they wouldnae leave me alone." His voice broke on the last word, squeaking uncomfortably high. "I had to."

Ewan lifted a raised fist, wanting to pummel the lad until the terrible feeling of betrayal left him. But he'd already spilled the blood of traitorous men this night and still his hunger for justice had not been sated. Rory and Fingal were suddenly there, flanking him. Ewan forced himself to release the boy, his hands shaking. The lad fell to the ground but scrambled up at once, his eyes lingering on the still bodies littered near the cart.

"What have ye done, ye great mongrel?" growled Fingal severely. The boy barely glanced at Fingal, but Ewan could see the shame written heavily upon his face.

Elias opened his mouth, his eyes glistening with unshed tears, but he shut it again in short order. He cleared his throat and wiped at his running nose with the back of his hand with a sniff. "I didnae mean tae dishonor ye, nor yet steal from ye."

"Looks tae me ye meant it," said Ewan with a disgusted scoff. "If ye hadnae meant it, then how do ye explain all this?" he demanded, pointing jerkily in the vicinity of the canvas covered crates.

Elias shook his head, as if in denial, his breath stuttering. "It—It's because of me da." He sniffed again, loudly, looking very pitiful indeed. "He gambled with the sheriff's men most nights in the alehouse, but he lost more than he could afford in the end."

In an anguished voice, Elias explained how, at first, his father's losses had been minor: daggers, small amounts of coin, a brooch. But then, deep in his cups and much too drunk to be thinking straight, his father had bet his horse. Such a beast was a prize that, if lost, would mean to the ruin of the family, as he could not earn his living without it.

"He lost," said Elias, forlorn. "So when they came tae me, without the kitchens when I was gathering wood for Alban, they said that, should I help them, they'd give me da 'is horse back. I only had tae leave the door open, aye? They didnae tell me what they wanted, but I was sure they would not harm anyone. The hall is full o' men in the night, and guards are posted in all the thresholds." He shrugged slightly, his eyes, which rested somewhere in the vicinity of his feet, lifted then to meet Ewan's briefly. Looking upon his laird seemed to pain him and he found his feet once more. "But once I agreed," he continued in a thick voice, "and I let them in, they demanded more."

"Mmph," grunted Ewan, his mouth drawn into a severe line. "What else have ye helped them tae cart away and sell?"

Elias dared to lift his face, his red-rimmed eyes sincere. "Naught else, Laird. I swear on my life. This, tonight, is the first attempt."

"And the last," said Ewan, leveling the lad with a steely glare. He did not know what to do with the boy. He couldn't rightly think of a just punishment with his blood boiling as it was.

Elias hung his head and nodded. "Please dinnae tell me mam."

Ewan might have laughed, were he not so full of disappointed rage. Here, the lad's laird had caught him in the act of stealing and he was more worried about what his mam would think of him. "I cannae promise ye such," replied Ewan with a shake of his head, his heart as cold as a stone. "First thing ye'll do is help us get these bodies into the cart. If ye can involve yerself in this mess, then ye can certainly help tae clean it up. After that...I'll think of a just punishment."

He should let Cressingham take him, he thought bitterly. Let the lad pay with his life.

*Edyth looked down upon the landscape as if she were a bird, gliding through the air. Indeed, she was a bird. Others like her were near, black and swift, the beat of their wings silent under startling caws.*

*The landscape moved beneath her; the rich fields with their gathered harvests, the stone walls separating them, and the beasts that roamed freely thereon. Her eye caught hold of a building in the middle distance, growing larger by the second. It was a great keep, brownstoned and well fortified, manned by armor-clad warriors standing guard.*

*As she passed over the keep, she saw a marching army, carrying the Scottish ensign of a red lion on a yellow field, drawing closer to the keep. These soldiers were heavily laden with swords, pikes, long bows, maces, and a variety of other weapons Edyth did not care to register, but also with them, came a great emotion. It swelled within her breast, growing so rapidly and with such sudden feeling that she would have faltered if she'd had bodily control.*

*"Turn away. Go." The thought filled her head, reverberating through her with great urgency, but she did not know to where she was meant to go. "To where?" she thought, eager and desperate to obey.*

*The answer came in the form of a changing sky. Clouds gathered, surrounding her. Indeed, the very sky appeared bruised. It roiled black, grey, and purple. She knew this sky, had been haunted by it for weeks on end.*

*The wind buffeted against her, but she could not fight against it. She was a prisoner to the elements, unable to go where she wished, nor could she push back against the force. She had the queer sensation of moving a great distance at unbelievable speeds. She could not feel the ground speeding past underneath her, but she sensed the passage of time and space, could sense the changing landscape below. Rivers and mountains, hills and valleys. Darkness then light, shifting as the landscape morphed beneath her.*

*Then, just as suddenly as she'd found herself aloft in the sky, she now found herself standing barefoot in the cold, silty mud. She was herself again, small and unsure. The mire squished between her toes, making her shiver with the cold. Wind lifted the hairs from her face and shoulders as thunder sounded, a rumble that ran through the long bones of her body to settle in her sour belly.*

*This place was entirely different than the brownstone keep she'd just left. She'd been here before. She knew this riverbank, knew the smell of the wet earth. Knew that when lightning struck, it would illuminate the storming sky, the river snaking before her, and the narrow wooden bridge spanning it.*

*This was not her river in Perthshire. She did not recognize the bridge, nor the vast expanse of marsh surrounding her. As if her thoughts brought the lightning to life, it struck, drawing sharp edges on cloud and the few lone trees just stubborn enough to make a life in the silty ground.*

*This time, however, where there had before been only empty landscape on the opposite side of the river, now lived hundreds—no, thousands—of winking helms, shields, and iron-tipped lances. Among them, too, were countless beasts, bedecked with chainmail. Horses. She'd only glimpsed these horrors, this cavalry, and then the light was gone, leaving an imprint of their shapes on the backs of her eyelids.*

*The wind picked up, twisting her chemise around her legs, her hair whipping against her face. She tensed against what she knew was soon at hand, readying herself for the onslaught. There, in the dark and cold, the screams began.*

*Battle cries rang in her ears, piercing and shrill. Swords crossed, the ringing of steel on steel so loud she had to cover her ears. It did not help. It never did, but still her hands pressed against her skull, desperate to block the hair-raising sounds of death; she winced as shapes moved around her. Men fell, their bodies littering the inky ground. Some gasped for air, others screamed in agony, her own cries lost in the cacophony.*

*Lightening flashed again, affording her a full view of the slaughter. Bodies were everywhere, stacked double, arms and legs severed. The water shone red, filled with the life's blood spilled therein. Bodies floated in the river, choked with corpses. She was going to be sick. She clenched her jaw and turned her eyes away. More bodies. Gutted men and horses. Everywhere she looked, death had visited.*

*Blessed darkness veiled her eyes once more; thunder rolled above. She could feel it sing through her bones, bringing with it a sense of dread so keen she thought she would lose her feet and fall to the earth to lie amongst the dead. She waited in the dark, her breath shallow and her heart racing.*

*"Stand!" came a warning thought inside her head. It was the same voice that had spoken before, a sprouting seed within her brain that quickly took root. It echoed inside her skull; she put her hands to her head once more, as if she could ease the ache with only a touch.*

*"What do you want from me?" she cried, pushing the heels of her hands into her eyes. Her head hurt. The pounding in her skull was making her sick. Pulling her hands away, she squinted into the dark, but she could discern no one person she knew. Frantic, she searched the smudged lines, half concealed in the bleak darkness for familiar faces without success. "I don't understand," she thought, desperate.*

*The ache had spread from her head to her chest. It was as a great weight—no, a vice that gripped her very heart. Sorrow filled her and she wept aloud, falling to her knees at last. The cold seeped into her chemise, the rank stench of rotting leaves and blood making her gag.*

Edyth awoke with a start, her breaths coming as fast and frantic as her heart was beating. She fumbled with the coverlet, throwing it aside, and crawled to the end of the bed, scrabbling for the chamber pot. Her stomach heaved, the first time in weeks, but she knew her stomach did not purge its contents due to her pregnancy. She could still smell the blood-soaked earth, could hear the desperate cries of beast and man alike. The ache in her skull had dulled but her chest still felt heavy with an unrelenting grief.

She wiped at her mouth and sat heavily on the floor, pushing the bowl away. Belatedly, she realized that Ewan had not woken her, as he usually did, when she had a rather gruesome vision. He was out in the woods again with Rory and Fingal, intent on catching a thief.

She wiped her eyes, feeling shaky, and moved to the ewer on the sideboard. She rinsed her mouth out with water and then drank her fill, her mind full of questions. She closed her eyes and saw the nameless men fall once more in her mind's eye, saw them as they were swallowed up in darkness of the battlefield and shivered anew.

What did it mean? She replayed the vision, committing it to memory. Where was the brownstone keep she'd fled? Where was the winding river at which she was commanded to stand? She could not recall any sigils, no telling markers that would give light to this mystery, save for the Scottish warriors who were marching steadily toward the castle they had then abandoned.

In the past, her dreams had been focused on saving Ewan; she'd seen his death replayed countless times. She could envision it still, should she wish to. These dreams were different, though. They did not command her to save anyone. Indeed, she was not shown any faces she recognized. She was only carried from one place to the next. Did it mean the soldiers were focusing on the wrong place? But what soldiers? What army?

She thought of Andrew Moray, holed safely away in Nairn with Cait's new family. Perhaps these dreams related to whatever he was planning. She could not know for certain. Edyth washed her face and rinsed her mouth out again, wishing she could talk to Cait in truth, and not in careful letters where words must be guarded as closely as treasure.

With shaky breath and trembling hands, she lit a candle and pulled out her writing implements. She would write Cait a story, one she hoped her sister-in-law would understand.

"Long ago," she began, for that is how all great stories start, "in a land not far distant, there lived a girl who could spin a story from wool. Her tapestries were revered by all who knew their value, for whomever looked upon them would see the great and terrible truths."

# Chapter Six

Not but a few days had gone by since the thieves in the wood had been thwarted when Alec came to Ewan within his study, eyes alight with excited fervor. "Forgive me," said the squire, his breathing labored as if he'd run a long way, "but I 'ave sommat that I think ye'd wish tae see."

Ewan, who had been speaking to Rory about his expectations when Cressingham made his eventual arrival, was in a sour mood. He ached in body and spirit, feeling as though it was all he could do to keep the very sky from crashing down around their heads. He leveled Alec with a look that plainly said, "what now?"

At this, Alec thrust a wadded piece of cloth into his hands, a grin spreading across his face. "Good news for a change, I hope."

Ewan glanced at Rory, who looked adequately intrigued, and lifted the strip of dark cloth, stained grey with sweat and grime and creased at the ends, as if it had been tied and untied countless times. He frowned at it, feeling as if he'd seen this before, but he could not quite recall from where.

"Earlier today," explained Alec passionately, "when ye were in the lists, a man came tae the gate asking for ye. Said as how he wished tae see ye expressly, but the gatehouse guards wouldnae let him enter until he gave his name and 'is purpose. When he refused and tried to get past the guards, he caused a bit o' stramash. The guards at the gate threatened tae put him in the dungeon unless he left."

Ewan nodded. "Aye, that's right." Johnne had already reported this to him earlier.

"Weel," said Alec on an exhale, "he came back."

"Where is this man now?" asked Rory.

"Gone," said Alec dismissively with a wave of his hand. "I was on duty atop the wall when he came the second time. Only this time, when the guards demanded he leave, I went down and spoke tae him through the portcullis." Here Alec affected an air of importance and said, "I told him as I was yer own personal squire and I'd deliver any message tae ye myself, forthwith, but that he couldnae enter lest he announced his business."

Apparently the secretive herald was not in possession of a verbal message, but a physical one. Alec gestured grandly to the limp cloth still clutched in Ewan's hand. "Do ye no' recognize it, milord? Does it mean aught tae ye?"

Ewan held it aloft, pinching a corner between his forefinger and thumb. He turned it this way and that, a furrow between his brows and scratched his bearded chin. The article was, indeed, very much like the long strip of cloth Graham, the giant tracker, wore to cover his poor eye. Graham, who had been missing since rescuing the Moray from Chester Castle in England, having missed the boat north. Ewan's heart lurched at the thought. If this cloth was, indeed, Graham's, then he was no doubt near, alive and well. He handed the cloth to Rory who grunted in thought.

"Aye, looks familiar enough."

"Mmph," agreed Ewan, his spirits daring to rise. "Might we have found our missing tracker? Or rather, he's found us."

Graham had lost the use of his left eye at a young age from a misfortunate incident whilst shoeing a horse. He wore the strip of cloth over his eye, angled and tied in the back, usually whilst in mixed company and in public rooms. Other times, he went without the cloth, but he always had it close to hand.

Rory made an interrogative sound in his throat. "Aye. Could be," he said.

Alec nodded enthusiastically. "Aye, that's as what I thought. I've seen 'im tie it on countless times."

"What else did this messenger say?" demanded Ewan.

Alec licked his lips, his eyes set on the corner of the desk and his brow furrowed in thought. "The messenger gave me the cloth and uttered one word. A name, I think, though I dinnae ken it. *Errett*, he said."

No one else saw this?" asked Rory, gesturing with the cloth. "Nor heard?"

Alec shook his head. "I dinnae believe so. I spoke tae him through the gate. No one came with me and I didnae speak to anyone about what he held. I came straight here."

"That's a good lad," said Ewan with an approving nod.

"But what does it mean, this *Errett*?" asked Alec, looking between his laird and the captain.

Ewan retook the cloth and carefully folded it before pocketing it. He looked to Alec, his eyes sparking with torchlight and relief. "Errett is the name of a shepherd known tae produce quality fleece. We spoke tae him last summer about breeding some of our stock with his favored rams."

Realization lighted in Alec's eyes. "And this is where he is? Graham is with this shepherd?"

"He must be," Ewan said with a suggestion of a shrug. "It's a long ride, but we can leave in the morning at first light." He turned to Rory. "Tell the stable lads tae prepare two horses. Ye'll be coming along with me, Alec."

Alec's answering smile was contagious.

The next morning, they rose before the sun. The stars were bright, twinkling down on them as if smiling. Ewan and Alec left the village of Perthshire behind, the sound of the swollen river following them as they found the westward road that would lead them to Errett and, hopefully, Graham.

The weather was changing. Mud already clung to their horses' legs and speckled their boots, but the recent snowfall was melting fast and, hopefully soon, would be gone altogether. Ewan thought, even with the sodden roads, they could make it to Carroglen by the early afternoon, save any disaster should fall upon them.

He'd wanted this time alone with his squire for some time, whom he loved as well as a brother. They'd saved each other in Blave when they'd been overrun by the English. But even without such a bond, Ewan would still honor him as a knight with all the privilege he could afford to give him. Alec was loyal and honest, and vastly *good* in a way that he, himself, was not. Altruistic and humble, Ewan admired the man he had become. Indeed, Alec would be of age soon and Ewan was making plans.

He broke the long silence by clearing his throat as they came upon a fork in the road. "Do ye mind that bonny parcel o' land o'er near Loch Tay ye so admired as a wee lad?"

"D'ye mean where ye took me on a boar hunt when I was naught but a page?" He chuckled softly. "I nearly shat meself when that beastie came up oot o' the scrub and spooked my horse. I'd ne'er heard such a ruckus."

Ewan laughed along with him. "Aye, the very place. If I remember aright, ye *did* soil yerself. Soiled yer bed because ye were too afeared tae go in the bushes after Graham's ghost stories."

Alec laughed. "No, that was the dog."

Ewan could not help his smile at the memory. Ewan had a habit of remembering Alec as he had been as a young lad, come to him from a family now gone. He'd come, motherless, to foster from a nearby village, his father eager to make something of his son. He'd had no money to offer as payment nor yet a way to see to the costly knightly accoutrements he would later need. But Ewan had loved him from even those first days.

He remembered Alec trying to hide his tears soon after his father had left him, late after the evening meal. Ewan's heart had gone out to the lad, remembering all too well his own grief at leaving home for the first time at seven. Ewan had soothed the lad's ache as best he could, telling him he must do his best to honor his father who was eager to see him shape himself into a good man.

Alec had roused mightily, his thirst to prove himself worthy of his lord's and his father's approval paramount. His father was gone now, and so he had no place to go, save for what Ewan bestowed upon him.

Ewan watched Alec in the saddle, noting how much he'd changed, grown in mind and stature, and in heart. Being out of the keep, away from the mounting troubles that surrounded him, Ewan could not help but feel as if a weight had been lifted from his shoulders. He cleared his throat, his heart feeling lighter than it had in weeks. "I noticed ye've been spending a lot o' yer free time with the kitchen maid, Ceana," said Ewan, chancing a glance at Alec.

The squire's face was carefully blank, but his ear, Ewan noticed, shone pink. When Alec said nothing, Ewan continued. "She's a bonny wee lass and yer mistress says that she's a quick study with the herbs and such."

"Aye," said Alec after a long moment, as if he'd been debating on whether or not to admit his knowledge of the girl. "Ceana has worked diligently tae learn the ways o' healing. She says as how she's enjoyed her mistress's attention and tutelage."

"She seems keen on ye, Ceana," remarked Ewan in as offhand way as he could, careful not to look at Alec and embarrass him further.

Alec said nothing for a long time, the footfalls of the horse's hooves the only sound filling the morning air. Ewan waited patiently, whistling a tune, knowing that before too long, Alec would not be able to stop himself from asking for more information. Sure enough, as they maneuvered over a rise in the road, Alec finally spoke: "D'ye think...that is tae say, how is it ye ken such a thing?"

Ewan grunted in an interrogative way and Alec continued, his words tumbling from him. "What is it that puts ye tae mind tae such a notion?"

His face was flaming, his hazel eyes darting to Ewan then away. Hiding his smile, Ewan pursed his lips as though in thought. "I cannae pretend tae ken much of women's secrets," he said philosophically, "but it doesnae take much tae read a lassie when she's keen on a lad." Ewan said no more, waiting to speak until after they crossed a stream, enjoying the torture he was inflicting on his squire. "But, ye'd best find oot fer yerself, aye? Ye're going tae need a wife tae help with the running of things once yer knighted."

Alec's shock was almost comical, his face blank and his mouth slightly agape as he processed Ewan's plans for him. Being knighted would mean he would be given a portion of property to hold and protect. And no doubt the thought of a wife had knocked the breath from him. Of course if he didn't wish to wed so soon, Ewan would not force him.

"What—The running o' what, milord?"

"Why yer lands, o' course. Near Loch Tay. The estate will need tae be properly maintained, the people seen to and the land worked in that part of the clan lands. I trust yer up tae the task?"

Alec's slack mouth twitched into a smile, his eyes wide and alight with happy surprise. "D—d'ye mean it? D'ye really mean tae entrust me with the running o' the land there?"

Ewan met Alec's eyes squarely. "I can think of no better man for it," he said seriously. "Graham is no' far from there, it would seem. We can tarry after, sae ye can look over yer new kingdom."

Alec's face, it seemed to Ewan, shone as brightly as the sun.

By the time they made it to Carroglen, the sun was setting and Ewan's stomach growled loudly, informing him it well past time to eat. They'd chosen to forego stopping for food and so they ate the unsatisfying fare they'd brought from atop their steeds: an oatcake and salted beef.

Despite the weakening light, they could still see workers in the fields. One of the sheepherder's dogs met them on the road, a black and white dart that they watched streak through the field like an arrow, through the brush, and up onto the road winding its way to the house. Its tongue lolled out of its mouth, smiling at them in greeting, and dutifully showed them the way to the master's gate.

The shepherds in the fields, driving sheep, called commands to their dogs. They did not pause in their work and did not seem to notice riders approaching. The road was long and poorly made, with ruts and swaths of mud that sucked at their horse's feet. They followed the dog, which seemed to know which places to avoid, happily covered in muck.

The farm was sprawling and dotted with outbuildings, all surrounded by fallow fields not yet turned green. Hay barracks were set here and there, where many sheep congregated, bleating for their fare. Ewan's head was on a swivel as if he might suddenly spot Graham behind one of the rock walls or some other barrier, but he did not spot him all the way to the house.

The house, for its part, was a single-story structure with a tidy roofline, the thatch without mold or hollow. The façade was whitewashed, the lower portion splattered with mud from the continually wet conditions of late winter.

"Where is everyone?" asked Alec, looking suspiciously at the house as if it held specters instead of farm folk.

Ewan shrugged and dismounted, his feet squelching, and said, "In the fields, I expect. Ye ken well enough how every hand is needed from time to time in the running o' a farm. Hello the house," he called.

Alec dismounted, turning a tight circle, his eyes roving from building to building. "D'ye expect he's in one o' these stables? Or in the house itself?"

But Ewan did not get a chance to reply for, just then, a young lad came upon them from behind, out of breath and red faced. "Finney, come 'ere boy! *Thig an seo a chù amaideach.*" *Come here you silly dog.*

Finney the dog, which had escorted them, and was currently sniffing Ewan's boot, immediately obeyed, its head cocked to one side as if waiting for instructions. The boy patted the dog's head, saying, "If it's Errett yer looking fer, milords, he's out in the field with the rest of the household. There are some ewes soon tae lamb and we're busy separating the mothers tae bring them in. He sent me ahead tae see tae yer comforts once ye were spotted on the high road."

The lad set his long staff against the rocky surface of the closest building and returned to take their horses. "Please make yerselves comfortable in the house. I'll just see tae yer beasts."

Ewan and Alec wiped their boots as best they could, stomping and scraping mud and muck onto a fence rail near the entrance. Ewan ducked as he entered, the lintel several inches too short for his own height, and they waited uncomfortably just inside the entrance as the lad led their horses into the shadowy haven that were the stables.

The house was empty and unlit so far as he could see and hear, so it was in an awkward silence that they stood in the dim. The lad didn't take too long. Soon, the door opened and he smiled at them rather toothlessly, saying, "Forgive the poor greeting, sirs. As I say, all the house are in the fields at present."

He moved further into the house, motioning for them to follow, and brought them to a small room furnished with a table and chairs. There was a hearth against one wall, full of dull embers, which the lad stoked back to life, tossing a billet atop. "Can I get ye aught else while ye wait?"

They accepted food and drink, which turned out to be bread, salted pork, and a few winter apples, and waited for what felt like a very long time before the front door opened. Heavy footfalls on the wooden planks further announced someone's arrival. Ewan and Alec stood just in time to see Errett, the master of this farm and, just behind him, the towering form of Graham, his one very blue eye fixed upon them.

Errett was a small man, well-tanned and weathered from his life out of doors, with a wiry frame corded with lean muscle. Ewan moved to them both, his heart full of glad relief. Underlying his relief there lived a fierce compassion for what Graham had undergone, for he clearly had seen trouble. Not only was he thinner than when he'd last seen him, but his boots were worn to almost nothing and his clothes fated and frayed. But he was whole and he was *here*, alive.

Ewan embraced his friend, who was a whole head taller than he was himself, feeling all the ribs along his side. They pounded each other's backs, saying nothing. Indeed, all the words Ewan wished to say seemed stuck, pushed together in a great lump in his throat. He cleared it and stepped away, letting Alec have his turn.

"Ye've grown, laddie," said Graham in his soft tones, appraising Alec with a kindly eye.

After several minutes of gratitude to Errett for feeding and sheltering his vassal, the shepherd left, bowing as he left them alone to see to his household. Ewan inquired of Graham's health as they sat down together near the fire, which Graham waved away with a broad hand. He told them all that had happened after he'd been separated from Ewan and Fingal so many months ago.

In an effort to draw the Chester Castle guards away from their escaped prisoner, he'd ridden east as Ewan had bid, but had been intercepted by a handful of guards, which had cornered him and held his horse. When his excuse for being out in the middle of the night was not accepted, they'd pulled him bodily from his steed, intending to bring him back to the castle or kill him where he stood. "Favoring life, I chose tae walk," said Graham wryly.

He knew that he could not go so far as to enter the castle and have any hope of escape, so he chose to cooperate and moved with a few of the guards on foot, who prodded him onward, all the while making plans. The rest of the party continued their search for Moray, riding out into the dark of night and leaving Graham with naught but two men as escort. That had been their mistake. "Two men tae the one o' me," said Graham, "even without my sword tae hand, would be no contest. But I had tae wait for the right time. They were armed and wouldnae have minded poking holes in me, no matter was I innocent or no."

They had bound his hands in a leather strip and had taken his sword and dirk, but they'd failed to notice his sock knife. "It was at least two miles back to the castle, maybe more," said Graham, "and them with their swords in my back, but after a time, they grew easier in their manner when I didnae fight nor gripe at them."

Graham sang softly as they went, apparently without a worry in the world as they moved toward the castle and planned his escape. He'd stumbled purposefully, falling to the ground on his elbows and his knees, and while he was struggling to upright himself, he'd deftly pulled his sock knife from its place and palmed it in his large, bound hands.

"The guards were both behind me, and had grown somewhat complacent in their duties, for I was easy in manner and all at ease and had been for a mile or more. They still held their swords, but they did not notice as I worked the blade between my palms through the leather, whistling all the while."

It had taken some time to loosen his bindings enough to slip a hand free, but there had still been time. The castle was not yet in sight but Graham, worried that they might chance a meeting of more guardsmen as they neared the keep, knew he must strike soon.

Whistling merrily, he turned with a sudden and brutal force, and stabbed one of the men right through the opening in his helm. He lost his wee knife in the man's eye socket and ducked as the second man swung his sword in the vicinity of Graham's chest. "I was lucky there," he said running a hand through his blond locks. "He took a hank o' hair from me with that swing."

He'd picked up the fallen man's sword and, after some effort, dispatched the other. "I took the second man's helm tae help disguise myself, should I need to so close tae the castle and with dawn approaching, made my way through the forests on foot. Missed the boat, o' course, and couldnae get into the port leastways, as it was crawling with soldiers, turning out crates and trunks in an effort tae find the missing Moray. Sae," he said with a shrug, "I moved north."

When Ewan asked him why he had not ventured to his uncle's lands, which were south from Perthshire, Graham explained that he'd been lucky to get a ride in a wagon with some tinkers, which were merry company, but heavy drinkers. "We travelled together for several days until one night, I drank too much and when I awoke the next day, we were near tae York and far off the path tae Caimbel lands. The roads from Berwick tae Edinburgh were swarming with the English. I couldnae risk asking for a ride again. My face is pinned tae nearly every township post I happened tae tarry in." He shrugged a shoulder as if walking from York to Midlothian was no issue at all in winter.

"But...how did ye survive? Where did ye sleep?" asked Alec, looking at Graham as if he were some great Greek god from the old stories.

"I kept tae the roads at night and oot 'o the heather, where I was sure tae meet my death in the cold. I stayed in stables and huts as I found them, thankful for any scraps I could lay my hands on." He frowned here, looking down at his dirty fingernails. "Stole here and there, when I couldnae get it honest. Most folk were kind and didnae notice who I was, but they didnae have the means tae transport me tae Perthshire."

They were all silent for a time, their minds replaying the tale Graham had just told them. He broke the silence first.

"But what news from Perthshire? I've lived these past long weeks in worry. I kent well enough that the Moray was still uncaught by the English—I've seen his face in the towns and villages alongside my own—but does he live?'

"He does," Ewan said succinctly. He then explained the difficulty in getting the sick man through the winter passes alive, and how they only awaited news from Cait as to when the man was ready tae raise his standard. Ewan also told him about the king's garrison that was presently being constructed on their lands, in view of the keep, to which Graham swore colorfully.

"What's more," added Ewan with a shake of his head, "We await conscription from Cressingham and appointment of a new sheriff any day. I fear it willnae be safe for ye in Perthshire, Graham. Ye cannae come home as yet." Ewan was sorry for that. He could see the disappointment plainly written on his retainer's face.

Graham nodded grimly. "I thought as much, which is why I contrived this ruse." Here he gestured about the room, making Ewan recall the piece of cloth that was currently in his pocket. He withdrew it, offering it back to his tracker. "I'm glad tae see ye, Graham, but there's little ye can do for me tae home. Do ye go north tae Cait and help where ye might until...until we can free ourselves from this canker. I'll supply ye with whatever ye might have need of."

He hated that he could not say when or how they would accomplish this task, only that they must. Graham, for his part, was ever faithful, saying, "Aye, Laird. I go where ye will."

# Chapter Seven

Iain Ruthven relaxed his clenched jaw as he walked the stony pathway that led to the Stewart keep. A solicitous servant led the way to the double front doors of the impressive limestone building from the stable yard, his quick steps loud on the frozen gravel. Iain had brought the group of lads as he'd agreed to, but he found no joy in it. He should be grateful that they were now safely hidden from Cressingham's clutches, but he did not trust Alexander Stewart. Not in the least.

The group of ten Ruthven lads followed in his wake, huddled together as if some great beast might come upon them and devour them. He could not blame them for their uncertainty. He felt the same desire to run and hide. He smiled inwardly at the thought. He supposed he was no better than any of these green lads, so inexperienced he was with intrigue and political scheming. Ewan was the better man here, but Ewan could not play the role of betrothed husband.

The marriage contract, weighty as a stone, waited in his satchel. Iain pictured it, the bold, flourishing ink listing his name alongside that of the Stewart lass, one Alice Marjory Elisabeth Stewart.

*Alice Marjory Elisabeth Stewart.* Even her name—all of three them—were as bland and commonplace as her personality. In their previous meeting, not one part of her had stirred the smallest bit of interest in him. Well, that wasn't expressly true. He'd been intrigued at the idea of the Stewart's daughter. He'd imagined her to be as formidable and cunning as her sire, but he'd been wrong.

She was dull, to put it plainly. She'd hardly said but a few words to him when her family had visited Perthshire in the fall. And while he was glad to see, at least from what he could tell, that she was indeed *not* like her father, he couldn't deny he wished for his future wife to have some spark of life in her.

To forego the alliance over something as trivial as personality would create a chasm between the two families. One that, in the coming storm, might prove fatal. He simply did not have a choice, no matter what his brother said. Iain would do his duty, even if it meant being saddled to the Lady Alice. A boring, colorless lass, who pissed in a pot more often than she spoke.

He schooled his features as they rounded a corner, passing half-melted piles of snow that had been cleared from the path. Despite his willingness to do his duty, he felt as if he had lost something important.

But how could you mourn the loss of something you never had in the first place? He rubbed his face with a gloved hand, regretting his words to his little sister as she'd cried over her own loss of freedom. *I very much doubt there's room for either of us to choose our lot in life. We, unlike Ewan, must take on the role of the respectable progeny.*

He was a hypocrite, plain and simple, but he'd hoped for...well, *more*. More what? More time? More attraction? He was young yet. He had no need to settle into marriage so young, yet here he was, contract in hand.

And while he hadn't shed any tears like his little sister had upon her betrothal, he could now appreciate her feelings. Unlike his sister, however, he sincerely doubted that he and his future bride would suit so well. Cait's husband had a personality, at least. *He laughed*. Iain couldn't recall ever seeing Alice smile. Not even once. He groaned inwardly, pushing such thoughts from his mind. It did him no favors to focus on such negative thoughts. The choice was made.

The heavy, iron-studded doors of the keep were thrown wide, having produced an impressive line of persons, all exiting the building in a decidedly formal fashion and taking their place along the topmost stair. They reminded him of a line of birds perched atop a branch, their shrewd eyes observing him.

Iain studied the crown of each head as they bowed or curtseyed, looking for his betrothed. She was not difficult to find, as the only other females were her mother and her younger nieces. Alice's light brown hair was loosely plaited and knotted at the nape of her neck and held in place by a black net. Her hair was a muted sort of brown, like a sparrow's wing. She held his gaze with unblinking, somber brown eyes held in a round, fair face.

She was not unattractive, he allowed. Only serious. Far too serious. Iain would have to make a game of pulling the lass from her shell. If only Ewan or Inan were here with him. They could take bets on how long it would take for him to pull a smile from her.

"Sir Ruthven," said her father, Alexander Stewart, one arm swept out in a grand gesture of welcome. His future father-in-law was tall and mostly built of sinewy muscle, save for the paunch he'd procured in these, his later years. Grey touched his beard and ran through his thick, dark hair, but he was otherwise spry and vigorous. And wholly intimidating.

The man had a knack of looking through you as if he was weighing the balance of your life and found you wanting. A heavy hand landed on Iain's shoulder, Alexander's voice full of earnest solicitude. "Ye'll recall my wife, Lady Morwen."

Iain bowed in a courtly fashion and took her limp lace-covered hand to bestow a kiss upon her knuckles. "A pleasure," he murmured in rote fashion, feeling nothing of the sort. Lady Morwen looked much like her daughter, though she was softer round the middle and had creases marking the edges of her mouth and eyes. She gave him a closed-mouth smile, soft and benign, which was more than he could say for Alice, who only stared at him without expression.

"We welcome you to Doune," said Lady Morwen, her voice as meek as a wee mouse. Her face was blank, but her brown eyes were assessing as they met Iain's own. "May the union of our families prove fruitful."

Iain wondered at what they'd hoped to gain from Ruthven aside from grandchildren, but of course kept that to himself. He could only think of one reason: control. Why else would the Stewart clan vie for an alliance through marriage when they were already aligned through his father's friendship?

"Ye'll recall my daughter, Lady Alice," said Alexander, his voice full of pride.

"Of course," he said succinctly, and moved to bow over Alice's proffered hand, brushing his lips briefly across her gloved hand. "Bonnie as 'er," he said automatically. Closer now, he could see that her aquiline nose and cheekbones were dusted lightly with freckles, her cheeks slightly pink from the crisp air.

There was nothing remotely playful or girlish about her that he could find. Alice only observed him with a mild detachment that confused him. She *was* bonny, he noted, and pleasantly plump. She engendered a womanly, mysterious charm that might beguile him had she thought to smile or draw him into flirtatious banter. But her complete and utter lack of curiosity in him, her future husband, made him wonder further about her family's motives. Haps she was only shy, he told himself. Or haps she was like her father and married him for some hidden purpose.

"These are my granddaughters," explained Alexander, naming them each in turn, each curtseying in prim silence. Iain smiled through it all, forgetting their names almost as soon as they were told to him. They said nothing. Indeed, Iain wondered if any of the women in this family had tongues in their heads.

"Come and get ye inside, out o' the cold," said Alexander. "My man will bring yer lads into the hall tae eat while we speak alone." He ushered them all inside and asked about the road and for news from Perthshire. Iain departed from the boys with a nod and a steely expression that he hoped conveyed his expectations of their behavior.

They were settled in a comfortable room, well appointed with lush furnishings, tapestries, and expensive beeswax candles. The Stewart was strutting like a cock in the hen yard, he realized. *See what riches we offer? See what prizes await the man who marries my flinty daughter?*

Iain took the proffered seat near the fire, seated adjacent to Alice who sat at the very edge of her chair, her hands folded in her lap, the very image of prim propriety. Her lips were full, her bottom lip pillowing out slightly, her eyes downcast to the vicinity of her knees. It aggravated him for some reason, this demure attitude that she always adopted. He forced himself to look away and focus on Alexander, who sat directly across from him.

"Much has happened since we last spoke. My laird and brother, Ewan, bade me tell ye that the sheriff assigned tae Midlothian has died."

"Did he?" asked Alexander with interest. "Yer brother's doing?"

Iain shook his head. "No man took his life," he answered truthfully.

"Would that our own sheriff follow in his footsteps," said Alexander dryly with a wry twist to his mouth.

Refreshments were brought and while they spoke, Iain informed them that King Edward had decreed that a garrison be built upon Ruthven land. "To house nigh on three hundred fighting men and assorted workmen."

"Retribution, haps, for the slight we gave him at the gathering," speculated Alexander, one brow lifted in question. Iain had to agree. The sheriff hadn't taken kindly to their meddling in his nefarious forms of justice against the people of Perthshire. "I wouldnae doubt it, in any case. Such a man wouldnae let the insult stand uncontested. I'm sure he filled the King's ear with tales o' potential rebellion."

Iain made a sound of agreement, shifting in his seat. "Aye. The man no doubt ran tae his betters, begging fer justice."

"How were the roads on your journey?" asked Lady Morwen politely as if such talk were inappropriate amongst such genteel ears. She was as finely boned as her daughter, short, with a small bump on the bridge of her nose.

Iain inclined his head slightly, acknowledging the honor it was to speak to the lady of Doune. "Fair as can be expected in such weather," he stated mildly. If these women would speak to him of nothing, he would do the same. On and on the polite conversation went, filling the stretched silences between question and answer. *How fares your mother? Well enough, I daresay. Was the harvest bountiful enough to keep you well fed? Aye, the Lord blessed us.*

The very idea that this was to be his existence for the remainder of his days seemed impossible. How did Alexander do it? How could he live with such a one, with nothing but polite propriety between them? Haps their behavior was only reserved in front of him, a guest. Haps behind closed doors the ladies of the household spoke volubly on all matters. He would endeavor to find out.

He wondered at what they might do, should he speak to them of more pertinent matters. His own house was one full of opinions from both sexes, which often led to long, invigorating conversation and argument. Lord, he missed Cait's arguments.

After at least ten more banal questions, Iain said, "Lady Morwen, I was sorry tae hear of yer conscripted lads tae the English. Do ye have plans tae recapture them?"

It was, perhaps, an impudent question, put to a lady who no doubt would have no thoughts or dealings with vengeance, but he held her eyes. Surely she had an opinion. No one could go through life without them.

Alice was, as far as he could tell, her mother remade. Looking upon Lady Morwen now, with the shock of such a question put to her, he wanted to take her by the shoulders and shake her until something honest fell from her lips. His own mother would have something to say about the conscription, that was certain. And Cait would have pestered him with questions and listened at doors to glean even the smallest bit of news or plans being made.

Disappointingly, Lady Morwen merely blushed and muttered, "I leave all such dealings to my capable husband."

"Of course," said Iain graciously, feeling accountably weary. This exchange drained the life from him. He turned to Alice instead. "I would hear what Lady Alice would do, should such a duty fall upon her. What is it ye'd do as laird, and yer charge stolen away?"

Alice's full mouth opened slightly, her breast lifting with the breath she drew in. Her cheeks shone pink, evidence of her discomfort, but he gloried in her reaction. Now he would have something of substance fall from her lips. But no, her eyes fell away, demurely affixed on the carpeted floor. "It would be imprudent for me to speculate on such an important matter," she said just as politely as her mother, her voice as soft as a summer breeze.

Iain could not help his disappointment but still he held out hope. He'd seen the spark in her eye, however brief, before she'd snuffed it out. He took a deep breath and tried again: "'Tis no' imprudent to speculate," he coaxed, "if one is invited to share their opinions."

Alice looked at her father, then at her hands. "I cannae say, milord. It would be intolerable for one such as I, with sae little experience in the world of men, tae offer such an opinion."

Iain grunted, his eyes darting to Alexander. He needed to get her alone, he thought, away from her parents. He hadn't failed to notice how she looked to them before speaking. It might have been unfair of him to expect more from her. What had he expected? A soliloquy on the merits of sacrifice in the name of keeping peace? He scoffed inwardly and said nothing more, resolving instead to sit in silence.

It didn't last long. "I've sommat I'd like ye tae see, Iain," Alexander said. Clearing his throat, he stood and walked to the sideboard, to an ornately carved chest. He opened it soundlessly and produced two rolled parchments, much battered as though they'd been handled heavily. "Have ye seen such in yer travels?" he asked, handing Iain the pages. "These were given tae me by Cressingham himself. Seems they're leaving them in each village they pass through."

Iain cast a curious look at his future father-in-law and took the scrolls wordlessly. The costly vellum sheets had been poorly cared for. Soiled by water or drink, the pages felt stiff in his hands. Indeed, a flake fell from the edges of the first sheet as he unrolled it, revealing a likeness of one Andrew Moray.

The image was skillfully made, but the artist had given Moray deepened eyes and a thick brow that hinted at a menace the true owner did not emulate. The broadsheet declared Andrew Moray an outlaw, wanted for crimes of treason against the royal crown. *Any person who gives shelter or aid to Moray, or any persons involved in his support, will be executed without trial.*

Iain's mouth had gone dry. His uncle, his brother, his sister...they were all guilty of supporting the outlaw. Intimately so. But this was not common knowledge and so Iain kept his face carefully neutral. "King Edward must be concerned, indeed, if he's wasting good gold on finding the man. What can Moray do, with his father in the tower? Does the son have power over his father's people?"

Alexander shrugged noncommittedly. "That remains tae be seen. Some say as he might. The Morays o' Petty are aligned with the burgesses—freemen, ye ken, who contribute tae the running o' the land and how it is taxed. They will no' wish tae follow King Edward, I think, and lose what freedoms they so readily enjoy."

Of course Iain knew that Moray was potentially dangerous for England, which is why his family had endeavored to help him. He set the page aside and unfurled the second sheet. He could not help his start of surprise at seeing the face of his brother's retainer, Graham, who had been unavoidably left behind in England when Ewan had helped to transport the outlaw from Chester Castle to Nairn. To the house of his sister, Cait, where he was currently convalescing.

Publicly, Graham's whereabouts were a mystery.

"This man, this Graham," said Alexander, his eyes carefully reading Iain's face, "was captured by the English. Cressingham said as he killed two English guards in his escape near Stamford Bridge. Do ye mind him?"

Iain's wame curdled. He felt as if he were being tested, as if Alexander knew all already and was only gauging Iain's forthrightness. He could not lie and say he did not know him for it was quite possible that Alexander knew or recognized Graham as one of Ewan's retainers. Iain nodded stiffly, his eyes roving over the image.

The artist had rendered Graham's likeness well: fair, one eyed, and hulking. But as with Moray, there was an added menace drawn in the line of his brow, in the set of his wide shoulders that did not exist in the kindly tracker. The swath of cloth wrapped around his head, covering his bad eye did not lend him any charms.

"It charges him as a murderous traitor tae the crown," said Iain quietly, feeling like his lips had lost all feeling. "As an accomplice in Moray's escape." Iain wanted to argue that Graham had sworn no fealty to the King of England, that he was merely a retainer of the Ruthven clan, but he knew that any person under Ewan's charge would be held to the same standard as their liege lord. Ewan had bent the knee and kissed Edward's ring, which meant all under his charge had made the same vow.

Iain resisted the urge to fidget in his chair and rolled up the page, offering it wordlessly back to Alexander.

Alexander's keen eyes pinned Iain to the spot. "Tell me true, Iain, what is it ye ken of these dealings? What game is afoot?" Iain saw from the corner of his eye how Alice's eyes lifted from the floor to stare at him. He did not meet her gaze.

Iain, as a rule, had not taken part in any of the carefully laid plans to help Moray escape the English. Ewan had been careful to leave him out of all his treasonous dealings lest Ewan die in his efforts as a traitor to the crown. If such a thing were to happen, Iain would denounce his brother and claim his loyalty to the King of England and keep the lands within their grasp. Iain was to take care of Edyth and their people. He was charged to live the lie should the worst happen.

But Iain was no fool. He could not divulge such a thing, even to Alexander, who hated the English just as fiercely as he did, no matter that they were allies.

He shook his head slightly in denial. "What crime did Graham commit that we would not? If you were captured by the English and held prisoner, would ye meekly do as you were bid? Would ye let them take yer life from you? No. I daresay ye wouldnae. Haps he is guilty o' killing the English solders, but they would have just as easily slit his throat or left him tae die a miserable death in some dank hold."

Alexander nodded once, his eyes never leaving Iain's face. "Aye, but what was this Graham doing sae far south? I mind him as one of yer brother's men. He wouldnae set foot on English soil save his master bid it o' him. Why was he in England, Iain, and sae near the escaped Moray?"

Iain frowned and swallowed his curt reply. "I am no' privy tae the reasons for being in England, nor can I say as what happened tae cause the death o' the Englishmen. I can, however, say that knowing the man, Graham wouldnae kill anyone if there had been another way."

Alexander, eyes narrowing, made a sound of disbelief in his throat. Pushing off the back of the chair he'd been leaning against, he said, "Tis a shame that ye're no' privy tae such information. Tis a strange coincidence, is it no', that Moray escapes from Chester Castle and yer brother's retainer is captured by the same guardsmen searching for Moray?"

Iain merely shrugged. He could not, would not implicate his brother in this. Alexander continued speaking, moving to sit opposite to him. "You asked my wife and daughter what they would do should they be chieftain. Ye asked if my lady wife planned to retrieve our lads from Cressingham. Why?"

Iain shrugged. He could hardly tell this man the truth of the matter, that he only wished to goad them into loosening their tongues. Iain forced himself not to glance at the ladies, sitting nearest the fire and searched his mind for something witty to say, some joke that would ease the tension in the chieftain, who Iain guessed, he had insulted.

Forcing his body to relax, Iain loosened his limbs so that he might appear completely at ease and appealed to the man's pride. "It is unlike the house o' Stewart tae take Cressingham's insult and it go unanswered," he said with a slight uplift of a brow.

Alexander's fingers tapped lightly on the arm of his chair, his eyes intent upon Iain, waiting. For what, he could only guess. Most likely the quickest way to cave in his skull. But no, after a long pause Alexander said, "Aye, ye've got the right o' it, *Mac-cèile*," his shrewd eyes telling Iain that this was not the end of their conversation.

*Son-in-law*, he'd called him. The title made Iain feel as though he were being swept along in a swift current, unable to find his feet.

The chieftain emptied his cup and set it aside, leaning forward in his seat as if to impart some great secret. Iain followed suit, leaning forward until their faces were a foot apart. Alexander's eyes were alight with an avidity Iain could not name. He appeared almost *mad*. "I might have a plot o' my own needing bold action," whispered Alexander. "If what I believe is true, and yer brother has aided the Moray, then I call upon you, future son o' my house, tae aid me now."

Iain's blood turned to ice. Alexander had indeed guessed at their dealings. Iain, for his part, had also guessed rightly. Alexander wanted the Ruthvens as allies to use in whatever scheme he'd dreamed up. Iain sat back in his chair, surveying Alexander over steepled fingers.

Glancing at Alice, who was presently staring into the fire, her hands clasped in a knot in her lap, Alexander said, "Alice's maid has a son who was recently conscripted by Cressingham. I would...*retrieve* him...and others, with the right help."

Iain narrowed his eyes, his dislike for this conversation mounting. "What is it ye mean tae do?"

Alexander's hard gaze cut through him, assessing, no doubt, whether he deemed Iain man enough—worthy enough—for such a secret. "Yer father, Malcolm, was a good man. I trusted him. And now as a son of my own house, I will trust you as well. I mean tae raid Cressingham's caravan o' stolen lads."

Iain could only stare. He *was* mad. Completely. He shook his head as if to clear it, then said, "But Cressingham will have a host o' men with him. How can ye hope tae get past any one o' them without being seen, much less take back yer men? Unless…" Iain eyed his future father-in-law, his circumspection turning to disbelief. "Ye cannae mean to kill them all, surely."

Alexander's amused huff should have been answer enough, but he continued. "Have a soft spot for Cressingham and his men, do ye? Worrit for 'em are ye?"

Iain narrowed his eyes in annoyance. "Ye ken I dinnae care one whit fer the man or his English cronies, but I *do* care a wee bit about the head that sits atop my shoulders at present. I'd hate tae have it misplaced."

This seemed to appease Alexander in some small way. A grudging smile curled upon his face, his manicured beard twitching. "Aye, and I wouldnae wish tae make Alice a widow sae soon. No, I dinnae mean to kill them all," he said brightly. "But I do mean tae strike fast and hard and take back what's mine. Or at least give the conscripted lads a chance at freedom."

The "too soon" comment from Alexander rankled Iain but he chose to ignore it. He sat up straighter in his chair, his mind trying to formulate a plan in which such a thing could be possible. "Even if ye can get past all the guards, which will be many, how will ye find yer people in the chaos? Don't ye think they'll notice who it is that's been taken? Surely they'll notice all the Stewart lads have been stolen away by Stewart men at arms. They're no' witless!"

"No, I daresay ye've got the right o' it," acknowledged Alexander. "Tae my mind, we must no' take anyone awa' from the convoy. We mun only strike the wagon train and draw away the guards, giving the conscripted lads a chance tae scatter. If they're canny, which they are, they will all hide awa and bide their time, getting home as they can. I daresay the Caimbels, MacNabs, and MacLarens will be glad tae see their lads return home as well. We'll go cloaked, with no heraldry. It must be secret. And it must be quick."

Iain stared at Alexander, not knowing what to say. It was bold, to say the least. He'd come here thinking to confirm wedding dates and dowry terms, but here he was, being conscripted himself, but to an altogether different event. One that would endanger his entire house.

He felt the weight of Alice's stare hot upon him like a brand, but when he turned his head to meet her eye, she looked away. He could only see heavy lashes touching a round cheek and mousy brown hair, braided as tightly as her lips.

"Have ye considered ye might need permission tae enter neighboring clan lands?" asked Iain.

Here Alexander shrugged, waving a hand as if it were nothing to trespass illegally on another clan's territory and commit murder. "There will no' be so many of us that they would even ken we're there. Besides, the place I wish tae carry this out, our clans are friendly."

"Mmph," grumbled Iain. *At least for now they are*, the thought sardonically. *They might not feel so friendly once Alexander committed treason on their property.*

"What have ye tae say in this matter, Lady Alice?" asked Iain. "Is your maid's son worth so many lives? If even one man is caught, yer house stands to lose much. And mine."

Alice took a careful breath, her dark eyes emotionless as she shyly met his eye. Was there no life to be had in this timid creature? God's teeth he wanted to shout in her face, to shake some life into her bones.

Finally, after a stretched silence wherein her innocuous expression did not change, she said, "I would gladly give my own life for him if it would bring him back tae his mother, but alas, I am but a woman and am without recourse. Excuse me," she said, shooting him an unexpected, icy stare, her ears gone pink. "The hour grows late."

Her mother, apparently sharing her daughter's discomfort, stood a beat after, and they left the room apiece, as silent as a breeze. He gaped after them. Well that was something at least. She'd spoken more than two words together that had nothing to do with his health or the lingering winter air. Still, she'd been as demure as ever, save for that the look she'd shot him. She did not favor him, it would seem. That was no surprise, thought Iain, though it did not fill him with any cheer.

"We will wait until the convoy is again on the move," said Alexander, as if he did not notice the exit of the strange creatures he lived with. How long did it take, Iain wondered, how many years did it take for the man to become so immune to silence and meek answers? But no, thought Iain. Alexander most likely encouraged their behavior. He liked the man even less.

"We've learned that they travel in a long procession," continued Alexander, "interspersed with men on horseback, several at the front and at the back. There are also guards that ride along the side o' the procession, but they are fewer in number."

"Ye've been spying, then?"

"O' course. I wouldnae ask such a thing from ye without a plan. My scouts report that the wagons are open and only some are adorned with bands tae cage their prisoners, not that they would need any. They dinnae need a cage when they've got crossbows. Run and ye'll get a bolt in yer back faster than yer next breath."

Iain understood perfectly. Ewan's scout had reported much the same. There was also the fact that the conscripted men would not fight against their captors if they believed their lord wished for their acquiescence. They would see it as their duty.

Alexander took a deep breath and continued. "We could cross through the northern pass and lay in wait near the Murray boarder if we're swift enough. The wagons are slow there, in the canyon pass, and there are many who walk that cannot fit in the wagons, slowing the procession further. It could be done."

"You wish to ambush them in the ravine, and them with a week's head start?"

Alexander nodded, unconcerned. "Aye. Ambush is the surest way to come away without casualties, tae my mind. They are not too far gone as yet, with how often they stop. Remember, they gather Scotland's sons at the larger villages they come to. And while their caravan is well guarded, it is slow and vulnerable if approached correctly. With a handful of Stewart men, we could take back what is ours and even free others. Our chances are better still now that we've got yer lads 'ere tae help us."

Iain inwardly recoiled, the feeling of being exploited returning in full force. It was with some effort that he next spoke. "The lads I brought with me are but green things, crofters and fisherfolk. They cannae be asked tae raid against hardened soldiers."

"I was once a green thing, as were you," said Alexander, as if Iain's concern was nothing. "Now is as good an age as any tae aquit themselves o' childish pursuits. They will be well protected in the canyon pass; besides, there are trails and hiding places aplenty tae hold all."

Iain shook his head. "I brought them here under the guise of protection. Protection for a price, which *I've paid* with agreeing tae wed yer daughter. Nay," said Iain, shaking his head. "Ye ask too much, chieftain or no'. My brother willnae agree tae put the lads in danger, nor will I."

Alexander narrowed his eyes in a rather unfriendly way. "Payment? Payment for my daughter's hand comes in the form of her dowry, which ye agreed upon, I'll remind ye. The raid is no' for payment, but a request." Alexander, ever the conspirator, must have sensed Iain's dislike and distrust, for he leaned away as if at his leisure.

Alexander waved a hand. "If ye willnae permit the use o' yer men, then so be it—" He sniffed, looking for all intents and purposes, much like a king ruling over his kingdom. "Yer skill with a sword is renowned. I've seen ye preform at the tourneys and at the gathering. I've no doubt ye'll be an asset tae my men in the canyon, even if ye go without yer own men."

"They're wee laddies, no' men," reminded Iain. "Nor do I have *my laird's* consent tae use them in such a manner. I am sworn tae my laird and brother, no' the house o' Stewart."

Alexander's eyes sparked. "Regardless, the question remains: will yer sense o' honor compel ye in aiding us? We have helped ye by giving a place for yer young men during Cressingham's conscription, as ye've pointed out. If ye willnae use them, so be it. I will accept yer choice. But what about you, *mac-cèile*? Will you lift your sword tae aid us?"

Iain tried very hard to swallow bitter words lest they tumble from his mouth. He had no desire to appear as the coward. And while it was true that with Alice came a sizable dowry, it hadn't tempted him in the least. What had brought him here had been the promise of safety for the lads of Perthshire. Agreeing to this scheme felt as though he was giving far too much to the man. Payment, indeed! He'd be paying for the rest of his life! Which, he thought rather derisively, might end very soon should he agree to this scheme.

It wasn't that he cared for King Edward or that he wished for the war in Flanders to be paid for with Scottish blood. Indeed, he did not. But he rather resented being manipulated into fighting. He could tell Alexander no, of course. He could and be branded as a faint-hearted coward. Especially since Alexander had guessed correctly that clan Ruthven was already deeply enmeshed in their own treasonous plot.

A terrible thought struck him suddenly. If he refused, would Alexander let slip his knowledge of Graham being a Ruthven retainer? The broadsheet had not said as much. Indeed, if such information had been well known, Ewan would have already been questioned or even arrested.

"What is your mind?" asked Alexander. "I can see ye're weighing it all oot in her heid. Is it battle yer worrit o'er? We'll give ye a good crossbow and pair ye with one o' my seasoned warriors, if yer in need o' such."

He felt himself bristle despite himself. "I'm no' fearful," said Iain, ice in his veins. "Pain of death doesnae concern me."

Alexander raised a questioning brow. "Then what's the problem? Do I no' have yer allegiance?"

Allegiance? He thought of Alice again. Did he owe such loyalty to her father? Yes, the man had given shelter to their young men, and in the past he'd helped with other issues, but did marrying the woman force him to agree to such an act?

They were allies, were they not? Had been for the whole of his life and before. And haps, he thought optimistically, regaining Alice's maid would win her favor. Surely proving he was a man of honor would garner some respect from the cold lady. She would have something to say to him then, surely. And what's more, Iain agreeing to raid the convoy did not strictly go against Ewan's wishes. He would be cloaked and unknown. He would only have to be careful not to be caught.

Drawing a breath he hedged, "I will aid ye where I might in this, but my allegiance is with my chieftain alone."

Alexander's hard gaze glittered with something akin to triumph. "Aye. I'm glad tae hear my men will have the aid of yer experience and the strength of yer arm." Alexander moved to pick up the decanter of spirit from the sideboard. He refilled Iain's cup then his own. "We will drink on it."

Iain barely tasted the whiskey, knocking it back then holding out his cup for another.

Alexander chuckled. "Do ye ken that yer mother and I were well acquainted afore she wed yer father?" he asked. "Aye, I courted 'er for a time." Alexander retook his seat, looking into his cup as if he could view in its surface the distant past, a smile playing about his lips. "Roslyn was no' only beautiful, but fierce. She had a tongue on her as sharp as any sword. Still does, as a matter of fact." His eyes lifted to Iain's, a look of respect within them. "I kent well enough she would raise lads as would respect and honor their wives. If anyone can be a husband tae my daughter, it would be a son o' fair Roslyn. It gladdens my heart tae ken my Alice willnae be wed tae a coward."

Iain did not know what to say. He felt sick, but there was nothing he could do but raise his cup in salute to his own mother.

Drinking after such a speech felt like a final surrender but he did it, feeling hollow and apart from himself in a way he had never before experienced.

"Tae fair Roslyn and her sons," said Alexander, lifting his cup briefly then taking a drink.

"Tae fair Roslyn," echoed Iain, his voice a rasp.

# Chapter Eight

The next morning, as Iain sat at the table in the hall, quietly breaking his fast with his clan members, he was surprised to find Alice approaching him.

Judging by the strained smile upon her face, at the way she walked as if she had a lance for a backbone, he rather thought she might have been ordered to seek him out. It bothered him to think that any lass would dislike him so well as to be obliged to speak to him, much less his soon-to-be wife. Her demeanor did not go unnoticed by the Ruthven lads around him. They cast him furtive looks but wisely chose not to comment.

"Milord," she said tightly. "Would ye be so kind as tae accompany me in a visit tae the chapel this morning? And, haps, to the mews after?"

Iain had no real affinity for prayers or for falconry, but agreed all the same. Haps, away from her family, he could pull a personality out of her. And haps the sun would not set this day and the oceans heave their bounds. Iain shoved those rude thoughts away. He'd sworn to himself that very morning that he would only seek out her virtues.

The contract was signed. He'd agreed to this union, no matter how backhanded her father had been. It wasn't Alice's fault Alexander had played him in such a way. Iain would not dishonor himself, his family, nor Lady Alice. He only hoped that she was not her father incarnate. There would only be one way to find out.

She departed on a curtsey, gone as quickly as she'd come, leaving him wondering. He'd slept ill, his thoughts teetering on the verge of the ridiculous. He'd awoken at one point with the sudden, burning thought that, haps, if Alice did not wish to marry Iain, that she might go to her father and beg his acquiesce in terminating the terms of the betrothal.

The last at the table, he finally set off to the keep's chapel, venturing down dark corridors. He got turned around once and had to double back, but finally he arrived at the ornately carved double doors of the chapel. Torchlight sputtered from a bracket beside the door. No windows graced the gallery, leaving it full of twitching shadows.

Unlike most places of worship, the keep's chapel room was small and intimate, meant only for family. There were no high ceilings that amplified every sound as most chapels did. The creaking of the door on its iron hinges signaled his arrival, but the veiled head of Alice did not lift from its bow as he entered.

She was kneeling near the front of the room, only but twenty or so paces from the back, close to the altar that sat between the benches and the vestibule beyond. There was only one window on the right side of him, spilling silver light across the bench seats. Candles filled the air with a haze of smoke that clung to the ceiling.

They were not alone. A priest also knelt in prayer off to the side near the window, his bald head bowed in contrition. Iain walked forward, the brisk, neat sound from his boots filling the space. He paused for a breath when he reached her pew, unsure. Alice, in this meek state, reminded him of the sparrow he'd first associated her with. She did not stir. She did not even look at him.

He made the quick decision to kneel with her, largely because he didn't feel like waiting in the aisle like a fool. Crossing himself, he found his place beside her on the small cushion but could not think of anything productive or sufficiently meek to say that might be pleasing to God. The only thoughts in his head were selfish and desperate, thoughts that put his honor into question.

After a time, the priest stood and exited through a door behind the altar, against the left side of the room. Iain had not even noticed it there, so shrouded in shadow it had been. Alice lifted her head after the door shut, the opaque material covering her head falling away to reveal her face.

Iain was alarmed to see moisture in her eyes. Immediately he searched for his kerchief, which he did not have, and felt lacking. *So much for winning her over with gallantry*, he thought. His heart softened looking at her large, soulful brown eyes. Even in the dim light he could see lines of gold that softened the darker features of her eyes.

He did not know what to say and he had nothing to offer her so he waited, feeling unsure and out of his depth. Tears of a woman were never a simple thing. With his sister Cait, it was easy: tease her, coax her from her melancholy until she forgot her sorrow. But that had been learned through a lifetime of experience. With Alice, he was in new territory.

In the quiet of the room, where only the soft sputtering of a candle as it suffocated in wax could be heard, Alice spoke: "I am happy to live alone," she whispered. "I would give myself to the church, if I cared for such things."

Iain's eye darted to the very large and ornate crucifix hanging on the wall before them, his usual teasing, crooked smile gracing his face. "Ye seem well enough devoted tae the church to my view. Ye're here, praying, are ye no'?" His smile widened and he looked down at her in a commiserating way. "Och, I ken yer mind now, lady. Ye've reconsidered yer previous heathen ways with the hope that God will save ye from the likes o' me."

Iain waited for a smile, a huff of a laugh, but Alice's eyes only stared blankly. His smile faltered and he recalled, once again, how it had been in Perthshire when she'd come to visit him in the autumn. He'd tried then to tease and to draw her out, but he'd been unsuccessful. He'd hoped at the time that she was only feeling unsure and shy, being in a stranger's home. But no. Nothing had changed. Disappointed dread welled up in him at the realization that this just might be Alice's disposition.

"God hears prayers of heathens as well as those of saints," she replied hollowly. Her eyes drifted to the carved crucifix, solemn and serious. Iain studied the side of her face; he could not read what she might be thinking or feeling. Haps if he plied her with strong drink, she might loosen her stiff tongue and they could have a real conversation.

The thought of this timorous creature drunk nearly made him snort. He schooled his face and tried again. "To which group do ye belong then? Heathen or saint?" Iain made a show of eyeing her speculatively. To his mind she looked, as ever, the embodiment of saintly nun. He could not imagine a more fitting role for her, yet she'd said she did not care for such a life.

"I cannae say, milord," she whispered. "Only God can judge."

He repressed a sigh. God help him, but he did not know what to do with such a strange creature. He was trying to speak to her, wasn't he? He was attempting to create conversation, but she stopped him at every turn. His usual easy banter with women was useless here. He would have to employ some other tactic.

Rubbing a long finger under his nose, his lips pressed tightly together, he grimly set to the task of being straightforward. "You must speak plainly tae me, Lady Alice." He tried to temper the irritation out of his voice but thought that he must have failed for the shocked look she now wore. "I have no wish to solve riddles," he explained further. "What is yer meaning when ye say ye'd rather live alone? Speak yer mind."

The first sign of life from Alice came in the form of blossoming cheeks. Her color changed from its usual pale tone to a rosy hue that stretched from the apple of her cheeks and spread to her ears. He could just see one of them through the gauzy veil she wore, mottled red.

"I only mean," she said in a strained whisper, "that I have grown accustomed to the idea of living alone. I've long since outgrown any fanciful notions of marriage that one clings to in their youth. Nor do I wish tae be a nun, which is the only course left to me."

Iain lifted a questioning brow, almost afraid to breathe lest it frighten away this new, bold creature. This was more words of substance strung together apiece than he'd ever heard from her. When she did not continue, he hazarded a question: "Why is a convent the only course left tae ye?"

Alice's brows knit together, shooting him a look that plainly showed she thought him simpleminded. "For someone who surrounds himself with women, it's a miracle ye ken so little of our lives."

Iain raised a brow. What did she mean he *surrounded* himself with women? But he let her words lie, instead saying, "I ken well enough what sort of lives women lead, but ye're the daughter of a chieftain. Ye'll no' want for anything. Surely yer father will not command ye awa' nor leave ye destitute. Ye have a home and a family, always."

Alice merely huffed softly, not looking at him. She bowed her head, her hands folded neatly on the bench before them. Had she dismissed him? He waited, holding his tongue, thinking he deserved an award for his exercise in patience.

He could not wait any longer. "So ye choose marriage tae a man ye dinnae want or need o'er endless prayers in a cold kirk. Is that it?"

Alice turned sharply to face him, the anger in her eyes giving him a righteous sense of triumph. "Dinnae pretend that you want or need me, sir," she hissed. "It is no mystery what a man such as you wishes for in a wife."

Iain could not help his ire. It had been slowly rising as the tide, sure and unavoidable. He was neck-deep in indignation; soon, he would not be able to hold back his frustration any longer and it would spill forth from his mouth in words best kept buried. "Ken my mind, do ye, then?" he growled. "Pray tell, what is it that I wish for in a wife?"

A none too discreet cough sounded from somewhere in the vicinity of the back of the room, drawing their eyes. Iain must have not noticed him upon entering the room, but there, in the back corner of the chapel stood another priest at a tall desk, a long quill hovering in the air.

Alice glared at Iain as if he had performed some depraved act—and in the house of God no less. The color on her cheeks changed from pink to crimson, her dark eyes narrowed. Iain stood, stepping out into the aisle. He waited, his hand out in invitation, but Alice merely stared at it, her chin thrust forward in defiance.

"I'm no' yer enemy," he said, irritated, but he let his hand drop. "Let us move beyond these walls." She nodded and stood on her own with the aid of the bench and followed him down the aisle. Iain's first inclination, despite his frustration was to tease, to draw her out over refusing his hand in worry for what the priest might say of such innocent touching.

He flattered himself that he was a quick study. He was good at all the usual academic and knightly tasks that he'd been obliged to learn, but he was even better at reading people. Almost from their first exchange, he'd learned that Alice did not respond to levity. At first, he'd taken it as a challenge; now, he felt only constrained and disappointed that she could not—would not—rally to his banter.

So far as yet, however, he had seen little aside from serious reflection and near-silent timidity from her. Except for today. She spoke to him, at least. She'd come and invited him to the chapel, he reminded himself. Aye, it looked as if it had cost her, but still she'd done it.

Whatever had come over her, he welcomed it. Haps he would not need to ply her with drink, but only make her angry enough that she lost her temper. Hap then, he might finally learn who Alice Marjory Elisabeth Stewart really was.

Their dual footfalls filled the small space as they exited into the dim of the gallery. They moved further down the hallway together and stopped, as if by some silent communication, in the shadowy space between torches.

Here, in the inky darkness, he thought she might feel safer. Here, with the walls close around them and the shape of their features softened to obscurity, he hoped she might speak. It felt to him as if they were in confessional. Haps she would feel the same and they could finally learn of each other. Iain bowed slightly, a hand gesturing toward her in invitation. "Speak," he entreated. "I listen."

Alice nodded stiffly, looking about her as if to check for hidden ears. "Let us have no pretense between us," she started, her tone careful and quiet, as if she were forcing calm upon herself. "This union is not borne of love. I have seen with my own two eyes how womenfolk flock to you, how they simper and hang on yer e'ry word as if ye hold their hearts in yer very hands." She made a face here, her nose crinkling with obvious disgust. She leveled him with a glare, her lip curling slightly. "I will no' be such a one. Abandon any hope of such a wife."

Iain didn't know if he should laugh or be insulted but he welcomed her anger, unjustly aimed at him or no. This was better than empty stares and silence. He refocused his mind. What did she mean, she'd seen lassies flock to him? He wasnae a mother hen. No one *flocked* to him. Nor did the ladies simper. Aye, he was...friendly. Sometimes he was a bit more than friendly, but Alice was painting him as a dishonorable wretch.

Not only this, but why did she assume that he was looking for a love match? It was preposterous. She was making far too many assumptions for his liking.

The slow intake of breath through his nose gave him precious seconds in which to control his tone. "Like calls tae like, aye? Would ye rather I be stiff and reticent? Would ye rather I was sullen and rude so that others would find it difficult tae entreat me?" He gave her a significant look, done with tiptoeing around her feelings. "Yes, madam," he said, "I have many friends, some of which, as ye pointed out, happen tae be women, but I'm no' what ye've made me out tae be, Lady Alice. I am no villain."

Alice was stiff, her lips pressed thinly. "Why then," she demanded, "when I came tae Perthshire...why did ye spend the whole of the games cavorting with any lassie that drew yer eye?"

Iain huffed a sardonic laugh. She wanted to speak of the festival? Och, he had something to say about the games. "Ye mean the same games that ye yawned through? It was all I could do tae come up with some way tae please ye, tae entertain ye, but ye said naught but twa words tae me."

"Ye're just sore that I didnae fawn all o'er ye like the others," she interjected, looking affronted.

Iain thought that, in another time and place, he might find this entire exchange humorous. He could not imagine Alice flattering anyone, least of all him, whom she seemed to despise for some reason. He could not account for it. What had he done to her to deserve such coldness? Such disdain?

"No one fawned," he said scornfully. His heart was hammering in his chest, so agitated he'd become. How could this small creature create such frustration in him? He turned back to the matter at hand, to her first declaration. "Ye've no need tae warn me against any lost hope of a love match between us," he informed her loftily. "Ye've made it quite plain ye dinnae wish for anything save silence. Why, it's all ye can do tae look me in the eye much less open yer mouth and speak."

Alice twitched as if the very word *love* was painful to her. "I'm speaking tae ye now, am I no'?" she demanded, lifting her chin stubbornly. "Nor was I raised for such a novelty as love, nor more than yerself."

Despite himself, he felt his irritation wane even as she glared up at him, her mouth twisted in scorn. What she said was true enough. Love had little place in arranged marriages but why bring it up? He didn't understand her at all.

But he'd gotten what he wanted, hadn't he? She was speaking to him at least. Well, he amended, she was shouting at him, but he wouldn't be picky. He'd take whatever he could get from her at this point.

All it took, apparently, was an offer for her to wax poetic over all his faults. She'd said he was too friendly with lassies. Accused him of base behavior. He frowned inwardly, unwilling to review any of his past deeds with a keen eye. He pushed the thought aside and said, "Aye, we may no' have been raised for such, but ye may come tae regret foreswearing such a possibility in marriage. Life is long, madam, and hard enough without adding further constraints. Will ye so easily cast off the possibility of affection?"

Alice's fine brows knitted together as if affection were equally foreign to her. He suppressed the urge to groan. Who was this person before him? "Most marriages have some form of affection, my lady," he said with only the slightest edge of bitterness.

Alice lifted her brows. "I suppose ye'd ken that well enough. You, the man who's rumored conquests cannae be counted on both our hands together. But I forget myself," she said in a falsely sweet tone. "None of yer conquests have been wed tae ye."

Iain laughed humorlessly, a bark of annoyance. She was insulting him in earnest now. He felt the tightly wound tether holding his anger in place snap. "Ha! Rumored conquests, ye say! And where have ye heard such a tale, Lady Alice? Idle servant's gossip or from yer own scheming family?"

Her face was full on red now. She visibly recoiled, her manner stiff and unyielding. "Scheming?" she demanded. "I dinnae need tae hear rumors," she hissed, her brows lifted to her hairline. "I saw with my ain eyes how the lassies followed ye around like brainless fools. I say, I willnae be such a one!"

Crossing his arms, he glared daggers at her. "Aye, I'm no' deaf. Ye said as much in the chapel."

"And why should I be such a wife? Why should I preen and simper and follow after ye like a great gowk tae appease yer pride? That is what ye wish for, is it no'?"

"Appease my pride? Is this what you think o' me? That I'm some vain sprag, desperate for any word that might feed my arrogance?"

Alice shrugged, looking stubborn indeed. Her arms were crossed, her breath coming short.

"What ladies can you mean?" demanded Iain, unwilling to give it up. "Speak now, Lady. I would have all yer complaints against me laid bare, for I'll no' wish tae revisit this conversation again in the future."

She waved a dismissive hand. "Ye expect me tae ken their names?"

They both fell deathly silent as the distant sound of footsteps and voices moved toward them. Alice shot Iain a warning look and tugged on his sleeve, pulling his eyes away from the two servant girls walking toward them, mere shadows in the low light at the end of the gallery. Alice walked briskly away, looking over her shoulder to ensure Iain followed. He did. God knows why. It certainly wasn't to feed his supposed immense ego.

She led him back through to the great hall, which was empty now save a handful of maids cleaning up after the morning meal, through the archway on the opposite side, and into the small sitting room he'd first been brought to upon his arrival yesterday.

As soon as he shut the door behind them, she whirled on Iain. "Ye called my family scheming!"

He nodded, leaning toward her slightly. They were mere feet apart in the sitting room. Were they more civilized, they might sit and speak calmly near the fire, but they were both far past calm. "Aye," said Iain with far too many teeth. "I thought yer parents would see we were no' a match when ye came tae Perthshire, but still they persisted. And when I wasnae keen tae sign the contract, yer Da cleverly contrives a way tae entrap me."

"Entrap!" she cawed, her eyes wide. "Entrap, he says!" A gasping, sputtering sound burbled from her, her fist going to her ribs as if there was a painful stitch there. She scowled as if she'd taken vinegar and muttered to herself. He watched as she waved a hand, dismissing his words as she paced on the ornate rug at her feet. When she turned back to him, righteous anger flowed from every line of her body.

"Ye wish tae speak of my visit tae Perthshire?" she seethed. "So be it! When I came tae meet you, my potential suitor, I wasnae prepared for what met me. I may no' have spoken but a few words tae ye but what did ye expect? I went there expecting tae find a gentleman, but instead I found a boorish lecher with a line o' lassies constantly surrounding yer e'ry move."

Iain's mouth fell open unbecomingly. "Lecher, am I? Be mindful of what you accuse, my lady." It was absurd! Never in his life had he a line of women flocking to him, nor hanging on his every word. The lassies in his village knew him far too well to pine over him. Yes, he flirted and teased.

He had many women who were his friends and while it was true that he'd kissed a few—alright more than a few—still he was no lech. Leastways he could not recall giving any such attention to any ladies whist Alice had visited.

"Do you deny it, sir?"

"I do deny it! Who was hangin' on my e'ry word, I'd like tae know."

"Why?" she asked with mock curiosity. "Sae ye can put her tae mind if ye e'er find yerself in need?"

Iain took a menacing step forward. She'd gone too far. He opened his mouth to retort but she merely waved a hand in his face as if she could dismiss her words as easily as a midge. "At the games," she continued "You were like a great peacock, basking in the attentions others gave ye. It was made clear tae me that ye're well acquainted with the womenfolk, that yer bed is rarely empty!"

"Made clear tae ye? Idle talk! Women crow just as loudly as men, never mind if it's the truth or no'," he announced, throwing his hands into the air. He took several deep breaths, glaring, and asked, "Who said such a thing?"

Alice, still pacing, bit out, "I heard some of the lassies in the crowd, bragging about who would have you next."

Iain huffed a laugh, shaking his head. "Look at me," he commanded. "Alice, cease this infernal pacing." The familiar use of her given name seemed to startle her. Reluctantly, she turned and found his eyes. With a great effort he tamped down his offense.

"Never would I take a lassie tae my bed and dishonor her or her family. They ken me far too well tae think I would. Aye, I've stolen kisses and..." He rolled his shoulder here, uncomfortable with saying just what liberties he'd taken. "And a bit more," he finished lamely. "But I cannae help wagging tongues nor more than you."

Alice scoffed as if this was only further proof of his wanton indiscretions with the ladies at the games. She turned from him, giving him her back. She was as prickly as a thistle, though, and just as stubborn to root out. He'd been entirely wrong about her. She was not quiet, nor demure as she was in public. He was having a difficult time consolidating the two very different versions of her.

They were, both of them, quiet for a long time, the only sound in the room that of their breathing slowly returning to normal. Finally, she broke the strained silence, still not looking at him. "I...I overheard you. In the hall when I went tae sup the day afore we left. You were there with a group of lads. Ye were...laughing at me."

Iain's thoughts fell away, his insides shriveling. He felt the very color leave his face. He did not have to think too hard to recall of what she spoke. The remembrance of his words came to him as quick as lightning; he had shamed her. A burning humiliation filled him.

His friend, Ranalt, had asked about the potential union between the clans, asking the sort of ribald questions puerile men enjoyed when teasing or talking about the opposite sex. Iain had laughed and had claimed he could not be tempted to such a plain bride even if she were as rich as the King of England.

He'd noticed her shortly thereafter and they'd quickly changed the subject. It had been a mistake. He hadn't meant his words to reach her. It meant nothing...just Ranalt teasing him and his answering in kind. His mouth worked, opening and closing as words failed him.

How was he to go forward? He could not deny what he'd said. He could not refute it with a lie, but nor would an apology ease the hurt he'd caused. He knew women well enough to ken that. She would most likely never forgive him for it.

But, at least, he could now understand her disapproval of him.

She was not done speaking. "Yer own brother chose a destitute Englishwoman over myself, whose family is in long-standing friendship with my own." She swallowed heavily and sat in a chair, her fingers knotted in her lap. "I am no' so young as I once was," she said, her voice suddenly soft. It wavered slightly. Something within his wame did the same. "I ken well enough I am unremarkable compared to other women, so I consigned myself tae live alone. Indeed, I confess that I would rather choose solitude over the church. Nor would I prefer a man who finds me wanting."

Iain had never felt so small. He licked his dry lips and moved to sit across from her, leaning forward in his seat as if to compel her to hear him. "I was wrong," he admitted, his voice full of regret. "I shouldnae have said such a thing. It was unseemly of me to take part in such cruel entertainment, and I'd beg yer pardon for what I said."

She did not look at him. He could not read her, but he could see her cheeks warm with the evidence of her outburst. Iain had no doubt he was of a similar likeness. Their knees were a mere foot apart. He could see very plainly the fine hairs that sprang from her temples like sparks of lighting, short and delicate. She had a very light smattering of freckles, the exact color of her hair across the bridge of her nose. Like a constellation of stars.

"Never again will such blasphemy leave my lips," he promised, his voice all but a whisper.

She pulled in a shaky breath and dared to meet his eyes, bronze and umber framed by sooty lashes, dark with emotion. They were clear of tears, but full of an emotion he felt matched his own injured heart. "Pretty words," she muttered, "but what of fidelity, husband? Will ye promise me such?"

He did not like her assumption that he would not be a loyal husband but he swallowed his want for offense and said, "I dinnae make frivolous vows, my lady. Aye, I vow fidelity and more." He paused, intent to finish this discussion here and now. He would lay it to bed for good, or so he hoped. "But, my lady, I *will* be courteous to those that entreat me, man or woman. Would ye rather I had ignored those that came tae wish me well in my sport or those that came to be entertained?"

Some part of Alice, whether it was the slope of her shoulders or the softening of her brow, changed. To Iain's eye, she seemed to melt, looking smaller and far less like the fierce woman she'd previously embodied. Slowly, her mousy demeanor returned and when he caught sight of her face as she looked to the opposite wall, unseeing, he could not name the emotion written within her eyes. He felt impotent with inexperience. He did not know if he should attempt to comfort her or keep his distance.

"I dinnae have the same easy bearing as others. As you," she confessed, looking into the banked fire. "I cannae make men laugh, nor charm them." She took a deep breath, her eyes meeting his. "When I saw ye at the games, sae easy with others but constrained with me, it was easy tae believe what those lassies said. I wished only that we could be easy with each other, but...." She shrugged. "I ken well enough that I cannae hold men captive with my charms. Indeed, I am plain. And then, when I heard you and yer friends laughing at me...." She trailed off, shrugging slightly, as distant as she'd ever been.

Iain felt suddenly and entirely ashamed at his previous assessment of her. Indeed, he had thought her plain upon first knowing her. Had held it against her as if it could justify his anger at his hand being forced. He'd thought of her as a sparrow, plain and plentiful. Unremarkable. And she *was* like a sparrow, but not in the same way he'd first considered.

An observer of such a creature, for instance, could well marvel at how the soft buff of feathers change subtly to all the colors of delicate grey and brown, at how the pillowy breast beckoned a soft touch, or how delicate features give way to fierce strength when defending their nests. For himself, he'd overlooked all the subtlety in her eyes, had not even cared to notice how they contained a myriad of colors. Dark at the edges, growing lighter toward the pupil with specks of gold.

When she was meek and uncomfortable, quiet and holding in her own thoughts, he could not see her. But he had seen her more clearly today. Had seen that she was far more than demure politeness and meek propriety. She was fierce and lovely, with her flushed cheeks, her full mouth, and her expressive eyes.

His gaze settled on her mouth, which had shot such well-placed arrows into his hardened heart. "Ye're quite wrong, my lady," said Iain softly. "Ye're no plain at all. Quite the opposite, in fact."

She did not respond and some other ladies might, with coy smiles or with practiced false modesty. She looked fully at him, her brow furrowed as if she did not understand him. As if he were a puzzle she could not quite work out.

After a short stretch of silence, Iain hazarded moving forward in his seat, leaning toward her so that he might impress upon her the sincerity of his words. She eyed him as one might a dangerous animal, wary yet curious.

"Ye claim our union cannae be one of love, but what of respect, Lady Alice? Is there room for such in our marriage?"

Alice picked at the cuff of her sleeve, her lips pursed in consideration. Slowly, she nodded. "I suppose it could, but respect can only flower where honesty and fidelity have first been planted."

Something like relief dared to enter his heart. Haps not all was lost. Haps she could forgive his slight to her. He felt the angle of his shoulders soften ever so slightly despite himself. "Hear me, My Lady." He waited for her eyes to find his own before continuing. "As I say, I dinnae take vows lightly. Trust that I will give ye honesty and fidelity. Respect is no small thing and I will honor it. All my days."

Her sharp nod came quickly. She drew herself up, as if preparing for some unpleasant task, her lips parted slightly. "Then be honest now, sir. Why agree tae this match if ye found me...as ye told yer friends, found the prospect sae distasteful?"

It seemed to Iain that asking such a straightforward question cost her greatly but still she met his eye, daring him to lie, to ply her with sweet words and flattery.

Iain would have to be honest. And while he did not wish to hurt her, any lie would be easily found because she already knew the truth. He hadn't wanted to marry her. Still, it wasn't as if she, herself, held any romantic regard for him. This thought lent him courage to speak truthfully.

"I've ne'r met anyone who glories in wedding a stranger," he said evenly. "I cannae say that I was eager tae enter into such a state with ye, nor more, it seems than you are eager tae wed me."

Alice was silent for a long moment. "Why, then? Why agree? For alliance only?"

No, it was more than alliance. Joining their families was the only way he could honor his father's memory, though he didn't quite understand why it mattered so much to him.

Aside from honoring his father, however, there was also the fact that he had no real choice in the matter. Not really. Faced with the possibility of his clan's lads being conscripted, marriage felt the better alternative, never mind his personal desires.

He chose his words carefully. "Remember, my lady, that we have both vowed honesty in the pursuit of respect." He waited for her slight nod before asking, "Did yer faither seek out an alliance with my family sae he could try tae use us in his plans against the English?"

A little line appeared between Alice's brows; her confusion was evident. "Use ye? In what way?"

Iain shrugged slightly, as if his clothes were suddenly too tight. "It is no secret that he wishes for an alliance in the coming storm—many clans would—but we are not so large a clan as others, who might make better partners. Perhaps yer father believes that, because we are small, we can be controlled."

Alice's expression betrayed no guile, only puzzlement. "For this reason ye accuse my father of entrapment?" Iain watched her carefully, intent to find a lie. She shook her head, looking mildly confused. "You gain much aligning with my family."

"Mmph," grunted Iain. "As ye say, we have much tae gain, and the house o' Stewart little, compared to other clans. Still yer father persisted. Why, he even endeavored to match Cait to yer Robert, a man twice her age and with a brood o' bairns."

Alice stared at him for a moment; he could see her mind working behind her eyes, searching for an answer. Was she searching for a suitable lie?

Finally she said, "Do ye forget that first an alliance was sought with yer brother, Ewan?" At Iain's shake of the head she continued. "When my father learned of yer laird marrying an Englishwoman, he was disappointed. Our families had been speaking of a potential union for some time and we felt—he worried—that yer family's sensibilities might change with the unusual union."

Iain did not miss the slip of her tongue. He raised his brows. *We.* "You worried as well? Worried o'er what?"

Alice, looking uncomfortable, pressed her lips together, her cheeks flushed. "I mean tae say," she said haltingly, "my family worried that an ally such as you, would now side with the English. Yer father was gone and Ewan married tae the English lass. People said as how she had no dowry tae offer and that she...well," she paused here, looking at her fingers. "Some said as she was not a suitable bride for such a man as yer brother."

The words were soft and barely heard. Iain had to strain to hear her over the sound of his own shallow breathing and the gentle whisper of the fire. She lifted her head, finding her voice with a slight shrug, her brown eyes direct. "We didnae ken what tae think, aye? But my faither knew well enough how Malcolm and Ewan doted on Caitriona. He thought as how, if yer Cait were married tae Robert, Ewan wouldnae sae easily forget the duty he owed tae Scotia. That he would choose more carefully his path, if his sister's livelihood was at stake."

Iain did not speak for several moments. "But Ewan married Cait tae the Thane in Nairn and still ye've sought out a marriage alliance. If ye're no' keen tae wed me, then why persist?"

Plucking at a loose thread on an embroidered cushion, she said, "My father says that he preferred a Ruthven son for me because he believed I would be treated well."

Iain sat back in his chair, considering her words. "There are many men who would treat a daughter of Laird Stewart well. Indeed, I ken that should his daughter be mistreated, yer father would do all in his power tae bring the offender tae justice."

Alice huffed softly, a whisper of laugh. "Aye, and it is with this same trust that he places me in the house of Ruthven, knowing that my husband would do likewise. Or so he believes."

Her doubt shamed him. And no doubt he deserved her censure and distrust. He was not sure how to move forward, but they must try for the sake of their happiness. "We cannae be free from the contract," said Iain carefully, "so we must come tae some other agreement. First, I would hear a return vow. We cannae expect such a boon as respect when only one half of the partnership has made the promise. I wish tae hear that ye'll speak truth tae me," he prodded.

Her dark, unblinking eyes made her look all the more like a bird. "I have spoken true," she said, a trace of displeasure in her tone. Ye would question my—" But she caught herself and nodded, her lips pressed together briefly. "Aye, o' course. Ye have my vow tae be honest and...and loyal."

He smiled slightly. "What a fine pair we make," Iain said with good humor, shoving aside his uncomfortable thoughts. It was all he knew to do, tease and make light. He sat forward in his seat once more and held out his hands, palms up. "How strange we are, tae cast off the idea of marriage, yet here we sit, making our own vows. Take my hands, aye?" he prodded.

Something in her eyes shifted away from the wariness he'd seen so plainly a moment before and, he thought he saw, a slight tug at the corner of her mouth. A ghost of a smile. It felt like a triumph. She followed suit and placed her hands into his own. Her hands were small and soft, the fingers square but feminine. He could see that she had a habit of biting her nails. He cleared his throat and said, "Now that our vows are complete, we can work toward a truce."

"A truce?" she asked, the hint of humor coloring her voice.

Iain squeezed her hands slightly. "Aye, in all civil matters of disagreement between two parties, there must be give and take. There must be compromise. We arenae the first such couple tae be united through contract, nor the last," remarked Iain. "Others have survived.

I daresay we will too." A smile, quick and commiserating lifted his lips, but Alice did not reciprocate. Indeed, her face was slack, her eyes trained on their hands. "Ee'n wars have been avoided through such means."

Alice nodded, ever serious, and lifted her gaze. "What is it ye suggest, then?"

"We have listed already our grievances," he said in a dismissive tone. "Already we ken of what we must work toward. We only need now tae find compromise. Haps we can make a way for each of us tae find happiness in this union. A way for each tae get something o' which we desire. D'ye agree?"

Alice considered him for a moment, her eyes searching his. "Agreed," she said after a beat. Pulling her hands away, she leaned back into her chair once again but this time, she looked over him boldly. "Yer idea has some merit," she conceded.

"Let us move forward now as friends, Lady Alice. Think on what ye might wish for in a union built of mutual respect. We can speak again when I return from the raid on Cressingham's convoy."

She stood and inclined her head respectfully. "Do be careful," she said kindly, and then she left him alone with his thoughts.

It was a long time before he found his way up to his apartments.

# Chapter Nine

C ait's letter arrived after the nooning meal, brought by a dusty, road
weary tinker, who had received the letter a month ago with a
charge to bring it south on his travels. From the state of the parchment,
he—and it—had been through a significant amount of tribulation. But
while the edges were crumpled and torn, the wax seal was unspoiled. The
tinker was summarily offered a meal and a bed, which Ewan assumed he
was now fully occupied with. Edyth did not spare the man a second
glance once he'd presented it to her, her mind focused solely on Cait's
awaiting
news.

"It's from Cait," she announced needlessly, her eyes unable to hide her
enthusiasm.

"Go on then and read it," encouraged Ewan with a nod. "I can see ye've
no wish tae wait until ye finish yer meal."

Shooting him a grateful smile, Edyth wasted no time in tearing
through the red wax seal emblazoned with the Ruthven coat of arms.
The ring boasting the family sigil had been one of the things that he knew
Edyth had placed within the stationary box she'd gifted to Cait on the
night of her wedding.

It seemed so long ago since Cait and William had parted from them,
but it had scarcely been seven months. So much had happened since

his sister's leave taking. The people of Perthshire had seemed to warm to his wife, for one, after her show of defiance against the sheriff at the gathering last fall. That pleased him greatly.

He doubted his people knew the whole truth of her dealings with de Biggar; those that did know only approved of the sheriff's death by her hand. That didn't mean he wanted that information to be common knowledge, however.

From his vantage, he could see that Cait's letter was gratifyingly long, packed with tiny, looping words that filled in every available inch of space, some of which curled up the side of the sheet when the end of the page afforded no more room. Ewan waited patiently for his turn to read the letter, helping himself to more food. As he was sopping up the juices on his trencher with a bannock, he noticed Edyth's worried brow.

"What's happened?" he asked, thinking that Moray's health had taken a turn for the worse. "Is something wrong?"

Edyth's bottom lip was tucked between her teeth, a rather somber look in her eyes. "I...it's nothing," she said with false cheer. She shrugged slightly as if to dismiss her obvious discomfort and gestured to the letter, her eyes not fully meeting his own. "It's only, do you recall that William has five sisters?"

No, he couldn't rightly say he recalled such information nor why this should trouble his wife. "Has something happened tae one of them?"

Edyth shook her head, her gaze fixed on the script in her hands. "No; it's no matter." She refolded the letter, saying, "Cait is enjoying the role of mistress in her new home but laments that fish is served at every meal. She says the winter has been overlong, but she enjoys her husband's people, especially his sisters."

Her demeanor did not fool Ewan. He made a noise of understanding in his throat and found her knee under the table. As an only child and a cast away from her own people, Edyth had grasped onto Cait's friendship like a drowning man reaches for salvation. They'd been fast friends, she and Cait. And now that she was gone, Edyth no doubt mourned her loss. "Take heart," he said, leaning in to kiss her cheek. "Cait

loves ye, *mo ghràdh*, and misses ye something fierce. Dinnae ye doubt it."
He nudged her with his elbow and gestured with his chin to the plum
tart that still sat, untouched, on her plate. "After the bairn comes, haps
we can go see her. Eat, Edie."

A reluctant smile broke out on her face. "Can we?"

"Aye, o' course we can. That is, unless something occurs tae impede
us." *Like war*, he thought darkly.

Edyth nodded, appearing distracted. She ran a hand over the small
roundness of her belly, which was still indiscernible in her heavy gowns.
She'd been sleeping ill of late. Her sickness had left her weeks ago, but
she complained of achiness often. And then, naught but a few days ago,
she'd started to bleed.

Ewan, who knew little of pregnancy outside of sheep and kine, did not
at first understand the alarm that his wife's maid, Gelis, had shown. She'd
brought him Edyth's chemise, wadded up into an indiscernible heap,
and had unfurled it like a winding sheet, showing him the spots of blood.
She'd begged him to command Edyth to lie abed, telling him that such
an occurrence, while not rare, if ignored, could prove disastrous.

He had insisted she lay abed, of course, to which she'd agreed, but she'd
quickly grown bored and disgruntled. There was no more swordplay,
nor standing for long periods of time in the storerooms or the stillroom,
which seemed almost like a punishment to her. Thankfully her bleeding
had ceased and although she was now out of bed, she spent most of her
time in the solar, attending to tasks that she did not enjoy.

"Any news for me?" he asked, setting down his cup. His eyes strayed
to her hand, smoothing the folds of her gown over her abdomen. "Are ye
well, Edie?" he asked, a large hand moving to rest over her own. They had
felt the babe move two nights ago, cuddled up under the quilts of their
marriage bed. Feeling the movement had chased many of their worries
away. At least for a time.

Edyth had explained that she'd felt the strange sensation of
movement—what she said felt like a little bubble of inward
activity—and had nudged him awake. She'd pressed his hand to the spot

and they'd both waited, breathless for several moments, until it came again. She had not felt the quickening movement since as far as he knew. He raised his brows in silent question, speaking a language that needed no words. She shook her head in response, the shadow of worry filling her eyes once more.

"I'm well," she said with forced cheer. Edyth handed him the letter with a nod. "Our friend regains his strength and is making plans to enliven the north men. There is no mention yet of particulars. Only vague ideas that will no doubt mean more to you than to me. She asks about my dreams. Asks for particulars." Here she shot him an apologetic smile. Wouldn't they all wish for such?

He was just about to suggest they retire to their rooms so she might rest and he read the letter when a shadow fell over them. They both looked up, expectant, and found Alec, his squire, standing before them looking grim indeed. Immediately Ewan's concern moved from his wife's melancholy to whatever disaster was assuredly currently unfolding. It seemed to Ewan that he could hardly catch a breath, so full his life had become with surprises and stress. He couldn't recall a time when he'd been full at ease in the last year.

Ewan prepared himself for some dreadful news. "Aye, what is it?"

Alec's hazel eyes were full of fear when he said, "Forgive me for the intrusion sir, but the guardsmen atop the gate bade me come and tell ye that a group of horsemen were spotted coming this way. They carry the sigil of England with them."

Ewan swore inwardly and forced a long breath in through his nose. No good news came from England. Ever. It would either be the treasurer, Cressingham come to collect taxes and their lads for conscription or de Warenne, delivering news of the new sheriff assigned to Midlothian.

He stood and took the letter Edyth offered him, then commanded a kitchen maid to take his wife to their rooms, pausing just long enough to kiss her. "Take yer plum tart," he called over his shoulder, hoping it might bring her a bit of happiness, even for a short time.

The bells were tolling now, signaling an important arrival. As Ewan and Alec made their way to the front entrance, he could see through the windows that the bailey was not full of rushing men at arms, frantic and unsure as it had been the last time officials from England had appeared.

It was filled, instead, with a smaller portion of the forty fighting men de Biggar and de Warenne had brought with them near Yuletide, filing out of his own small garrison. His own men—far fewer currently housed here than were under his command—were also assembling themselves at the gate, upon the wall, and in the buildings that lined the bailey, looking grim-faced and surly.

Relations between his own retainers and those assigned to help with the construction of the king's garrison had improved somewhat since he, Rory and Fingal had dispatched what was left of de Biggar's own personal guard. Questions had arisen, of course, as to where they'd gone off to, but Ewan had said little save that their charge had called them away to other parts unknown. Their current assignment, however, was to stay buried together in an unmarked patch of earth outside of the village.

Elias, the lad who had helped them into the kitchens had been spared. After careful consideration, Ewan had kept him alive, but he reasoned that the lad could not be left here, where a slip of the tongue could bring trouble. He sent the lad off to apprentice in the high places as a shepherd. Sheep kept secrets, as did his seasoned master of sheep. The lad had been so grateful to have kept his head that Ewan doubted he would ever speak of his shame.

The remaining English guardsmen that were not assembling currently in the yard were out in the woods with the craftsmen, cutting his timber and carting stones. He'd seen some of them from the windows as he made his way to the yard, each pausing, turning from their work to gaze toward the rise of the road.

"How large is the contingent of men?" he asked, thinking he might have trouble finding enough beds for the night.

"Johnne counted only eight, but they carry the banner of the king."

Ewan nodded, feeling a small amount of dread leave him. Only eight, but still far too many to his liking.

"What is your command?" asked Alec softly from behind. "Would ye have me guard her ladyship?"

Ewan glanced away from the window and took in his squire's appearance. He'd grown so much in the last year. He was only an inch or so shorter than himself. His eyes were earnest and eager, willing to do whatever was commanded of him.

Ewan grasped his squire's shoulder, squeezing it slightly in affection. "Aye, do." Edyth would not be in any danger, he didn't think, but he appreciated the concern and his willingness to offer his protection. "See tae my lady wife and tell her no' tae worry. I will come to her and report in due time what has transpired."

Alec nodded and turned around, leaving Ewan standing at one of the windows overlooking the bailey. Gathering himself, Ewan forced determination that he did not really feel, and made his way to the gate, passing men at arms, straight backed and ready for command.

Ewan considered what might be in store for him. If it was Cressingham, there was little he could do that he hadn't already endeavored to put into play. The young lads had been removed, thanks to Iain and the Stewarts. Any left would be trained men, who had a much better chance at survival, no matter how sorely he would feel their absence.

And if it was the new sheriff.... Ewan's dread increased tenfold. Conscription, he could handle. But a sheriff, if he turned out to be anything like their last, was a perpetual thorn in his side. The last sheriff had been a tyrant. And with Edyth's dreams of late, he was constantly on edge, guessing what they could mean. He shook his head and moved to the stairs, thinking of what he must do should the worst happen.

Haps what Edyth was seeing in her dreams had to do with whatever was presently riding toward his gates. But if she could not make sense of them, then how could he be expected to? He pushed his thoughts aside and mounted the stairs that would take him atop the gatehouse, the early spring wind cutting through his beard.

The bell had ceased its tolling. Rory was there with Johnne, one of his retainers, who were watching the horsemen approach. All were silent as they reached the wall, their eyes narrowed and their thoughts plain. They, too, did not anticipate anything good from this sudden arrival of men carrying the English ensign.

These newcomers, whomever they were, pulled up short of the gate, their horses blowing and dancing on the spot.

"Little fanfare," muttered Johnne. "No large contingent of men or steward of the King by his side. It could only be a message," he suggested.

Ewan saw he was right. No de Warenne and no Cressingham were there, but still, he did not relish any message from the English.

One of the men dismounted and removed his helm, displaying his greying, cropped hair. "Hail," he called, lifting a gauntleted hand to where Ewan stood upon the parapet. "We have come from Edinburgh, to deliver Perthshire's lawman. We would speak to the lord of this estate."

A stone settled in Ewan's wame; he had to try very hard not to curl his lip.

"So few men he brings," whispered Rory, so those assembled below could not hear.

"He is no doubt counting on the men de Biggar already deposited here at Yuletide," Ewan responded, a sour taste in his mouth.

"What will ye say when he asks about the missing soldiers?" asked Johnne.

"Lie, I expect," responded Ewan.

"Haps they come with fewer men because this man is less of a spleeny, fat-kidneyed puttock than the last," speculated Rory further.

Ewan grunted his response, thinking his luck would most likely prove otherwise. That would remain to be seen. The group of new arrivals were dressed in chainmail and long surcoats, emblazoned with the English lion and covered in mud from the thawing roads. "I am the lord of this keep," called Ewan. He gestured for Johnne to open the gate, saying, "We will hear you."

The wooden planks under his feet trembled as the portcullis gate was opened to the strangers. Ewan frowned, reflecting on his quick admittance for the strangers as he made his way down the stairs. The last time a sheriff had arrived, Ewan considered shooting the party full of arrows, so little did he want them on his soil. Now, he opened his gates, knowing it was futile to resist.

Rory was close behind him, but Ewan could not help but miss Iain, who had a talent in reading men. "Order refreshments from the kitchens," commanded Ewan to a page who stood in the shadow of the gate. "Bring them to my study within the garrison. That's a good lad."

As the boy ran off, Ewan's eyes fell upon the men as they handed off their horses to the stable workers. They moved toward him, their heads on a swivel and they took in their surroundings. All save for the man at the front. Ewan blinked at him, feeling a strange jolt of surprise at the recognition.

"Sir Ruthven," said the man, bowing sharply, a small smile only visible from the twitching of his voluminous mustache. His short hair was nearly all grey now, save for his eyebrows and facial hair. They were still as black as charcoal. He was not as thin as the last time Ewan had seen him, but he was still lithe, with the body and bearing of a soldier.

Ewan knew the man well—or at least he *had* known him.

"Lucas," said Ewan on a breath, hardly believing what he was seeing. He had saved this man's life in France.

Lucas, who had fought for Edward, had been captured by the French and held as a prisoner of war while their betters negotiated trades. But the men in Ewan's company had had other ideas. They'd beat him severely, denied him rations, and left him in the mud to bleed or freeze to death.

But Ewan, who was sick to his soul of blood and death, had taken pity on the man. Ewan had shared his own meager rations, had bound his wounds, and had provided warmth for him where he could until, weeks later, his superior officers had taken him away. They had given him back to the English in exchange for some of their own captured.

"You survived," said Ewan unnecessarily.

Lucas bowed his head. "Aye, though dying would have been the easier choice."

Ewan's mouth twitched slightly. A little over two years ago, when Ewan had gone each morning to check on the man and found him yet still alive, Lucas would remark that it would just be easier to die. When Ewan challenged him to do just that, Lucas would reply that he could not, for it wasn't in his nature to give any Frenchman satisfaction. Every day that he was a prisoner, this was their exchange. And every day, Ewan expected to find him dead come morning.

"Sir Lucas Olifard, at your service," he said neatly in his rich baritone that Ewan so well remembered. "Is there a place we might speak?"

Ewan mentally shook himself. He was being stupid, standing here in the yard gaping like a simpleton. Sir Lucas no doubt would wonder if he'd been hit on the head too many times if he did not string more than a few words together. "Aye. O'course. Please, follow me."

Ewan led the way to his own small garrison, stopping long enough to command an awaiting page to escort Sir Lucas' companions into the barracks, where they might rest and clean themselves as they saw fit. Rory would intercept them soon enough and ensure their further comfort while Ewan spoke above stairs with their commander.

"It has been some time since I last saw ye," said Ewan upon entering the office. He gestured to a seat opposite his desk, saying, "By what fortune do I find ye here?" Ewan took his own seat, wondering what to expect. He could not trust the man, who came to control and force King Edward's law upon them, yet he could not view him as an enemy.

*And yet.* And yet while Ewan wished for no sheriff whatsoever, he considered that if his people had to be governed by the English, that Lucas could possibly be their best option. The man owed his life to Ewan, after all. Surely he would honor the debt and treat his people honorably.

"Yes, I've been serving in Dumfriesshire, but am happy to have been commissioned here, in Midlothian, well away from the skirmishes in the south. An unhappy business it was there," Lucas confided. "We were constantly in danger of attack out upon the roads and while my own men were not harmed, there were stories of huts being burned over soldier's heads. We've had arrows shot at us here and there, but we've been otherwise fortunate. We had our horses stolen a fortnight past, which vexed me greatly." Lucas shook his head here as to show his disapproval. "Still, if that is all I can say happened, then I will count myself lucky."

"I think ye'll find that stolen beasts are no' so uncommon amongst Scotsmen," commented Ewan with good humor. "We consider the trading of stock tae be a most honorable pastime. Consider yerself properly welcomed tae Scotia."

Lucas' mustache twitched. "As I've heard. I'd rather not arrows fly at my head, all the same."

Ewan nodded. "Och, weel, from my experience, yer a difficult man tae kill. Tell me what happened after I saw ye last."

Lucas, seemingly at ease, told Ewan of how he returned home to England to his wife and two young children—both boys. Lucas, as an experienced soldier, was commissioned to Scotland last April, after the battle of Dunbar, where he was tasked to build a fort near the west coast, at Dunure. "I was successful in that venture, so I was sent here, to oversee the building of His Majesty's garrison here upon your own fair lands."

Lucas fumbled with the latch on his satchel and pulled out an official-looking letter which he promptly handed to Ewan. It was only a formality: the commission of Sir Lucas here in Midlothian and its parts surrounding, which included Perthshire, giving him the authority to conduct business in the name of the King of England pertaining to governance of His laws. Not only that, but Sir Lucas was also to oversee the building and maintenance of the garrison.

Even though it was Lucas and not de Biggar here upon his lands, still Ewan felt a familiar resentment bubble up inside him. He did not consider himself an English subject, no matter that he'd bent the knee and kissed Longshank's ring.

"I saw that progress has been made on the garrison," remarked Lucas. "You must be very pleased with the honor His Majesty has bestowed upon you."

Ewan did not feel that he could speak so he only nodded. It was true. The foundation stones had been laid despite the cold weather, and all the necessary building accoutrements prepared: scaffolding, great ramps and pulleys, and a number of other tools that Ewan could not name. It would not take long.

"I would speak with the master carpenter as soon as possible. Would you introduce us?"

Again, Ewan nodded, unable to trust his voice. A hollowness that had settled within his breast when he'd first learned of the garrison had only grown as the building itself had. With each bucket of dirt gathered for the earthen works, with each tree that was felled...each stone that was set into place, that space within him seemed to expand and swell. He hated the sight of it. A scar upon his otherwise beautiful landscape.

"We can go now, if you wish," said Ewan once he felt he could trust his voice.

Lucas shook his head. "Not just yet. I would say something more to you." He paused, his brows furrowing, thinking. "I would not bring it up, save for our history together. I know you to be an honorable man; our time together in that hell taught me as much." He cleared his throat and Ewan tensed, already anticipating what he might say.

"De Biggar," said Lucas, his eyes as blue as the summer sky, "reported that you were...meddlesome." He waved a hand at the last word, as if the word were insignificant. "He said as you wouldn't allow him the freedom of governance that his titles permitted him. He claimed that you threatened him."

Ewan felt all the color drain from his face. He weighed his options quickly. He could lie, but what would be the point? There were countless witnesses to what had transpired. Besides, Ewan had not been in the wrong. He inclined his head, admitting to the accusation. "Aye. I did threaten him. He was caught in the act of theft. Not only that, but he was heavy-handed in his so-called justice against my people. I made my opinion of his treatment quite plain."

Ewan shifted in his seat, unwilling to recant all that he had done, which had been much. "Ye ken what it is like with some men," he added. "Men who get drunk on their own importance. De Biggar was such a man."

Lucas seemed to consider Ewan's words. After several heartbeats he said, "Yes, I've experience with such men." He leaned forward, his eyes searching Ewan's face as if he could read his thoughts if he tried hard enough. "Did you kill him?"

Ewan huffed out a soundless laugh. His lip twitched as he shook his head. It would be just like Lucas to not mince words. "No," he answered truthfully, his eyes guileless. "But I'd have liked to." After a heartbeat he added. "He died while I was away, visiting my mother." That was a lie. Ewan was, in fact, helping Andrew Moray to escape imprisonment.

Lucas surveyed him for a few more seconds, his piercing eyes seeming to look through into Ewan's very soul. Finally he sat back in his chair and said, "I have heard many rumors. You know how tongues wag, but I would hear from you how was it that de Biggar came to meet his end."

Ewan shrugged. "As I say, I was not present to witness his death. Some say apoplexy, others poison. Only God can reveal such a thing. He was found without the gate, his body spoiled tae the beasts o' the forest."

Lucas made a sound of assent. "Yes, that is one story I heard told."

Ewan did not say more. He did not want to know what else Lucas might have heard. It no doubt was full of supposed witchcraft brought on by Edyth. At least, that's what de Biggar's man in the forest had alluded to. He'd hoped that with his death, so too would the rumors of Edyth die, but it seemed that he was not that lucky.

Ewan forced his features into one of benign indifference, fearing to ask questions about what else Lucas might have heard regarding his wife. He did not wish to appear as if he was worried about idle gossip, which he, as a rule, was not. Only when it came to Edyth. Only then did wagging tongues catch his ears.

Lucas looked about the room, eying the display of weapons upon the walls. "This is your own personal garrison? How many men does it currently house?"

Ewan did not wish to answer, but he knew he must. Lucas would know for himself, now that all his own soldiers as well as those appointed to their lands by King Edward now shared the space. Craftsmen also were housed within these walls. All in all, he was outnumbered and quarters were cramped.

It would get worse after the king's garrison was complete. He would be completely overrun then, with nigh on three hundred promised. "I have sent many home during the long winter months tae tend tae their families, but there are fifteen here that have sworn allegiance tae me. There are some forty craftsmen and soldiers together sent by the king also housed here. Some of them have secured lodging within the village as well."

Lucas nodded and made to stand, turning his hat over in his hands. "It seems all is in order. I've no further questions at present. I would ask you to acquaint me with this garrison and introduce me to the men under my charge, if you would."

"Of course," said Ewan, quickly exiting his chair.

He'd just gotten to the door and opened it, his arm outstretched as if to gesture Lucas forward when the man paused, placing his hat upon his head. He smiled at Ewan, his eyes alight as if they shared some private joke. "Some say de Biggar was cursed by a witch. Can you imagine? Superstitions run deep even amongst educated men, it would seem."

Ewan forced a chuckle and followed Lucas down the stairs and into the barracks, feeling as if all the air had quit his lungs.

The garrison was near to empty with the majority of the men out in the field, working under the garrison architect's direction, but there were a few men scattered about, seeing to their duties.

Ewan showed him all the rooms, then showed him the lists and other outbuildings within the walls of the keep. They had just entered the great hall when Edyth exited. Her face was flushed and her eyes bright with some emotion.

"Oh, there you are," she said as greeting. "I came to learn—" She cut herself off, noticing that Ewan was with a stranger. She curtseyed, her cheeks pink with embarrassment. "Forgive me."

"This is the new sheriff, appointed to Midlothian," announced Ewan, giving her a significant look. Would she ever do as he bid? He pushed the thought aside, saying, "He has come tae observe the building o' the king's garrison and tae meet the men under his charge. Sir Lucas, this is my wife, Lady Edyth."

Sir Lucas bowed neatly over Edyth's hand with smiling eyes. He pressed a quick kiss to her knuckles then, straightening, said, "Sir Ruthven has secured himself a most lovely English rose, it would seem."

Edyth's eyes darted to Ewan's then back to Sir Lucas, an uncertain look in her eyes. Ewan could easily read her thoughts. She wanted to know why the new sheriff was within the keep. She wanted to know if she should be afraid. He settled a hand at her elbow and walked them all inside.

"Sir Lucas is an old acquaintance from France," he explained. "We were brought together by some difficult circumstances. I'm most surprised tae find him here, upon our lands, but he would be a welcome guest, even were he not appointed here by the king."

Edyth's fixed smile did not change as she welcomed the new sheriff to their home. She curtseyed once more, looking very much like she would rather be anywhere else in the world. Ewan cast her a questioning look and leaned forward to press a kiss to her cheek. "Dinnae trouble yerself, *mo ghràdh*," he whispered.

Edyth nodded jerkily, smiling at Lucas. "Please take your leisure. I will have food and drink delivered to you."

"No need," replied Ewan. I've already sent for some, but I'm afraid it was probably delivered while I was giving Sir Lucas a tour of our barracks. I'm afraid I quite forgot. No, dinnae ye go and fetch it. I'll send a kitchen boy. Come and join us."

After a few domestic necessities were seen to, Ewan, Edyth and Lucas found themselves in the small room off of the great hall, their food suitably delivered and quite alone. Lucas wasted no time with polite conversation. He accepted his horn cup of ale and said, quite pointedly, "Where is yer wanted man? Graham, I believe his name was...the escapee from Stamford Bridge."

Ewan, who was in the act of drinking, nearly choked. He sputtered, his ale weeping down his chin. Edyth patted his back, her eyes unable to hide her fright.

"I have seen his broadsheets in Edinburgh and further south. If you harbor him within these walls, it would be better that ye tell me now."

"I cannae say where he is," rasped Ewan truthfully, "nor have I seen broadsheets declaring him a wanted man."

Lucas surveyed him carefully, assessing him. "As I say," he said carefully, "I know you to be an honorable man. I will trust you because of our past, but I would ask to hear why your man was so far south, so close to Chester Castle."

Edyth looked between them, her face pale, and sat very slowly into her chair, her cup forgotten. "He was there on my behalf," lied Edyth easily, surprising Ewan. He did his best to try and look as if this was not new information to him. "As you noticed, I was not born or raised in Scotland. There are old ties there, in England."

Sir Lucas lifted a brow, an invitation for her to continue, no doubt. Edyth cleared her throat, smiling softly at their forced guest.

"Perhaps Ewan has told you that I'm a fair hand at physicking?" she asked. "No? Well, if you're not too terribly busy with other duties, I'd be happy to show you the herbal garden that I've been cultivating since I've been here. Do you enjoy gardens, Sir Lucas?"

For his part, the sheriff surveyed Edyth with a polite interest, nodding and responding when spoken to, but otherwise waiting for Edyth to get to the point. "There is a plant that grows very well near Manchester which I do not have here in my garden," explained Edyth. "My dear friend wrote to me some time ago, inviting me to come and gather all that I wished but," here she gestured to her rounded belly, a blush blossoming on her face. "Well, as you can see, my husband is not so keen for me to go. He suggested that since Graham has a keen eye for small details and can tell the difference between Lady's Mantle and Feverfew, he bade him go in my place."

Edyth leaned forward and selected a few pieces of salted meat to add to her plate, talking all the time. Ewan had never seen her lie so well. "I'm sure you've seen the herb of which I speak, being from England yourself. The stalked marsh orchid that blooms in wet fens...do you know it?"

Sir Lucas shook his head. "No, no, I cannot say that I know it by name."

Edyth smiled at him warmly. "I'm sure if you saw it you would know it. I've been told that it can tolerate much drier meadows, but no matter how many of Scotland's fields and marshes I've searched, I've yet to find it."

"And this tracker, Graham...was sent by you to dig up the roots in winter?"

"Precisely," said Edyth, her large, guileless eyes meeting the sheriff unflinchingly. "Though I am sorry to learn that he has met trouble doing my bidding. I could only use someone as talented and discerning as he to complete such a delicate task. No other servant would know how to identify the stalked marsh orchid in its dormancy. I do hope he found what he was looking for."

Sir Lucas shifted in his seat, his eyes darting to Ewan then back to Edyth.

"It's unlikely that he will have been successful, my dear," said Ewan in a placating tone. "If he was arrested, they would have confiscated any treasure on his person." It was difficult for him to keep a straight face, but he just managed it. It would be a miracle if Lucas believed a word!

Edyth affected a look of disappointment then started in on a long-winded, one-sided conversation detailing the variety of uses of common herbs, ending with a promise to look at one of Sir Lucas' men who'd been complaining of restricted bowels. Edyth boasted that she knew just the cure for such an ailment, her smiling eyes drifting to Ewan. Indeed, she did know a cure. She'd dosed Rory with the remedy last year and he'd shat for three days straight.

She excused herself, saying that she would go and prepare the necessary medicines and have a servant deliver it to him on the morrow. Ewan's affection for Edyth grew as he watched her exit the room. She'd made herself out to be the exact kind of overindulged, yammering simpleton to send a servant on a merry chase for a flower in the middle of winter as ever there could be.

Sir Lucas cleared his throat. "Lovely wife you have, Sir Ruthven."

"Aye," he said, his smile growing. "I quite agree."

# Chapter Ten

Iain was cold, pressed up against a black pine, his toes stiff and his nose dripping. Himself and a dozen of the Stewart retainers had ridden into the gorge pass in the foothills of Trossach mountains two days ago.

The weather, although miserable, turned out to be in their favor. Even for March, the late blizzard was unexpected. Thick, fat flakes fell like so many shooting stars, to cover the pine boughs and the trail. Any tracks they'd made had quickly filled with fresh snow, muffling any noise they made into an engulfing silence. They'd long ago extinguished their fires, lying in wait, for the caravan to come into view, huddled in their assigned places within the evergreens, plaids over their heads. Iain was, in a word, miserable.

Their scout, the Stewart master of horse, had informed them only an hour ago that he'd last seen the caravan making their way toward them in all haste toward the next village, no doubt in search of some shelter from the storm. Thankfully, the Stewarts knew this valley well and had chosen their hiding place carefully, where rockfalls had nestled within the low places, creating perfect hiding places.

Iain was leaning against a tree, small bits of pine boughs stuck in his bonnet and plaid to help disguise himself, bow in hand. He squinted through the falling snow and strained his ears for any sound of an approaching wagon, a bark from driver, or jangle of harness. The snowfall had all but stopped by now. Little flurries danced in the breeze like little, errant gnats. The only sound was the occasional muffled *thwump* of snow as it fell from branch or the sporadic caw from a crow.

His could not feel his face, but Iain told himself it would be over soon. The plan was for him to keep hidden and wait for half of the caravan to pass him by before he was to strike. Their arrows would be the signal for those farther ahead on the trail to strike the head of the proverbial snake, as well as signal to the others at the tail to move forward with purpose.

The lads further down the gorge road, those waiting at the front, were to dispatch the drivers and detach horses from wagons. Meanwhile, Iain and others would send a continuous volley of arrows from the trees upon the guardsmen so as to give others the time to cut any bindings. They were to strike fast and not linger, even going so far as to split up and lie low in a nearby cave to ensure they were not followed back to Stewart lands.

They'd come the day before to scout out the entire area, to view the nearby villages and to trace the hidden trails that snaked and wound through the rocks, trails that led to cavities within the mountains. He was on one such trail. It was narrow and completely covered with snow, but he could still see the indentation of where it lay, albeit buried, leading the way up and over the ravine lip.

Iain blew heat into his hands, which were stiff and cumbersome. It wouldn't take long, he told himself, and then he would be well away, done with his duty and done with the cold. He wiggled his frozen toes in his boots, trying and failing to bring warmth to them.

Iain was a fair shot with a bow and preferred it in a situation such as this, but he worried over his aching fingers. He had just decided to remove his gloves and shove his half-frozen fingers into his oxters when a movement caught his eye. It was Brian, one of the Stewart's men, waving at him from across the road, his head poking out from around a large pine growing on top of a boulder. In his hand, Iain saw he held what looked like a flask. It shone dully in the cloud-covered sky.

While whiskey might not warm his extremities, it would warm his belly and, perhaps, make him forget just how cold he was for the time being. But just before he moved from his place to accept the proffered gift, the doleful cooing of a dove sounded through the otherwise silent ravine. This was the signal they'd been waiting for to inform them that the caravan was close. Iain could not see around the bend in the road, nor could he hear anything over the buzz of snow silence, but still he readied himself, readjusting his footing and the crossbow in his hands.

It felt like a long time in the wind and anxious quiet before he heard the distant, low rumble of wheels pushing through snow. If he strained his ears enough, he thought he could hear a man—a driver perhaps—encouraging some beast, but the sound was snatched away in the wind before he could discern any meaning to the words.

Iain pulled a handful of bolts from his quiver and stuck them in the snow at his feet, reassessing for at least the dozenth time, his hiding place. He, himself, was standing on a bank above the road, which was sparsely covered in spindly broom branches and two black pines. Neither of the trees were as wide as he would wish for. They wouldn't shield him completely from enemy arrows, but from this height, he had the advantage of a first strike. The guardsmen would likely not have arrows nocked, nor would they notice him as he knelt in his snow-dusted plaid, ensconced behind icy broom until it was far too late.

With fumbling fingers, he loaded a bolt and pushed against the stirrup with his foot, maneuvering the bowstring into place. He'd been given one of the Stewart's crossbows, which was quite different from his usual short bow. It was lighter and less clumsy than what he was used to and easy to hide and use in tight quarters. These were benefits to be sure, but so too, the machine was vastly sensitive and still unfamiliar to him, despite his practice with it in the yard at Doune. Iain had nearly pierced the arbalist's foot in the practice yard when his finger had accidentally grazed the trigger.

Remembering this, he was careful to keep his hands free from the trigger as he waited, counting the minutes, his eyes sharp upon the bend in the ravine that hid the oncoming travelers. It felt like an age had passed before the sounds of the moving caravan grew in proximity. Someone he could not see barked an order for haste, their words carried to him on the wind. That was good. The direction of the wind was in the Stewarts' favor. Hopefully sounds of the ambush would not alert the last portion of the party until it was too late to run or to come to their comrade's aid.

A horse snorted; the incessant grating of the wagon wheels turning over rocks and ice filled the silence, making his heart flutter with nervous anticipation. He flexed his cold right hand and readjusted his crossbow, aiming it carefully through the scrub.

As the head of the caravan crested the hill, he saw that the first wagon was fitted with flat, iron bars in a way as to create a cage. And within the cage were a huddled mass of bodies, plaids covering their heads, each body leaning into another for warmth. Two guardsmen escorted the wagon, one on each side, their long swords winking above their shoulders and crossbows, which were strapped to their saddles, laden with heavy furs across their shoulders.

He watched, unmoving, barely breathing, from where he crouched in the snow, as the wagon moved past him, the guardsmen looking weary. One of the guardsmen spoke to the driver, who grunted in response, and snapped the reigns with a flick of his wrists. The horses responded, pulling the heavy burden a fraction faster into the depths of the shadowy ravine.

Next came a group of men on foot, unbound and wrapped tightly in furs and plaids. They were unarmed from what he could see and were overseen by another set of guardsmen who followed closely behind atop horses. These guardsmen were grim and silent, diligently looking over the rocks and bracken that lined the canyon walls. When one of the guard's eyes slid to where Iain was concealed, he held his breath for fear that his foggy exhalations would give himself away.

The man's head turned away, though, unseeing what was awaiting them. Iain kept his eyes on the guardsman, ready to strike him down if he noticed one of the Stewart men along the path. Nothing happened, however. They were too well hid, or haps the men in convoy were snow blind after so many miles of winter. Either way, the procession filed past them, the prisoners staring bleakly at the road or wagon before them, their shuffling footfalls reverberating against the ravine walls.

Iain's arms were aching from holding the bow still for so long; his fingers were mostly numb. He longed to blow into them, or to put them under his arms, but he could not dare to move or readjust himself, lest he cause snow to fall from the icy branches of his hiding place.

He was charged with waiting for the third wagon to pass, which the scout had informed him, was the estimated middle of the procession. No wagon appeared, however. Only a sizable gap after the men on foot. The guardsmen did not seem bothered by it, however. They didn't even look behind them.

Iain strained his ears for sounds of battle, or anything else that might explain the break in the line, worry overcoming his discomfort. Was something wrong? He could scarcely feel the cold now, his apprehension growing as the space behind the first wagon and the marching men lengthened. Iain ached to stand, to get a better view over the crest of the rising road. *Wait. Dinnae be hasty.*

He bit his lip, reviewing the plan in his head. They had anticipated the convoy to be of one body, where they could strike all at once, fast and hard, then retreat. Iain's eyes found the hiding place of the other man from across the road, where his head could be seen poking out around the side of the rock hiding him. The man must have felt his gaze because their eyes locked briefly. The man raised a gloved hand, pointing at the back of the last guard, his intent clear. He wanted to shoot them now.

Iain shook his head. *No. Wait.* There were no cries of pain or signs of battle taking place as yet. He could not discern if the sounds of the wagon were from the one already passed or if was the next in line on the other side of the hill. He dared to rise part way from his crouch so that his companion could see him more clearly and chanced a look over the hill, where he thought he saw the helm of a rider just poking above the line where road met sky.

He settled back down into his crouch and, with a slight gesture, motioned for the man to wait. He did his best to ignore his frantic heartrate. He'd been on raids before, of course. He'd stolen sheep and cattle, had raided crofter's carts, as well as lifted the rare horse from neighboring clans, but this was different. This was treason.

He was pulled out of his thoughts when the man across from him, hidden amongst the shale and debris from a rockfall, shifted his weight, sending a slow cascade of shale down the slope. Stones tumbled and slid toward the road in a muffled clatter, snow sliding to reveal the slate beneath.

To the guardsman now cresting the hill below, it could have been natural, an act brought on by the wet conditions, but like any well-trained man, he could not ignore what he'd heard. Iain watched, his breath held, as the guardsman urged his horse forward, moving far ahead of the mule-driven wagon full of conscripted men and boys. The guardsman pulled his sword from his back, his gaze turned up the slope to where the Stewart man was now aiming an arrow at him.

The guardsman's eyes widened, his mouth opening in a cry of warning as the arrow flew. It pierced through the man's leather armor, near his heart, but it was not fast enough. The guard's shout of alarm to his comrades was as a crier's bell, loud and piercing. Nothing happened at first. The man driving the mules did not seem to be aware of what was happening until the inspecting guard fell from his horse into the road before him.

From this vantage point, Iain could easily see the driver's puzzled expression turn from one of concern to one of alarm in a matter of seconds. Iain hesitated. So far as yet, the driver had not ceased the wagon's procession. The huddled line of walking men were just now cresting the hill, not yet fully exposed to those waiting to save them. Another bolt was fired from across the ravine, hitting the wagon driver.

*Damn him*, thought Iain rather unfairly. They were exposed now. The carefully laid plan must be abandoned.

The driver fell forward, the weight of his body falling onto and pulling the reins. The mules cried in protest, rearing into the air then bolting forward in panic. The wagon full of men heaved as the wheels overtook the fallen driver. They jostled about, their own cries of alarm mingling with the mule's disapproval. The sounds of chaos rebounded in the ravine, echoing back to him. All was chaos.

The conscripted men on foot scattered, shouting and scrambling up the embankment or back down the hill from whence they'd come. But with no weapons to hand, and the walls of the rocky mountainside slick with snow and loose stone, Iain feared they would not get far. They would likely be caught by the coming guardsmen, still unseen.

The guardsmen that had only just recently passed them doubled back, the conscripted men in their charge forgotten, screaming their outrage and orders.

Thinking fast, Iain trained his bolt on the guardsman closest to him, who was shouting orders at the top of his lungs. "Attack! Arrows! Someone get those reins! Push the lads through, ye whoresons! Get them gone!"

The cage farthest ahead that had first passed jerked as the horses pulling it were pushed all the harder. Iain feared they might get away, but he could not worry over them. Hopefully the ambushing Stewarts further down the line would be able to catch the drivers and dispatch them.

Iain trained his arrow at the rider who'd been shouting orders. The man was currently pulling men off the sides of the ravine, where they'd been attempting to escape onto higher ground. Still atop his steed, the guard deftly grabbed onto cloaks and plaids and yanked the would-be escapees from their perches in the rocks. Some of them had made it far enough that they were nearing the top of the sloped wall, scrambling over boulders and clinging to trees as they pulled themselves upward.

Iain released his breath and pulled the trigger on his crossbow. With a force Iain was still unaccustomed to, the bolt shot forward to pierce the guardsman's back, near his left shoulder. The man fell forward and, unable to hold on, fell from his horse, which promptly ran off, eyes rolling. Hastily, Iain set another bolt, his hands shaking, and took aim once more.

He had seen death by violence, of course. But no matter how hard he practiced in the yard with his fellows, when it came to actual combat, his hands shook and his heart beat as if it would like nothing better than to pound right out of his chest. Iain did not know how Ewan had spent two long years in France, fighting against the English and still come away whole.

It was with this thought, that he pulled the trigger once more, felling the staggering, swearing guardsman. He reloaded without thought, ignoring the blossoming pool of blood beneath the man now holding two of his arrows, and took aim once again.

"Arrows! There! Kill him!" This from another guardsman that had been at the front of the line. He'd spotted one of the Stewart men and was helpfully pointing his sword to a spot, halfway up the ravine, to where the man was partially exposed. An arrow whizzed past the guard's head, barely missing him from the looks of it. He ducked, lifting his shield, which was already pierced with two arrows.

The Stewart man in question, no doubt feeling that his best option was to quit his spot now that he was exposed, chose swords over arrows. He leapt from his place upon the ravine wall with a shrill war cry and fell atop the guardsman. Iain looked away, intent on his next victim.

Conscripted men were darting everywhere, running, dodging, fighting with their fists. Iain could not tell if the sounds of battle were just here, in front of him, or if all parts of the caravan were now under attack. They needed to leave. There was ample distraction now for the conscripted men to flee. They only lacked a means of escape.

Iain let his bolt fly, which hit a horseman in the thigh. He screamed and grabbed onto the appendage, dropping his sword, which he had been using to cut down runaways as they ran past. A conscripted man who was running by stooped and deftly picked it up, running toward another guard with deadly purpose.

Iain watched, grinding his teeth. Damn it, but someone had to lead them out. They did not know the secrets of the ravine, as he'd been shown. They would die on the walls or be recaptured if he did not do something. He stood, pulling his plaid from his head to further expose himself and waved his hands. "*Dhòmhsa*! To me! This way!"

He did not to see if anyone followed. He did not dare stay in his place any longer, now that he'd revealed himself. Already arrows flew at him, hitting rocks and broom. Clambering laterally across the ravine wall on a sheep's trail, barely discernible from the fresh snowfall, Iain dared a glance over his left shoulder. It was working. Several of the conscripted Scots had noticed him and were following him from below.

So too were Cressingham's guardsmen, however. He redoubled his efforts, scrabbling around a jutting boulder. An arrow just missed his left ear, whooshing so close to him that it made his stomach flip.

Up ahead, the trail split off into a fork. One leg of the fork led to the ravine floor, and the other led up and over the lip of the gorge, to the open ridgeline. He needed to lead them there, where they could push more easily into the Trossachs and hide. Arrows continued to find him. He flinched as one embedded itself into the snow exactly where his hand had been only a second before. He'd been shot by an arrow before. In the leg. By Edyth. He did not welcome such pain again.

Iain swore softly under his breath as he rushed forward, the trail slippery. He stumbled and fell twice in his haste before he finally made it to the fork in the trail. Pausing here, he turned and waved his hands once again, grateful to see that the Stewarts were canny enough to aim at Cressingham's bowmen currently aiming for him. He waved his hands again, drawing more eyes. "To me! To me!"

And then he turned tail and ran up the trail that would lead to their freedom. Or at least, he hoped it would end in such a way. He did not look behind him again. He dare not. Stumbling and scrambling over rocks, climbing with the aid of both of his hands in the steepest portions. There were trees here and there that could provide him cover, but Iain did not slow, his lungs burning. Not until he made it over the crest of the ravine, thick with leafless oak, did he slow to a stop, heaving for breath.

He paused only for a moment, just long enough to ease the stitch in his side, to calm the quaking in his limbs, then he was off again, cutting through the shin-deep snow, back to the lip of the gorge, eager to view what was happening in the ravine below.

It took long moments of desperate breaths and anxious thought, but when he finally made it to a place where he could see, he was gratified with what he saw. The ravine was mostly empty now. At least ten guardsmen lay dead or dying. They'd been stripped of their warm cloaks and weapons.

But best of all, the conscripted men were free. They ran together mostly, like a flock of starlings, for the mouth of the ravine, where Iain knew more Stewart men were hidden away. So were more of Cressingham's wagons, but there was little he could do about that now. He ran back to the trail, eager to see who had followed him.

The wood was mostly quiet now. He could not hear screams of dying men, nor could he hear signs of battle still being waged. Not over his own breathing and the pounding of his heart in his ears. When he made it back to the trail, he saw a cluster of shapes coming over the rise. Iain pulled his sword with haste then lowered it. These were not Cressingham's men.

The young man in the front of the line, upon seeing Iain, tensed, drawing to the stop, but then he relaxed as he registered that Iain was not a uniformed guardsman that had been escorting them to the sea, but a rebel. Iain eyed the group of four lads that had been lucky enough to escape the debauched plot. "Are ye hale? From where were ye taken?" Iain asked, looking past them for more escapees.

None came. *Only four?* Iain's stomach sank to the vicinity of his knees. While he was happy for even one to have escaped, he would not deny to himself that he'd hoped for far more. Still, there were other routes the conscripted lads could venture down. Haps those trails were full. He hoped so.

"Clan MacLaren," said the first young man. He was wide in stature with muscled shoulders that bespoke of his skills as a blacksmith's apprentice or some other physically demanding occupation. "In the village of Balquhidder Glen." The lad was bleeding from a cut at his temple, but he seemed otherwise well. One of the other boys, Iain noticed, was holding his arm close to his body, looking green. This boy was shorter, far skinnier, and had the look about him of a rabbit that had been chased down by a fox.

The other two lads were well clothed with heavy furs draping their shoulders, following quickly behind the other lads. "We are all well enough," answered the blacksmith boy. They all looked at Iain expectantly as if he held all the answers to every problem they were now experiencing.

Iain repressed the urge to curse and looked past them, down the pathway from which they'd just come. "We need to move. Were ye followed?" he asked as he turned.

The boys trailed him immediately, reminding him of ducklings waddling after their mother. "Others followed, but they took the lower trail," answered one of the boys from the back, his voice reedy and unsure, his brown eyes wide with equal parts fear and hope.

"Do ye ken Balquhidder Glen?" asked the largest boy. "Is it far from here? We've been travelling for days on end, stopping at different villages to conscript more men. We've lost our way, I'm afraid."

Iain glanced at these "men", his lips pressed tightly together, taking high steps through the drifted snow. "Come on, quickly now," he urged. After a beat, he said, "I dinnae ken yer village." At seeing their disappointment, he added, "But I ken well enough where yer clan resides. Yer lands abut a southern portion of my uncle's lands."

The only sound for several moments was that of crunching snow, their huffing breaths and gusting wind. "Where are we?" asked the lad with the hurt arm. Iain estimated him to be about ten and five years. Mayhap younger. He was bollocks at judging age.

"We are on the cusp o' clan Murray, in the feet o' the Trossachs," responded Iain.

Murray was just north of clan Lindsay. He quickly calculated the distance to his elder sister, Aldythe, and immediately dismissed the idea. It was days away and in the wrong direction. "We'll have tae find shelter for the night. There's a cave east of here," Iain announced. "Or we could go west intae a nearby village, but the place will likely be crawling with Cressingham's men. I like our chances in the wild better."

There were grunts of assent from the lads at this. "Aye, there are guardsmen left alive," said one of the lads. "They're chasing down others that escaped the mouth o' the ravine."

Iain nodded. "The cave it is, then."

There were several outposts, places Alexander had prepared for his men, to find shelter in once the raid was over. He hadn't made concessions for all the conscripted, of course. How could he? He'd only wished to distract the guards, give the stolen lads a chance to scatter and escape. If they were canny, they would make it back to their respective homes on their own.

"Stay close and go canny." Iain assessed the lads, weaponless but at least properly dressed for the late winter storm that had blown in. "Here, take this," he said, handing the closest boy his dirk. "Just in case. What're yer names?"

The lad now inspecting Iain's dirk spoke for the group. "I'm called Hamish. This is Jam—"

Iain cut the boy off with a sharp motion, but he needn't have, for the boys had heard the noise as well. All heads turned back toward the crest of the hill where sky met snow, where a hidden sheep's trail snaked through the bracken and rocks, covered in their tracks.

While they'd made progress away from the trailhead, they were easily seen in the leafless, sparse wood. Even had there been decent cover, their tracks were as good as a trail of breadcrumbs.

Iain strained his ears. Was that a boot in the snow or only his imagination? No, there it was again. The rhythmic sound of boot striding in snow and shifting rock. Iain wasted no time. Unslinging the crossbow and his quiver of bolts, he handed them off to the largest of the boys. The lad reached out an eager hand, his reddened fingers wrapping around the wooden shaft, eyes wide in what was unmistakably delight. Iain did not let go, searching out the lad's eyes. He'd been young once too, and knew all too well how well he'd have liked such a toy at that age.

"Take this and hide," commanded Iain, his voice gruff. The boy nodded and pulled slightly on the bow. Still Iain held fast, staring into the lad's eyes. "And mind yer aim," he said. "If I happen tae catch yer bolt, I'll be verra angry indeed."

The boy nodded emphatically and ran to a nearby oak, snow flying behind him, the other lads close behind. Lord, he hoped they were smart enough to split up and not all try to hide behind a single trunk.

Iain put the boys out of his mind and pulled his short sword, turning just in time to see two of Cressingham's men crest the hill. They spotted him immediately and ran forward.

"Hold!" shouted the first of them, hurrying his pace, his companion not long behind.

Iain's answering smile was more of a grimace as he loosened his sword arm, swinging the blade in a tight circle. The steel cut through the air with tight whistle, a sound of which he never tired. His blood sang, his muscles loosened.

Iain much preferred it this way, sword to sword rather than crouching in the snow. He set his feet, the cold forgotten, and flexed his neck sharply to one side, popping several bones in a thoroughly satisfying way. "Welcome tae my mountain," said Iain as the men grew closer, his arms stretched wide. "Come closer sae I can greet ye properly."

# Chapter Eleven

T he guards were not heavily armored. They wore studded leather jerkins over their gambesons in place of the heavier, costly plate armor. More vulnerable, yes, but also easier for them to maneuver in. As for Iain, he was not much better protected. Still, his odds were good.

Both men were breathing heavily, having just run up a sheep's trail. Both men were wild eyed and, from Iain's estimation, quite put out by the goings on. He motioned them forward, all the while mentally cataloging their every move. He immediately noticed, for instance, the way one man favored his left leg, how the other man was short and wide, and therefore would be harder to push around.

"Hold! Drop your weapon!" said the first of the two. They slowed to a stop in front of Iain, their eyes glinting in their bacinet helms. The first's beard, the color of straw, was crusted with ice and snow, his teeth bared in menace. "Ye'll be coming with us back tae Cressingham tae be sentenced for your crimes against the crown."

Iain shook his head slowly, his lips pursed as though in thought. "Nay, I dinnae think I will. If ye wish tae have me, ye'll have tae kill me first."

The second man, chest still heaving from the climb, lifted his sword, his breath fogging before him in quick bursts. He took up his place beside his companion. "Gladly," he breathed, his cracked, chapped lips pulled into a grimace. Iain smiled in an unfriendly way, noting that the man seemed anything but eager. In fact, Iain rather thought the man had had quite enough of the goings on. He would be easy to discourage, which, in a fight, was as good as poison.

Iain's appraisal of his foes took only a matter of seconds, enough time to know how he would proceed. As if waiting for Iain to finish, the shorter man raised his sword, screaming, and charged him.

Iain adjusted his stance and dodged the man's swing with only a little effort. The taller man was also involved, moving as if to flank Iain on his left side, but Iain turned his body toward him and lunged, sword outstretched. This man would have a longer reach. Iain would have to keep one eye on him at all times.

Their swords connected, the edge of the blades sliding along each other with a hiss. Iain spun away, back toward the shorter man on his right, a flurry of motion and disturbed snow. Iain's back was partially to the shorter man, but he had anticipated him taking advantage of such, and met the man's incoming downward blow with a block that jarred his bones.

The force of the strike staggered Iain and he backed away. Nearly falling, arms outstretched for balance, he barely kept his feet, but smiled as if they were friends, sparring in the yard and not out for blood. Both men pursued him, stalking forward with purposeful, quick strides. The man with the beard growled, "Surrender, *neach-brathaidh.*" *Traitor.*

Despite knowing that some Scots aligned themselves with England, it still took him by surprise to find himself fighting men borne of his own homeland in defense of its young. Flexing his wrist once more, Iain replied, saying, "*'S e mac do dh'Alba a th' annam. Dè th 'annad?*" *I am a son of Scotland. What are you?*

Iain, his lip curled in disgust, lifted his sword and beckoned them forward. The tall man moved first, his blade cutting the air, and came upon Iain with great force, but Iain had been ready for him. Their blades sang in the freezing air, their grunts swallowed up by the sound of steel on steel.

Iain had been right. The man's reach was far, but he was also putting so much force into his swings that he could quite easily lose his balance. Taking advantage of this, Iain took a quick step back, leaning away from the wide arch of the blade intent on taking his head from his shoulders. The momentum of the man's sword pulled him along, his weight on his toes. Iain crouched and swung his foot at the man's unbalanced legs. The guard fell with a spray of snow, cursing.

The shorter man was on Iain instantly. He had to roll to miss the thrust of sword aimed at his chest. The whiz of a bolt blew past Iain's face, barely missing him. It lodged in the snow, the fletching of the bolt just visible above the powder, mere inches from his face. He growled and rolled to his feet, his sword blocking an attack by the shorter man just in time.

"Mind yer aim, ye wee scut!" he shouted into the man's face, who, no doubt, thought Iain mad.

The shorter of the men came at Iain again and again with punishing strokes. Iain's sword arm was growing weary, his shoulder cramping. He needed to end it, and soon. He could not see where the taller man had got to.

This time when the short man attacked, Iain stepped into the strike, narrowing the distance between them, and caught the man's sword with his own. He shoved the shorter man as hard as his could, sword against sword, his teeth set in a tight grimace.

"What will ye say tae yer betters, once I kill ye, Traitor?" growled Iain. He pushed against the man will all his might, his face inches from the other man. "What will yer forefather's think of yer betrayal?"

Of course the man did not answer, but he eyes sparked in anger. The guard yelled in Iain's face, spittle flying. Iain, ever the opportunist, bit him sharply right on the nose. It wasn't pleasant, for either of them, but it was enough for the man to falter.

The man cried out in pain as Iain's sword pushed his opponent's weapon aside. The guard raised a hand to his injured nose, his mouth agape in outrage. Iain did not waste time. Pulling the dirk from the man's belt, he drove it into his belly. He crumpled, falling onto his backside, his breaths coming fast, his face gone white.

Iain struck hard and fast, the flat of his palm on the pommel of his sword, the other wrapped around the hilt. Putting all his weight behind the strike, Iain buried the blade into the man's leather-armored chest, straight through to his heart.

Heaving for breath, he yanked the sword free and turned, expecting the second man to be on him, worried that he was about to feel a blade bite into his flesh. But he was met with no resistance. A dozen paces away, the taller man was hobbling. Two bolts from the lad had landed, piercing him through the right knee and another in the thigh.

The man staggered, his sword arm drooping, the injury staining his breeches red. Droplets of blood colored the churned snow in a trail reminding Iain of holly berries.

Iain walked toward the man, wiping his mouth on his plaid-covered shoulder. "In a bit o' a tight spot, it seems," said Iain conversationally.

The man grunted and very carefully sat down, heaving a great sigh as he did so, his mouth set in a rictus of pain. "I cannae fight with this." He gestured to the arrow sticking grotesquely from his knee, his skin as nearly white as the snow.

Iain crouched and retrieved the man's sword, which was within easy reaching distance. It could be a ploy, this weakened state, to draw Iain into an expectation of surrender. Iain allowed himself a moment to catch his breath, feeling lightheaded and giddy from the fight. Blood raced through his veins, humming in his ears.

Iain gestured toward the man's injuries with a thrust of his chin. "I ken that hurts like hell itself. My brother's wife shot me through last year." He could not help the smile that tugged at his lips. Lord she was a terrible shot. "The ague nearly killed me."

The soldier, grimacing, said nothing, breathing through his clenched teeth. They were silent for the space of a few heart beats when the man said, "What are ye tae do with me, then? Kill me? Ransom me?"

Waiting for his breath to calm, Iain appraised his opponent. He supposed he would have to kill the poor buggar. It would be the smart thing to do, even if the man could not get far as he was. He would most likely freeze to death or be eaten by beasts in the night. It would be kinder to end his life now, for he had no intention of bothering with the tedious process of ransom.

"Our captain holds some of yer lot down in the valley," said the man, as if trying to persuade Iain. "He's bringing them tae Cressingham. Haps they'll consider a trade if ye bring me down tae them."

"Is that what ye'd do, were ye in my place?" asked Iain incredulously.

The man merely smiled tightly. They both knew what the guardsman would do. He would kill Iain outright and walk away. But if he was telling the truth, if the convoy had captured some of Alexander's clan's men, there would be trouble for certain.

*Damn.* He could go and try to free them, but he was a lone man now, with four lads to think of. Iain stood, frowning down at the guardsman. Even if he tried to trade this man for any of Alexander's men that had supposedly been captured, the likely outcome would be that he, himself, would become a captive. He could not fight against what was surely a hornet's nest of Cressingham's guardsmen below.

Iain sighed and hefted his sword. "There's nothing for it. I'll make it clean and fast. Turn yer head, aye?"

The man's dark eyes did not register grief or regret, only bleak acceptance. He turned his head away, revealing a pink patch of neck above his gambeson. He mumbled a prayer under his breath and Iain waited for him to finish. "Amen," they both said together. Once the man had crossed himself, Iain took a deep breath and swung mightily.

*Nairn*

The noblemen were, as always, whispering in circles about their most recent plans to raid Dundee Castle in the coming weeks. To Cait's understanding, Dundee was a strategically important holding in controlling the Great Glen and the northern reaches of Scotland that had been taken by King Edward shortly after the Battle of Dunbar.

One of their allies, a supposed English loyalist, had informed them that King Edward, growing weary of the rebellious Scots, had tasked the sheriff of Elgin to get his fellow Scotsmen in line. This sheriff and Edward's principal Scots follower—Sir Reginald Cheyne—had called a meeting amongst the nobles that had sworn fealty to England.

"No doubt to demand they call their retainers and stamp us out," Moray had said upon hearing this news.

"Longshanks didnae much care for the gift we gave him last month," intoned William with good humor. This remark caused the other men at the table to chuckle in appreciation. They had, with the help of a handful of Burgesses, burned English ships moored in the harbor, set to make way for Flanders.

Cait felt the familiar flare of anxiety that always came with the men's boasting. Pride so often fed careless choices. Would that these conspiring men take their victories with a mite less self-importance.

Cait surveyed the room, trying to recall the names of the people assembled. There were more men coming and going now...messengers at all hours delivering news.

"Aye, the Sheriff o' Elgin makes plans tae meet in Inverness at the end of the month. T'would be a shame were we tae miss it." More chortles met this comment. Only Moray seemed unamused.

One of the men had brought with him the invitation. Said letter was now on display in the center of the table and had been read, reread and deliberated upon so many times that Cait had it memorized. Simply put, King Edward had charged his officers to stamp out the rebel Scots that so infuriated him. Cressingham and de Warenne had their hands full enough as it was and could not be bothered to rout them out, it seemed.

Such was the duty of the Sheriff of Elgin, apparently, who called all the great men to a meeting in Inverness.

"Surely ye dinnae plan on going," said MacDuff, his twitchy mustache all aflutter.

"No," laughed Moray. He sobered, rubbing a finger under his nose, his eyes focused on the letter between them. "At least no' openly. There are some 'ere as may go. It would be good tae have knowledge of their plans. I wonder if they suspect it's me who's behind these attacks?"

A murmur of agreement ran through the circle of men. Moray continued: "If chance favors us, we might attack some unlucky English loyalist on his way back tae his holding."

The silence that followed his statement was as a living thing, pushing against Cait's wame. Every time they planned a raid she felt giddy and sick. The men would leave, William included, and she would wait silently, full of empty-bellied terror until they returned. And even when William was to home, the constant worry did not leave her. She lived, as it were, from moment to moment, in breathless anticipation of being found out.

She looked to William, who did not seem to share her reservations. If he was not eager, he was willing. She bit her lip, thinking of the last time he'd left. She'd helped to plait his hair and paint his face with charcoal so as to be better hidden in the night. The moon had been high and bright, and she'd worried the entire time he'd been gone that his light hair would be seen. She'd regretted not covering his hair in soot and ash along with his face. But he'd returned home to her, bloodied, full of righteous reprisal and lust.

There was much deliberation hereafter as to which noble would be the best to strike. Most were interested in one castle in particular, however: Dundee. The lord of this castle was newly appointed from King Edward himself, a Sir William Fitz Warin.

Cait wrung her hands in her lap, her mouth gone dry. There were many players here and still those who were yet undecided in their loyalties.

Many nobles' sensibilities were simply not yet known, one of which was the Lady Euphemia of the Great Glen.

Her husband was currently imprisoned in the Tower after the failed attack in Dunbar and the countess was eager, it seemed, to appear loyal to King Edward in the hopes that he might free her husband. The lady, however, had done little to stop the rebellion that they had secretly perpetrated in her own territories, thus placing her English loyalty into doubt. They simply did not know if they could count on her.

Someone at the table suggested she be cornered, haps even stolen away on her way home from the scheduled meeting in Inverness and questioned. "A kind of ransom, but no' for coin, aye?"

"She has no' yet made her alliance known," MacDuff countered with a brisk shake of the head. "It would foolish tae attack such a one and lose potential soldiers. Why should she choose the Moray after being treated in such a manner?" he asked. "Nay, we must only go to the meeting and watch her carefully."

William's long mouth turned down in thought, his brow furrowed. "We cannae sit idle and wait for the lady to make her choice. She might n'er show her hand. Just because she attends Cheyne's meeting doesnae mean she backs England."

There were several grunts of approval at William's statement.

William's words sparked an idea in Cait's mind. Wiping her palms on her knees under the table, Cait cleared her throat. She still was not used to playing an open part in all these schemes and preferred to listen rather than talk, but the men had not regarded her unkindly as yet. "I could..." Cait started, shrugging one shoulder, "...I could go tae the meeting with my husband and endeavor tae acquaint myself with the lady. Haps she will be more open with me, a woman?"

Lachlan, a narrow-shouldered man set across from her with a nose that was far too large for his face, tapped his fingers on the tabletop. His ample eyebrows quivered as he considered Cait's words. "Mmph," he grunted. "The idea has merit, tae my mind, though it's no' my decision tae make." He looked to William, then Moray.

Moray shook his head. "Tisn't needful," he said dismissively. "I thank ye for yer willingness, Mistress Cawdor, but the Lady Euphemia will choose her husband. She will do whatever she can to show England she wishes her husband set free."

"Did she have a good relationship with her husband, then? Do ye ken this woman?" she asked. William placed a hand on her knee under the table, effectively stopping her bouncing foot. She hadn't even realized she'd been doing it.

"It's what a loyal wife would do," William offered, a note of pride in his voice as he cast her a fleeting glance. "But we cannae know with any real surety what she will choose, no matter if she loved her husband. The question is, does she love her own neck more than her country?"

The table was silent for what felt like a long time before MacDuff spoke, his eyes settling on Moray. "Either way, ye must decide if yer ready tae openly attack and raise yer standard, Andrew. We cannae keep debating how others might act. It's *you* who needs tae choose, aye? Raise yer standard and openly fight, or keep up with these wee raids?"

But Moray did not get a chance to answer, for in that moment, argument broke out amongst the men. They shouted over each other, some offended that MacDuff would disparage their efforts, others in agreement.

Cait waited, tracing the woodgrain pattern on the tabletop when a guardsman approached the table. Indeed, not just the table, but Cait herself. He bowed neatly near her elbow, his helm held in the crook of his arm, asking for forgiveness in interrupting them. She bade him speak and the noise around the table fell away. They were used to messengers coming in and out at all hours, but never had a message been intended for Cait.

"There is a man here as says he wishes tae speak tae you, Mistress," said the guardsman, sotto voice. "He claims tae have come from Midlothian."

Cait, confused, looked to the doorway of the great hall and saw there a silhouette of a man she knew very well. A man whose shoulders she had sat upon as a girl to better see the games at festivals. Her heart leapt in joy, her mouth falling open with happy surprise. Seeing him was as though she was seeing the hills and forests of her home. She pushed out of her chair so quickly that it toppled over.

His name fell from her lips like a prayer, her throat tight with sudden emotion. She fell into him, wrapping her arms around his middle, her head against his heart. He was thinner than she remembered. He stroked her hair, speaking words she did not fully hear.

When she pulled away to gaze up into his familiar face, she saw more clearly now how much he had changed. His face was carved more deeply with lines of trial and sun and wind. He was naught but bone and sinew, his blonde beard long and streaked with grey.

"Graham," she said on a breath, her eyes stinging. "Ye look right hackit."

He smiled with good humor, his good eye wrinkling merrily. "Och, that bad, am I?" He looked over himself. "A clean shirt'l do me, I 'spect."

Cait blinked away her happy tears. "I'm right glad tae see ye, Graham. How is it ye're here?"

He shrugged one shoulder, his eye roving around the room, settling on the table behind, full of men. "I ran intae some trouble near Chester and thought as I might find a place tae rest here, if ye'll have me."

The sound of more chairs moving on the wooden planks filled the room as the gathered men stood.

"Chester?" asked Cait, confused. "But why have ye come *here,* so far from home?"

"He'll be an outlaw now, I expect," said William from beside her. He clasped hands with Graham and welcomed him to their home. "And in good company."

They sat together at the table and Cait ordered food and drink to be brought while Graham explained his purpose for being so far north.

"Himself as said I wasnae safe in Perth, what with the new sheriff sae watchful of the goings on there after de Biggar turned up dead."

Cait said nothing but she had a sneaking suspicion that the previous sheriff had not died by chance. She had only heard from a previous letter from home that the hateful man had died and her family had been, at that time, without the imposing rule of a sheriff. No details had been given as to the purpose of the man's death. Her family would not be so careless as to include any incriminating information, of course, but Cait suspected Ewan had had quite enough of his backhanded dealings.

Cait refocused her thoughts on the giant tracker at her side. Graham explained much of what he'd been told by Ewan, pausing briefly to wet his throat, "Himself as said that the garrison is halfway complete with nigh on forty men working sae diligently each day. Once it's complete, they expect it tae house close tae three hundred of His Majesty's men at arms and craftsmen."

MacDuff huffed and folded his arms across his chest. "Three hundred! It will be difficult indeed to rout them out once they're properly outfitted."

Cait felt sick to her stomach. An English garrison full of English soldiers living on her homelands. "Can anything be done?" she asked, looking to William. "Can we help in some way?"

"This is yer brother's home?" asked Moray, looking pensive. "Ewan, is it?"

Cait nodded. "Aye, the very same. The man who risked much tae bring ye tae safety," she reminded him, lest he forget. He hadn't, of course.

Moray pursed his lips and leaned back in his chair, looking by all accounts at his leisure. "Aye, I think it's time tae raise the standard, MacDuff. We shouldnae let our friends suffer so."

MacDuff slapped the table in celebration, making Cait start in surprise. "That's a good man! But which shall we attack first? Dundee or this garrison in Perthshire?"

"My Laird will soon be absent," informed Graham, "gone tae Doune for his brother's wedding."

Cait's heart leapt to her throat. Iain was getting married. Edyth had written of his betrothal but the event had been a distant thing to her; she'd held out hope that she might be able to attend, but with their carefully planned raids and her home full of scheming men, she could not leave. She would not endeavor to travel so far without William or at least a contingent of men, which would be impossible at present. They were all needed, every last one.

Moray was silent for a time, thinking, his eyes cast into some unseen future. Finally, he said, "It must be Perthshire first. Then we must take back control of the Great Glen. Its security is paramount. We will help Mistress Cawdor's brother and with any luck, he will still be in celebration at Doune and therefore blameless in the eyes of Midlothian's sheriff."

Cait's nerves increased tenfold. It was time. All their planning and scheming in the dark, secret places of their home would now be made bare to the world. Moray would raise his standard and draw all eyes. William took her hand under the table, his eyes intent upon her.

"Now is history made, here at our table," he whispered.

Cait, who had to try twice to swallow, merely nodded.

# Chapter Twelve

The path to the cave was lost to Iain since the snowfall, the trail that had been shown to him was now swallowed up into a smooth ocean of white. The only disturbance to the scene were the yellow straw of grasses and the grey humps of stones that were not completely buried. He knew he was going in the right direction though, evidenced by the landmarks he'd memorized to find the shelter again.

"That tree there," said Iain, his voice sounding muffled in the blanketed environment. "Aye, the tree with a split trunk. Ten paces to the right and ye'll find the start of a wash, where the water empties into the gorge. That's where we'll find our shelter."

The boys, who had not complained of the cold or the distance, who had trusted Iain as if he were a foster brother, hurried toward the split tree. "Here," shouted one of the boys excitedly, pointing at the crest of the hill, where the earth gave way to horizon. The boys gathered there, at the edge of the wash and waited for Iain.

The rush of rain and snowmelt in years past had stolen away the earth, leaving behind boulders and shale in a steep trail that fell into the gorge far below. About a third of the way down, there was a scrubby tree desperately clinging to what soil remained between the rocks. "There," said Iain, pointing. "There is the entrance to the cave."

Being boys, they did not think of the danger of traversing the distance from the edge of the ravine on which they stood to the mouth of the cave. They eagerly climbed down, their cheeks rosy in the watery sunlight. Iain followed, his hands slipping on the wet rocks.

The cave was not tall enough for Iain to stand but the boys could walk if hunched. Iain would not complain; it was deep and dry, and shielded them from the wind. They pushed their way in, their breaths filling the tight space and Iain found the prepared supplies left there by the Stewarts: dry wood, grasses, flint, a sack containing oatcakes, and woolen blankets.

It was not difficult to light the small fire, filling the space with an orange glow. Littered on the cave floor were small bones of some animal and the ashy remains of a previous fire. The boys settled around their newly made fire on their haunches, their hands so close to the flames Iain had to warn them. "Ye'll cook yerselves and not know it."

Once he'd seen them settled, he explained that he must go back out and look for the Stewart men the soldier he'd felled had mentioned. "I must go and see if he was speaking true. I'll be back soon," he promised at their stricken faces.

"Will ye take us tae our clan when it's safe?" asked the lad with the hurt arm.

Iain nodded. "Aye, that I will. Do ye rest now and eat what ye can."

The way up from the cave was not as harrowing as the way down, but Iain knew the next time he came, it would be all the harder. He dreaded coming again and fumbling his way in the dark to the mouth of the cave. There was always the hope that he would fail and fall to his death, he joked to himself grimly.

Iain hurried up and over the edge of the ravine and backtracked, following their footsteps in the snow. He passed the fallen soldiers and found, once more, the sheep's trail that would lead him to the bottom of the gorge. He slowed here, careful to quiet his steps and pause to listen hard for any sign of people every few feet.

He'd made it to the fork that would bring him to his previous hiding spot and turned in the opposite direction, which would lead him to the mouth of the deep valley. It was dusk and the shadows were long, but he could clearly see the dark shapes of bodies interspersed in the snow below, could see the splatters of blood upon the rocks and drifts, and could make out the churned mud of travelers.

Straining his ears, he could hear nothing save for the occasional *thwump* of melting snow as it fell from a tree limb. The soldier he'd felled earlier had only said that his captain was holding some of Alexander's men in the valley. Which way should he go? Part of the convoy had gone ahead—through—and some had not yet made it to the opening of the ravine by the time he'd moved from his hiding place.

He could not sit here, idle, and try to puzzle it out. Indeed, there was nothing to puzzle out. He had only two choices and he chose to go out of the mouth of the ravine, toward the portion of the caravan that had not yet appeared to him.

Bodies were fewer here, away from where Iain had lain in wait. He dared to pick up his pace, pulling the crossbow from his back. If he happened upon a group of soldiers, he could survey them from a distance and, should he feel he could strike, would do so.

He followed the edge of the ravine, hugging the wall as best he could and sticking to the shadows. The ravine floor where it met the wall was littered with fallen boulders and rotting trees. He walked for what felt like a long time with his nerves frayed, listening for any sound that might herald the enemy when he came upon the first of the bodies. He nearly stepped on one of the conscripted lads, whose face stared blankly into the darkening, cloudy sky. There were more scattered here and there, bolts piercing their bodies.

Iain could not help but feel culpable. Their attack had brought death to them on swift wings. He could argue that they would have died in Flanders just as easily, but the regret was not so easily removed. He could not say to which clans these lads belonged. Their families would wonder what had ever happened to them.

Iain's dislike of Alexander increased, thinking of him at his leisure back in Doune, out of the cold, locked safely behind stone and iron. How easy it had been for him to command his men to take such a terrible risk.

He thought then of Alice, of her desire to return her maid's son to his rightful place. He did not know what the lad looked like. He didn't even know the boy's name. What a shamble this endeavor had turned out to be. He felt sick with regret. Pulling his eyes away from the boy at his feet, he forced himself onward. He would see for himself if what the solider had said was true.

There was a turn in the ravine before it opened up to a wide, sweeping valley but in the foreground, naught but fifty yards away, sat three wagons, filled with conscripted lads, heads bent and silent, their breaths clouding the air.

Feeling conflicted, Iain considered his options, which were few. Not only were they caged, but worse, there were at least a dozen guards surrounding them. One of the wagon wheels had broken and they were now barking orders for those who had been locked away inside to get out and walk. They were going to leave the wagon behind, it seemed, and force them to their feet. Iain cursed under his breath, ducking behind a tree.

There was no way he could kill these men on his own, even if he could somehow climb up the ravine behind him to get a higher vantage point and pierce them with his—he checked his quiver—eight bolts. He scowled.

How was he to know if they even held Stewart men? He could not, unless he went among them, which he could not do. He would be consigning himself to death. No, he could not save these conscripted lads nor save the men the soldier claimed had been captured, no matter how much he wished to.

The soldier could have been lying, of course. He could have easily been only trying to lure Iain into a trap, but there was no way to know. He could not wait here for the convoy to start marching again so he did the only possible option left to him: return to the cave and see the boys to

the border of their clan lands and pray God that they did not get more
bad weather or run into more soldiers.

By the time Iain made it back to the cave, the lads were huddled together,
three of their faces slack with sleep. One boy, the lad Iain thought might
be a blacksmith apprentice, had met Iain at the mouth of the cave, his
eyes wide and full of desperate fear. The lad lifted a knife in defense.

"Easy, *mac*," soothed Iain, showing him empty hands.

The lad relaxed at recognizing Iain, his breath stuttering out of him.
Iain nodded, understanding well the desperate feelings the boy must be
suffering. As tired as he must be, still he'd foregone the pulling lull of
sleep in the warmth of the cave to defend their little ragged troupe.

"Will they find us?" whispered the boy, his eyes black, his face white to
the lips. "Will they follow our tracks in the snow?"

Iain did not think so but he would not take any chances. "Ye've done
brawly, man. Rest now; I will take second watch. I will wake ye should I
need yer arm."

The lad nodded, his eyes sparking with gratified pride. Iain could see
it shining out of him, like a beacon in the dark.

Iain had settled himself against the side of the cave, his plaid pulled
tightly around him, with only the soft sounds of the fire for company
when the boy returned, hunched.

"Here," said the boy, thrusting out his hand. "We saved ye an oatcake."

Iain took it with a nod of thanks and watched the boy amble back to
his spot by the fire, his heart feeling too large for his chest.

# Chapter Thirteen

The spring sun was pushing through the clouds, melting the late snow. The buds on the trees were bursting with verdant color but still no Cressingham convoy had made it to Perthshire. Ewan could not account for such a blessing but he was not naive enough to think he would escape conscription altogether. Something must have waylaid them.

He couldn't help but hope that some lasting ailment afflicted the man. Haps he'd run back to England to get warm. Haps they would be lucky enough for the man to catch the ague and he'd soon be dead. Ewan scoffed lightly at his own thoughts. Would that they could be so lucky.

Bad news did come, however, late in the day in the form of a messenger. Meg's message, brought by a green lad who looked barely old enough to shave, had been a welcome addition to their supper. Or at least he'd wished it to be. Despite the messenger's age, he carefully and articulately stated his responsibility to speak to the Lady Ruthven alone. Ewan showed the messenger to the room off of the hall where they could speak privately but the lad, hesitant to speak in front of Ewan, had to be persuaded by Edyth.

"There is no need to conceal any message from my husband. Any message given to me privately will be restated for his benefit by my own tongue."

The lad, who took his charge seriously, eyed Ewan distrustfully, but was ultimately convinced to impart the news for the sake of his mistress's need for haste.

Edyth's cousin, Meg, who was married to a MacPherson, was calling for aid. "The English came and demanded several dozen kine, goats and sheep tae feed the soldiers from my laird's stocks. The MacPherson denied them, o'course. The long winter was hard on our beasts and with the birthing season soon upon us, we need every head we can tae sustain us."

Of course, the laird's refusal had not been taken with gracious acceptance. Instead, they found themselves fighting for their very lives. "They said as how, if they were denied, they'd take it all from us and burn the roofs o'er our heads while we slept."

Ewan understood perfectly. War required soldiers and soldiers needed meat as much as anyone, but the great machine that was King Edward's army was making more and more enemies at home as the days progressed. The MacPherson, just as he, himself, had responsibilities to his people first. A good leader must see to his own house first over all else. "Did yer laird leave any alive?" asked Ewan.

The messenger shook his head, his round, youthful face, full of righteous pride. "Not a one. Himself wouldnae let them steal the food from our mouths but defending ourselves cost us. Several of our warriors were killed and many more lay abed and our auld healer is overwhelmed."

Meg's own husband, Garrick, had been gravely injured in the fight and, worried that he was not getting the care he needed, she'd begged The MacPherson to send one of his messengers to fetch Edyth.

Ewan frowned, thinking of Edyth's pregnancy. While he sympathized with The MacPherson's plight, he did not feel comfortable allowing Edyth to travel. Not when her pregnancy was so tenuous. The roads, besides, were another issue. Dangerously muddy during the day and then freezing at night, the carriage was bound to get stuck, a wheel or axle broken, or the horses injured.

Ewan shook his head in a regretful manner and said, "Och, I can well imagine the pain ye must be feeling, but I cannae in good conscience send my wife at present. She—"

A desperate sound left Edyth, forestalling him. The confliction she felt was clear on her face. "How can I deny my aid?" she asked, her hands going automatically to the swell of their child. Her eyes swiveled from the messenger to Ewan, full of concern. "I fear I must go. Haps if you come with me and we are careful...." She trailed off, her eyes betraying her own worry.

Ewan, not wishing to have this conversation in front of the messenger said, "Weel, ye cannae very well travel now, so late in the day." Ewan placed a hand on her elbow. "Let us see tae the lad's needs; he's travelled far and would no doubt care for a full belly and a soft place tae rest."

Edyth nodded, solemn, her mind clearly heavy with what was to be done, and followed them out of the room. She did not return to the dais to finish her meal, however, but retired to their rooms, Gelis following close behind.

After getting the lad fed and settled, Ewan made his way to find Edie. She would want to go to her cousin, of course. He knew her well enough to know that she would worry herself sick if she did not do something to help. But how could he allow it? How could he allow the days of travel, cold and blustery as the days still were, even in a carriage?

He found her in her rooms with her aged maid, packing a trunk. "No, I don't want to take too much, Gelis. We must travel light."

Ewan shut the door behind him, making both women look up from their work. Gelis, curtseying, excused herself, setting a bundle of cloth on a chair as she passed him.

Ewan waited for the door to close behind the maid before moving to his wife where she knelt on the floor, surrounded by clothes and accoutrements. His boots sounded loudly on the planks, his gaze cast over the mess she and Gelis had made.

"Sae ye've decided," said Ewan. "Ye're sure?"

Edyth looked close to tears. "I confess that I don't know what to do. She looked down at her abdomen, her mouth set in a frown. "Being prepared for a journey felt better than doing nothing," she explained with a soft shrug.

Ewan looked in her trunk, which was half full of cloth, sachets of herbs, and her mother's red leather journal, full of herbal remedies. "If I stay," she explained, "there is the risk that Meg's husband will die. But if I go..." her voice wavered and she met his eyes again, the green of them vibrant with emotion.

"Ye risk much," finished Ewan for her.

She nodded, the tears in her eyes spilling as she blinked. They fell onto the billowing fabric of her gown.

He disliked that she'd been crying, hated what she must be feeling. He reached a hand across the divide of the open trunk. She took it, whispering. "What should I do, Ewan?"

Ewan sighed and joined her on the floor. "I ken well enough that ye think of little else save for the child, but we must also account for all possibilities afore a choice can be made."

"Are there many public houses between here and Meg?"

Ewan gave her a look of regret. "There is only one. There are crofter's huts, but..." he trailed off with a shrug. "I cannae say what comforts they could provide aside from a hay bed in a barn or a spot on the floor near the fire."

Edyth nodded, looking crestfallen. "There is also the issue of Hugh Cressingham and his men roving o'er the countryside," reminded Ewan. "I cannae say where he is at present. Our scouts said as he should have been here by now." He sighed softly, his mind distracted with that potential issue. "I'd rather no' leave Perthshire and him come while we're away. Besides, we are tae travel tae Stewart lands soon for Iain's wedding. I dinnae think we should risk travelling twice."

Edyth pulled her hand away to pick up a slipper from the floor. She held it, her fingers playing with the laces. "I could go alone to Meg while you go to the Stewarts. Or rather, I can go with Gelis and a guard." The suggestion, he could tell, was given halfheartedly. She did not wish to be parted from him any more than he wished to be parted from her.

Ewan shook his head. "If ye decide ye mun go tae Meg, I will be there with ye. I willnae leave ye, Edie." She nodded, sniffing. "I ken well enough what it is ye're feeling," said Ewan, "but there is more tae think of than Cressingham or where ye'll bed for the night. It's three days of travel in *good* weather tae MacPherson, which we dinnae have at present. Rains will likely have washed out the roads in at least two places, as they do each spring."

Edyth was silent for a long moment. "We can ask the messenger boy. He got here by himself with no trouble."

Ewan nodded, acknowledging that truth. "Aye, we can at that, but remember that he came on horseback all the way, pushing hard, and he's no' breeding as ye are."

Edyth smiled slightly at the picture he'd painted of the messenger boy being pregnant. She sighed. "Yes, of course, but Harris is gentle. He never balked or ignored my commands when I came alone from England."

"Aye," agreed Ewan. "He's an excellent beast and I'm glad of it. The real question, Edie, is whether or no' ye're willing tae risk yer own life and that o' the child's. I will do as ye wish, *mo chridhe*, and go with ye every step o' the journey, whatever yer choice."

Edyth considered his words, her bottom lip tucked between her teeth. "Either way, there will be anguish. If I don't go, Meg will suffer, and her husband."

"Aye, they might at that." He said nothing more, waiting. He looked over her frame, which had never seemed so frail as it had before. She had always seemed to him as strong as her will and while not indestructible, she had always been resilient. Enduring. When he'd found her last year she'd been wounded, beaten and utterly spent and yet unbroken. He'd vowed to protect her, to shield her with his very body should she need it. But he could not protect her from this.

In this he was utterly and unnervingly powerless. There was *nothing* he could do to keep her safe from the very real danger that now lived and grew within her. Women died in childbirth. Often. He recoiled mentally from the very thought. Imagining her being ripped from him, especially from something he'd caused, was unbearable.

"I'm afraid," he admitted, his voice naught be a whisper. He licked dry lips, searching for the words. "I would remain at yer side always, but I cannae should the worst happen."

Edyth's own feelings were reflected in her eyes. She reached for his hands as if to lend comfort, but he could see her attempt to hide her own fears from him. She forced a smile, her soulful, green eyes telling him far more than her words. Lifting his hand, she kissed his knuckles, tears welling. "Fate chooses whom she takes and when, Ewan."

If her words were meant to reassure him, she'd failed. He scowled, the panic at the thought of her sudden death seizing him. Pulling her into his lap, he wrapped his arms around her, one hand resting on her burgeoning stomach. "Dinnae say such things to me, Edie. Damn fate and tae hell with providence. I willnae hear o' it."

She let out a soft huff, a wry laugh against his neck. She inhaled deeply, taking in the scent of him, and kissed the hollow at the center of his throat. "If I've learned anything from my visions, dear husband, it's that we cannot stop fate, no matter how well we wish to."

"Mmph," groused Ewan, his heart sick and full to bursting with worry.

"What is it ye always say to me? Let us not borrow trouble?" She pulled away to better look into his eyes. Her hand found his cheek, cold and starkly white against the russet of his beard. "Let us worry only over what we can control," she said. "Let us put our energy into helping Meg."

Ewan deflated slightly. "Sae ye've decided then."

Her expression was one of regret when she said, "I must go to Meg, my love. And you must bring me there. But first, let us see Iain. I would...I would see him again afore he's wed."

Some part of him, some hidden place within his breast tightened uncomfortably at her words. She wished to see Iain once more, in case the worst happened. In case she died from birthing the child she carried.

Some part of him hated himself for what he'd planted within her belly. They'd both been ignorant of the potential cost, wishing for a child, only thinking of the happiness one might bring to them. Never did they consider the toll. And now one was coming, but he feared the price would be far too dear.

He nodded against her hair, unable to speak just yet, so close were his emotions to the surface. He would do as she wished, what her fierce, honorable heart demanded. He would ignore his fears and his doubts. He would do as she bid because she was more dear to him than anything else in the whole of the world. His hands roved over the lines of her body, which had grown softer in the last months, committing the feel of her to his mind even as he prayed.

*Lord, keep her safe. Dinnae take her from me.*

She lifted her face to him, as if she knew his mind, and pulled his mouth down to hers, her own emotions, still so raw and close to the surface, evident in her kiss. It felt like a goodbye, somehow, an acceptance of their potential parting. He tightened his hold on her. "No, Edie," he said. *"Cha bhi mi dealaichte bhuat." I will not be parted from you.*

# Chapter Fourteen

The weather was turning fine, and with it, the trees budded bright green. The snow from the late blizzard hadn't lasted long, swelling the rivers beyond their boundaries, and turning roads to naught but muddy trenches.

The smell of the warming earth perfumed the air, lightening Iain's spirits despite his current mood. He had only just returned after great effort from the raid, having taken great pains to bring the boys he'd come across to the border of their lands. He was tired and his mind burdened. Not yet had all of the Stewart men returned home from the raid. Nor did he think they would.

Alexander had sent out a small group of men to go and search for their lost brothers in arms, but Iain had little hope of good news. He'd told Alexander about what the man he'd killed had said, how he claimed his captain held some of the Stewart warriors in the valley. How he'd ventured out in search of those men and what he'd witnessed.

Alexander had not been happy, of course. He'd cursed and agonized over it all. He'd regretted Iain not being able to confront the soldiers escorting the convoy but understood his inability to do so. "They willnae betray us," said Alexander with confidence. Iain knew well enough that any man could be broken if the correct force were applied but he said nothing. He could only hope Alexander was right.

As it was, he was now walking with Alice to retrieve her falcon. She wished to show Iain the talent of her bird by taking her on a hunt, which was as good as a distraction as any he supposed. They were to be married in three days, and were expecting his family that very evening. Even his mother was coming with his uncle and a small contingent of his retainers. He hadn't seen his mother since Cait's wedding last year and was surprised at how eagerly he anticipated her arrival.

"It will be fine weather for your family, I hope," said Alice as they made their way to the doors of the mews.

Iain nodded absently, his mind preoccupied. "Did ye think on our truce?" he asked, darting a glance toward her. "I would hear now what it is ye'd wish tae garner from our union." He waved a hand as if to encompass the whole of the world. Alice only appeared thoughtful, her eyes set upon the path before them.

The sound of their footfalls on the wet gravel filled the vacant space for a time. "What can a maiden such as myself wish for, aside from security?" she started, glancing his way. "I wish tae have a place," she said with more force, as if finding her confidence once more. "I wish for my comforts tae be thought of and seen to, but moreso, I would have my opinions be valued by my husband."

Iain grunted in assent. That seemed easy enough. He would have offered her those things already, willingly. In fact, he was somewhat surprised that she would feel the need to ask for such. Hadn't he made it clear to her, yet, that he respected her and wished for her happiness?

Still, he agreed, feeling that she should ask for more. "And have ye thought of how we shall live? Do ye wish tae live apart? I have an estate in want of a lady. I could stay in Perthshire, where my brother has need of me if ye'd prefer I reside there." He paused, considering what comforts she might stand in need of, and him ignorant to them.

He stared at the toes of his boots as he considered. "O'course there are servants there, at the estate in *Caol Ghlinn Amain*. I've no doubt yer hand upon them would only improve their prosperity, but if ye have need o' something, all ye must do is ask."

Alice slowed her steps, staring at him. "All I must do is ask and ye'll make it so?" she asked incredulously. Her disbelieving smile sent a thrill through him. A smile, even if it was borne of skepticism was a triumph he would not soon forget.

He could not help his answering smile. "Dinnae get too greedy, now my lady," he said, shooting her a knowing look. "I cannae give ye the moon, nor more than I can force the rain away, but if it's within my power tae deliver yer wishes, I'll endeavor tae see it done."

Alice pretended to consider his words, watching him out of her periphery. He could see her studying him, gauging him. "'Tis an arrogant man, indeed, tae make such vain promises."

Iain pretended to be offended, sniffing in distain. "N'er have ye need of a blade, my lady. Yer tongue is just as deadly."

Her smile grew, pulling Iain's eyes. She was lovely when she smiled. Truly. He wondered that he'd ever thought her plain.

Their playful banter fell away as they walked in companionable silence. After a short time, Alice said, "Ye wish for a marriage in word only, then? Ye wish tae live apart?"

Iain shrugged, thinking automatically of his brother and Edyth. A seed of melancholic envy had planted itself in his heart, though he could now say how or when it had occurred. He only knew that if he did not endeavor to cut it out now, it would only grow into a great weed that he could not pluck out entirely, no matter how earnestly he picked at it.

He and Alice were not his brother and sister-in-law.

But no, he did not wish for a marriage in name only. Indeed, he wanted much more, but they were strangers still, their relationship still tenuous. Part of him wished to console, to whisper hope into his heart. *We simply do not know each other. In time, we can be one.* But another part of him knew that hope was a dangerous thing. Fragile and cutting all at once.

He reminded himself once more that Alice had said she would not love him, would not entertain even the mere thought of anything more. Save respect. He did not think he could live in close quarters with a wife who could not offer more than polite regard.

Coward that he was, he chose his words carefully. He did not wish to cast his impossibly desperate thoughts before her only to be met with contempt. Haps he truly was as she said, arrogant and in constant want of praise. Why else would he fear her rejection?

He did not meet her eye. "I dinnae wish tae bring ye intae the troubles of Perthshire. There is a tenuous peace, balanced on the edge of a blade there at present. The new sheriff isnae a tyrant, leastways that I can tell, but there is trouble between the English stationed there and my brother's retainers. I must help him at home, for a time, but then I will have to return tae my own estate." He waited, for what, he wasn't sure. When Alice did not speak, he added, "But I...I think for respect and esteem tae grow between us, we must live together. At least for a time."

He left out how his brother planned to join the Moray as soon as his standard was raised. Once done, no army on earth could hold Perthshire against the wrath of King Edward. Aye, Ewan was shrewd and endeavored to play both sides like their father would have done, but Iain feared that once Ewan's hand was shown, all would be lost. Iain could not be made complicit, lest they lose all their lands and titles.

When Moray raised his standard, Ewan would march through their clan lands, quietly gathering the men he did not wish housed at the keep for this very purpose. This left Iain behind in Perthshire, keeping to the running of the lands and people as if nothing of import was taking place. He was to buy them time, and when Ewan's treason was discovered, Iain was to condemn his brother's actions to the sheriff.

At least that was the plan, though Iain had no taste for it. Iain did not know how he'd get the strength to stay home while his brother defended their home and lives, to die on the field of battle. Iain could not sit idle, commanding the sowing of fields and breeding of sheep, as if he had no other care in the world. How could he do it, while his brother bled?

But this was not the whole of the reason he would return to *Caol Ghlinn Amain*, for Alice would be there. And she might, quite possibly, be all that was left in the world to him should things not go to plan.

It was with these dark and muddled thoughts that they arrived at the mews. The master of falcon, Archie, was there, attending to his duties. Cheerful as ever, he asked if his lady wished to take her *seabhag* out for a hunt.

"Aye, Archie," Alice responded. "But first I wish tae introduce Sir Ruthven tae all my birds."

Archie bowed and led the way, lantern held aloft, down the aisles of cages. Most were empty, some holding rabbits, but others were occupied with birds. They passed by shadowed silhouettes of gyrfalcon, goshawk and sparrowhawk, whose large, yellow eyes stared solemnly back at them. All of them were handsome in their own way, but Iain rather thought the largest of them, a gyrfalcon, the most stunning.

He paused at its cage and the others slowed. Archie chuckled. "Aye, he's as handsome as anything. Catches the eye, he does. Powerful, too, but he's no' as subtle as milady's wee pet."

They moved on, taking the light with them and Iain was compelled to follow.

They stopped at the end of the aisle, where a relatively small bird, with large black eyes rimmed in gold lived. It chirruped softly in greeting, the candle flame reflected in its ebony pupil. "This is *Buadhach*, my lady's peregrine falcon whom she's trained since she was but a fledgling," instructed Archie.

Alice smiled softly at her bird through the rungs of the cage. "She is small and light, but graceful and deadly." Alice crooned to her bird, whose head canted to the side as if waiting for instructions. The bird's wings fluttered as it dropped from its stoop within the cage to the floor, which was filled with rushes and droppings.

"Are all these birds your own?" asked Iain, looking around the space. All in all, he guessed there to be at least eight birds housed within the space, but he could not be sure. The light was low and some of the cages were covered.

She shook her head. "Not all. Some belong tae my brother Robert."

"This wee beauty 'as taken a liking tae milady," said Archie. "I think it's because they have similar temperaments." Here Archie winked as if sharing some cheeky secret that was lost on Iain.

Alice made a small sound of what Iain took for embarrassed pride. "We can be in each other's company without demands. It is a rare thing to be at ease with another soul."

How true, thought Iain. He regarded the flushed look of Alice in this space she so clearly loved. Even in the light of the single lantern flame he could not help but notice how her eyes shone with pride and anticipation.

"Aye, that," said Archie, nodding. "And ye're both underestimated. Be wary of the quiet ones they say, eh, milord?" He laughed conspiratorially, nudging Iain with his elbow.

Alice's face flushed even a deeper shade of pink. Iain appraised the man. Haps he could learn more from other people than he could from the lady herself. "What can you tell me of your lady? She will not boast of herself."

Archie's demeanor turned serious, the corners of his eyes wrinkling in thought. "Och, no. She wouldnae do so. Not in her nature tae boast, is it?" He gestured to the bird with a whiskered chin sitting in the golden halo of light. Its grey wings and white breast dully shone under the single flame. Iain wondered suddenly what it would look like in the open air, free from its cage.

"*Buadhach* 'ere is a simple lass. There's no showy, feather-shredding battles as some other raptors. There is only the quiet hunt and a victim, unaware that it is about tae meet its death. She is the unsuspected war master."

"And this is how you view your lady?" asked Iain, glancing at Alice, who was presently ignoring them both, looking uncomfortable. "War master?"

Archie pursed his lips slightly and winked at Alice, though she pretended not to notice. "Och, aye. Tae be sure. *Buadhach* may appear small and weak compared tae other birds, but she 'as a mind on 'er that can run circles around most men. Haps milady is no' so bloodthirsty or as fast as our friend here, but she is equally underestimated."

Iain rather liked the happy image the falconer painted of his lady. Haps in time he, himself, would come to know her in the same way. Iain lifted a brow, his eyes intent on Alice. "A queen without an army," he remarked, the corner of his mouth lifting in a teasing smile. Alice, looking flustered, urged them onward.

The next cage they came to was of at least a dozen doves and pigeons, the delicate white of their bodies glowing in the halo of the lantern. "These are our messengers," explained Alice. "We've trained them from the egg to carry little trinkets and messages to amuse ourselves. They come in handy, too, when the distance is far and all human messengers are otherwise occupied."

They gazed at the birds for a long moment, Iain's mind on the puzzle that was his bride. He wanted to know more. "What do we hunt today? Dragons?"

Alice's eyes glittered as Archie raised the lantern. "Dragons?" she repeated, a smile in her voice. The corner of her mouth twitched upward, his eyes catching upon the movement as well as any hawk might a mouse in the field.

Iain looked to Archie, a teasing note in his voice. "Or has yer mistress slayed all such beasts?"

Archie chuckled warmly. "Aye, dragons and firedrakes and all manner o' beasts. Any left have fled for fear of their very lives."

Alice, for her part, seemed out of sorts with their easy banter. She drew in a breath as if to speak but, apparently unable to choose words, gave up with a shrug.

Archie took up the conversation for her. "The day is soon upon us when ye'll be marrit." He walked them further down the aisle, lantern leading the way. "T'will be a blessed day, tae be sure."

Iain inclined his head graciously, his eyes straying to the now silent Alice. Haps he'd teased her too much. Haps the reminder that she was to marry him in a few short days jarred her out of her pleasant mood.

Alice bowed her head, her face hidden in shadow, her hand skimming across the bars of an empty cage as they passed, her brown eyes black in the low light. "Hood my falcon and gather all else that is needed for the hunt, would you, Archie?" she asked softly. "We go now tae the stable yard."

It did not take long to get saddled and mounted. The stable lads were already industriously occupied in their preparations when they arrived. They rode in easy silence through the trees, the quiet beauty like a balm to Iain's soul. He filled his lungs with the smells of spring and let the sounds of errant bird song lighten his heart.

He glanced at Alice, who seemed lost to her own thoughts. He wondered about her maid's son. About the issue of Cressingham's men capturing some of their warriors. He thought of Archie's flattery of his lady.

Iain waited until they were in solitude, the falconer and their escort too far behind to hear them. Clearing his throat softly, he said, "My lady...War Master." He could not help his small smile at the words. He could not deny that it pleased him to think of her in such a way. He fancied that he'd seen a bit of what Archie spoke of in the keep's chapel and in the antechamber after. "I would hear yer opinion on what course of action should be taken. If you were laird o' this clan and with the chance of your treason to be made known, what is it ye'd command?"

Alice cast him a look he could not read, but it turned thoughtful as they rounded a bend in the trail. "I cannae rightly say, milord."

"Yer man says otherwise, dragon slayer. Come now, we are alone as well as we can be and I willnae laugh nor scorn yer words. What would ye do after a failed raid with less than a third of yer conscripted lads come home and a handful of yer warriors captured?"

She appeared as though she considered his words, her thoughts turned inward. After a long moment with only the jangle of harness and the breath of the beasts under them, she said, "We cannae know for certain that they're captured." He could see from the unhappy set of her mouth, however, that she did not believe her own words.

"Ye think that it was only the poor weather holding them? That they are out in the heather, afraid or unable to come home?"

Alice shook her head in a way that showed her regret. "Nay, Sir Ruthven. I cannae believe such, though my heart wishes it tae be true. We must consider that they are captured or dead. I'm no' sure which outcome would be worse."

Iain nodded, steering his horse through a swollen stream, thinking once more of the dead he'd seen scattered upon the ravine floor. The horses splashed loudly in the stream, kicking up muddy water onto them both, which Alice summarily ignored. "Still no word from yer maid's son, then?" he asked with a heavy dose of apology in his tone.

"Nay...he did not return. Not as yet."

His heart went out to the poor lad. He could have very well been any of those that had died during their attempt, or he could be in some English encampment. Or yet still, aboard a ship heading to the continent where he would most likely die upon some foreign blade. Like Alice, he did not know which fate was worse.

With nothing else to say, he could only offer his apology, wishing he had better words.

On they rode, through glen and copse, the silver sky peeking through budded limbs. Since their truce, the silences between them were no longer taught and uncomfortable. Not only that, but she'd smiled today. Twice. A small flame of hope licked to life within his breast. Haps, in time, they could be wed in all ways, and not in name only.

"Ours makes a solemn hunting party," she said in apology. "I dinnae like tae bring the dogs or the lads with their horns. I...I much prefer the quiet the forest and the glen provide. I hope ye'll still be entertained with only our small party."

Iain looked behind them and saw Amos, a stringy man who spoke more to horses than he did people—Iain had liked him immediately—and Archie beyond. The latter held Alice's falcon on his gauntleted fist, smiling as brightly as the sun. Iain could see it even from this distance, which had to be at least fifty yards.

"I often hunt alone, myself, or with my brother. There is much tae gain from nature and solitude."

Alice's brown eyes sharpened onto him. "Aye. I quite agree." After a moment of stretched silence, Alice said, "Ye asked me what I might do, should I be the chieftain o' the Stewarts." She licked her lips, her brown eyes darting to Iain and then away again. "I must confess that my father did ask me, before the raid, what I would have him do. I mourned for my maid, ye see, and I encouraged her son's retrieval."

Haps Alice was more of herself now, or haps he could just read her better, but he could plainly hear the remorse in her voice as she spoke.

"My father does ask it of me, from time to time," she continued, "tae offer what advice I might give. He thinks with his mouth, ye ken, and I have a talent for listening. He is...grateful for my opinions but does not always heed them."

Iain grunted his understanding, urging her to continue. "Aye, and so what counsel would ye give now, War Master?"

Once more the corner of Alice's mouth twitched as if itching for a smile. It was progress. Haps one day he might even hear her laugh. She shrugged. "I ken only what I've witnessed. Women are ever in a position to watch and learn, Sir Ruthven—"

"Iain," he corrected. "If we're meant tae me married, then surely ye can call me by my name."

Her cheeks flushed but she inclined her head in acceptance. "Iain." The color went all the way down her neck, making him smile. If using his name made her blush, he couldn't imagine what kissing her might elicit. He pushed the thought aside, laughing at himself. She would probably faint.

"As I say," she continued, "I've observed that power in the wrong hands is easily corrupted, and all the more dangerous when in the grasp of simple-minded men. Cressingham has grown arrogant; indeed, all of King Edward's great men, Surrey, Cressingham and de Warenne cannae see past their own greatness. Especially now that their sovereign is in

Flanders and leaves them to their own devices. They are unchecked and, therefore, all the more dangerous."

"Mmph," grunted Iain in agreement. "Archie was right, I see," he flattered. "A keen mind, indeed."

He watched as the flush reached her ears with prideful glee. Haps drawing out blushes from this lady would be as pleasant as pulling laughter. Alice chose not to comment on his complement, only saying, "I thought ...I hoped that Cressingham would no' think anyone would dare tae take back from him what he has stolen. I thought we could—" She shrugged, her eyes filled with apology. "My ill advice was heeded by my enthusiastic father and now it has cost us much. Not only did we fail to retrieve all of our clan's men, but now the real fear is that Cressingham kens the raid was perpetrated by my family. By my ill advice"

They were riding close. Iain dared to reach out and touch her elbow, offering solace if she would accept it. "We are all of us made fools from time to time, my lady. We cannae always be right. Even the greatest of men. Be at peace. The plan was a good one."

Alice glanced at where his fingers grazed her elbow, any feelings on the matter shuttered to him. He let his hand fall away, feeling as if he'd pushed her too far. What was he doing, anyway? He knew Alice's heart. She'd bared it to him honestly afore he left on the raid. She did not want him.

They rode on in silence for many minutes until they came to a wide glade, rich with the bright green, tender grasses of spring. Alice stopped her horse without word at the edge of the sweeping landscape and Iain followed suit. "This is where we will hunt," she announced with quiet reverence.

Iain dismounted and hesitated in offering his service. Still, it was the gentlemanly thing to do. After only a slight hesitation, she leaned toward him, her hands settling on his shoulders. He pulled her carefully down and set her upon her feet.

She had a woman's shape hidden under her billowy gowns. Gone were the slender angles of youth, replaced with soft curves. She was a woman grown and full ripe with life.

She let go of him immediately and he stepped back, remarking on the landscape. "This is a bonnie glen. D'ye come here often, then?"

Alice nodded, her eyes sweeping over the meadow grass, newly green. "I come here often with my birds tae train." She glanced at Iain, her eyes losing some of the worried look they'd harbored during their serious conversation.

"Yer admirer draws near, War Master," remarked Iain, gesturing a hand to where Archie was steadily approaching from behind. The falconer held the bird proudly, his elbow cocked at an odd angle, a black hood covering the bird's head. Amos took their horses with only a nod, leading them away.

Alice's face shone brightly with promise, staring fixedly upon her beloved pet. Iain watched as she pulled on her own gloves, which were folded in her belt, and took Archie's burden from him with a soft murmur.

The bird went readily and waited patiently as Alice removed the hood from its head, exposing its large, yellow-rimmed eyes. It blinked with some keen animalistic knowledge, clicking its beak. Alice whispered to her bird, brushing a knuckle against its breast.

"This is a good place," Alice said softly, glancing at Iain briefly. "Rabbits willnae be able to resist such tender shoots. The doves and pigeons will be searching for the wee insects that linger after the dew has dried, drawing them in."

"Here, Lady," said Archie, handing Alice a lure, a leathery bundle made to look like a bird attached to a long hempline, wrapped around a rod.

Alice took it in her left hand and walked into the glen a few paces. "Watch as *Buadhach* finds her prey."

The bird's jesses were untied and *Buadhach* was released with avid anticipation. There was a brief glimpse of white, downy feathers under

its wing as it took flight, and then it was gone. Iain watched as the bird
drove itself higher, its powerful wings beating smoothly in a uniform
rhythm, carrying itself into the trees. It settled amongst the spindly
branches of a towering beach, not yet budded out; Iain thought that
if he looked away, he would not be able to find it again, so small and
indistinguishable it was against the silver sky.

Alice spoke almost reverently. "She will ensure her own safety first and
foremost, watching the sky for larger raptors, then she will focus on the
task at hand."

The master of falcon ensured their entertainment by walking through
the forest to their right, beating a stick against a targe. Disturbed by
the ruckus, several birds flushed from the thicket with disgruntled cries.
Alice tracked the movement with a finger, saying. "There is a partridge!"

The falcon took flight with a graceful push of talon and pull of wing,
her delicate feathers fanned out to catch the wind. Up, up, she climbed
until she was a mere dot in the sky, far above them. "She sees her prey,"
said Alice with reverence, "even at such a great distance. See how she
floats on a mere breath of wind?"

Iain, who had been looking at Alice's avid face instead of at the sky,
forced his eyes back to the spectacle. Indeed, *Buadhach* appeared as if she
floated upon an unfelt current, her wings outstretched in an effortless
drift.

And then, quite suddenly, the bird was falling, diving through the
distance that separated it from its intended target. It streaked downward
at spectacular speed, its wings tucked close to its body and knocked the
covey out of the air. It fell, powerless, to the field below.

The former, seemingly at ease and in no hurry, gracefully returned
to her master's outstretched, gloved hand. *Buadhach* chirruped softly,
blinking expectantly, and was rewarded with a piece of raw meat from
a drawstring bag that Alice had thought to place in hand while the bird
hunted.

"No feather-shredding defeats as with the other birds of prey," said
Archie sagely as he came upon them. "She is like some men, ye ken. There

are those that 'ave no need tae boast in their strength, but only let their deeds speak for them. Their kills are honorable and exact. So it is the same with wee *Buadhach*."

Archie left them, intent to find the fallen partridge, leaving them alone. "She is beautiful, is she no'?" asked Alice, gracing her bird with a rare, tender smile.

Iain had to concede that the bird was, indeed, beautiful, with its large dark eyes and the bright lines of gold that lined them and colored its beak. "What else does she hunt?" asked Iain, watching Alice's smile.

"All sorts," she said. "Mostly smaller birds, but peregrines have been known to attack larger raptors in defending their nests."

They watched the bird hunt and demonstrate her skill until Archie's bag was half full and the falcon had lost interest in the feed. Iain and Alice were left alone, save for the escort that had quietly accompanied them, Archie wishing to return the bird to her bower and the dead coveys to the kitchens.

Iain was surprised to see that a plaid had been laid on the far side of the meadow, a basket of food provided for their outing. Iain could not deny that the day had so far been pleasant, if not quiet. Alice did not speak much, preferring instead to watch the world around her in silence.

But he did want to know her thoughts. He wanted to know something about her other than what he'd observed. He did not know what to say, however, so he settled on their mutual interest as they settled on the plaid under a towering beech. "Will yer father send out scouts again tae look for the lost conscripted lads, d'ye think?"

Here Alice shrugged and looked far afield. "Haps." After a beat, she said, "He didnae speak tae me of such things. Only of our marriage."

Iain paused in lifting a piece of bread to his lips. "What is his counsel?" asked Iain, suddenly wary. He still did not fully trust Alice's scheming father, thinking that haps his advice to his daughter would be that of duplicity and advantage.

Alice leaned forward and chose bread for herself, not meeting his eyes. "Only of my duty." She blushed slightly and bit into her fare, avoiding his eyes.

As Iain chewed thoughtfully, he wondered at her words. Duty could mean many things, one of which might be to endeavor to turn her new husband's mind to her father's wishes. "Of what duty could a father demand of his daughter, newly given in marriage?"

Alice's blush deepened, her eyes darting to his then back to the fare spread before them. "He spoke of my duty as a wife, not as a daughter."

Iain understood then. Her duty to her husband—to him—would be to obey, to produce a son, and to have the running of the household. He looked at Alice carefully from his periphery, noting how the sun found the golden hues in her hair, like light sparking on a spider's gossamer thread. He could not fail to notice, either, how uncomfortable she was. She could not even meet his eye. He frowned, thinking of their wedding so soon upon them and what Alice most assuredly would not welcome.

Though it was her obligation to submit to him, he could not ask such of her, knowing how tenuous and newly won their truce was. A truce laid on a foundation of respect could not survive where obligation lived.

"Thank you for agreeing tae help on the raid," said Alice, changing the subject smartly. "My father was right to choose such a man for me. I heard as how ye helped some ye found return tae their own borders."

"I am only grateful that my own clan's sons have been kept safe by the kindness of yer father," he replied diplomatically.

They ate in companionable silence the rest of the time, only speaking mildly of the turning weather or of her birds. No matter how cleverly he jested, he could not win another smile from her.

Cait stood in the courtyard of her home. Their retainers, a handful of Burgesses' sons, and her own husband were preparing to leave for Perthshire, to raid and kill and burn. Her stomach was wound as tightly as a fisher's knot, her blood running cold. She could not bear to think of bringing such destruction upon her own fair home, but she'd begged the Moray to spare her keep yesterday, had pleaded that he not harm her family or any of their people.

Andrew had only said he could make no promise. They would contest any who fought against them. And while she understood it must be this way, still, she could not calm the quiet tremor in her hands or in her heart. Were they doing the right thing? William said they were, said that they must strike now, before the garrison was full of the king's men. And while she well understood, still her heart leapt to her throat, imagining the destruction that would befall her beloved home.

William had held her all the night long, attempting to quieten her fears, and he had for a time. She'd fallen asleep in his arms at least, too exhausted to worry any longer. But with her waking, with the perpetual rising of the sun, so also rose her fears.

The stable lads were bringing out the horses, squires and pages fetching weapons and provisions and strapping them to their master's steeds. All were busily employed, some laughing at some unknown jest. None seemingly sharing her fears. Graham, at least, was staying. He stood beside her, tall and stony, and just as quiet as they surveyed the yard. The great men had decided that Graham should stay behind, worried that he might be identified, and Ewan be found complicit in their dealings.

Moray would ride out with his banner, declaring for the world to see that he was at war against the English scourge that inflicted their lands. A page brought the banner out to Moray's squire, who would carry it aloft along the road: three white stars on an azure field. Seeing it filled Cait with equal parts pride and trepidation.

William, properly suited and armored, came their way at the edge of the yard, his dark blonde hair hidden under chainmail. His spurs sang with each step, his blue eyes alight with promise. "How can my lord husband be so fearless and confident?" asked Cait.

Graham grunted beside her. "He feels every emotion you do," he said softly. "But he must no' give it place within him, lest it take root. One cannae go intae such circumstances with doubt in their heart. Such is the way of any warrior; he must only do, and not give place to hesitation. Go swiftly and strike hard without thought of what might be should he fail."

He paused, both of them watching as William stopped to speak to one of his retainers and then to his sisters. They were milling about, close to the railed fence of the yard, waving and laughing at a page who had tripped and fallen in a mud puddle. "Do not let him see you weep, nor let him see yer doubts, *fear beag*," continued Graham. *Little one.* "Let him leave without the burden of your tears."

Speaking of tears only seemed to call them forth, but she nodded and swallowed them away. "I am glad ye'll be here with me, Graham. I dinnae think I could bear the waiting without you."

Graham did not respond as William was upon them, squinting in the sun. "All is ready. We take our leave."

Cait forced a smile and kissed his mouth. She could not embrace him, so cold and bulky he was from his armor. "*Bi gu math. Thig dhachaigh thugam gu luath.*" *Be well. Come home to me swiftly.*

"*Is ann le deòin a thilleas mi thugad.*" *It is with eagerness that I will return to you.* He turned to Graham and shook his hand. "Take heed o' my wife's comforts ere we are parted. If," he said, raising his brow with meaning, "if the worst should happen, see tae her safety. Protect her."

"With my life," answered Graham solemnly. Cait's heart beat wildly against the cage of her ribs, her eyes stinging. Fear gripped her, easily envisioning the pains she would endure should William fall. She rapidly blinked her tears away and forced cheer.

"There will be no need," said Cait. "Ye'll return swiftly, as I command, for Graham cannae play the role of husband and friend. Only you."

William bowed and took her hand. He pressed his lips to her cool skin. "As ye command, my lady." He winked at her, his mouth lifting with good humor. "Farewell for now, sweet Cait.

And then he was walking away, retreating into the yard full of mounted men. Cait felt suddenly as if there was not enough air. She pressed her hand to her breast as if she could slow her heart's rapid rhythm with a touch.

"We have the worst of fates, Graham. I have ne'r been good at waiting."

Graham huffed a laugh, lifting a hand to wave goodbye. William turned and found them with his eyes as the men and horses moved from the yard. Cait lifted her hand as well. "Waiting will go easier if we occupy ourselves," he said. "Go and fetch the sword Edyth gifted ye and let us see yer skill."

Cait smiled, her eyes pinned to her husband's back as they filed from the yard and through the gate. "Aye. I will change and meet you in the lists. Dinnae go easy on me Graham. I would welcome the oblivion borne of fatigue."

# Chapter Fifteen

As planned, Iain's family arrived within a few hours of each other. First his mother, Roslyn with her brother, who was much improved since the last he saw her. Mourning the loss of her husband, Roslyn had lost much of her usual vibrancy. And while she was still quick witted and had kept a sharp eye on his little sister, she had seemed a lesser version of the woman that had raised him.

But viewing her now, he could not help but notice that her bearing was once again full of confidence. Gone was her mourning habit and veil, replaced with an ornate crispinette, winking with pearls in the bright light of the courtyard. He smiled at her plaited hair, at the vein of grey boldly streaking through it.

Her brother, Niael Caimbel, was just as he remembered him as well, steely eyed, shrewd, and slight, with hair the color of a raven's wing. Of course he was a little changed. In his later years he'd thickened round the middle slightly and grey now touched his beard and at his temples, but all in all, he was the same man. Formidable in an altogether different way than Alexander Stewart, his uncle could quell a man with silence.

Iain kissed his mother's cheeks, his heart lifting in a way that he hadn't expected. "Mam, how well ye look," he'd told her, meaning it. "How many offers of marriage have ye received since living with Uncle?" he teased.

She scoffed and said, "Dinnae ye wish such upon me!" But Iain knew she was not truly angry; she smiled and held her hand against his cheek, asking him if he planned to shave before he was wed.

He hadn't had much time to spend with her, as Lady Morwen was keen to take her away and show her their estate with a promise to return her to Iain when it was time to eat supper. Only an hour before the meal was to be served, came his brother and Edyth, followed by her aged maid, Gelis. He wondered why they hadn't taken a carriage, but all other thoughts fled his brain as Ewan helped a noticeably pregnant Edyth from atop her steed.

Iain could not help but stare at the roundness of her middle that no amount of pleated, billowing fabrics could hide. She was, to Iain's mind, all the more beautiful. Indeed, her skin shone as brightly as her warm smile.

She embraced him, the surprisingly rigidness of her middle pushing against him and said, "How blessed we are to see each other again so soon." She looked into him in that strange way she had, as if she could read his very thoughts, and said, "Have you come to terms with your choice then?" Her green eyes pierced into him, and he pressed her hands before kissing her cheek in greeting.

Iain considered his answer, examining his feelings. Surprisingly, somewhere between agreeing to come and marry Alice and everything that had happened on the raid, and their truce, the sharp edges of his resentment had been dulled. The carefully nursed dislike he held within his breast for the entire enterprise no longer filled him with such anger.

"My attitude has improved," he admitted with a wry smile, "and none is more surprised than I."

Edyth smiled knowingly up at him and said, "I should like to meet this lady once again, who has the power to change even your stubborn mind."

"Opinions are easily altered, Sister, when given all the facts. We have a truce, the lady and I," he added at her lifted brow. "Should ye wish to speak with her, she is in the women's solar with my mother and Lady Morwen. I daresay ye'll have tae overcome yer fear o' embroidery if ye venture in with them."

Edyth did not get a chance to reply for Ewan was there, clasping his forearm in greeting. "Brother, how fairs the house of Stewart?"

Iain bowed slightly, knowing what Ewan was really asking. *What's wrong?* Iain had not realized his concern had been so evident, but to Ewan, perhaps he could not hide any depth of feeling, no matter how well he buried it. Regardless, Iain schooled his features and responded, "Not as tranquil as wedding guests would hope for, I'm afraid."

"Mmph," grunted Ewan, narrowing his eyes in speculation. "Let me see Edyth settled and then we can speak."

"These are the lists," explained Iain unnecessarily, nodding toward the enclosure, filled with churned mud and sand. They paused, watching as some of the Stewart men spared with the Caimbel retainers that had escorted their mother. They each leaned their elbows along the fence line and spoke in quiet tones as Iain related to Ewan and Niael all of what had transpired since he'd arrived. Ewan grew quite still as Iain told him of the failed raid and the possibility of Stewart captives.

"Cressingham will come and take his revenge," said Ewan. "We must make plans as tae secure our own safety. We must no' stay sae long in celebration, as we had planned. If one of these captured men lets slip that Alexander was behind the raid, or that ye were involved...." He did not finish his sentence. He did not need to. Iain knew quite well what would happen. Cressingham's wrath would be great, indeed.

Their uncle grunted his agreement. He huffed softly, his mouth turned grimly downward. "We didnae see Cressingham nor his soldiers on the road north, but that doesnae mean they arenae far away."

Nodding, Iain said, "Aye, we mun get them awa' safely soon after the ceremony."

"I might as well no' bother tae unpack my trunks," grunted Niael.

Iain gestured to the sparring men before them. "At least ye've thought tae bring some men with ye. Where is your contingent, Ewan?"

Grimacing, Ewan said, "At home with Rory. Edie and I leave here for MacPherson." He then explained the trouble that had brewed there recently, and their need of Edyth's skill. "I can see now why Cressingham has no' come tae Perth, demanding conscription," said Ewan. "He's got his hands full enough as it is with the MacPhersons and the Stewarts." Ewan shook his head, looking worried. "I'm glad ye made it out, Iain. That could have gone poorly."

Niael grunted his agreement. "Even if the raid against the convoy wasnae as successful as the Stewart had intended, I'll no' disparage a man taking a stand. He was right to. Cressingham and de Warenne have both grown far too aspiring for my taste."

Ewan and Iain exchanged a look, knowing that their uncle no doubt had some plans in motion already. Or at the very least, he knew of some great plans underway.

With little encouragement, their uncle then told them about how one rebel, a Sir William Wallace, had been rumored to kill the Sheriff of Lanark. "He's gathrin' men, is the rumor. Robert Dundas says as how he meets with the lowland nobles, asking for aid. Some are with him, but others…" He shook his head, disgusted. "Ye ken well enough how they squabble and argue o'er who as should be the rightful king."

Iain did know. It was easy to agree on the matter that King Edward had no business in Scotland, but what came after his expulsion caused a great rift. "Where does this Wallace plan to strike?" asked Ewan, pulling Iain from his thoughts.

Their uncle lowered his voice, his eyes roving for any who might hear, then, seeing they were unheeded, said, "Dundas, Hay and the Comyns, they say as how the Sheriff of Elgin, is called to suppress the rebels with whatever army he can gather."

Ewan swore softly under his breath but he was ignored. Their uncle continued, "We've got this Wallace fellow in the lowlands and Moray in the highlands. Tis my mind that these two powers should unite, for I fear this sheriff might make it very hard indeed for our rebels tae continue should the English-loving nobles fall in line."

"Cait's letter hinted that Moray sent out a messenger for that very purpose," interjected Ewan. "Andrew is interested in Wallace's plans, if he has any, but the messenger hasnae yet returned."

Iain made a sound of regret in his throat. The messenger could have been waylaid by some unforeseen circumstance, but more likely, he was long dead.

"Wallace has plans," offered Niael. "Didnae ye hear as how King Edward released some of the noble houses from the White Tower, only tae send them off tae fight in Flanders?" At their negation, he continued, "Weel, Wallace and the Lord Douglas raided Scone and took it from the returning, newly reappointed lord. Killed him outright for choosing that murderous king o'er his own people."

"William the Hardy, d'ye mean?" asked Iain, his brows raised nearly to his hairline. "D'ye man that scunner has switched sides on us again?"

Niael waved his comment away. "He willnae be the last, either. Discomfort is a great motivator and King Edward kens well how tae bring it about." He shrugged slightly, as if to dismiss the suffering to come. "I've heard tell o' a meeting tae take place, called by this Sir Reginal Cheyne, this sheriff of Elgin. He bids all sworn vassals of Edward tae meet in Inverness Sunday next." He turned and looked at Ewan sharply. "Did ye get yer missive?

Ewan ran a hand over his weary face. "Aye, I heard this message from Lucas, the sheriff currently overseeing my lands days afore I received my invitation." He shook his head. "Are ye going, then, Uncle?'

Iain thought his brother had aged at least five years in the time since he saw him last so full of burdens as he was.

Niael squinted at someone in the sparring yard, his eyes following their movements with a critical eye, and said, "Aye. I will be there, along with our usual friends." Iain knew this to be the Comyn, Hay and Dundas, amongst some others.

"How is it I'm only now hearing of this meeting?" asked Iain of his brother. While Iain knew he had no right to be upset—he'd been embroiled in the Stewart family for weeks now—still it rankled him to no end that he was in the dark in all this.

Ewan only gave him a pointed look. "It doesnae matter. I willnae be there." At Iain's questioning grunt, he said, "Edie. She is no' well. I...I fear tae leave her side."

"What of her dreams? Do they still plague her?" asked Iain.

Ewan huffed out a humorless laugh. "Ye could say so." He rotated his injured shoulder, his eyes distant. "She sees an army moving from place to place, but she doesnae ken the names or places she sees. She's drawn them for me," he added, "but it's hard tae ken with any real certainty."

"Have any guesses?" asked Niael, looking pensive.

"I do," answered Ewan, pushing off the rail. He ran a hand through his hair, grown long. "A brownstone keep, sprawled o'er a rocky outcropping set against a vast expanse o' water on one side. She says as how it was felt larger than a river." He shrugged. Could be Loch Lomand or Lock Ness...mayhap even the Firth. There are a handful of castles that might fit that description."

Niael grunted his assent. "But what else do we know? Haps we can puzzle it out together. What have ye heard from Cait?"

Ewan shook his head, shrugging slightly. "Cait writes only tae say that Moray is well and is gathering followers. Edie has written back, describing her dream, but we've yet tae receive an answer. How they'll make something of it, I dinnae ken."

"What's more," added Ewan "the army of Scotsmen she sees marching upon this unknown keep quit the place. They simply...turn around and go elsewhere, without a single sword drawn, tae another body o' water. This time it's a river. She's sure o' that much, at least." He laughed without humor. Iain couldn't blame him. There were no doubt thousands of rivers in Scotland. Ewan shrugged. "She says as how it's wide and winding, with a narrow wooden bridge spanning it. Does this mean aught tae you?"

Iain could only shrug. Niael pursed his lips, his mind working behind his cunning eyes. In the end though, he shook his head, saying, "As ye say, there's no way of knowing for certain."

"What of you, Iain?" asked Niael. "With Ewan unable to go tae the meeting in Inverness, will you go in his stead?"

Iain shot his brother a disparaging look, disliking his part in these political machinations more and more. "Och, seein' as how my role is tae show unwaverin' loyalty tae the English king, I should make it my business tae be there." He sighed and, thinking better of it, said, "But won't they think it odd that it's me that come and not my laird, the Earl of Perthshire?"

Ewan's uneasy manner, hampered by worry, gave Iain pause. Ewan shrugged as if dislodging an unfriendly hand. "Ye'll give my regards tae the sheriff o' Elgin and explain that I didnae wish tae be parted from my lady wife, so near her time of delivery."

Niael had many questions about their plans once Ewan's treason was known, which they readily shared. If their uncle could see a flaw in their strategy, he did not say. Indeed, he approved of Ewan's forethought and attempt to keep their holdings.

"Ye'll stay in Perthshire instead of at yer estate in *Caol Ghlinn Amain*?" confirmed Niael.

Iain scratched the back of his neck, thinking. He wasn't sure yet what Alice wished. She hadn't confirmed that she wished to go live alone in the northern estate. It was a strange feeling indeed, to suddenly remember that he had charge of another entire person. One who depended on him in all things. "I suppose she would come with me," he said uncertainly. "Though haps I should deposit her in *Coal Ghlinn Amain* first and I return tae Perthshire alone."

Iain, watching as one of the men sparring fell backwards into a rather foul-smelling puddle, added, "Would it appear strange for a newly wedded husband to abandon his wife in a lonely house with only servants for company?" Some part of him felt guilty doing so while another part of him thought it would only give him relief. She would be safe, at least, holed away and far from danger and he would have no need to hear her disapproval of him.

But that is not the sort of marriage he wanted. He glanced at Ewan; soon to be a father, his wife warm and her very heart written in her eyes for all to see. She loved Ewan. And Ewan loved her. For certs the weed of envy in his heart had taken root. He feared it would be impossible to remove.

"If it's advice yer after," said Niael sagely. "Ask the lassie which she would prefer and see that her choice is honored." He left them then, moving under the fence rail to go spar. "Geordie, I'll have a go," he shouted. A page ran forward with a practice sword.

They were quiet as they watched their uncle prepare himself for a sparring match, each in their own heads. It was only after the steely clanging of swords began that Ewan said, "Tell me true, how goes it with Lady Alice?"

Iain shrugged slightly, though Ewan's eyes were still fixed on the match in the yard.

"She...she speaks more," he said lamely. Then he smiled, thinking of how she's shouted at him and accused him of loose behavior. "We've made a truce."

Ewan grunted, catching his eye. "That bad is it? Surely it didn't come tae blows," he teased.

Iain laughed softly, leaning his forearms against the topmost rail of the fence. "She seems tae be under the assumption that I prefer the company of simple-minded women because I crave their baseless praise." He glanced at Ewan, whose concerned frown had given way to a smile.

Ewan chuckled. "So she is as clever as her father boasts," he remarked. Then, sobering, said, "Tell me of this truce. I would learn of what ye've promised in the name of peace."

Iain's smile faltered. It was all well and good to tease but the truth was...disappointing. It shamed him, embarrassed him, to speak of it to his brother who had married for love. But still, he told Ewan the whole of it, even explaining his frustration at the hopelessness he felt. "I cannae say how I should move forward. Should I hope for more or leave it—and her—be?"

Ewan's strong hand found his shoulder, giving it a squeeze. "Sometimes I think that fate has a sense 'o humor. Life has a way of giving us exactly what we dinnae want, yet what we are given is sae often exactly what we need. In time, we can see the fruits of providence plainly."

It did not comfort Iain to hear from a man who had eagerly wed his bride, that in time, he might be glad for his choice. "And how long before I am glad for the lesson fate gives me, brother?" asked Iain.

Ewan shrugged. "Ye're ever a resilient pursuer, Iain," reminded Ewan. A smile tugged at his mouth. "May yer betrothed make ye work hard for any affection. I daresay ye wouldnae enjoy it otherwise."

Iain's answering grunt was all the reply he would give. He pushed Ewan off center, but he did not fall. "Come, let us go speak tae Mam and Edyth, and make our plans." He paused and then added, "And I will speak tae Alice about where she would live."

They walked in stride back toward the keep. Ewan rubbed a finger under his nose and quietly said, "Can ye no' recall that Edyth and I argued afore we wed? Aye, we have love between us, but it did not come all at once."

Iain glanced at his brother, waiting for him to continue. He did: "Haps yer memory isnae sae keen from the ague that affected ye then, but our road together wasnae an easy one. There was trouble aplenty, what between Dunbar and the church chasing her." He made a motion with his hand as if to dismiss these significant trials. He stopped and looked Iain in the eye. "What I mean tae say, Iain, is that it's difficult indeed tae go through such pains together and no' find a friend at the end o' it all."

Ewan started walking again and Iain followed, his mind full of desperate questions and few answers. He knew what Ewan said was true. It was how many of his most enduring friendships had started. Trusting another man to keep his feet and not abandon you in a fight was hard won and the friendship lasting. But short of going into the lists with her each day and training with her, he wasn't sure how to encourage her trust.

# Chapter Sixteen

The next day came early and was full of listless waiting on Iain's part. He knew that for Alice, her day would be long and filled with careful preparations. But for him, he only had to wash and shave, and dress in his best clothes, the entirety of which could wait until moments before the ceremony began as far as he was concerned.

They were to be wed in the village kirk, where any and all could witness the blessed event. He passed servants scrubbing the floor of the great hall, the sleeves of their dresses rolled up to their elbows, their skirts soaked with grey, dirty water.

Iain felt uneasy in spirit and no matter how hard he worked himself in the lists that morning or how thoroughly he prepared himself for his leave taking, he could not account for the feeling. Haps it was only his nerves. It would make sense, with him being wed in only a few short hours, but he didn't think that was the cause. Not fully, at least. It was as if he'd forgotten something very important that he could not call to mind, no matter how well he strained his mind.

The feeling was still with him as he was washed and was rubbed down with finely scented oils from France, dressed and combed and bothered to the breadth of his patience. Finally, having had quite enough, he refused a wee flower that a servant was attempting to put in his bonnet and made his way to the kirk.

Ewan, who had been with him through all the pampering, was also eager to leave the keep and walked with him to retrieve their mother and Edyth, who were deep in discussion in the great hall. It sounded to him that they were discussing childbirth, which was as grotesque as watching a tooth being pulled to his mind.

Together they took a carriage into the village in deference for Edyth and Roslyn. Iain could not remember a time that he had felt as jittery and cramped in the small space. The enclosure was silent all the way through the streets save for the squeak of the wheels and the rhythmic clopping of horse hooves. When they pulled to a stop at the front of the kirk, the steps were lined with villagers, intent on viewing the spectacle.

The church itself was as fine as any Iain had ever seen, with elaborate lead-lined glass windows and ornately carved statues lining the walls and standing guard in every alcove, looking properly forlorn. He'd only ever seen one other church like it in Edinburgh, this one on a much smaller scale, of course. Iain took a deep breath and forced his feet forward, down the long center aisle, past the pews filling with guests, and toward the priest standing at the altar, his family following close behind.

The priest, a very tall and thin man with pale eyes and a propensity for muttering to himself greeted them. "Aye, excellent. Excellent," he mumbled after each introduction was made. "Stand here, if ye dinnae mind. The bride is arriving just now. Aye, excellent. Very good. Wait 'ere."

The empty-bellied feeling Iain had experienced all the day increased tenfold once he stood apart from his family and the priest ambled off to parts unknown. Not knowing just what to do with his hands, Iain found himself smoothing absent wrinkles and readjusting the angle of his belt.

His tunic was the best he had, a rich red of the best spun wool their ewes produced and saffron hose to offset the color. His Ruthven plaid was carefully pleated and thrown over his left shoulder and pinned in place with their clan sigil.

He touched the pin briefly as he tried to calm his nerves. It had belonged to their father, whom he had had a tenuous relationship with the whole of his life. Malcolm had been formidable to say the least, and had held his children to the highest of standards. Ewan had always seemed, at least to Iain's mind, the son who could do no wrong. As for himself, well, his father had loved him, he was sure. He wasn't the type of man to show such affections, but he did boast of Iain's skill on the field when it was deserved, or of how diligently he set to any given task.

That had been enough; at least he'd convinced himself he'd been content at the time. But now that his father was gone, laid to rest under the kirk in Perth, Iain was still left wanting. Once Iain had taken the vows and had been knighted, he'd expected some sort of display of pride from his father. Instead, Malcolm had called him into his office and gruffly shoved a deed of land toward him from across the table. "This is yer's now, Iain. I'm granting it in hopes that ye'll make something of it."

It had been a portion of their lands that bordered MacThomas, which had no estate upon it. No home, nor much of anything save for dark forest tucked up against the mountain and sweeping fields. Still, he'd endeavored to make something of it, knowing what his father intended. It was just another test. Another task to push and stretch him.

Iain did not begrudge his father's ways. He had gone happily to the place and had hired men to help him clear the land from what he'd earned in tourneys and used the timber to build him a modest estate. A home as dark and silent and as far removed from everything he loved that he found, in the end, that he could not occupy it.

Haps now, with a lady there, the halls would not seem so desolate. There were servants there, presently keeping it in order, but he did not go there unless expressly needed. He preferred to spend his time in Perth, where laughter and life lived in the very walls. Or at least it had. Aldythe had left five years ago, and then Cait, and now even his mother had abandoned the place. Haps the memories were too much for her.

"Let us begin," said the priest, who was suddenly before him. He realized with an internal start that Alice had also appeared beside him, her family in tow. The priest gave them all instructions, indicating where Lady Morwen and Robert and his daughters should sit. Iain barely paid them mind. Alexander stood there, his brown eyes glittering with pride.

Alexander lifted Alice's hand and placed it into Iain's. "This beloved creature is now under yer protection. I expect ye tae keep her well and love her." There was no menace in his voice, but Iain still felt the weight of the charge. It was as if a mantle had been placed around his shoulders, heavy and unfamiliar. He spoke of love, a word that seemed to haunt his thoughts of late. How ironic that he would charge Iain with the action when it was his own daughter that was so repelled by the idea. Even so, Iain inclined his head in acknowledgement, saying nothing else.

Iain glanced at their joined hands, his eyes travelling up her arm to settle upon her face. She was as lovely as he'd yet seen her, with her fair, round face and her dark, intelligent eyes gazing back at him. So too she seemed to him as distant as a star. Glittering and beautiful, but impossible to hold. And, he realized with a slight shock, that he did, indeed, wish to hold her.

Not only in the physical sense. She was his wife and they would be expected to produce children at some point, but it was more than that. He wanted to win her. He wanted her estimation of him to change. Her view of him as a pompous philanderer had at first made him scoff, but now, he could only feel a desperate desire to prove her wrong. He wanted more than a marriage in name only.

"Aye, excellent," muttered the priest once more, taking his place before them. The chapel's quiet seemed to press in on his ears. He felt as if he were suddenly under water. The weight of every eye rested on his back; he felt rather than saw Alexander seat himself in the pew just to his right where Lady Morwen and the rest of the Stewart family waited.

Iain could not understand why he was so jittery. In all his time as a lad, battling between clan raids, in his duties on the boarders of their lands, in shouldering the heavy responsibilities his father had placed upon his shoulders, never had he felt so unbalanced.

He could do many things. He could boast on the strength of his arm and prove his talent with a sword. He could jape and smile and woo, but this woman beside him made him guess and falter.

The priest bid them take each other's wrists in their right hands while he tied them together with a white cloth. He spoke to them plainly about the purpose of marriage and how they must, together, build a life that would be pleasing to God. Iain dared to find Alice's eyes but she looked only at their hands, her skin dazzled with jeweled color from the stained glass windows.

The priest blessed them, making the sign of the cross over their linked hands. He turned to Iain, calling him by his full name: "Sir Iain Madok Caimbel Ruthven, do ye troth by yer honor and by the spirit of God that resides within ye, tae give yer hand and heart, without sin or shame, tae this woman?"

Iain licked dry lips. He searched her face, looked over this small, curvy creature outfitted in the finest blue silk he'd ever seen. It must have cost a small fortune. Her headdress was a simple golden circlet set over a white veil, her dark hair bound in an intricate plait. *By his honor.* Yes, he would honor her as best ye could. "Aye, I do so pledge my troth."

Alice's dark lashes fell over her eyes at his words, as if accepting that their fate had been sealed. Indeed, if there had been a way out of their contract of marriage before, there was none now.

Iain refocused his mind. He listened as Alice was made to repeat the vows and then it was done. The priest was addressing the church as a whole about that sanctity and sacraments of marriage. When the priest fell silent, Alice stared up at him expectantly. He did not hesitate, though he felt as if he were outside of himself. He bent at the waist and brushed his lips against hers carefully, tentatively, the final seal to their union. She was his and he, hers.

He did not feel any different. The weight of the vow had not yet fully settled upon him. The priest removed the wrapping from their wrists and they walked down the aisle, her hand feather light, resting in the crook of his elbow. Well-wishers congratulated them, all beaming and full of emotion.

"Now," shouted Alexander to the wedding party without the church, "we celebrate! To the keep!"

A raucous cheer carried them to the carriage awaiting them. The throng of people he did not register pushed them along as a wave in the ocean. He was merely flotsam, landing in a bedecked carriage, the colorful ribbons and bows as bright as jewels.

The conveyance might not have been so uncomfortable if Alexander and Morwen had not joined them, the former of which spoke unceasingly of their alliance finally coming to fruition. He spoke of his wishes for Iain to remain in Doune for a time to make plans for defense, of how he might best utilize Ruthven men should an uprising officially begin. "With the king fighting on the continent, Cressingham, Surrey, and de Warrene have the run of the country," he confided in a fatherly tone. "Edward couldnae stay their hands, even should he wish it from so far away. We cannae sit idle; we must make our own plans while we have the chance."

Iain regarded his father-in-law warily. The man wasted no time at all in endeavoring to enlist him in further treasonous plots he could not afford to be embroiled in. "Ye'll have no use o' Ruthven men, Sir Alexander," said Iain, "unless my brother expressly allows for such. He alone is chieftain, and he alone will decide if and when we will fight."

Alexander, red faced, clearly had much he wished to say on the topic, but Morwen shushed her husband, saying, "A wedding celebration is no place for war making, husband. Can it not wait until the morrow, my dear? Aye, on the morrow ye mun speak tae both brothers at once." She patted his hand, her face a perfect replica of the usual benign and serene expression he'd first noted in Alice.

She continued, her voice full of cheer, "Let us speak instead of happier things." She looked to her daughter, saying, "Yer maids have filled your trunks tae be sent on tae Perthshire. How sweet it will be tae enjoy yer groom's family for a time afore ye set off tae be mistress o' yer own home."

Iain glanced at Alice, not sure if this was her desire or her mother's. He would have to speak to her about it tonight when they were alone. It was with a bit of alarm that he realized that the next time they would be alone would be in their shared chamber that evening. Hesitation entered then, not knowing how best to navigate that inevitable situation.

Yes, she was now his wife, but the thought of her simply *allowing* him to touch her because it was her duty to do so rankled him. Hadn't Alice said her father had spoken to her regarding her duty? Was she presently preparing herself for his unwanted touch?

Alice, for her part, bowed her head obediently. He eyed his new mother, watching her smiling eyes as she viewed her silent daughter. Iain could not help but wonder what Alice would become away from her childhood home.

The rest of the way to the keep was made in silence. The heat from Alice's body radiating into his own where their shoulders and hips touched upon the bench seat. By the time they entered the great hall, the sun was starting to set, burnishing the cold, grey stone a vivid gold. The torches had been lit; they flitted merrily in the soft breeze.

Alexander bade them follow him through the front doors of the keep to the small antechamber he'd first been brought, the same room in which he and his bride had made their own vows. The lady Morwen stalled in the hall, speaking to a maid about some domestic affair, leaving them alone with Alexander.

"I would bestow yer gift on ye now, away from the gaggle o' merry makers soon tae arrive," he announced, indicating that they should sit. He then moved to the same ornate box at the sideboard, his back to them. Alice moved to sit closest to the banked fire. The long train of her veil trailing down her back pulled the golden circlet askew as she sat; her face erupted in flame, her hand just catching onto the lopsided headdress before it fell.

Iain took the circlet from her cold fingers and sat beside her, watching as she readjusted herself, tugging the gauzy fabric out from under her. She was embarrassed, he could see, so he placed the circlet upon his own head. He leaned close to her ear, saying, "This is only the first of yer foes I will vanquish, my lady."

She shot him a look of embarrassed gratitude and then her father was back, standing before them holding a fold of vellum emblazoned with seals and ribbons.

"Here is the quitclaim of land belonging tae Alice, and now you, Sir Ruthven, upon yer marriage."

Iain did not move to take it. "I make no claim upon my lady wife's property. As it belongs to her, it will be her choice should she acquit such tae me."

Alexander raised surprised brows. "Ye'll no' assert yer right?"

Iain could feel Alice's stare heavy upon him. "As I say, I leave such matters to my capable wife." His words were chosen with purpose; they were the same words Lady Morwen had used in deference to her husband's authority.

Alexander's eyes darted to his daughter, the stony expression on his face not quite able to mask his surprise. After a slight hesitation in which the man seemed to gather himself, he bowed neatly before them and offered the quitclaim to its rightful owner, his daughter.

Wordless, Alice took the proffered gift, seemingly at a loss. Iain had not intended to make such a gesture. It had not entered his mind to defer to Alice until that exact moment, but now that it was done, he knew he'd done right.

Not waiting to be dismissed, Iain stood and offered his hand to Alice. "There is a celebration in want of its players, my lady. I'm happy tae escort ye, or would ye rather tarry here?"

Alice, staring in a stupefied fashion at the land title in her hands pulled her eyes away to gaze up at him. Iain could not read her well enough to know what she might be thinking, but he waited, his hand outstretched, feeling unaccountably vulnerable.

It was not as though a refusal to take his hand equaled betrayal, as if she owed him obedience or even her fellowship after his gesture. Indeed, she owed him nothing at all. But still, somehow, a refusal to take his hand would matter to him.

Blessedly, she did not make him wait long. Slipping her hand into his, she allowed him to help her up and out of her seat.

In the dark of the gallery, outside of the great hall, Alice tugged on Iain's hand, indicating she wished to stop.

"Iain," she began, then paused. With a little shake of her head as if in disbelief, she lifted her eyes to his, nearly black in the dim. She stood on her toes and he, thinking she wished to whisper lest her father hear, leaned in. It was with some surprise that he felt the soft warmth of her lips against the corner of his mouth.

She immediately pulled away and left him, striding toward the stairs instead of entering the hall. He stared after her and felt rather than saw Alexander's presence loom up beside him.

Glancing at Alexander, he saw that, he too, stared after the retreating Alice. "Shrewd of ye, *mac mo thighe*," he said softly, "tae garner her trust with such a grand gesture." The way Alexander looked at him, as if proud of the successful outcome of some scheme Iain had contrived, pricked his ire.

Iain drew himself up, pulling in a long breath through his nose as he met Alexander's eyes. "Ye were right about one thing, *Athair-cèile*."

At Alexander's questioning brow, Iain continued. "A son o' fair Roslyn will indeed endeavor tae honor his wife. I have no motive, save regard." With that, he swept through the entrance into the great hall, intent to find his family.

At least a hundred candles were lit, filling the space with a gilded light that seemed nearly otherworldly. The hall was full of tables and benches, and upon the dais, in the place of honor, was set the full body of a glistening, roasted pig. The noise in the room was as a thousand bees, a happy hum of conversation that bolstered his spirits.

Maids were ready with pitchers of ale and expensive wine, all with bright smiles and a gleeful mood. There were minstrels in an alcove near the dais, already plucking merry tunes. Not far away against the eastern wall, near the minstrels, he saw his brother and mother exiting through an arched doorway. Iain did not know the keep so well as to know every doorway and gallery, but he knew this exit. They were headed to their apartments. Roslyn would be leaving presently with her brother, Niael.

On his way, he passed a seated Edyth, who smiled kindly up at him. He gave her shoulder a soft squeeze as he passed and followed his brother and mother through the doorway.

As he suspected, they were mounting the stairs. "Mam," called Iain, wishing he'd spent more time with her. Time, as always, seemed to run short. "I thank ye for the honor of yer company, though sae little of it I was able to enjoy. I'm only sorry ye must leave."

"Congratulations," she said, smiling. Roslyn was a proud woman, tall and straight despite her age. He felt a swelling of gratitude for the woman that had helped to form him. She'd shaped and molded him as best she could, despite his antics in his youth. Now, after Alexander's frank appraisal of his mother, Iain could not help but agree with the man, no matter how well he disliked him.

Alexander had been right. Roslyn was fair, in all the ways a person could strive to be. Suddenly emotional, he pulled her against his breast, eliciting a small sound of surprised delight from her. "Can ye no' stay long enough tae eat at least," he asked, dropping a kiss on the top of her head.

Roslyn pulled away and looked at him sharply. Her critical eye traced over the lines of his face, her hand coming to touch his forehead.

He laughed. "Och, I'm quite well."

"Afraid tae be left alone with his wife, I suspect," said Ewan, a smile in his voice.

Roslyn ignored this, saying, "Yer uncle is instructing the stablemaster now of our imminent departure. We take with us the lads brought tae Doune to escape conscription."

Iain nodded, feeling that was best. "Cressingham willnae return tae Caimbel a second time in search of would-be soldiers."

She gave both of her sons a meaningful look. "Best be wary; if Niael is alarmed, there is reason tae tread carefully."

She turned and placed a hand on Iain's cheek, a soft smile in her eyes. "May yer union be a happy one. The lady Alice is blessed, indeed, tae have such a husband. I can think of no better man in all the world." She paused, all softness gone now and, in her usual blunt tone, said, "Ye've chosen tae love her this day, Iain. Dinnae ye take the vow lightly."

He could only nod, feeling the weight of her words. *Love*, she'd said.

Roslyn laughed softly. "Aye, love. Tis naught but compassion and forbearance, which ye have in spades...when ye wish it." She pinched his cheek and gave him a look so full of certainty, it made his throat feel suddenly tight.

She stepped away and, turning her gaze to Ewan, asked, "When will ye depart for MacPherson? I think it best if ye dinnae linger." Her eyes darted toward the door leading into the hall, where the muffled sounds of the celebration continued. "Niael's disquiet coupled with yer lady wife's dreams, I confess I find myself ready tae leave. She told me as how she dinnae sleep at all last night for the dreams that plagued her." Roslyn sighed, the shadow of worry filling her eyes. "I willnae tempt fate. Nor should you, boys. I would tell ye tae leave this night, but that would be impossible. Tolerable from me, an auld lady who cannae be too far gone from her bed, but no' for the groom."

"We will both leave on the morrow," said Ewan.

Roslyn nodded and smiled at them both. "My sons," she said rather breathlessly. "How proud yer faither would be, seeing what ye've become." She paused, her hand groping for Ewan's arm. "I am a proud woman, and have much to boast on with such worthy children." Taking hold of Ewan's arm, she said, "Come Ewan. I grow weary. Take me up tae my rooms, sae I might complain at the way my maid has packed my things."

Iain watched as they disappeared around the bend in the stairs, his mind a muddle. He supposed he should not worry over her safety with Uncle Niael and his men escorting her. Still, he wondered when he would have chance to see her again.

Iain reentered the party, pausing at the door to take in the extravagance. Alice had returned while he was speaking in the stairwell. She sat at the dais looking placidly down at the room full of people, her hands hidden beneath the table. Lady Morwen was there on her left, leaning in to speak to her. He should go and sit with her, but first he must speak to Edyth.

He found her where he'd last seen her, sipping on a cup of cider. "Are ye well, sister?" asked Iain as he joined her. He could see her weariness, her eyes tired and rimmed with purple circles.

"I am," she said, her hands automatically going to the roundness of her belly, smoothing the fabric over the swell. "Congratulations, dear Iain."

Iain nodded his thanks. "Mam told me that ye slept ill last night...that ye dreamt again. I would ask ye tae share what ye saw."

He saw her hesitation, her eyes roving around, afraid, perhaps, of who might hear. Iain waited patiently, refilling her cup from the pitcher placed on the table. The green of her eyes was remarkable. Like the verdant moss that covers the forest floor and just as soft. Finally she spoke, her voice low.

"I dream much of war, but last night was strange. There was no battlefield. There were no screams of men or beasts." She paused, licking her lips. Her eyes, which had been distant, focused upon him once more. "I saw the shadow of an ax fall against a backdrop of stone." She shook her head, her mouth slightly open as if searching for words. "I...I can't say what it might mean, Iain, but what worries me is the feeling that came with it. It was...I was full of sorrow. Of dread. I wept upon waking, though I could not say why."

A weight settled into his belly. He knew well enough what she'd prevented at the Battle of Dunbar last year. He resisted the desire to pester her with questions. She'd said she was not sure what it meant and if she did not know, it would be pointless, indeed, for him to speculate. It did not ease his mind, though. "Ye'll leave tonight then?"

A look of regret flitted across her face, her hand going for her cup. "Ewan wishes to leave at first light. He wants me to rest. I do regret our hasty retreat."

Iain shrugged, forcing a smile. "Ye'll be staying longer than Mam at least."

Edyth did look sorry. She squeezed his hand suddenly, her face lifting as if remembering something important. She pulled away to search her pockets. "I have a gift for you," she announced, handing him a lumpy handkerchief. "And I hope you appreciate the work I put into it, for I loathe embroidery above all other occupations." Her smile was warm and genuine and completely contagious.

He opened the cloth, which he saw was stitched with fine and carefully crafted needlework. In one corner were two rams, their curling horns bedecked with thistles, battling. So much he saw before his eyes fell upon the article in the center: a polished, oval stone, grey save for the veins of green and white that ran through it in thin ribbons. He stared at it even as the lines of it lost their edge, his eyes misting with emotion.

The stone itself was of no worth. There were thousands just like it that had been shaped by the river winding through the center of the village of Perthshire. The current had forced all rough edges away, leaving the silken, weighty thing now resting in the palm of his hand.

"So you can have home with you, wherever you go," she said, a finger lifting to touch the stone. "Isn't it remarkable, how it feels to the touch? Soft yet unyielding." He found her eyes as she said, "Much like you, Iain." She folded his fingers around her gift and graced him with a kiss. "Your heart is your greatest strength. Do not hide it away."

Iain did not know what to say so he only cleared his throat and pocketed the treasure. "Ye're right. Ye're complete shite at needlework."

They both laughed, even as Edyth pushed his arm. He grew serious quickly, though, and touched her shoulder. "No better gift could e're be granted. I thank ye, Edie."

Edyth, looking touched, motioned toward the dais. "Go, Iain, and see to your bride."

# Chapter Seventeen

The celebration had lasted for hours; Iain was full of wine and meat, but he hadn't drunk so much as to be free from discomfort as the priest approached their table. Alice had noticed him too; he felt her stiffen in her seat. "The time has come," said the priest solemnly, bowing slightly in greeting, his cheeks flushed with wine.

Iain watched, his feelings conflicted, as Alice was summarily whisked away by a host of married ladies he did not know, feeling strangely detached from his body.

Alexander took advantage of her newly vacated seat, sitting close and smelling strongly of drink. He spoke to Iain of rebellion and risk, of allies and enemies but Iain did not hear him. His mind was on his wife, above stairs, being prepared for her marital duties.

For the whole of his adolescence, he and his friends had spoken of this particular aspect of marriage as if it were a benediction from God himself. The act of consummation was, for all lads of such an age, the ultimate goal and the only boon they could conceive that came with the odious obligation of marriage.

But now that Iain was here, he could not conjure the same immature, excited thoughts as he had as young lad at the prospect. That's not to say that he didn't want to consummate his marriage. On the contrary.

Alice was his wife and he had grown rather fond of her. No one was more surprised than he at this discovery.

He'd liked the feel of her in his hands the few times he'd touched her. Over time, he'd learned just how impassioned she could be, how she tempered her quick mind with a slow tongue. A lesson he could well learn.

And he was a man, wasn't he? Wanting to take one's wife to bed was as sure a wave rushing to shore. But what Iain had not anticipated, what his younger self could have never conceived, was the hesitation now ruling him.

Iain's body was at odds with his mind, each wanting to be master, each equally valid in their arguments. The prospect of taking Alice, as was his right, sent his blood to racing. He thought of her full mouth, of her sparking eyes when he'd driven her to anger, of how he itched to fill his hands with her soft curves. Of the willing kiss she'd bestowed upon him a short time ago.

The church and the law marked her body as his, but the very idea of taking her mouth and using her body because it was simply his right to do so repelled him. Even a year ago he would have scoffed at the idea of foregoing his marriage bed out of deference for something so fleeting as feelings.

But that had been before he'd been witness to his brother's marriage. Before he'd seen the way he and Edyth looked at each other, at the evidence of their love for one another. Iain did not want Alice to *submit* to him. He wanted Alice to desire him. He wanted the root of jealousy he'd so diligently endeavored to pluck from his heart to finally wither away.

Not only did these thoughts pervade his mind as the priest returned to escort Iain above stairs, but also those of a far more serious concern. Pinned to the back of his mind, ever present, were the growing concerns of Edyth's dream, of Alexander's urgent whispers, of the meeting in Inverness that he was to attend in Ewan's place, and last, as he stood outside of the bridal chamber—so known by the ribbons draped over the lintel—he thought of Alice. And dared to hope.

Alexander knocked on the door loudly, calling out to the women hidden within. "Come! The time 'as come for the blessing o' the marriage bed!"

The door was flung open amidst giggles and blushes from Alice's friends, the room alight with dozens of candles. Iain's mouth had gone quite dry but he followed the priest into the room, his eyes falling to Alice immediately.

She was perched upon the end of the bed, the voluminous, velvet curtains open, looking as pale as the sheepskin rug at her feet. She was dressed in a richly embroidered robe the color of wine. Her hair had been let down, cascading over her shoulders in loose waves to pool on the coverlet. He hadn't known her hair was so long. Indeed, he supposed there was much he did not know about her.

He only half listened as the priest directed those in attendance to remove his surcoat, belt, and his boots, which he suffered through with as much dignity as he could muster. His face was surely aflame with the indignity of it all, but he sat, finally, next to his wife in his liene and his hose. He belatedly remembered to cross himself as the priest first splashed Alice with holy water, then himself.

They both watched in a sort of benumbed stupor as the party exited, full of celebratory glee. If he felt unsure, he couldn't imagine Alice's feelings, timid creature that she was. But no, she wasn't so timid, he reminded himself. Letting out a careful breath, he eyed Alice in his periphery. She was staring at her hands, small and knotted, upon her lap.

"Good e'en tae ye, Alice," he said absurdly, as if they hadn't just been sitting together all evening.

Alice copied his salutation automatically and then the silence resumed. He could not think of anything sufficiently witty to say to break the awkwardness filling the space, but he had to say something. "The gifts your family bestowed upon us were quite generous."

Alice nodded, not meeting his eye. "My mother is good with a needle, is she no'?" She was referring, he guessed, to the ornately stitched bunting, proudly displaying their two family's sigils side by side: two rams battling on a field of crimson for Ruthven and a pelican feeding her young in the nest for Stewart. Iain rather liked the Stewart motto, despite his dislike of her father. *Virescit Vulnere Virtus.* Courage grows strong at a wound.

"I've thought of another requirement to uphold our truce," said Alice somewhat forcefully, as if she feared she would lose her nerve if she waited any longer to speak.

Iain made an interrogative noise and she continued, taking a deep breath as if to draw courage from the very air. Iain saw her hesitation, could hear her anxiety in the slight waver in her voice. "I wouldnae wish for my husband tae take an excess o' strong drink."

Iain thought back to what he'd imbibed during the celebration. Was she making some judgement on the wine he'd savored?

Alice continued, "Some of my father's retainers, when deep into their cups, they grow stupid with...with lust." She faltered on the last of her sentence, no doubt imagining Iain's own lust-filled thoughts. She wouldn't be wrong, he thought wryly, taking in the scent of her.

She'd been rubbed down with what smelled like rose oil so that she glowed softly, as if the warm radiance of candlelight came from within her. The intoxicating scent filled his nostrils. Her hair looked as silken as her wedding gown had that evening and he itched to touch it. He closed his hands into fists instead.

"Did one of these drunken men try and seduce you, my lady?" asked Iain, a smile in his voice. "Heaven help them if they tried. I'm no' sure which would be the more formidable. Yer father's wrath or yer own."

Alice responded with the small smile he'd come to so appreciate, surveying him from the corner of her eye. "Drunken men do no' seduce, sir. They grope and drool."

Iain's eyes were fixed upon the small turn of her mouth. "What is this?" he asked in mock surprise. "My lady jests!" Alice shrugged slightly with apparent pride in her successful jape. "Och, my lady, ye've naught tae fear from me in that regard," he assured her. "I grope and drool even without drink."

Alice's crowing laugh, a sharp bark in the relative quiet of the room took him by surprise. Hands flying to her mouth, Alice's face went from white to crimson in a beat. His smile grew. "She laughs!" he cried. "By the saints, she laughs! Come, my lady, I must hear it again." He pulled her hands away from her face, seeing for the first time her full, radiant smile. He stared, transfixed upon the sweep of her full mouth, at the apples of her cheeks lifted in gaiety and knew he must have more.

She was beautiful when she smiled. And for Iain, knowing that her laughter was so hard won, it felt like a gift bestowed upon him. He wondered in that moment, how many other men had witnessed such a triumph, for that is how he regarded it.

It did not take long for her to command control over herself. Her smile softened, a quiet sound of amusement trailing away to nothing.

Her fingers were warm in his hands. A thrill of some unknown emotion sent his heart to racing at the innocent touch. They both looked down upon this small union, their amusement subsiding. Iain gave her hands a small squeeze before letting go, saying, "All the same, Alice. I accept yer terms of the truce."

They were quiet for a time, the sounds of the celebration muted and far away. It sounded as if a group of raucous party goers had taken their celebration out of doors. Muffled sounds of raised voices could be heard coming from the closed window from the yard below.

He ran a hand through his hair, thinking of what else he might say, and then latched onto the memory that he must speak to her about where she wished to live. Now was as any good a time as any, he thought, and pressed forward with far more certainty than he felt.

"Since we speak of vows," he said, as if calling a meeting to order, "I must ask where it is ye'd like tae dwell. In the carriage yer mam said as how yer things were being sent on tae Perthshire, but is that, truly, where ye wish tae go?"

"I tarry where my lord husband tarries," she said with a slight frown, as if confused by his question. "D'ye ye no' wish for me tae go with ye tae Perthshire?"

"It is my wish for my lady wife tae sojourn where she wills," answered Iain. "Our truce began with the intent of compromise. I have business in Perthshire for a time while my brother is away, but if ye'd rather forego such tedious matters, and retire in *Caol Ghlinn Amain* alone, I will see it done."

Alice was staring at her knees, a furrow in her brow. She opened her mouth as if to speak but no words came. She chanced a glance at him, her brown eyes dark and rich. After a beat, she said, "Does Ewan no' have a steward and captain tae see tae the keeping o' his estate?"

Iain hesitated, not sure of what to say. The short answer was that, yes, of course he did, but could he—should he—entrust his Alice with their plans? Could he say that he was meant to go home to Perth, and remain there, for the benefit of their duplicity? Once Ewan's eventual plans to join the Moray were in motion, it was imperative that Iain convince the sheriff residing there that Iain did not hold with his brother's treasonous act. He was to publicly condemn and renounce Ewan, and to take control as chieftain.

And while Iain wished to trust Alice, he could not. Not yet. She was the daughter of a cunning man. Not only that, but she, by her own admission, had been involved in her father's schemes no doubt for the whole of her life. Was she as deceptive as her sire? Looking over her, he saw the mantle of solemnity she so loved to don return. He could not read her.

The room was silent save for the quiet hiss of wick and wax, of his own breathing, and the odd shout from below. She gazed at him with her clear eyes that spoke of her intelligence. "There is something ye're no' saying," she said softly. "Have we no' vowed honesty, Iain?"

A breath of wry laughter left his lungs. "Aye, that we have." He stood abruptly, feeling the need to move, to think. He needed to clear his head, to put distance between the warmth of her body and the intoxicating aroma that emanated from her. "There are secrets," he admitted, shooting her a glance as he walked to the chest his clothes had been laid upon. "But they are no' my own; ye mun no' press me." Surely a daughter of Alexander Stewart would understand.

Without thought, he started to dress, sitting on the chest to replace his socks. He did not know why, but suddenly he felt that he must. He should leave here and return to his own rooms before he forgot himself and did something stupid like kiss her. Was she a Delilah, intent to use her feminine whiles in hopes of gleaning information? But for what purpose? She and her family were loyal to Scotia. Weren't they?

But Alexander could no doubt play both sides of the political divide as well as any other man. Just as they planned to. *What could her father gain by learning their secrets, though?* thought Iain. He would not throw the house of Ruthven to the wolves with his daughter ensconced within its walls, would he? Unless Alexander used the secret knowledge of their plans against the crown for blackmail. Alexander could extort them easily enough with such knowledge and Alice would be the puppet master, leading him around by his bollocks.

He heard rather than saw Alice's movements, her footfalls in the rushes shuffling as she came toward him. Looking up from his dressing, he paused, waiting for what she might say. She was only a short distance away, looking for all the world like an innocent, with a halo of light behind her from the fire, limning her with a golden aura.

"Keep yer secrets, husband, so long as they've naught to do with me...with us." Her voice was slightly strained, her eyes following his moments as he pulled a stocking over his heel. "Why this attitude?" she asked him. "Are you leaving?"

Iain stood and draped his surcoat over an arm. "I think it best."

Alice's neck flushed with heat. He stared at the exposed expanse of flesh where her robe had opened, at the deep neckline of her undergarment just showing through. Drawing herself up, her shoulders thrown back, Iain watched, transfixed, as she tugged on the knot holding her robe in place.

She let it fall to the floor, revealing herself to him. They'd dressed her in a thin chemise, wide necked and decorated with fine lace that her pink skin shone through. Iain took her in from head to foot, lingering on the round swell of hip and full breast, noting the small tremor in her hands. She was beautiful and tempting and she was his for the taking.

He took the two steps necessary to reach her and lifted a large hand to her cheek. She gazed up at him, her eyes full of hope and fear. "Yer a brave wee thing, I'll give ye that," he whispered. Just a kiss, he told himself. Just one touch. Just one, and then he would go where he could think more clearly.

Haps he was too far gone in lust and wine. Haps he'd spent too much time talking of intrigue with his uncle and Ewan and now that was all he could see. Alice might not have any ill intentions, but he could not puzzle it out here, where her very scent drew him to her. He could feel the rapid rise and fall of her breasts where they brushed against him; it was nearly his undoing.

A loud knock sounded, making them both jump. "Iain," a muffled voice said. A voice Iain knew as well as his own. He shot Alice a look and moved to open the door. He heard rather than saw Alice cover herself.

It was Ewan, his face markedly distressed, immediately alerting Iain that something was not right. Of course something was wrong. Ewan would not come and interrupt for nothing. Glancing over his shoulder to confirm that Alice was more fully covered, Iain dropped his hand from the door and beckoned his brother enter.

After the smallest of hesitations, Ewan did so, his steely eyes hard with resolve. "Be at ease, Ewan. We are not yet fully wed. What's amiss?"

Ewan looked like a caged animal, rigid and bunched up as if ready to pounce on anything that dared get too close. He went to the window and pulled back the heavy drape. "Forgive the intrusion," he said, "but the ruse is up. Soldiers from Cressingham's army have arrived demanding Alexander. Grab only what you can carry. Servants will send the remainder on tae Perthshire."

Alice gasped and joined Ewan at the window. "Why?" she asked. "How did they get past the gates?"

"The guards no doubt drank too much. It is a celebration," suggested Iain, taking Ewan's place at the window. Privately he wondered at whether Alexander had been betrayed, but he held his tongue, not wishing to upset Alice at such speculation.

There, far below, dozens of torches blazed in the courtyard, the orange light of the flames reflecting dully against plate metal armor, on sword and shield. English soldiers, intent on justice, no doubt, for the raid on the conscripted convoy. They'd been so intent in their conversation that they'd missed any noise from below as celebration.

"I was going down tae get some tea for Edyth when armed guards came upon me in the gallery. I stopped one...they said as how someone breached the gatehouse." Ewan's anxiety was palpable. "Thank God Uncle has left with Mother already."

In the silence that followed Ewan's statement, Iain could hear distant shouting, muffled and discordant. Alice's hands clung to the window coping; her knuckles were as white as her face. "Where is Da?" She turned in a whirl of hair and fabric, unable to hide her panic.

"I cannae say," said Ewan evenly, hurrying to the door. "I must bring Edyth safe away, Iain." He paused and, giving Iain a significant look, added, "Make haste." Iain nodded his understanding. Iain could not be made complicit in the raid upon the conscripted convoy. It would ruin all of their plans. "I willnae wait long," Ewan added. And with that, he left them, the door shutting reverberating in the stillness of the room.

Alice stared at him, her eyes wild and full of worry for a long second. "What will become of him? Of you?" she asked. She immediately went to her trunk and pulled out a satchel. She stuffed random items into it, rushing to the side table to grab a comb.

Iain did not wish to say. Whatever Cressingham was doing here, it would not end well for the Stewarts. "I must go, Alice." He ran a hand through his hair, thinking fast. "I can send for ye later, when things settle...."

"I am coming with you, husband," she said, pausing in her packing long enough to find his eyes.

"What of yer mam...of yer nieces?" Iain knew that Cressingham would not simply leave Alexander here. He would be arrested no doubt, or killed.

Alice's shocked and terrified eyes hardened into bleak resolve. "Whatever it is as happens, I am no longer daughter o' Alexander Stewart. I am Alice of *Caol Ghlinn Amain*, wife of Iain Ruthven."

A slight thrill shot through Iain at her claim.

"Go," she commanded, seeing that Iain still stood there, gaping at her. "I will gather some things and meet you at the chapel. There is a hidden way out of the castle from there."

Iain agreed and, after gathering his things, opened the door, the sounds of distress snaking their way up the stairs. The house sounded as if it were in complete chaos. Women were crying, people were running, someone was shouting below stairs.

Iain had brought very little with him and so it did not take but a few scant minutes to gather his belongings. He did not waste time with removing his fine wedding clothes. He took extra care in strapping his sword belt around his hips and made quick work in finding his favored knives. He secured them on his body and had just opened the door to find Ewan there with Edyth, fist raised to knock.

"Good," was all Ewan said before turning and stalking down the corridor, Edyth's hand clutched tightly in his own. "The maids and other servants are meeting us at the stables. Radney makes ready the horses."

"Alice says to meet her in the keep's chapel. She will show us a way out."

The sounds of a fight were louder now as they descended the stairs. The steely clangs of swords, of angry shouts and cries of pain raced up to meet them and spread through the halls. "Get yer wee knife tae hand, Edie," instructed Ewan levelly as they neared the bottom.

Although they could hear a ruckus, they met no one at the bottom of the stairs and so they made their way through the gallery toward the chapel. Indeed, as they passed the arched entry toward the great hall, they could see through the vastness of the room and beyond. The tables were empty of merry makers. Goblets and plates of food remained just as when he'd left them for his marriage bed. A cat was perching on a nearby table, happily feasting on some bit of fowl. Beyond, lay the front doors, one of which was thrown wide. Black shapes of men lurked upon the stoop, but they did not linger to watch or make sense of what was happening.

The musicians were gone, their precious instruments abandoned. Instead of melodic chords strummed on the psaltery, they could hear quite plainly the commanding, booming voice of an Englishman outside in the yard.

"Which way?" asked Edyth, peeking her head around Ewan's shoulder.

"Follow me," said Iain, leading the way. He walked them across the deserted great hall to another hallway that he knew would bring them to the chapel.

There were two servant girls, huddled and crying in an alcove that shrieked with alarm as they passed.

Ewan shushed them harshly and said, "Pray where is your master?"

One of the girls lifted a shaking hand to her mouth, clutching a rag, and sputtered, "Sir Cressingham took him into the yard. They commanded that he confess his sin against the king but he would not."

The other girl piped up. "He wouldnae say, so they struck him. But when they threatened t—to hurt his son, Robert, he confessed all."

The first girl elaborated: "Himself as said as that Robert was innocent and that he, alone, commanded his men to attack the convoy. I fear for his life," she cried. "What will become of him?"

Ewan shot Iain a look that said, quite plainly, they would be next should they wait around long enough. "Keep yer heads," commanded Ewan. "Get ye tae yer rooms and dinnae speak o' the guests that have come, lest we, too suffer Cressingham's wrath." They girls nodded and stood on shaky legs, hurrying away into the dark of the corridor.

The chapel was not far and as they neared, Iain saw Alice move from the shadow of the door. She stepped out, cloaked and lightly burdened with only one bag for travel.

Edyth grasped Alice's hands. "Where is your maid?"

Alice shook her head. "I dinnae think it wise tae go in search of her at present."

Ewan grunted his approval and motioned for Alice to lead the way.

Alice seemed to gather her resolve, swallowing her nerves and squaring her shoulders. "This way," she said, motioning them into the chapel.

This room, too, was empty, save for the low burning candles and flickering shadows. They followed Alice silently down the aisle between the pews and through a door nestled into an alcove behind the altar upon which sat the holy sacraments.

"This door will lead to an exit along the side of the keep," explained Alice, her voice as soft as a caress in the dark causeway, her face swallowed up in darkness. Iain could only see the white column of neck and shine of pearlescent cheek as she turned her head to speak to them. "We can easily be seen on the way tae the stables, but...." She faltered here, her breath hitching. "But haps we will no' be seen with...with the spectacle in the yard."

Edyth made a sound of regret in her throat, but she did not move to touch her. Iain did not know how to comfort her. He could only think of their few swords against such an army. How could he protect his newly made wife from such?

"Mind yer feet. There is no light here for a ways," instructed Alice, pulling him from his thoughts.

They fumbled through the dim. Only one torch burned around a corner, out of direct view, Iain's hand on his Alice's elbow. When they finally made it to the outer door, Alice paused. "We will be hidden from view for only ten paces or so, then when we clear the side of the chapel, we will have full view of the courtyard on the left."

Iain, for his part, was amazed at her composure. Yes, she was clearly distressed, but there were no tears or fearful sobs as from the servants they'd passed.

Her hand rested on the latch but Edyth waylaid her. "Wait. Have you...does your family know you're leaving with us?"

Alice's eyes darted to the door, the shutters hiding her feelings falling away. "I managed to s—scribble a note. They will understand."

The look of sympathy that Edyth gave Alice nearly undid her. Tears pricked, glassy bright even in the poor light, and something in Iain's chest tugged uncomfortably.

"Too right they will," intoned Ewan, but not unkindly.

Alice nodded and, filling her lungs, opened the door.

The assault of sound hit them hard. Alice staggered at the cries that filled the night air. "Mercy!" cried a woman, tearful. "Mercy, my lord!"

It had to be Lady Morwen or, haps, one of Alexander's granddaughters. Iain grasped Alice's elbow, leaning close to her ear. "Ye needn't do this. If ye change yer mind, just say the word." He was thinking of Lady Morwen, who would lose a husband and a daughter within the same hour.

Alice's only response was to shake her head and take a step out of the keep, and into the cacophony of chaos.

# Chapter Eighteen

T he courtyard was well lit. The dozens of torches held by
Cressingham's men made sure of that. There were at least thirty
men there, all dressed in His Majesty's uniform. Plate armor and
chainmail clad each, they looked as though they were going to war, not
to a wedding feast. Indeed, Cressingham had come prepared for strict
resistance, but had found none.

Ewan, holding onto Edyth's hand, crept quickly and silently to a
wagon, which was set near a tree thirty paces from the chapel exit. Iain
and Alice followed, sticking to the shadows the best they could. They, all
four, huddled there, behind the conveyance, waiting for the page's signal
that all had been prepared. "It'll be a lantern," explained Ewan quietly,
his eyes on the torch-lit yard, full of Cressingham's men.

Iain focused on the wide steps of the Stewart keep where a stoney faced
Alexander glared down at them, his hands bound and a noose around his
thick neck.

Among Cressingham's men, Stewart vassals were scattered in the
crowd gathered on and around the steps of the keep, pale faced and
robbed of action. They had been at the wedding feast, dressed in their
finery and without their swords. Daggers would not be enough to
prevent massacre here.

Along with Alexander stood Robert, pale in the face and twitchy-eyed in the bright halo of the torch that hung against the wall. Behind him, in the shadow of the heavy doors stood two of his wee daughters, arms wrapped around each other. Lady Morwen was there as well, her stricken face not focused on the crowd in the yard but upon her husband's furious form. Iain's stomach turned over.

Ewan gestured with a jerk of his chin toward the back of the crowd, where three Stewart men slunk away into the dark.

"They're heading toward the armory," whispered Alice, her face as pale as a winter moon. Her lips trembled as she spoke, Indeed, Iain could feel her entire body trembling with fear and cold from where she stood, though they were not quite touching. Putting an arm around her shoulders, he chuffed her arm, bending close to whisper in her ear.

"If Cressingham has come and no warning sounded...." He trailed off, his eyes searching the curtain wall about them. He could see no men posted, not that they would stay there now that they were invaded. Still, it made him wonder.

"They are dead," she breathed, her lips white. "They wouldnae betray their laird."

"Haps they were too deep in their cups," offered Edyth, though even to Iain, her consolatory excuse seemed thin. "Or haps they have quit their places to formulate an attack," she suggested in a hiss.

Iain did not think so. If they had been alert and able, they would have signaled Cressingham's arrival long before he'd ever come to their gates. Regardless of what had happened or how, Iain knew the outcome. The Stewart men, unarmed as they were, had little choice. They would be cut down if they sought to protect their laird. They could fight and die, or they could do nothing and live.

The urge to flee hit Iain hard. He looked to Ewan, who's eyes were fixed upon some distant spot to their right. A ringing of steel cut through the murmuring crowd, pulling every eye.

Cressingham stood on the steps, his sword drawn, the three black swans on his great surcoat appearing as coiled snakes from this distance.

Robert was holding his mother now. Iain could only see half of her face, pressed as it was against her son's chest. Her mouth was open, and from it, a most agonizing, haunting wail spilled forth, making Iain's skin pebble to life. Iain doubted that he would forget such a sound. It was agony personified and it terrified him.

"Ewan," he hissed, his eye fixed upon Cressingham. "We cannae linger."

"Hsst," warned Ewan. "I await the lantern light from the stable yard. We cannae risk leaving now and being seen if we must tarry in the stable. We must go only when we are ensured the horses and made ready."

Grimacing, Iain looked down at his wife, her eyes pinned to her father. She did not cry. She did not make a sound, but he could clearly see the terror etched on her face and the stiff posture of her body.

His heart galloped within its cage. What was he to do? He was no longer a lone man, but a husband. This stoic, terrified woman was his responsibility. He could not stop Cressingham's justice. It would impugn him...haps his interference would even cause his own death or that of his brother's. And yet. And yet his honor and his knightly instinct demanded that he stand and fight.

Iain's eyes found Robert again, holding his wailing mother. His girls, ranging in age from ten down to six years of age, sobbed in each other's hair, clinging to each other as they watched their grandfather's shame play out.

A man holding the end of rope presently tied around Alexander's neck tossed the long line up and over the torch bracket suspended above the steps. Upon a word from Cressingham, the man pulled the line taught, his armor clinking and singing with his movement. "Ye're charged with treason against His Majesty, the King of England," shouted Cressingham. He looked over the crowd and motioned with his sword to some unseen person standing therein. Two men were brought up upon the steps, bloodied and bruised. One appeared to be missing his eyes, if the bloodied cloth stretched over them was any indication. They'd been ill-used—tortured.

A soft sound escaped Alice and Iain instinctively held her tighter. She did not resist his comfort, as little as it was. Cressingham continued: "These are retainers of clan Stewart," he announced to the crowd, as if they did not already know. Iain recognized them as some of the men that he had gone with on the raid. Men that had not come home. A woman cried out, no doubt a mother or wife of one of these tormented men. "These men have confessed their treason, as commanded of them by their liege lord, Sir Alexander Stewart, Laird of clan Stewart!"

A subtle shift rippled through the gathered crowd. There were no cries of outrage nor a move made to fight. Iain felt rather than saw their acceptance. What could they do? The keep was full of villagers and poorly defended soldiers from the celebration. It angered Iain that Alexander had been so careless.

Iain's thoughts fell away as two men took hold the end of the rope and heaved, pulling Alexander's body up by the neck. His toes barely touched the stone of the topmost step, his back bowed and his face red, eyes bulging.

Alice turned her face into his side, refusing to watch. It was Edyth that gasped, a mewling sound of protest falling from her throat. "Let us go, Ewan. Please," she begged.

Cressingham lowered his sword and the rope holding Alexander aloft slackened. He crumpled to the ground, coughing and sputtering, his bound hands clawing at the rope digging into his flesh.

"I will ask you a final time," shouted Hugh de Cressingham. "Other clans have been interrogated, yet they claim innocence. "I will ask you only once," he growled. "Who aided you in committing treason against your sovereign? Tell me, and I will show your people mercy."

Alexander was able to rise to his knees with great effort. Lady Morwen was sobbing so hard she wretched. Alexander swayed on his knees, his face red and his eyes streaming. A soldier helped loosen the rope around his neck so that he might speak. He coughed and spat blood upon the steps. His eyes roved around the yard. He looked to his son, Robert, holding his wife not but a few paces away, lingering there.

Iain tensed, worried that he would, in his weakness, give up the Ruthven name. Alexander tore his eyes from his wife and son, his granddaughters, and pinned Hugh de Cressingham with a steely glare. "We are *Stewarts*," he rasped. "We dinnae call for aid. We, with our few, destroyed yer convoy. I alone caused—"

His words were cut off as Cressingham signaled for the man to pull the rope. Alexander was lifted up off the steps once more, his toes an inch from the ground. An ugly, wet sound escaped him. Enough. Iain would not stay here, signal or no, and force Alice to witness her father's death. He looked to Ewan, whose dark eyes registered such silent fury he worried he would forget himself and charge the keep. "We mun fly, Ewan. Now."

Edyth's face, he saw, was tracked with shining tears. He looked back just in time to see Cressingham replace his sword into its scabbard and pull his dirk. "Look away," Iain commanded, turning Alice's face into his chest. She was crying, he heard her efforts to hold in her sobs. With great, gulping breaths, Alice tried to hold herself together. He did not falter. Sweeping Alice up into his arms, he quit their hiding place, forced to go slowly in the dark.

Alice was light, so much like the wee sparrow he'd first associated her with, quaking in his hands. He did not bother with looking over his shoulder to see if Ewan and Edyth followed.

His thoughts were interrupted by a grunt and the sound of something wet and heavy hitting the stone steps. This was immediately followed by Lady Morwen's keening cry that raised the hairs on the back of Iain's neck. Alice shuddered against him, her arms tightening around his neck and shoulders.

"Wheesht, *eun beag*," he whispered, though Alice hadn't said a word. She stifled her cries against his chest, her fist held tightly against her mouth. He could feel her tears soaking through his sark. "I will see ye safe, Alice."

He did not look to see what was now transpiring. He could well hear the commotion and knew without seeing that his father-in-law was dead.

Disemboweled, from the sound of it. He tried to tune out Cressingham's demand that Robert pledge his fealty to King Edward else he die as his own father had.

Cries of men, women and children seemed to cling to the very trees and outbuildings. They rang in his ears, but Robert's voice rang louder still, reverberating in his ears.

"I s—swear on my life and on...on my faith that I will forever more be faith...faithful to England and its king."

Iain dared to quicken his steps, his eyes set on the dark smudge of the horse stable fifty yards away. And then, blessedly, a lantern shone in the darkness, a quick unfurling of yellow light as the shutter was pulled free and then replaced.

"There," breathed Ewan. "They are ready for us."

When they reached the stable yard, a dark shape approached them, Archie, dressed in black so as not to be seen. "My lord," he hissed. "All is prepared. Come, I beg use o' yer hands tae lift the fence rails."

He led them into the dark of the structure, where Iain's pageboy Radney and Edyth's maid, Gelis waited nervously. They were huddled in a stall, sharing the space with an old mare, a lone lantern fighting off the darkness.

They stood when Iain whispered their names. Radney hurried out of the stall, silently lifting the lantern off a peg set into the wall and took them to the back, dark spaces of the stable. "I packed yer things and those of yer mistress. Her falcon is just here." He motioned them forward to where horses stood ready near a back door that led out to a fenced paddock. Alice's falcon was in a wicker dove's basket tied to the back of her saddle. "She'll no doubt be put out after such treatment, but..." he trailed off, looking uncertain.

"Ye've done well, Radney. Help get Gelis upon her steed, aye?"

Iain set Alice down. Pale and shivering, she stared blankly, her face a mottled red, the tracks of her tears bright even in the single lantern flame, sparking silver.

Iain pulled the plaid that had fallen from her shoulders more tightly around her but was at a loss as what to do for her. He could only think of his own grief at his father's passing, which surely paled in comparison to what his wife now felt. *His wife.* It still seemed too new and foreign to him, and yet here she was, trembling silently, her life in his hands. He put an arm around her, encouraging her lean into him.

Ewan returned, having removed the rails from a section of paddock fencing and lifted Edyth onto her horse. "All is made ready," he said quietly. He lowered his voice, speaking to Edyth privately. She placed her hand upon his cheek, her eyes gone soft. Ewan must have made some sort of request of her because her whispered, "I promise," reached his ears. Iain helped Alice up and onto her horse, grateful they'd had the sense to send Roslyn off hours ago. Hopefully they were safely on their way south, toward Caimbel lands.

Edyth sat a short distance from he and Alice, the swell of her pregnancy protruding from the opening in her cloak. In her eyes was such a look of tearful empathy that Iain's heart lifted in hope. If anyone could help Alice through this difficult time, it would Edyth. She'd lost her mother to the witch's noose and her father to a knife blade in the street. Haps they should also go to MacPherson lands so Edyth might soothe the broken pieces of Alice's heart, for he certainly didn't know how to affect such healing. He felt stupid with uncertainty.

But no, Ewan would have need of him in Perth. "Can ye ride alone?" Iain asked of Alice. "There's no shame in sharing a horse with...with me, if ye wish it." He worried she would have difficulty seeing through her tears and he felt like a cad, leaving her alone.

Ewan walked Edyth's horse out into the night. They were swallowed up silently, leaving them alone. Alice's swollen, red eyes met his, her breath stuttering as her body grieved.

"I see what ye meant," she said thickly. "Yer brother and his wife, they have respect and...more."

Iain nodded, not understanding why she would speak of this now. "Alice, tell me true. Am I doing right, taking ye awa' from yer mam?"

He worried that stealing her away in this fashion that, in time, she would resent him. He was giving her no time to say goodbye. "I...I can return later and retrieve ye, if ye feel ye must stay."

"Stay and watch as my father's body decomposes upon the gates of my childhood home, d'ye mean?" Her voice broke on her next words. "Watch as Cressingham makes an example o' my house? He willnae let my father find rest. He will make the most out of his treason—my treason—as a warning tae others. No, Iain. Let's away."

He took a step closer, placing a hand on her booted foot. The touch felt far more intimate than any previous touch, even though he'd only just carried her bodily away from the carnage in the yard. "But what of yer mam, yer nieces?"

Alice shook her head, fresh tears filling her eyes. She looked away. "Robert willnae leave them here after such violence. He will send them awa', and me with them should I stay. Doune no longer has place tae hold me."

She was right, he realized. Cressingham, or at least his soldiers, would not leave this place in a hurry. Not without making an example out of them all. He hesitated for only a fraction before mounting Alice's steed behind her. Alice's place was at his side.

She did not protest or shy away from him. Indeed, she seemed to not have even noticed. He waited for Radney to tie a lead from their shared horse to his own, riderless one, and then he was ducking under the lintel into the cold, night air.

They went slowly, Radney beside them on his rouncy, listening for any who might have followed them. Iain's head was on a swivel, his senses sharpened. Once they made it across the long, sweeping meadow at the back of the stables and into the thicket of trees, Iain gave Radney instructions to separate, go south, and meet them at their usual camp on the other side of Blairdrummond. "If someone should be following after, I wouldnae make finding us sae easy," Iain explained.

He gave further instructions that, if someone did follow the lad, to carve his mark into a tree at the camp, then to travel further south into

Caimbel lands. "Dinnae ye lead them into Perthshire. Bide, instead, with my mother."

Radney was a good lad. He did not falter or show fear. He only took the flask of sprits Iain offered him and took a different path in the moonlit forest.

He watched the lad go until he disappeared between the trees and then turned in the opposite direction. "Will he be alright?" asked Alice, her voice thick. "Will he be quite safe alone?"

Iain took a breath. He'd been doing his best not to dwell on the very questions Alice now asked. "He's young, aye, but he's a canny lad."

They made their way carefully in the dark of the forest. It would be an easy thing to injure a horse going as they were without a trail, but the moon was high and full and they had little choice otherwise.

They came upon Ewan, Edyth, and Gelis only a few minutes later, looking like specters in the deep wood. Harris, especially, who was a beautiful, dappled grey, shone brightest. "We part here," said Ewan unnecessarily. "We'll take the Westerton trail over the ridge and then find the northern road tae Meg."

"I know a way we can go," offered Alice, her voice barely above a whisper. "That keeps us from roads."

Ewan nodded, his eyes lingering on Alice for a moment. "I am...I am sorry, Lady Alice. Sister," he amended. "*Rach le Dia*," he offered. *Go with God.*

Edyth moved her horse closer to them, reaching out her hand toward Alice, who accepted it in a numb fashion. She stared at the contact as if she could not quite reason out what was happening. "Alice," said Edyth softly. "Endure this trial as best you can." Edyth's green eyes looked nearly black and bottomless as she searched Alice's face. "When you feel you cannot go on, let Iain carry you." With a light squeeze of the hand, she moved away and they were gone, swallowed up by the dark.

It moved Iain to hear Edyth speak in such a way; he wanted Alice to trust him in the way that Edyth had trusted Ewan. He filled his lungs with the cold sharpness of the forest, of the roses that scented Alice's hair.

"Edyth lost both of her parents tae violence," he explained shortly, his voice a rasp. "Lay yer head, lassie. Do ye rest a piece. I'll keep and guard ye."

They walked in the dim for over an hour, Iain cautious in the changing light as the moon rose. He started slightly, thinking Alice was asleep, when she spoke. Her breathing had slowed and her head rested heavily against his chest. His chin brushed her head, snagging her hair in his stubble. "D'ye think we'll be safe from them?" she asked, fear in her voice. "Cressingham and his men? Will they come for us?"

He did not want her to be afraid, but he would not lie to her. He considered his answer carefully before saying, "I imagine ye could answer that better than I could. Will yer Robert tell them of my involvement in the raid?" asked Iain.

Alice shook her head against his chest. "He wouldnae reveal us. He wouldnae let my father's death be for naught. He—my father's—last words were that he, alone, committed treason." Her unspoken words hung in the air. The raid had been undertaken upon her request to save her maid's son. An unsuccessful raid that had resulted in her father's death.

"It wasnae yer fault," said Iain gruffly. "Alice, d'ye hear? It wasnae yer fault. Yer father made the choice all on his own."

"And for the love of a daughter."

Iain lifted a hand instinctively to her arm, wishing to offer comfort. "For love of his clan," he replied, squeezing her softly. "But ye're right. He did love ye. Fiercely."

# Chapter Nineteen

They rode for several miles under a low moon covered in clinging clouds. Alice had finally stopped crying but every so often he felt a tremor run through her as she sat against him. Sharing her horse had been spontaneous and instinctive. Iain did not know what to say or how to comfort her. It would be a very long time, indeed, before she forgot the grisly manner of her father's death. If ever.

Iain's horse was dutifully following behind. Every so often, deep in his thoughts as he was, Iain would forget it was even there and, hearing it dislodge a rock or trample a limb, Iain's heart would leap into his throat, sure someone had followed them. He regretted not having easy access to his weapon, what with Alice seated before him, her backside wedged between his legs and her back flush against him, but nor could he lament her presence.

It was a cold night and their shared body heat was enough to keep off the chill. Not only that, but he could not deny that he liked the weight and feel of her. Iain thought rather sardonically that his wedding night had not turned out how he'd imagined. Not for her either.

They'd avoided the roads, choosing instead to take a longer path through a ridge of the mountain range that brimmed the northern border of Stewart lands. Alice had said nothing save for once suggesting he take a left fork in the trail rather than the right. "There was once a hunter's shelter this way," she'd muttered, and then she'd said no more.

And now that they were miles away and the moon was on its descent, he searched for words to comfort or distract Alice, telling her about his home in *Caol Ghlinn Amain*.

Iain maneuvered the horse through a black stream and, leaning close to her ear so she would hear him over the sounds of horses in the water, said, "I think ye'll like Amain. Ye willnae find a bonnier situation in all o' Scotland tae my mind."

At Alice's interrogative noise, he continued. "The great glen stretches for miles at the feet o' the mountains. Tis full o' merry blossoms in the early summer sae that the very air is full sweet with 'em. Even the stag and the hind dinnae wish tae leave it; they bed doon amongst the sweeping fields of swaying grasses all throughout the year. And while the house isnae sae imposing and fine as Doune, tis grand enough tae my mind."

"I look forward to seeing it," said Alice, her voice small. "Does it have a name, your house?"

Iain urged the horse down a rather steep embankment where the usual trail had been washed away. "Lean intae me, lass," he instructed. Then, after they were back on the proper trail, added, "I didnae name it, no. I left that honor for my future wife." Saying such a thing out loud made him feel vulnerable in a way that he could not understand. She was that wife, this surprising creature set between his legs, now brought low with mourning. He swallowed away his apprehension and said, "*Your* honor, my lady."

Speaking this way felt somehow like a surrender, though he could not say to what he was conceding. He'd spoken true. She was his wife and allowing her to name their home had been his wish since he'd first built it.

Alice, for her part, did not speak for some time. The silence stretched on between them, but it was not taught and rife with insecurities or resentment as their first silences had been. Indeed, not since their argument in the chapel had he been uncomfortable with their silence.

After what felt like a long time she said, "An honor o' which I'll endeavor tae be worthy," she said with formality. "We are nearly there," she added.

She was right. It hadn't taken more than another half of a mile before they came upon the abandoned hunting camp. The "shelter" as she'd called it was no more than an open air bothy, or had been.

Iain supposed at one time it had had four walls and a stable roof, but the fallen tree through the middle of it had rendered it now useless. Iain dismounted and looked closer at their refuge, squinting into the interior through the dark.

"Looks tae me we'll be sleeping under the trees." He glanced at her, gauging her thoughts. He did not suppose she was used to sleeping on the cold, hard ground.

He helped Alice dismount. Even in the low light, Iain could see the glassy shine of moonlight in her eyes, sparking like stars. If she was disappointed in the shelter, she did not show it. "Not much of a marriage bed, I'm afraid," she said apologetically.

Iain huffed a soft laugh, a shock lancing through his middle at her quip. "No, I daresay it's no' so grand as ever we'll find, but it's better than some."

She watched, waiting, as Iain perused their meager possessions in search of bedding. "I've my plaid and a fur. We...er, we might have necessity tae bunch up close tae keep warm." For some reason, he felt his face heat like was a green lad o' ten and six. "I dinnae think a fire wise."

"No," Alice was quick to say. "No, I dinnae think it wise."

Together they found a rather springy bed of mosses and ferns a short distance away, partially covered by a large black pine. Alice began clearing sticks and rocks while Iain saw to the horses. Before long, Iain returned to find Alice laying out their meager bedding, his plaid on the bottom and the fur on top.

"We can wrap the ends o' the plaid over atop the fur, since it's so much larger," she explained without looking at him.

Iain nodded, scratching the back of his neck briefly before moving to remove his boots. As he bent down, he saw Alice look around her for a suitable place to seat herself to remove her own boots. "Och, sit 'ere lassie. I'll help ye with that." Alice agreed and, sitting upon the bedding, waited as Iain knelt before her.

It was in silence that he palmed the heel of her foot with his left hand and placed it upon his thigh to find the laces and hooks that ran along the inside length of her ankle. Her woolen skirts were finely made and soft to the touch as he lifted them away, her petticoat beneath a frothy white. He was proud to see that she'd dressed for cold; her long grey cloak was even fur lined along the hood.

Alice's ankle boots were finely made, just as everything else she wore. Embroidery in what looked to be gold thread wove in a delicate design along the toes. Iain patiently unwound the leather lacings from the hooks, his fingers slipping slightly on the last, before he pulled the boot off. Her stockings were as bright as the moon and as soft as a rose petal. He followed suit with the next boot and then pressed warmth into her toes, rubbing his large, warm hands against her stockinged feet.

"Th—thank you," she muttered into the dark, breathless. He could not tell if he was making her uncomfortable with his touch, but she did not pull away or chastise him.

"Best keep yer cloak tight around ye," he said in response. "Here, let me help ye in."

He lifted the fur and waited for her to climb atop the plaid and position herself before covering her again.

He looked about them, thinking it would be best for him to stay awake and keep watch, but Alice held up a corner of the fur as if in invitation. The wind blew through the boughs, filling the space with the sound of rushing waves come to shore. He worried he would not hear someone's approach if he slept. Alice visibly shivered, saying, "Will ye no' come in and get warm, Iain?"

The sound of his name, spoken so softly felt like a plea. And after everything she'd been through this night, he found he could not deny her, even had he wished to. He would wait until she fell asleep, then he would stand guard.

Alice did not lean into him for warmth. He could hear her breathing coming fast. He groped for her hand, cold and small and engulfed it in his own. The spring air wasn't so cold that he could see his breath, but it was uncomfortable enough that a bit of added warmth was welcome.

They lay there, staring up through the boughs of a pine, watching the clouds blow past. He wanted to comfort her as much as he wanted to kindle warmth between them, but he was quite simply afraid to touch her further. He didn't want his attempts to be perceived as wonton advances.

"I'm sorry about yer father," he whispered to the sky. "If...if ye need tae cry or, or speak o' him, I will hear."

Alice was quiet save for a muffled sniff, indicating that she was already crying. His heart swelled with sympathy for her. He could not imagine what she must be feeling. Without asking permission or waiting for an invitation, he simply did what seemed natural, and turned toward her, pulling and gathering her against his chest. The small gasp that followed did not seem to him as alarm or even protest, only surprise, and so he let his arm more fully relax across her middle, her head pillowed on the bicep of his other arm.

As he'd suspected, Alice was soft and comfortable to hold. The heat of her breath against his neck warmed him further. He would have a difficult time, indeed, of staying up to keep watch. Just until she falls asleep, he told himself. She quaked in his arms as she tried to hold back her grief.

"Ye dinnae need tae hide yer grief from the likes o' me, Alice," he said softly into her hair. "Weep all ye need; there is no shame in it."

A sob tore through her throat at his words; he reflexively pulled her tighter against him, feeling the full weight of her anguish. Her hand fisted in his surcoat, absorbing the tears she readily shed. Iain stroked her hair, speaking softly of her father's duty and of his bravery, of her own stout heart. "I can well see tae the heart o' ye, Alice, here and now, and it is a lovely thing tae behold. A heart that doesnae love the sword, but only what it defends, is well favored. Rest now, *gealbhan beag." Little sparrow.* "I'll see ye safe."

At some point Iain fell asleep, and Alice with him. He woke with a start at the twittering of a bird in the grey of dawn. It was a miracle that no one had come upon them in the night. He was stiff and a rock was pushing into his scapula, but he was warm and loathe to wake his sleeping wife who was presently draped across his chest. Her hair clung to his stubbled chin, one arm thrown across his middle.

"Awake, *gealbhan beag.* The day is upon us," he rasped.

She did not move but he heard how her breathing changed as she came to consciousness. So too he felt an awareness come upon her in the pull of her muscles, as if drawing strength to run.

"Stay here, if you would, and I fetch food from the saddle bags."

Alice pulled away, looking shy and uncertain, saying nothing, and gathering the fur more closely around her. She looked like a wee rumpled mouse in a haystack, he thought, with her hair in disarray. Rummaging through the saddle bags not but a few short steps away, his breath clouded the cold morning air. Iain pulled two apples and a hank of hard cheese in a linen sack from one of the bags and a waterskin from the other and turned back to his shoddy marriage bed.

He hesitated, lingering above her, but Alice, cheeks stained red, opened the shelter of the covers for him, inviting him in to share her warmth once again. He handed her the food and the waterskin then pulled the plaid more securely around their shoulders. "I'm sorry it's no' such a grand feast as ye might expect on our first morning together as man and wife," he said, not really sorry at all. He rather liked that they were alone in the wild together, despite the circumstances that had brought them there.

He felt a further blossoming of their friendship that had heretofore been absent. Something he could not name had shifted between them, though he did not believe it had anything to do with their vows in the kirk yesterday. "Cheese, my lady," he offered, holding the wedge out to her. She pinched off a corner, making tiny pieces crumble into their bed.

"Thank you."

"See now, wife, how yer husband spoils ye already with breakfast in bed?" he teased, taking a bite of cheese for himself.

Alice smiled weakly, pinching off more cheese from the rind. "Thank you, Iain," she said meekly. Her eyes were puffy and pink from her grieving and her face pale, but she met his gaze squarely. "I mean thank you for...for everything."

Iain took a careful breath through his nose and swallowed his bite. "Cressingham...it is a wretched man as would take a father's life in such a way, for all his loved ones to witness." He reached for her hand, cold and small, her blunt nails chewed to the quick. "Hear me, Alice," he said, his voice grave. "I will pull my sword in defense of yer heart, my lady, should ye wish it. I am yer man and it is my duty tae do so. Ye must only speak and I will answer."

Looking overcome, she blinked her eyes rapidly and dropped his hand, lifting her fingers hesitantly to his face, where a lock of hair blew into his eyes. She pushed it away, her brown eyes searching his face as if, in the moment, she saw him for the first time. Her boldness surprised him but he welcomed it. "Vengeance belongs to God," she all but whispered. "But I cannae deny—" She swallowed whatever words she was going to say and let her hand fall to her lap.

"My father died well," she said, pulling her eyes away. "Few men could do so, I think, and no' plead or grovel." She closed her eyes, no doubt repressing the tears that threatened. After a moment she collected herself and said, "I do wish for Cressingham's death. He has stolen away my clan's children and now my father's life."

Iain put the apple he'd been holding down on the fur covering their laps and took her hands. "I will be yer sword and yer shield, Lady Alice. By my life and the strength of my arm, I will have vengeance upon Cressingham for what he has stolen awa' from ye and yers."

Alice squeezed his hands. "Not on yer life, husband. Dinnae swear such."

"Grown fond of me already, have ye" he said, his mouth quirking into a half smile. "I knew well enough t'would only be a matter o' time."

She shook her head, an answering smile tugging on the corner of her lips. "Have yer vengeance, she said, returning to solemnity, "but not at the cost of yer life. I dinnae wish tae mourn another."

"Whatever ye wish, my lady, I will see it done," he promised. "Here, finish eating. I will see tae the horses."

The way to Perthshire was not terribly long, but because Iain wished to stay off the roads, they had to take a longer route. They'd ridden separately the rest of the way, stopping as needed to see to Alice's needs and eat. It had rained most of the second day and all through the night and when they got to their camp, there was Radney, waiting. He reported quietly to only Iain that he hadn't been followed, but as he'd skirted the edge of the trees as they'd left the keep, he thought as how he'd heard fighting within.

Iain wondered at that. Haps the Stewarts had fought back. He'd seen those men slink off, supposedly in search of swords, but he did not dwell on the prospect. There would be no way for him to know and he didn't care enough to risk finding out.

All three were wet through, so it was with the hope of warm beds and dry clothes that decided they ride through the night. Alice impressed him. She did not complain or balk at the long hours in the saddle. She was a good rider, in fact, and aside from needing to stop to let her falcon hunt, made no requests.

They'd made good time. All of Perthshire was industriously engaged. They passed many people on their roads who were surprised and happy to see him. When they were only a few miles away from the keep, Iain bade Radney ride ahead to inform the household that he brought his lady wife with him and to prepare a chamber for her.

He slowed to a stop as they crested the last hill that would overlook the wide, snaking river, the sprawling village that spanned the water, the sweep of meadow and field newly planted, and last, the tall, square keep atop the hill. No, not just the keep, for in the center of a once-verdant meadow now sat the jagged scab that was the half-built garrison.

"It used to hold only sheep," said Iain, indicating the meadow holding the king's garrison. "Now it holds a different sort of animal."

Alice shielded her eyes against the sun, her face a mask. "How long?" she asked, "How long until it's complete?"

"Ewan says by the harvest."

"That soon?"

"Come, a warm meal and bed await ye, my lady."

# Chapter Twenty

Iain kept to his own chambers for the first three days, not willing to venture into Alice's rooms after she retired for the day. And while they spent their days companionably enough, he'd left her quite alone in the long hours of darkness.

So it was with some surprise that Iain found Alice outside his bedchamber door the fourth night at the Ruthven keep, looking uncertain and underdressed in a robe and slippers. Her knock had sounded just as meek as her bearing. Somehow he shared in her uncertainty despite how their friendship had grown.

Perhaps uncertainty wasn't the right word, Iain mused. They'd spent the majority of the last few days in each other's company. He's shown her the estate, he'd introduced her to his people, they'd taken her falcon out for a hunt, and walked in the orchards each evening before supper. He'd teased her and she'd smiled. Laughed, even. He found his mind continuously drifting toward his wife whenever he was away from her.

But each night after supper, Alice would retire above stairs and he would stay in the hall, debating within himself on what he should do. Tonight, he'd drank with Johnne and Inan, speaking of everything and nothing at all. Drinking for Iain was a rarity, who always wanted a clear head, but it was the only way to distract himself from his increasingly confusing and altogether inappropriate thoughts. If one could have inappropriate thoughts about one's wife. He didn't know. Father Thale could certainly tell him, not that he really wished to know.

It was not only the banquet her full mouth offered, her pillowy bottom lip that so drew his eye. Nor was it only now that he noticed her long, sooty lashes that brushed against a rounded cheek. It was more than that she was woman, soft and so full in his hands; he'd seen a glimmer of her heart and mind, so carefully hidden from view.

He'd seen with what fervor her mind latched onto the training of her falcon and how she took such pride in her father seeking out her opinion. He'd called her War Master, as if it might shame her somehow. But he had only shamed himself. Her mind was bright and quick despite her shyness. And she was as bonny this night as he'd ever seen her.

But Alice was in mourning for her lost father and was certainly in no state of mind to welcome him to her bed. Despite that, here she stood, dressed for bed, her loose hair framing her face, looking like an angel come to save him from his bleak thoughts. Did she come here like this on purpose? Did she know how this would torment him?

"Forgive me," she said on a breath. "My maid has forgotten to replace my candle and I wondered if you had a spare."

Iain did his best to hide his disappointment and opened the door wider, swinging his arm out in welcome. Their chambers were across the hall from each other, so it made perfect sense that she would come here instead of bothering with waiting for a maid to bring her a fresh taper or going below stairs. She had not come here for him and certainly not for anything to do with marital rights.

"Aye, ye're welcome tae whatever I have, my lady," he said opening a drawer and pulling out an unused candle.

She took it, looking bashful, his eyes catching hold of her bottom lip as she tucked it between her teeth. He looked away, unwilling to feed any more of the wanton thoughts that had plagued him throughout these last few days and nights. He couldn't count the times he'd thought about what it would be like to taste her mouth in truth. He mentally shook himself, handing her the candle, careful not to touch her.

She took the proffered gift but did not move, her eyes darting around the space, taking in his private quarters. He suddenly felt ashamed of his slovenly behavior. He'd tossed his sword belt and surcoat onto the chest at the end of his bed, but they'd slunk off and now lay in a pool upon the floor. So too had he carelessly deposited his boots at the writing desk near the window.

Belatedly, he noticed how his liene was halfway untucked from his hose, wrinkled and stained from the ale he'd accidently sloshed onto himself. He ran a hand through his hair, feeling unfit for company compared to her angelic presence.

"I received a message from Robert," said Alice, "by way of a carrier pigeon. He sends his regards and says that my belongings are packed and ready tae be sent on the morrow." Her eyes found the wet spot of ale besmirching his shirtfront. "Have ye heard aught from yer brother?" she asked, finding his eyes again.

He shook his head. "Not as yet. If there is trouble, he will get word tae us. Dinnae ye fash."

She nodded and, glancing behind her at the closed door, seemed to steel herself for some terrible task. Drawing in a sharp breath, her shoulders straight, she said, "I would...I have a question I wish tae put tae ye regarding...regarding our truce."

That damn truce. He regretted it in some ways. Yes, it had enabled them to stop finding fault with each other, but it signified still a barrier between them. But Iain could not think of any other demand she could possibly add to those they had already been agreed upon. Already they'd vowed honesty and fidelity in the pursuit of respect. So too had he promised her not to take an excess of strong drink. Had she decided, then, that she was ready to live apart from him? He frowned at the thought.

"I only had a few cups o' ale with the men after supper. No' whiskey."

Alice surveyed him, looking slightly confused. "No, my lord—"

"Iain," he corrected. "We are husband and wife are ye no'? Ye have leave tae use my name."

She blushed but pressed on, "I dinnae speak of ale, mil—Iain." Gathering herself once more, she lifted her chin and said, "I would ask why it is…. Rather, we never resolved the question of what it is ye wish for in this union." She let out a frustrated huff and corrected her statement. "I mean tae say…D'ye want a wife in name only, Iain?"

He stared down at her, his heart quickening. Of course he wanted more, if that was what she was, indeed, speaking. He'd woken up in the middle of the night enough times since their wedding, talking himself out of crossing the short distance between their rooms to ever deny such. He'd be a liar and worse.

He appraised her, this small creature who had far more nerve than himself. Still, he chose caution. He could not presume. "Of what do ye speak, Alice?"

A flush crept up her neck, drawing his eyes to the exposed skin at her throat. Her neck was long and supple, and begged to be kissed. He'd thought about pressing his lips to her skin for days now. He pushed the thought aside and found her eyes again.

Careful with his words, Iain said, "What I want doesnae matter. I am yer servant, madam."

Looking slightly crestfallen she fiddled with the candle in her hands, her feelings shuttered to him. Had he offended her in some way? He felt impotent and stupid with inexperience. Every other lass he'd wooed had been so different from Alice. They'd flirted and hinted and teased in an elaborate dance, a dance he knew all too well. But with Alice, his footing had always been wrong, the music discordant and his steps clumsy. He did not want to take another wrong step.

The night air coming in from the window had turned cold, signaling an oncoming storm. Indeed, he could see the gooseflesh pimple to life along the column of her neck. Making his way to the window, he closed the shutters and drew the drapes, but when he turned back again, he was met with a startling sight. Alice's robe had slipped from her shoulders, exposing the scoop neck of her chemise. His eyes strayed from her neck to her collar bones and further still to the swell of her breasts.

He knew he was staring but he couldn't seem to stop. Did she know how well she tortured him? His hands itched to touch her, to run his hands through the cloud of her hair and to taste her mouth, to claim it. He'd yet to do so. The polite kiss in the kirk was akin to what he might give his mother or sister.

The thin chemise she wore did little to cover her. He could see the outline of her body silhouetted against the fire, could see the slow rise and fall of her breasts against the white fabric. He bit back a groan and looked away, unwilling to give his fertile imagination further fodder.

"What is it?" she asked, her voice tight. "Will ye no' even look upon me?" She exhaled through her nose, her lips pressed tightly together. "What is it ye find so repellant?"

Iain turned sharply to her, his mouth agape. "Repellant?" he scoffed. He took a step closer, noticing how she faltered. "It's been many days now that all I can think about what it might feel like tae touch ye, tae fill my hands with ye, tae taste...." He broke off and pushed his hands through his hair. "Ye said...at Doune ye said in the chapel as how ye wouldnae allow for such intimacies in our marriage. Ye said as how I shouldnae expect such in our marriage. I thought that I could shoulder that. At the time I thought I could honor your wishes."

She took a tentative step toward him and said, "In truth, what I said is that I wouldnae follow ye around like a brainless gowk and simper at yer e'ry word."

Iain smiled, daring to hope. "Aye, and ye've kept that promise."

She answered him with a smile of her own saying, "And how do ye feel about honoring such a demand now, husband?"

All the blood seemed to have left Iain's brain. He could not think of a witty reply. He only answered what his body demanded and closed the distance between them. He took her into his arms greedily, pulling her body flush against his. He could feel all of her soft curves against him in an exquisite kind of torture and took her mouth hungrily. A sound escaped his throat that he did not recognize. Somewhere in the recesses of his addled mind a voice warned him to slow down, to temper his ardor, but it was too easily ignored.

She met him with equal measure, her hands in his hair, pulling his mouth to hers again and again. He heard her sharp intake of breath as his mouth found her throat, his hands splayed across the expanse of her back, forcing her closer. Her back arched, her drooping robe fluttering to the floor, her breathing harsh and irregular. Nothing in him was gentle as he had intended to be, as he'd hoped he might be, but she did not yield to him. Indeed, her strength was a match for his own, urging him onward.

Somehow he found them suddenly on the floor, their hands pushing and pulling at fabric that separated them. He yanked at his shirt, which had hung up around his neck, and once he was free, he opened his mouth hungrily upon her neck once more.

That voice came again from the foggy recesses of his mind, warning him of his actions. It was too fast, too savage. He must go slow and be gentle with her, but there was nothing gentle about Alice now. She was war master and fierce falcon one moment and all tenderness the next. He was at the mercy of her, at the feel of her silken skin, that seemed to burn him wherever he touched.

Her mouth was warm on his throat and she strained eagerly toward him, his name on her lips. Her body was soft and yielding to his own, their legs entwined, hands running along smooth skin, the swell of muscle and the furrow of a bent knee.

A knock on the door roused them from their lust. Both lay frozen in sudden fear, as if they were children caught in the act of stealing. They stared, wide eyed at each other, then the door. Iain lifted his hands from her, pulling away as if ashamed. He *was* ashamed. He'd come at her like some wild savage, some berserker who could not manage his own desire.

He stood on shaky legs and lifted Alice's forgotten robe, offering it to her. The knock sounded again, this time with the muted voice of Alefred. "Iain! Are ye in there, man? Ye're wanted below stairs."

"Aye, I hear you," he said, his voice gruff. He found his shirt and put it on. "Aye. I'll be down soon." He frowned at the door before returning his attention to his wife. Alice, for her part, seemed dazed and, if the color high on her cheeks was any indication, mortified.

He crouched down next to her, finding her eyes. "I'm sorry, Alice. I shouldnae have come at ye like that."

Alice met his gaze. Her lips were swollen from his kisses, her hair in wild disarray. She'd never been lovelier. "I'm no' sorry," she said softly. She took his hand, her own trembling slightly out of shame or unspent ardor, he could not say. "I would add another tenet tae our truce, husband. I dinnae wish for a marriage in name only."

Iain tucked a strand of hair behind her ear and kissed her, softly this time, and said, "As ever, my lady, I am yer servant."

# Chapter Twenty-One

Iain listened impatiently to a complaint from Inan, one of Ewan's retainers in their own small garrison office. It was not long after they'd broken their fasts and already there were complaints. As ever, there were problems in the cramped quarters of their small garrison between what Ruthven retainers remained and those appointed there by the English.

"I cannae prove it, but I ken it was that weedy varlet Frederick as filled my boots with pig shit."

Iain resisted the urge to pinch the bridge of his nose and said, "Aye, as ye've said, but by yer own admission, ye cannae prove it. And now that ye've descended upon 'im and encouraged Bram and Rab tae join in, ye've started an all-out war."

Inan's mouth opened in outrage. "Sae ye think it's right for them tae harass and jab and insult our honor, and we must take it without recourse? It's more than the boots! They've been provoking us for weeks on end, making snide remarks and gestures. They've made our duty time into one o' torture, and ye say we must take it all with a smile?"

"Nay, that's no' at all what I'm saying."

The bell tolled wildly, interrupting them. Their eyes met, staring at each other for one brief moment, their bodies gone rigid. As one, they both sprang from their places and ran for the door. The stairs were narrow and dim, but they both made it down to yard in record time. Someone was shouting, their words drowned out by the peal of the bell, warning them of some unknown danger.

Iain could smell the trouble before he could see it. A reek of oily smoke on the air, thin but present. It was enough to raise the fine hairs along his arms. Fire was dangerous and deadly, but he could see no trouble from where he stood in the yard, surrounded as he was with the curtain wall. It was no mere kitchen fire, though. Of that he was certain. It smelled foul and *wrong*. Was it Greek fire, lobbed at them from one of Edward's favored war machines? But no, he could see no such devastation from where he was. Nor would that make sense. Why would Edward order a garrison to be built upon their lands only to then come to destroy them?

Iain sprinted across the yard, dodging people who ran in a confused state, and climbed a ladder that was set against the wall, his head on a swivel. Others were already there, standing atop the wall, but they were not looking toward the keep, at some devastation, but out toward the forest. The fist currently squeezing his heart lessened slightly.

He joined the men at arms at the parapet and from there, he could see the trouble clearly. "Damn you, Ewan," he muttered angrily. Everything always happened when he was away. The great, hulking shape of the towering king's garrison was aflame. The blaze licked up the vertical timbers, across planks and scaffolding and into the newly constructed rooftree.

The master carpenter's carefully constructed pulley systems were demolished, broken apart by some unseen violence, in a heap upon the ground. Not only that, but crates of tools were upturned, scattered. Large beams had been placed against the doors, one end rooted into the mud, the other pushing against the heavy iron-studded doors to keep them shut.

And even from this distance, Iain could just hear the screams of men. He did not know if they were from men trapped inside or those gathered around, without, throwing ineffectual pails of water onto the doors. His gut twisted.

"God help them," he muttered, feeling sick. He was about to quit his place and race to aid the men already gathered around the structure—at least they attempted to gather. The flames were no doubt so hot that they could not get close. They were too late. Far, far too late.

"There!" shouted one of his companions from atop the wall, Iain followed his pointing finger to the far side of the blaze, nearest the dark forest. The shapes were difficult at first to make out, what with the bright flames dazzling his eyes against the morning sun, but he could see them now. Men were scurrying, fleeing into the woods. Indeed, some of these bandits—or whomever they were—had been seen and were engaged in swordplay. An intermittent flash of steel sparking like the sun on water between tree and fen.

"Is that...is that the Moray's crest?" asked the man beside him. "Just there," he added, pointing his gauntleted hand to the left-hand side of the skirmish Iain had been watching.

Iain squinted through the smoke and saw the flag unfurl in a soft up current, revealing three white stars upon a blue field. It was. It was the Moray ensign.

"What would ye have us do?" asked someone from atop the wall. "Shall we go down and meet them?"

Iain looked round, careful to identify his companions. He saw none of the sheriff's men, nor any of de Warenne's laborers. They were Ruthven men, all. "Weel," said Iain, frowning. "Aye. We mun take tae the field in defense of the King's garrison but take ye care tae dress slowly. I'd hate for the sheriff to get the better of an answer tae prayer."

They stared at him, clearly not understanding. He lowered his voice needlessly. None would hear them from where they stood. "See how the Moray leaves our keep intact? See how they draw the sheriff's men out to fight? Let us give the pretense of support for our appointed sheriff, but we willnae lift our swords against our saviors. Go now and meet me upon the field to assemble."

Iain dressed with the aid of his squire Hamish, a brawny lad heavily muscled and careful with words. It didn't take long and before he wished it, he was leaving through the side gate toward the engulfed mass of flame and char that had been the king's garrison.

The sound of cracking beams, the roar of hungry flame, and that of falling debris from within masked any cries that might have come. Looking at it made Iain's wame curdle. None would be left alive. None could survive such devastation. So intent was his study of the destruction that by the time Iain had made it halfway down the long slope, he failed to notice the soldier coming his way. They collided, their shoulders crashing together, nearly knocking him off balance.

The man he hit was coughing, his face so covered in soot that Iain barely recognized him. It was his brother's captain, Rory, looking green under the grime masking his face.

"Easy, man," said Iain, catching Rory as he stumbled.

"There were men inside," he wheezed. Iain stared at Rory's singed beard and eyebrows.

Iain did not want to think of the pain and fear they must have felt. "D'ye ken who...how many?"

Coughing mightily, Rory shook his head. When he could speak, he said, "Laborers and some o' the sheriff's men. I happened to be without the walls when the bells sounded." Iain handed Rory the flask from his belt, who took it gratefully and medicated himself several times. "I couldnae leave any man tae that fate, no matter which master he serves." Rory grimaced, his teeth startlingly white in his sooty face. "I couldnae get in. The second floor collapsed and they...I couldnae get in."

Iain could not fathom the courage it would have taken for Rory to even attempt to enter into that hell, who knew well the pains inflicted by fire. His sword hand would never be the same from the fiery injuries he'd sustained from Sheriff de Biggar.

"It is Moray," informed Iain quietly. "His standard flies even now as the sheriff and his men pursue."

"Moray declares war against England," said Rory with some reverence.

Iain looked about him, only barely registering the people scurrying from place to place. "Ewan must be told," he said, his eyes falling back on the captain. "He willnae wish tae leave his lady wife, but this—" he gestured here to the chaos down the hill. "He should ken what trouble has beset his lands. He should be told that war is made this day, here upon our very soil."

Rory nodded. "I will take my leave presently." He gripped Iain's elbow. "Be wary, *bràthair*."

Iain nodded. "Aye. Go canny."

The king's garrison was a towering pyre, the shadows of timbers looking as blackened bones in the shadows of licking flames. Sparks flew into the sky like so many shooting stars, sparking embers dying as quickly as a breath. Ash floated on the air, sticking to eyelashes and in throats.

The people that had gathered round the destruction stood in stupefied horror, empty buckets hanging loosely by their sides. Most of them were laborers hired by de Warenne and commanded by the sheriff. Iain ordered them to go within the walls of the keep and rest. "It is lost," he cried over the roar or ash and flame. "Leave this place. Find refuge as we pursue our aggressors with vengeance!"

The handful of red-faced people left, looking alarmed at seeing the Ruthven men assembling in full battle armor upon the ruined landscape. He looked into the forest, where there could still be seen here and there a struggle of swords. He jogged to his brother's men, laden with sword and shield, mace, and halberd. There were not many Ruthven retainers living here now, so crowded was their place with the sheriff's men also in residence. But also, Ewan had wished to only keep fifteen of his retainers here, the rest living in their homes with their families throughout their lands. Now that the Moray had raised his standard, Ewan would call upon them in secret to join the cause.

Iain did not know what choice to make. He could not stay within the keep and do nothing. The sheriff would suspect his duplicity. Nor did he wish for the Moray or his men to perish after their efforts to free them from the king's garrison. He must go with his men into the forest and fight. But for which side should he command the warriors to give aid?

He looked to the forest, thinking of his father, of Ewan. Malcolm had been laird, and now Ewan, not him. He had been follower always, happy to do what he was told and relieved that he did not hold such a responsibility. But Ewan was not here. It was himself who must choose for their people. Iain looked to the men gathered, prepared to go to their very deaths at his command. He could not command them to spend what time they had left in the world in the aid of the English.

"Hear me," he said. "I am no' yer laird, and yet I ask ye tae go intae these, our forests, and kill all o' de Warenne's or the sheriff's men as ye might. It must be all; there can be no witness of our treason lest we lose our tenuous hold upon our lands. Do so and free ourselves from the English hold. Free our lands from those who would suppress our heritage, for they have sown the seeds of their own demise. Go, do battle, and avenge our brothers!"

A cry rent the air as the assembled warriors lifted their weapons into the air. "Vengeance!" they cried. "Courage!" And then they ran the distance from the sloping field that had once held grazing sheep, into the gutted forest that had once rung with birdsong, not with death.

Here, now, within the sparse trees, the only sounds were that of battle, of grunts and gasps and of the ringing of steel.

Iain spotted one of the sheriff's men not a long way off, only one of the forty soldiers appointed to oppress and make claim of their lands, grappling with a Scotsman. He did not know this Scotsman, but he could tell that he was the weaker man here. If left alone, he would slowly succumb to his opponent.

The world dissolved around Iain until there was only these two men, their grimaces white in darkened helms. Iain's short sword was light and eager, answering even the smallest of his commands. He pulled his dirk in his left hand, eyeing the grappling men.

Iain made haste and came up behind the two combatants, locked in a deadly struggle. The English soldier's back was open and vulnerable to his attack. It was not difficult to find the weakness in the man's armor. He knew well where the edge of blade would do the most damage. Just as he came within striking distance, there was a look of surprise, a shock of fear at potentially being overpowered that entered the Scotsman's eyes.

The tip of Iain's dirk sank into the Englishman's kidney, his back bowing in a rictus of pain before he fell. Iain was gone in an instant, not bothering to waste precious time. He moved between rock and bush, from tree to tree, stepping over bodies both dead and those still clinging to life. One man weakly lifted his gauntleted hand as he passed, crying "Mercy." Iain could pay them no heed. His attention was solely focused on the next of grappling combatants. He watched them fight, still a ways off, watched helplessly as one of the sheriff's men drove his sword through one of Moray's men as he lifted his sword, piercing him through the pit of his arm and down, into his lungs or heart.

The English soldier turned, his eyes registering and recognizing Iain as a friend, pointing his sword deeper into the timbered forest. "There! Make haste, Sir Ruthven. The Moray and his men ran to the trees!" A look of confusion entered his eyes then as Iain did not follow to where his sword pointed but, with fixation, moved steadily toward him.

The man faltered, lifting his sword defensively but his feet were wrong, his balance lost. Unprepared for Iain's betrayal, Iain took his head without resistance. The man's helm, head and all, rolled down the slope, blood painting the spring grasses pushing through the grey leaf mold a gruesome red.

Iain looked about him, seeing others of his brother's men grappling with de Warenne or the sheriff's men, others yet killed those that had been injured but had not yet succumbed to death. Satisfied that none so far had escaped back to the keep, he moved deeper into the wood.

It was not long until he saw, some way ahead, the sheriff. He was grappling with none other than William, the Thane of Nairn. Iain recognized him by his great surcoat, whereupon was depicted a rearing horse and lion. The sheriff was a good match for his brother-in-law. He met every powerful blow from William with apparent ease, though Iain saw how he struggled to take the offensive.

The thane was on the slight upper slope of the hill that eventually met a branching waterway, trickling toward their wide river, his sword swinging repeatedly towards the sheriff's neck. The sheriff was keeping him at bay, but he was tiring as he fought to keep his feet on the slippery slope. They had been grappling for some time, Iain was sure. Their swings were slower, their breathing ragged. Indeed, the tip of the sheriff's sword was not so quick to rise and meet William's powerful strikes.

Sir Lucas ducked a well-aimed blow meant to take his head from his shoulders. The edge of William's sword scraped along the sheriff's helm. It was enough to knock it askew, temporarily hindering Olifard's view. William took advantage of the staggering sheriff, pulling his dirk with fluidity. The dirk was airborne for the briefest of moments before William caught hold of the hilt and, turning his wrist, drove the knife into the throat of Sir Lucas Olifard, appointed sheriff of Midlothian.

Iain continued toward his brother-in-law as the sheriff slid and rolled once down the slope. There he stilled, in the branch of the stream's frigid water. The sheriff had been, by some people's estimation a good man. Leastways that's what Ewan had said. Still, he had come by appointment of an usurping king.

Blood covered William's dirk, his hand, and splattered his surcoat. William registered Iain immediately as he came upon him, nodding in greeting as he caught his breath. William replaced his bloodied dirk into its scabbard, looking about him for more danger. None were upon them, the fighting being deeper in the woods by evidence of the shouts and steely rings of sword upon sword. "We thought it best no' tae give ye warning," William said in lieu of a greeting.

Iain nodded, catching his breath. "My treason is made clear. We can leave none alive."

William nodded grimly then turned toward the sounds of battle. "Then let us commence in cleansing these lands o' the sassenach plague."

Ewan, Edyth and Gelis arrived at the MacPherson keep in the early afternoon. The gate was closed, the guardsmen leery of them despite them being alone and clearly unable to do any damage. Still, they bade them wait without the gate while the steward was informed of their arrival. Edyth's back hurt and her hands and feet were so swollen she wondered if they'd ever return to normal.

Ewan helped her to dismount, careful to hold onto her while she found her legs again. It didn't take long. They were welcomed in short order. The attitude in the yard was subdued, as she would expect. Edyth could not help but contrast this visit from the last time they'd come. Her cousin and her family had been waiting outside the keep, eager and full of smiles. Now, the atmosphere was quite the opposite.

What people *were* present were anxiously engaged in their duties and did not give them even a passing glance. The keep itself was dark-stoned and sprawling, with marks of soot from the torches staining the walls in increments around the face of the building. They were, all three, brought into an anteroom within the keep to await Angus MacPherson, laird and father-in-law to Meg.

Angus was a tall man and wide, with great, hulking shoulders and a full belly to match. His deep-set eyes glittered in the anteroom's candlelight, his mouth set in a grim line. Ewan greeted him as if they were old friends, clasping forearms and speaking words Edyth did not even try to discern. She was so uncomfortable from their long journey that she had little energy to spare for anything beyond keeping her feet.

Gelis was taken away by a maid servant to show the old woman where her mistress and master would stay. Edyth barely registered her departure. Then, without a word, Ewan scooped her up into his arms and carried her through a wide, torch-lit gallery, up a flight of stairs, and into a finely furnished apartment.

Edyth barely spared the room a glance, only having eyes for the four-poster bed piled with quilts. Angus' deep voice reverberated in her skull as Ewan nestled her onto the wool stuffed mattress. "I will send the midwife tae tend tae yer lady wife once she is finished with the ailing. She looks as if she might need some tending 'erself."

"She is only weary from travel," said Ewan, though Edyth knew him well enough to hear the worry in his voice. Her eyes were too heavy and her body too exhausted for anything more so she happily succumbed to the dark that awaited her.

She slept late, waking after dawn. Ewan was gone; she was alone with the cold sun streaking across the rush-strewn floor. But no, Meg was there, depositing something in a large trunk in the corner of the room.

She turned at Edyth's stirring. In her eyes, Edyth could discern Meg's delight at seeing her come, answering her call, and the dark circles of exhausted worry that plagued her. "Cousin," Meg said on a breath, finding her smile. She came to Edyth and helped her from the bed, hugging her tightly. "I prayed you would come." Meg held Edyth apart from herself, looking her over. Warm hands found the fullness of Edyth's belly, holding her child.

"Your son is much like his father: big."

Edyth smiled. "Yes, I feel it. I can barely breathe some days." Edyth kneaded the heel of her hand at the base of her ribs where the child often enjoyed pushing his foot. "I eagerly await his arrival."

Meg nodded knowingly, laughing lightly. "I know well of what you speak. But your time for delivery is still some time away, is it not?"

"Yes, a month, I think."

Silence filled the space between them for a time, Meg's hands learning the feel of Edyth's pregnancy, her eyes solemn. Edyth stilled Meg's hands. "How is your Garrick, Meg?" She held her breath, worried that her cousin's husband might have died in the time it took for them to arrive.

"He...he lives still, but his wound is grievous. I worry the ague will take him."

Edyth, who well understood such fear, bade Meg help her dress so that she might tend to him, which she swiftly and industriously saw to. "I brought you one of my gowns to wear. I know you brought little in the way of possessions, and it will suit you well in this stage of your confinement."

Edyth could hear the smile in Meg's voice at the word confinement. Edyth's confinement was turning out to be anything but, and that suited her just fine. She could not think of a worse fate than to be holed up in a chamber for weeks on end with no one but lady's maids for company. It would be torture.

Garrick was in a chamber at the opposite end of the long gallery, propped up on pillows, his face sallow against the white linen sheets. "Where is his wound?" asked Edyth, placing the back of her hand against Garrick's forehead. It was burning up, his eyes roving under his eyelids.

A sword sliced the inside of his arm. Just here," said Meg, pulling back the coverlet. His right arm was heavily bandaged and red with weeping blood soaking through. "We packed the wound with wood ash and bound his skin together with strips of cloth. The skin is too swollen to take a needle or thread at this point." Meg shook her head slightly, her eyes resting upon her husband's prone form. "I endeavor to pour tonics down him, but he does not wake often and most of it spills from his mouth." Meg's eyes misted with tears. "I fear he is already lost to me."

Edyth moved to the opposite side of the bed, to stand beside her cousin, to better see the wound. "Help me remove this bandage," she said softly. "Then I will see what needs to be done."

Meg lifted her husband's hand up into the air so that Edyth could more easily unwind the binding. She held in a gasp as the last of the fabric fell away, revealing a six inch long cut on the inside of his arm, following the length of his bicep. It was crusted with congealed and blackened blood from the wood ash they'd applied. Edyth looked closely, her nose a mere few inches from the wound.

Pressing gently against his flesh Edyth watched as yellow pus oozed from a rather gruesome pocket of his wound. A soft groan escaped Garrick at Edyth's ministrations, his cheek twitching in mild protest.

"I can see no bone, which is good, but this discharge is a distressing sign. It is likely why his fever lingers." Edyth frowned in thought, trying to call to mind what her mother had used in such cases. It did not take long for her to recall a wheelwright employed in her childhood village that had been injured in accident involving a chisel. Her mother had bade him soak his hand in hot water laced with spirits. "Not all is lost, Meg," said Edyth. "Go quickly to the kitchen and fetch me an oblong dough bowl, one large enough to cradle his arm. Bid yer cook tae also open the stores and bring me a crock of whiskey."

Edyth walked to the fire and opened the kettle that was hanging without the fire on a hook and looked into its depths. "Send up the lads from the kitchens with another billet of wood and more water, too please." Meg, looking eager, nodded and left Edyth alone.

*Please God*, prayed Edyth. *Let this work.*

# Chapter Twenty-Two

It was four days later when Garrick's fever finally broke. He was weak and frail, but Edyth had said as how she thought the danger had passed. The relief was keenly felt by all, even Ewan, who hadn't spent near the amount of time or effort on the man. And while others of the MacPherson warriors had not been so lucky as Garrick, Edyth's relief was palpable.

A score of days had passed since the battle so the majority of the injured were well on the mend, industriously employed where they could be with only moderate incumbrances: arms in slings or walking with the aid of a crutch. These men came to Edyth and the midwife for their bandages to be changed and their wounds assessed throughout the day, but the bulk of their time was spent with those lost to fever.

Garrick's swelling was greatly reduced by the evening of the fourth day, but when Edyth mentioned applying needle and thread to his wound, Ewan had begged her to wait until the morning. She was plainly exhausted. He, himself, was tired and he'd only trailed along and helped, feeling out of his element.

He did well playing the errand boy, bringing Edyth needed items and helping to lift limbs and bandage wounds as often as needed. It was grueling work, which gave him an even greater appreciation for his wife's talents, but it also made him worry.

He gave her a sideways glance at the dinner table, unhappy with how little she'd eaten so far. Her trencher was near full of food and he'd only seen her take a few small bites. He was just about to insist she go to bed and stay there all day tomorrow if needed when a kitchen lad approached them. He hovered uncertainly behind Meg's chair, looking unsure and shy. Ewan glanced briefly at the sweaty boy, distracted as he was with how tired Edyth looked.

Meg, following Ewan's gaze, noticed the lad and, turning in her seat, addressed him. "Aye, Rabbie? Is there aught you need of me?"

The lad leaned his aromatic body closer. "Himself bids me tell ye that there's a visitor waiting for one o' yer guests in the anteroom. He asks—" the lad licked his lips, his eyes roving to Ewan's face only to dart around the table then settle back on Meg. He lowered his voice, "He bids me quietly request that Sir Ruthven come with all haste."

Ewan raised his brow and stood, giving Edyth a look that plainly said, "eat," and, wiping his mouth on a linen cloth, rose to follow the boy. The lad was quick and quiet, the slap of his shoes loud in the dark hallways. The lad, Rabbie, he reminded himself, led him toward the front doors of the keep, but he turned down a hallway just short of the doors and brought Ewan to a small room made for waiting visitors.

Ewan was brought up short when he saw Rory there, impatiently grim faced and covered in dirt-caked sweat, smelling strongly of smoke. His face was smudged with black, as if he'd slept in the kitchen ovens. "Laird," said Rory, not bothering to wait for the boy to exit. He grasped onto Ewan's forearm with his good hand. "Iain commanded I come. I've ridden all day and night tae reach ye. He asks that ye come back tae Perthshire. We've been attacked."

All the air seemed to leave the room. "What?" he gasped, his mouth falling open. "Who?" Ewan demanded. "When?"

Rory's tiredness was apparent, his voice void of emotion. "It was yesterday morning, soon after the morning meal. The men were busy in the lists and the craftsmen already well underway in the garrison. We didnae...its wasn't until the bells tolled that we saw the garrison was aflame."

"A fire?" gasped Ewan, his mind immediately conjuring the image of a gutted, blackened heap that was once his home. The thought nearly brought him to his knees.

"Aye. The Moray...they came and blocked the king's garrison doors, locking many inside...."

The very breath seemed to have left Ewan's body. He felt as if he'd been punched in the gut. "The garrison? What of the keep? Of our people?"

Rory wiped his grimy brow with the back of his hand, his eyes tired. "The keep was intact when I left, as was the village. The sheriff's men had ridden out to meet the Moray as I left, scattering them into the trees. Sir Olifard...he pursued the Moray and his fighting men."

Relief surged through Ewan upon hearing the keep and the village was left untouched, but what of Iain? What had he done? "Did the sheriff demand Iain fight against Moray?"

Rory could only shake his head. "I cannae be sure. As I left, I saw Iain gathering Ruthven retainers upon the field below the king's gutted garrison."

Ewan swore, running an agitated hand through his hair. If the sheriff demanded Iain fight against Moray, he would be going against everything they'd worked toward. Surely Iain would not do such a thing. But how could he refuse without showing their hand?

Full of anxious energy, Ewan turned to the door and flung it open, Rory quick on his heels. He would go to his chamber and gather his things. If he left now, he could be back in Perth before nightfall the next day if he met no trouble. Haps he could see to the issues at home and then make it back by the week's end. It would be grueling, but he could not leave Edie alone here for long, but nor would he take her back to Perthshire in her current state.

Rory spoke quickly in lowered tones as he followed, their shadows long and sharp upon the whitewashed walls. Servants jumped out of their way in the narrow space, pressing themselves against the walls as they passed.

"The Moray has raised his banner," said Rory. "He fights no longer in secret. Will ye go out and meet him?"

Ewan stopped dead in his tracks, looking into his captain's weary face. Yes, the time had finally come, but damn it all if it was at the worst possible moment! While he'd made himself and the Moray the promise that he would do all he could to aid in ridding the English scourge from their lands, Edyth's time would be soon. Mere weeks away. He did not wish to leave her. The very thought of it made his heart constrict painfully.

However, if what Rory said was true, if the Moray had, indeed, declared war upon the English in this stunt, then Ewan's next course of action should be perfectly clear. He should, as Rory suggested, gather his men quietly as he'd planned and ride out to join forces. He should leave the running of Perthshire to Rory and Iain, but now that it came down to it, he faltered. Was Iain ready? Was *he* ready? He swore again, knowing it didn't matter. War had been declared. They must, all of them, do what was required.

"I must know how Iain engaged. Against which army and how many fell or were injured. This will dictate my next course of action." He lowered his voice. "If he sided with Olifard, as he was supposed to, then we will proceed as previously discussed." Ewan swallowed, his heart beating a quick rhythm against his ribs. They started down the gallery again at a quick clip. "If not," Ewan said, "and our treason is made known to Sir Lucas, I fear we have already lost Perthshire."

Rory did not respond. He didn't need to. He well knew the fear Ewan was feeling. Once they made it to the stairs that would lead to their apartments on the second floor, Rory asked, "Shall I find Lady Edyth, Laird? Will she be accompanying us?"

Ewan hesitated, his foot hovering over the third step leading to the upper floor and looked down at his ashen-faced, filthy captain. He couldn't, wouldn't, drag Edyth back to such turmoil, and at such a risky pace as he would need to set.

"No," he said succinctly, guilt fisting his heart. "She...must stay, but please, do go fetch her from the hall where she's supping with her cousin. I must...I must tell her goodbye."

Edyth came up the stairs as quickly as she might, though she was not as fast as she once was. Indeed, the very breath seemed to be stolen away from her and she had to stop at the top of the tightly wound staircase, using Rory as an anchor.

"Are ye well, Mistress?" he asked, sounding concerned and not a little afraid. Indeed, the look on his face told her quickly that he was far out of his element, dealing with a largely pregnant woman. "Shall I leave ye here tae go and fetch my laird?"

Edyth could not answer, so desperate for air had she become. She didn't understand what was happening, only that something was gravely wrong. Her hands went automatically to her protruding belly, which had grown hard with her exertion.

"No, Sir Rory. I am well enough," she said on a breath, "only encumbered. Pray speak. Tell me why you have come and in such a hurried fashion." She could not help but notice how very soiled he was.

Rory helped her to walk the distance to their apartments, telling her all the while what had transpired. Edyth's heart leapt to her throat. Now that she was aware of what had brought him here, she could easily smell the lingering smoke that clung to him that she'd assumed had been mere campfire. "Are any injured?"

Rory shook his head, dismissive. "I cannae say as yet, if any at all. There were craftsmen and soldiers still working when the fire was lit." He wiped his brow with the back of his hand, carving a path in the mud and grime so that his bronzed skin shone through. "They as certain 'ave perished," he said with a grimace, "but I cannae say what happened after I left...Iain commanded I ride here in all haste tae tell my laird the news. I cannae say who might have been caught up in the frenzy, but there was some fighting in the wood as I rode past."

A weight settled into the pit of Edyth's belly, as heavy as a stone. It made it hard to draw breath. "Dear God," she uttered, clutching Rory's arm.

They found the room in disarray as Ewan threw items, seemingly at random, into a canvas bag. He looked up at their entrance, red faced and harried. "Edie," breathed Ewan. He seemed at a loss for words. The anxious disquiet rolled off him in waves; she could feel it even so far away from him as she stood in the doorway. "Come, *mo ghràdh*. We must speak."

"Rory told me." She hastened to the bed alone, Rory choosing to stay without and moved to help Ewan pack. He did not let her; Ewan took her hands, his eyes full of urgency and quiet torment.

"I dinnae ken how I shall leave you, but I fear I must." His fingers, which were usually warm had turned cold against her skin, his heart in his eyes.

Edyth embraced him, all sharp lines and restless energy held in check. He was full to bursting with the need to act. She could feel his displeasure, his fears, and his desperate attempt to hide them from her. "I will be well guarded here," she promised him. "You needn't worry over me."

He let out a huff of disagreement. "Needn't worry?" he repeated, incredulous. "Full well ye ken I will do naught else in your absence."

She smoothed his hair, her fingers digging into the dark curls she so loved and kissed him briefly. "But you must try," she said, upon pulling away. "There are larger concerns at present that need your full attention."

Ewan's eyes searched her own. He did not need to voice the question that lingered in his eyes. She could see it written plainly. One way or another, the possibility of them being parted this night forever was undeniably high. Childbirth or from the sword, either one of them could succumb and the other would be left alone.

"Promise me," Ewan whispered fiercely, pulling her against him. She could feel his heart beating furiously against her breast. "Swear tae me that this will not be the last."

Tears pricked her eyes, but she blinked them away. She turned just enough to kiss his cheek, then the corner of his mouth. Suddenly he was pressing his own mouth fully to hers with a fervent intensity. It felt far too desperate, much too much like a goodbye. Edyth's heart shrank in hopeless fear.

She could not stop the tears that fell from her eyes, no matter how diligently she tried. They streaked silently down her cheeks, but she ignored them. His hands roved up her arms to delve into her hair. When they broke apart, their foreheads touching, their breath mingling, Ewan said, "I dinnae wish to leave ye, Edie. It feels a sin tae do so, and yet neither can I bring ye into the hell brewing at home."

She nodded against him. "You are laird as well as husband. Our people have want of you and for good cause. Do not agonize on the choice, Ewan. It cannot be helped."

Ewan kissed her once more, a delicate sound of remorse escaping him. "If ye willnae swear tae it, then I will command ye, *mo leannan*. Ye must live, Edie. D'ye hear?" He shook her ever so slightly, his heavy hands settling on her shoulders. "Live. You and the child."

Edyth smiled sadly, knowing the words were pointless, but speaking was impossible. A knot in her throat prevented any words. She tried not to think of him or Iain, or any of their clan in peril and concentrated on the feel and smell of him, so immediate yet fleeting. As soon as he left her she would mourn their loss, they would drift away like smoke from a candle and be lost.

He kissed her once more as if he could not help himself then forced himself away. He stood as a drunk man, as if he felt the earth sway beneath his feet and called for Rory. "Come," he called, his voice gruff with unspent emotion.

When Rory entered, Ewan said, "Ye'll stay 'ere with yer mistress. I lay this charge at yer feet, Captain. Watch o'er yer mistress well. With yer very life."

Rory's thoughts were hidden, but Edyth thought she discerned disappointment at being left behind to mind his laird's lady wife. The emotion was so fleeting that Edyth thought she might have imagined it.

Dutiful as ever, Rory bowed, one fist lifting to his heart. Of course there was little the poor man could do if Edyth's childbed proved her demise. Nevertheless, Rory vowed, "On my honor, Laird, I will keep and guard her."

Ewan ran a hand through his hair, his eyes darting around the scattered articles of clothing. "I think I've got all I need."

"Laird," said Rory, looking vastly out of place with his sooty, road-weary clothes. He was not wearing armor save for a leathern jerkin, but it was splattered with mud and stained with what looked very much like blood. "There is more news that I havenae yet shared." He licked dry lips, his serious eyes never leaving his laird. "Upon my travels here I found a portion of the Comyns marching north. They said as how Sir Reginald Cheyne, the sheriff of Elgin pressed the Comyns to march on Moray and stamp out his rebellion."

Edyth's quick intake of breath was ignored. Ewan paused in his packing, his eyes dark. Rory continued, "Only they said as how they had no intention in fighting the Moray. They wish to meet as friends."

Ewan grunted, clearly not believing this news. "How is it this sheriff of Elgin kens the Moray is behind all these night attacks?"

Rory's mouth twitched slightly as if itching for a sardonic smile when he said, "Och, weel, they werenae so careful with their last raid on the lord of Castle Urquhart. They ambushed him in the middle of the day as he was on his way back to his keep."

Ewan grunted and said, "What these Comyns say and what they will do are two entirely different matters. We must only wait and see where their true loyalty lies."

"You think the Comyns will not side with Scotland? That they will play the Moray false?" questioned Edyth.

Ewan shrugged, busy with strapping on his sword belt. "Ye ken well enough how it is amongst the clans. We can agree that Edward shouldnae be king, yet we'll squabble amongst ourselves on who should rule once he is defeated." He pulled the bag over his shoulder, his eyes a weight on Edyth, his face pale. "We must only do what our conscience bids and let the consequences follow."

# Chapter Twenty-Three

By the time Ewan made it to the border of his lands, he took a circumventive route through the northern edge in the vague hope of coming across sign of Moray's contingent moving back north. Meeting them had been too much to hope for, however, and he'd wasted precious hours in vain. There was sign of people traveling, evidenced by the tracks in the spring mud, but they were long gone.

Ewan crossed himself, thinking of what hell he might find upon crossing the bridge into Perthshire, and pushed on. It was nearly dusk by the time he made to his holdings and he slowed his horse atop a rise that would overlook the valley.

The blackened husk that had been the king's garrison was like a scar upon the landscape, still smoldering. Faint lines of smoke curled into the air; he could not smell it as yet. The wind was at his back, but he imagined he could smell it all the same, acrid and sharp. It sat there below his curtain wall amid a field in what had once been surrounded by beautiful trees.

He squinted against the long shadows, thinking he saw people moving about the base of the once-towering structure. It would do no good lingering here. He must go home and see what fate awaited him. His steed, tired as he was, carried him dutifully down the winding length of the ridgeline and across the bridge that spanned the river.

Instead of riding to the keep, however, he rode toward the garrison, where he assumed there would be laborers collecting what might remain of use. Haps there he might learn what reception he would have upon entering his gates. Would he be traitor or laird?

A little over seven months ago he had taken this exact route, exhausted and outraged at coming home to find the monstrosity of the unwelcome addition to his lands that was the king's garrison. He'd agonized over his impotence, over his choices that had brought about sheriff de Biggar's swift retribution. But now it was nothing but a smoking pit and he, once more, come home to uncertainty.

The six people milling about the base of the ruined structure were indeed de Warenne's laborers. They shifted stone and wood, their hands and faces blackened with ash and soot, to try and—as far as Ewan could guess—gain entrance into the ruined building. They looked up as he dismounted. "By what course do I come home to find such destruction?" he asked, careful with his words.

One man with hands like shovels and just as dirty spoke from the group at large. He bowed slightly, which gave Ewan some hope. If he was discovered as duplicitous, this man would not bow to him, surely. "Bandits came, they did," he said, his words whistling slightly through a gap in his teeth. "Andrew Moray, some as said, my lord." Here his lips thinned in disapproval of the hated man. "Burnt men alive, they did. We're trying tae get what's left o' 'em out for a proper burial, as is their due."

Ewan frowned as he looked over the collapsed structure. They would find little within save dust. "Was a hot fire?" he asked, to which the man nodded. "I doubt much that any person will be found. Still, do as ye like. I will send the priest down tae bless the ashes."

Ewan's conflicted feelings battled within his breast. Truly, he did not like death. Especially where innocents suffered needlessly, and yet.... And yet he could not deny that in his heart of hearts, hope splintered through his doubts and fears. Would that God would allow him to be free from the English stain upon his lands and still keep what was his, given to his forefathers from King David himself.

"Why are ye here alone?" asked Ewan, hoping his careful questions would lead to more information. His next thoughts were of Iain. He needed to learn how his brother had acted. "Has my brother no' commanded that ye're helped?"

The man's eyes travelled to the edge of the ruined forest a fair distance away. "They've been busy themselves, aye? Gatherin' the deid from the forest and about. A fair number o' men that need tae be buried still."

Ewan forced breath into his lungs, careful with his features lest they give away his fears. He made an interrogative noise in his throat, following the man's eyes. The rich forest that had once skirted the field was ruined now. Nothing but scrub, stubs of stumps and a rough road where oxen had dragged the timber were left, but beyond the remains of the once-forest lay woods still, heavy with shadow. It kept its secrets. He could not see any man, dead or alive.

"The bandits left none alive," said the man. "The sheriff commanded his guardsmen to scatter and capture them within the forest. Yer brother took what Ruthven warriors as he could spare and stormed into the woods after but...." He trailed off, his eyes meeting Ewan's with obvious fear. "As God as my witness, it was as if a bewitched wind came along with the bandits, giving them swift feet, for so few o' them could be killed."

Ewan refrained from asking how it was this man, a laborer, could have known such details as they transpired, seeing as how he would not have followed Iain or the sheriff into the woods. Such gossip was useful, however. Let them think that Moray had such power and ability beyond blood and bone. It could only help their cause, this fear of the supernatural.

Ewan nodded. "My brother is left alive?"

"Och, aye, my lord. He has commanded all within his charge left living tae gather and bury the dead. They've been hard at work all the day, and still within the woods. Leastways, I 'ave no' seen them come out again."

The man seemed transfixed as he gazed into the long shadows of the silent forest at the edge of the field. "An ill wind comes from the trees, my lord." He shivered in the gentle breeze and crossed himself. "Be wary, good sir. Take pains tae guard yerself from evil spirits afore ye venture intae such a place."

Ewan nodded solemnly, his own eyes attempting to read the long shadows of the forest. Such superstitions were common and to be expected, but as a man well acquainted with death, he knew some of what this man spoke. He, himself, had felt the same strange charge upon the air when lingering in a place where lives had been stolen, where blood soaked the earth.

Ewan thanked the man and left his beleaguered horse to one of the laborers with instructions to bring him to the keep's stables to be cared for. Turning his back on the curtain wall of his home, Ewan sought out his brother, his mind full of questions and desperate hopes.

He heard voices before he saw the people they belonged to. He followed a track of a wagon which winded its way through foliage and trees. Ewan could see the prints of men and beast alike in the disturbed earth and could smell the sharp iron scent of blood.

Deep into the woods he found Iain and seven or so of his retainers, pulling and lifting bodies. Two men apiece, one at a fallen man's ankles and another at the head, carried and lifting the dead, to toss them into the back of the wagon. The wagon was full, a dozen or so bodies were heaped atop each other in a gruesome collection, the two set of oxen yoked together waiting patiently at the front, their wide eyes roving with their distaste of their load.

Iain spotted Ewan as he and Johnne lifted a dead man, a look of surprised relief plain upon his face. "One, two, three," he said, swinging the body back then forth again to carry it swiftly on the wagon bed. Once the body had landed, he wiped his sweating brow with the back of his gloved hand. "Just like ye, brother, tae join us when the work is near complete."

Ewan spared him a fleeing smile, relief suffusing through him at seeing his brother and so many of his retainers hale and sound. "The ground must still yet be dug for ours. I have strength enough for that come morning."

Iain looked up through the bows of the trees to the purpling sky. "Aye, we are out of light and must end this. We will have need to finish the job come morning."

"How many?" asked Ewan.

"We have lost four of our own," said Iain softly. "They have been brought intae the kirk already and are washed clean by the priest and my lady wife. As far as the sheriff goes," said Iain, his eyes looking dark in the shadow of the trees, "we couldnae leave any alive to witness our treachery. The sheriff and all his—and de Warenne's men—lay here," said Iain, sweeping a hand around him to encompass the forest at large. "Count them, as ye like, brother, and sleep easy. Only laborers are left, and they not observers of what befell the men in the wood."

Ewan nodded, his heart stuttering at the news that Lucas had been killed. He knew that it couldn't be helped. He was the enemy, after all, but still...he had been a friend. Thinking of the man's wife and sons left alone in the world made his heart grieve. "Where is he? Sir Lucas...his wife and sons would wish him home with them, and he a knight, should be buried with full rights," explained Ewan needlessly to no one in particular. "I will make arrangements for his transport come morning."

"I thought ye'd best bring him tae Edinburgh at least," said Iain with a nod. "He's also up at the kirk." After a pause, he added, "We were careful to speak of the Moray's strength and skill, at the numbers that beset us," continued Iain. "With luck those laborers that linger will take the news with them as they venture home and speak of our misfortune in each village they encounter."

"Who of ours? I would pay my respects," asked Ewan, looking from face to face. He needn't have asked. He knew well his men and saw who was missing. A fist seemed to squeeze his heart at finding Alec missing from their group. Still, he would have the fallen men's names spoken aloud here, amongst the enemies they had taken part in defeating. He swallowed the sudden emotion that had knotted in this throat.

"Inan," said Iain with regret. "Rab, Willie, and auld Henry." Iain, seeming to understand Ewan's pain, added. "Alec is in the keep. My lady wife tended tae his wound as best she knew how. Only a cut on his arm that needed stitching," added Iain hastily, lest such news unsettle Ewan further. "I thought it best that he be left at the keep tae sharpen swords than tae pull the threads loose with the effort required here."

Ewan frowned and nodded, processing the information his brother had relayed. They had lost only four of their men and, so far, their treason was unknown.

Unable to finish their work in the dim of the forest, they set the oxen back toward the keep, the slow pace bringing them to the now abandoned, gutted garrison. "We'll no' bury these," said Ewan. "Let us burn them here."

They made quick work of unloading the wagon between them, and with the oxen unencumbered and returned to their places, they waited as two men and the priest came. With them they brought the necessary torches and oil, the former casting eerie, orange shadows across their faces and those of the dead. Their eyes, unseeing and clouded, did not reflect the light. It made Ewan ache to cross himself in protection. Ghosts would haunt him. It would be a long time yet afore he forgot this sight.

"Pour the oil," instructed the priest, emotionless. Ewan watched as Johnne doused the fallen soldiers with splashes of oil from the pail. The priest said the prayers and they, all, watched, transfixed, as the torches were thrown atop the heap.

Each man brought their forearm before them to shield their faces as the oil caught, the heat instant and savage. Black smoke, darker than the heavens, billowed up in a sickening pillar. The dead would be turned to ash and, carried upon the wind, would be driven to where God willed them.

These dead men who had sworn to take his very lands from him, they would now belong to Scotland. Their ashes would be swallowed up by the earth. It was a rightful end.

"Damn any man who dares take what is ours," muttered Ewan, his eyes fixed upon the macabre pyre. "May they get the same."

Weary to his very bones, Ewan sat in his office, his mind full to bursting with what he might do next. He must see Lucas shrouded, bound and carted off. He would bring the man himself to Edinburgh as he gave his report to what officers were there of Moray's unsolicited attack. Hopefully, with showing Sir Lucas the respect he deserved, he might conceal his true loyalties. At least for a time.

Rumor was that Cressingham was still in Scotland, though he was not sure where. He wasn't in Perthshire, thank the saints. Still, others said that he had taken a ship to Flanders with all of King Edward's conscripted men.

He would find the truth of it for himself. He had to, afore he called upon his men, one by one, and bade them join him against the English. He would speak to Dundas and Hay, his southern allies as well. They should be made aware of what transpired here and his future plans.

He pinched the bridge of his nose, wishing the ache in his head away. A fleeting thought caught hold of him, to seek his wife for a cure before he recalled that he had left her in Balgowan. *Left her*, as he swore he would never do. He hated himself, sick to the marrow of his bones. It could not have been helped, he told himself. She was not alone, after all. She had Meg and the MacPherson midwife to look after her. And Rory would rather give up his own life than fail his charge.

But even as he thought it, he knew better. As faithful as his captain was, he could no more prevent her death than he could. He ran a weary hand through his hair, feeling sick and prayed God that the midwife would be enough.

A soft knock sounded upon his study door; he grunted in response, too burdened with worry and with plans of what he must do to speak.

It was Iain. He came in and sat upon the desk, very close to Ewan, gazing down upon him without words for a long time. "She will be kept safe," he said finally, his voice soft and full of feeling that stirred Ewan's heart. "Dinnae doubt it, *mo bhràthair*. Dinnae give credit tae yer fears. Ye mun only do now what honor demands. Go forward, without thought of yer wife, else distraction claims all our lives."

Ewan felt like weeping. He sat back against the rail of his chair, not meeting his brother's eyes and agreed with only a nod. "I will leave on the morrow and deliver Sir Lucas," he said gruffly. "Johnne, Fingal and Alec will accompany me. I'll send Johnne back tae ye with what news I find."

"And then ye'll join the Moray," said Iain. It wasn't a question. Silence stretched out between them as Ewan gathered his slippery thoughts. He rolled his shoulder slightly out of habit more than pain. "I'm tae remain, am I, and play act the faithful English subject? I would rather be at yer side, sword in hand, than play these politics."

Ewan sighed. "We've been through this. This course was decided long ago, Iain. And ye have a wife now tae keep and comfort."

Iain's mouth twisted slightly, his eyes showing acceptance at the reminder. "I do at that," he said, his hazel eyes sparking with some hidden emotion. It made Ewan curious, this look of his brother's, but he did not pry, only asked, "How is she?"

Iain shrugged and pushed off the desk, moving to the slitted window against the side wall. "As well as she can be, as a witness tae such violence against her own kin."

Ewan could well imagine, as his own wife had lost both of her parents violently, and both on the same day. But he did not know the Stewart lass as he did his own stoic wife. Still, he offered what advice he could. "Only give 'er time and distraction, if ye can."

Iain grunted, still looking out the window, his eyes fixed on some far distant point. "I have made her a promise, Ewan," he said, his usual easy manner and lightness of speech abandoned. "I will have my vengeance on Cressingham in her name." When Ewan did not answer, Iain met his eyes, his face blazing with the weight of such a promise. "I have sworn it to her and will see it done. I cannae stay here and play the meek brother. I will not."

When Ewan opened his mouth to protest Iain cut him off. "I willane foreswear my oath, brother, and lose what respect I have gained in Alice's mind and heart."

"Am I no' yer chieftain?" asked Ewan without venom. He did not have the energy to be angry. His heart was too soft in his grief.

Iain pulled his dagger and held the tang in his fist, the bite of the sharpened edge no doubt nigh on drawing blood. "Aye, chieftain. I am yers," said Iain, impassioned, "for I've kissed this holy iron and with my own tongue have I said the vow in God's own church, but I am also brother...and now husband. So too have I pledged my sword in vengeance against my wife's enemy. And by God I will have it."

Ewan stared at Iain, his mind full of desperate thoughts. How could they both leave Perthshire together, and leave it open to demise? How could he risk Iain's life upon the battlefield? He was strong and skilled, yes, but he had yet to see real war. Ewan had lived and breathed it for two long, agonizing years. He'd been sick to his very soul of the whole business. He'd spare his brother the ghosts that haunted him still, if he could.

Iain continued, a thin trickle of blood sliding down from his closed fist to the point of his blade. A drop settled there, much like a tear; it grew and trembled at the tip, silently falling to the rush-strewn floor. "I am with ye 'til the end, *mo cheann-feadhna*, even unto death, but I will have my vengeance."

Ewan closed his eyes, weary and full of feelings far too close to the surface. He could deny his brother retribution, could forbid his part in freeing Scotia from the English plague that had beset them, but he did not want to. Iain had just as much right to die for what lived in his heart as he, himself, did. Ewan opened his eyes, deepest blue and sparking with fervor, and leveled them on his younger brother. "I cannae deny ye go if ye will it, Iain. Let it be together, then, that we meet our fate."

# Chapter Twenty-Four

The roads into Edinburgh had started out quietly enough. They passed farmers, sheep and shepherds, and clusters of travelers as expected, but as they drew closer to the port city of Edinburgh, traveler had given way to men at arms. Their banners blew stiff in the wind as the columns rode past them on the stony old Roman highway, brisk and purposeful.

Ewan did not know all of the ensigns that they encountered, but he had no doubts that these were those who were loyal to England. Each time they had drawn to the stop as they encountered the men at arms, one man would pull away and question their purpose upon the roads. Ewan, stiff and annoyed at being asked, had wanted to respond with irritation. What business of theirs wherefore he went? But he'd had the presence of mind to use the encounters to their advantage.

It would serve them well to further spread the news of Moray's attack with such men. He exaggerated his own losses, claiming half of his retainers had been lost. "And so we deliver our noble sheriff, Sir Lucas Olifard, murdered in defense of our lands, and make our claim against the fiend, Andrew Moray of Petty."

Each man had shared their grief at his loss and their hope that they could route out the villain and then they were gone, off to their own places to cause harm and bolster Edward's objective. It sickened him to watch them go off with such violent purpose, Scotland's own sons willing to kill their own in favor of a foreign king. But they carried with them now a message: The Moray is come. The Moray will fight against Edward's rule.

Sir Lucas was swathed tightly in a shroud and bound with a hempline in the back of the wagon. Fingal and Johnne drove the horses, stoic and quiet, while Alec followed behind, and Ewan at the head.

The brownstone city walls were heavily guarded at every gate and so they were bade to wait in a long line of would-be visitors to the large city. Goats bleated and pigs rooted in the prolific mud, the sun high and cold. Finally it was their turn and with little fuss they were, some of them, escorted to the castle garrison to report their loss to John de Warenne, the so called Guardian of Scotland.

Their wagon holding Sir Lucas was left at the bottom of the hill in the square and guarded by Fingal and Johnne. Alec, looking tired but eager followed faithfully behind his master, quick to offer his aid should he be needed. He wasn't, at present, but still Ewan wanted him near should he need him to deliver a message to the men at the wagon.

They waited in the dark anteroom of the castle's garrison for what felt like a very long time, watchful as armored men, messengers, and pages came and went. Ewan's stomach growled and his throat ached for drink, but he did not send Alec away to fetch refreshment. Not yet. "Remember," said Ewan quietly. "Make good use o' yerself. Keep yer eyes open and make note of anything ye might see that can be o' use tae us."

Alec was to be his eyes while he spoke to de Warenne, who would most likely pay little heed to a squire.

Finally, they were escorted to a whitewashed room, tiled and rush strewn. He could not believe his luck upon entering. A large table centered in the middle of the room was covered in a large map, upon which was clustered several different wooden carvings symbolizing calvary and infantry alike in differing colors. Ewan tore his eyes away from the map and found de Warenne's red-rimmed eyes and pinkly raw nose observing him from where he stood on the opposite side of the table.

Ewan made a courtly bow, to which de Warenne grunted his welcome. As Ewan hoped further, the man moved from the table, no doubt wishing to draw Ewan's eyes away from the secrets the map held.

"Sir Ruthven," said de Warenne in his reedy voice, motioning with an arm to direct him to a set of chairs near a brazier on the opposite wall from the map. He sniffed loudly and wiped at his noise with a kerchief. "Come and warm yerself as well as ye might. This hell-hated pit is eternally frigid." He shook his head mournfully, his mouth set in a distasteful line. "I cannot recall a time I was warm in this detestable prison."

It was no secret that the Earl of Surrey did not enjoy the Scottish climate. It was rumored that twice now he had retreated to his southern home in England only to be sent immediately back again by his king.

Ewan did not dare glance at Alec behind, who he knew stood at attention near the door, ready as always, to be commanded. He hoped his squire was able to see the map well enough to determine locations of the whittled figurines from where he stood. He could not look, however, to gauge the distance without calling attention to his purpose.

"By what intent do I find a chieftain here, so far from his duties at home?"

His words felt like an accusation or a rebuke. Ewan frowned and shared the sad news of Moray's attack. De Warenne's response was immediate and full of fury.

"Damnable, hateful rogue!" he spat, his fists clenched tightly on his knees. "You say you saw his ensign? The Moray brat has declared war against us?"

Ewan shook his head. "Not I, milord. I was no' tae home, but delivering my wife tae visit her cousin in Balgowan. It was my brother, Sir Iain, who fought against the Moray alongside Sir Olifard." He was careful not to say they had been at Doune, where this man's compeer, Cressingham, had taken his retribution against Alexander Stewart. Ewan did not wish himself nor Iain to be implicated in anything involving the raid on the conscripted convoy. They may well know of their wedding, but he would not offer more information.

"I bring Sir Lucas' body sae that he might be given the rights owned tae him as a servant o' the crown." Ewan paused, affecting a solemn visage and added, "I would have him returned to his own parish where he might be laid tae rest near his family." It was not difficult to pretend sadness. He was, indeed, saddened at the loss of life, but he could not deny that he was glad of the garrison's destruction.

"Care so much about a sheriff appointed to your lands, do you?" asked de Warenne sharply, smelling a lie.

Ewan met his shrewd, grey eyes squarely. "I kent the man from my time soldiering in France. He was...wounded," he said, leaving out the details that they had fought on opposing sides of the ongoing conflict. "I fed and clothed him as I could until he was sent home tae convalesce. It was with great surprise and pleasure that I found him upon my lands. So, aye, I do care about the loss. He was a good man, Sir Olifard."

De Warenne grunted, still looking as if he wished to withhold his judgement. Ewan did not blame him. "He fought alongside my brother and my retainers against the outlaw, Moray," continued Ewan. "He is no' the only friend I've lost tae that man. Many of my retainers were lost in their fight tae keep the garrison, but it was tae no avail. The security and honor of the garrison our noble king bestowed upon my lands is naught but rubble."

De Warenne's face flushed hotly, livid. He swore, his lips pressed tightly together as if he would hold further blasphemy within himself. "Naught is left? What of the laborers? What of the craftsmen I paid?"

"Some were burned alive, I hear, though I cannae say how many or who they were." Ewan did not have to pretend at his disapproval of the innocent's deaths. "In any case, there is nothing left of them but dust and ash."

"All?" de Warenne raged. "All the guardsmen?"

Ewan stared, careful with his words. "So it would seem. D'ye think they would run coward?"

De Warenne for his part did not answer, his thoughts turned inward, his eyes distant. "Infernal knave! Whelp!" he ranted. "I should have his father killed to teach the fiend a lesson." His breath came short, his face crumpled together in disgust. In time he calmed and ran a hand over his face. "Nay, I cannot kill the father. He would be hailed as martyr and only rouse the country further against us."

De Warenne, seeming to become suddenly aware of his loss of decorum waved a hand at Ewan, dismissing him. "Aye, Sir Ruthven," he said distractedly. "I will see that our honorable sheriff is returned to his rightful place." He stood and Ewan copied him, bowing in farewell.

As he passed through the door, Alec fell in after him. They did not speak, not until they were safe away, hidden behind the closed door of their shared room in the Rose and Crown public house.

Alec had ordered their food and drink, which was brought to him forthwith by a flaxen haired maid who had an eye for Alec's fine form. She curtseyed as they left, her eyes fixed brazenly upon his squire, whose ears burned red.

Fingal went to the door and, opening it a crack, peered through. "We're alone," he said upon returning to the small table holding their fare.

They reached for their preferred morsels, speaking around their food. "Well?" prompted Fingal. "What news?"

Ewan looked to Alec, giving him a significant look.

"It appeared as though there is a large company of calvary assembled, or to be assembled, near the Kilsyth hills. Leastways that's what it looked to me." He shrugged and took a large bite of brown bread.

Ewan frowned in thought. "Falkirk?" he suggested. "Or Cumbernauld?"

Final grunted. "That's two day's ride...at least for a small contingent. It'll be moreso fer such a sizable company of cavalrymen."

"What of infantry?" asked Ewan, filling his horn cup with ale from the stone crock. "Did ye hap tae see where they were assembled?"

Alec shook his head, chewing industriously. "Mmph...there were far more cavalrymen than marching troops so far as I could see, but there were some I could see here, at the mouth o' the Firth o' Forth. And there were others north, near Dundee, I'd guess."

Ewan grunted. "That would make sense. The Great Glen is readily held by the English. Ye'll be sure tae tell all this tae the Moray. Tell him also, that I go tae gather my men at arms tae fight alongside him, wherever that may be."

Fingal agreed, promising to send word.

Alec frowned thoughtfully into his horn cup. "Tae where will we send the men, my laird, if we dinnae ye ken where the Moray would strike next?"

Ewan swallowed his bite of bread and said, "They will have a place with Cait until more is known. And then we'll meet them upon the field, wherever that may be."

Edyth's appearance in the kitchens was met with surprise, but she ignored the servants' stares. Having never been one to sit still for too long, the expectation that she convalesce in her borrowed chamber for the coming weeks was asking too much. She needed to keep her hands busy, and her mind off of Perthshire.

Meg well understood her need to move, of course, and did her best to distract Edyth with walks in the gardens or playing games in the women's solar, but Edyth was growing bored with such entertainments after only a week. With so many hours in the day, she could only sit for so long. There was work to be done, and Edyth was happy to help. With her cousin busy with the running of her household and caring for her children, the walk to the kitchens had been a welcome, solitary distraction.

Edyth stopped in her tracks in the doorway of the bustling outbuilding, her hand smoothing over the billowing fabric that covered her protruding belly as she took in her surroundings. The kitchen, like with most estates, was separate from the keep, but the MacPherson's kitchens were less modern than what she was accustomed to. There was no oven set into the hearth, for instance, so bread was baking straight within the dark coals.

The room was large and square, and had been repaired with lime, but there were no windows, so the light came from the fire and from the torches set into the walls. The result of this was flickering, unsteady light, long shadows, and darkened corners. Everyone seemed to work well despite the lack of illumination, even in the intense heat. Edyth fanned a hand in front of her face, both from the heat and from the smoke that lingered thickly in the air.

The lilting cadence of Gaelic married with the homely sounds of chopping, stirring, and the clanking of iron pots as Edyth made her way between two long tables, heading for the still room on the opposite wall. Her hands itched to hold the pestle in her hand.

She had just reached the door, nodding to people as she passed them, when the muscles holding her child contracted, her skin growing taught and hard. It did not hurt, but she stopped all the same, waiting for it to pass.

Being a stranger to pregnancy herself, did not preclude her from knowing what to expect. Cramping such as she was experiencing was to be expected, especially as a woman neared the birthing. The thought both excited and terrified her. While she wasn't alone, she missed Ewan. It wasn't usual for a husband to be present during labor, but she'd aways pictured him near. Certainly not days away. But it could not be helped, so she buried the desire to see him, to hear his voice, and distracted herself in the only way she knew how, work.

The contraction lessened and Edyth moved forward, trying to settle her mind. She pushed open the door and was met with the earthy scent of dried herbs, as familiar and as comforting as a mother's touch.

Would that she could have her mother, if not her husband. Both were impossible. *But you have Meg.* Yes, she had her cousin, which was a blessing she would not easily forget.

Edyth took a long breath through her nose and lifted a white apron from a peg near the door. She was not alone. Meg, who was experienced with childbirth, and the elderly midwife, Ada. Meg as a dear friend but years apart had loosened the tight knot holding them together. Their time here, aiding their injured after Cressingham's soldiers cut them down, had brought them closer again.

The stillroom had a narrow window, high along the outside wall that prevented her from seeing out of doors, but it let in the necessary light that one needed for preserving herbs. She inhaled deeply as she perused the rack suspended from the ceiling, full of hanging plants.

Yarrow, meadowsweet, angelica and other plants dangled on long stems, some nearly touching her head. She passed them by, looking for nettle or raspberry leaves. She recalled her mother giving a tea of such to pregnant women, claiming that it would ease their labor. She found none, however, and finding it a good excuse to venture outside, she quickly procured a basket and a pruning knife from a low shelf.

The sun was bright and the weather fair, if not hot for early July. Edyth squinted as she perused the grounds, her hand shielding her eyes.

"What is it ye're looking for, mistress?" asked a woman.

Edyth turned to her left and blinked at the small woman kneeling in the kale yard, close to the rock wall, digging in the dirt. Wrinkles covered her heavily freckled face, her lips turning inward from a loss of teeth. The kertch on her head could not quite cover the silver in her hair, little whisps springing free, waving in the breeze. It was Ada, the midwife.

They'd worked together helping the injured but hadn't said much to each other in the course of their duties. But now that most of the men were healing and did not require such constant attention, haps they might have more to speak on.

"Hello," said Edyth nodding her head in greeting. "I'm looking for raspberry leaves. Do you have any here?"

The woman stood without difficulty, and straightened to her full height, which put her a few inches below her shoulder. "Aye," the woman said, her eyes heavy upon Edyth's very pregnant belly. "But no' here, lass, in the kale yard. We've got a wee patch o' the canes our yonder, but ye shouldnae go by yerself, and pregnant as ye are. Ye should be abed."

Edyth took a breath to stop her immediate reply. She did not want to sit. She didn't want to be holed up in a room for weeks on end. "I appreciate your concern, but I've got weeks yet afore my babe arrives. I would spend what time I have left out of doors rather than a stuffy room."

The old woman moved to stand closer Edyth, her steady steps incongruous with her aged body. A gnarled, dirt-crusted hand slid atop Edyth's round belly; her eyes narrowed as if she were trying to listen to a whispered conversation. Her hands moved with surety, pressing on a hard lump of foot or buttock pressed against Edyth's side. The applied pressure encouraged the child to move, producing the familiar sensation of inward stretching. It was a strange and wonderful sensation of which she never grew tired.

"Mmph," the old woman grunted after a time. She lifted the hem of Edyth's skirts to look at her ankles, muttering softly under her breath. "Do ye suffer from headaches?"

Edyth nodded, resisting the urge to step away. People didn't often touch Edyth, let alone lift her skirts. "Yes, off and on. Most likely due to lack of sleep."

Ada sent her a sharp look, her wrinkled eyes narrowing further. "Ye dinnae sleep well?"

Edyth sighed, not wishing to go into the nightmares that often plagued her. "Not always, no."

"Have ye been bleeding?" asked the woman sharply. "Or felt giddy, like ye might be sick?"

Edyth felt the blood leave her face and rush to her heart. It beat faster with sudden concern. "I have, though not in the last few weeks."

The old woman grunted; her blue eyes that were so light as to appear nearly white narrowed on Edyth. "And yer feet are swollen. Get ye up tae the keep, lassie, and put yerself abed."

Edyth opened her mouth, not to argue, but to beg for more information, but the woman shooed her into motion. Edyth was not a midwife; her knowledge of herbal cures was growing, but her understanding of everything that could possibly go wrong with a birth was limited. Was her child in danger? Was she?

"Get ye up tae yer rooms and settle yerself. I'll come tend tae ye," promised the old midwife. Edyth cast a look over her shoulder, her heart heavy with worry. Ada watched her go, her mouth pressed into a thin line.

The hallways in her cousin's keep were narrow and dark, with few windows, but there were torches set at regular intervals throughout, guiding her to her given room. She passed by her cousin's room and did not pause to check on her husband, though she knew she ought to at least see if he'd kept his tea down.

With the help of Gelis, Edyth removed her slippers and her gown, instantly feeling lighter in just her chemise. Gelis opened the shutters, letting in a stream of sunlight, while Edyth resisted the urge to pace. "Will ye no' lie abed, mistress? Ye look as white as milk."

Edyth ran her hands over the tautness of her belly, her mind straining to recall any pertinent information her mother might have mentioned regarding her own symptoms. She could think of none, and lay upon her side in the bed, where she stared at the shaft of light cutting through the room.

"I'm fearful," she admitted to the silent space. Her whispered confession somehow calmed her, as if admitting her feelings would give way to a solution. No solution came to mind, however. Instead she thought of Ewan, wishing for him now.

"Och, ye needn't be afeared, mistress," said Gelis soothingly. "I'll go and fetch ye some water, then, shall I?"

Edyth hardly heard her maid leave, thinking instead that she would need to tell Meg what name she intended for the babe, lest she died in childbirth. Haps she should write a letter to Ewan should such a tragedy occur. It would comfort him, to have her heart written so plainly and tangibly on a page. She imagined him reading it, could see the pain that would overwhelm and consume him. Her own heart lurched.

"Stop being a ninny," she chided, wiping tears that had erupted so readily onto her cheeks. She had only just moved to the edge of the mattress and swung her feet to the floor when a knock sounded. "Come," she said, hoping she didn't sound weepy. She wiped her face once more, erasing any evidence of her weak moment.

Meg entered, concerned, followed closely by a maid, carrying an arm full of linens. "I spoke to Ada, Edyth. No, please lie down," she said, coming to sit at the edge of the bed. She laid a hand on Edyth's ankle, her eyes narrowed as if she were struggling to unknot embroidery thread. "Yes, I quite see. How are you feeling?"

Edyth shrugged. She'd been feeling fine, save for the usual aches and heaviness that accompanied late pregnancy. "What's wrong?"

Meg squared her shoulders and met Edyth's eye. "Ada is very skilled. I trust her completely. She says there is cause for concern and that you must lay abed. She's in the stillroom, mixing you a tea of chamomile, raspberry leaves and cohosh."

Edyth glanced at the maid, who laid her burden on the table near the window. "What are the linens for?"

Meg patted Edyth's knee, speaking as one does when trivializing a horror. "It's naught tae worry over. Ada likes to be prepared is all. She will come and inspect you, but she feels that your time is soon at hand." She smiled here, looking more like herself and less tense.

Edyth grasped her cousin's hand. "Tell me true, Meg. Why the cause for concern? The babe shouldn't come for weeks now.

"Ada has seen much in the way of pregnancy and birth," affirmed Meg, as if this was an adequate answer. "If Ada says to lay abed, then we'll see that you do." She smiled brightly, as if doing so could chase away Edyth's worry. It didn't work.

She would just have to wait for Ada then, and ask her.

It did not take long. Ada ambled in, followed by Gelis carrying a tray with ewer and a kettle. Edyth sat up despite the grunt of disapproval from Meg.

"Mistress," greeted Ada in her wavering voice. "I've made ye a powerful tonic. Ye mun drink it up, aye? For the sake of yerself and yer bairn."

"Why?" asked Edyth, even as she took the proffered drink. It's musky, stale odor seemed to sit in the back of her throat, making her cough. It would surely taste as terrible as it smelled.

"Aye, it's right nasty, but ye mun drink it all, then again in a few hours."

"Why?" she asked again. "Please tell me what's wrong."

Ada nodded and motioned for Gelis to set down the tray. "Get the kettle on," she advised, then ambled closer to Edyth. She lifted up Edyth's hand in her own vein-riddled one with surprising strength. "I've seen in the past, mothers whose feet bloat like a fish and it's naught tae worry o'er. But some who have also complained of headaches and bleeding, weel, they have sometimes lost their lives. And those of their bairns."

Edyth's mouth fell open, aghast. "Why?"

Ada shrugged, looking closely at the pulse hammering away in Edyth's neck. "I cannae say, but they sometimes suffer from spasms and then n'er wake." She made a sound of regret in her throat. "It may no' be such for you, lady, but I'll no' risk such. Drink this tonic. It will bring on yer labors."

Edyth's breaths were coming short. It was too soon. "But..." she said, tears springing to life, "Is this not just as dangerous? To force the baby to come before its time?"

Edyth remembered well an instance when she, herself, dosed a woman with a tonic meant to help and instead the woman had died. She would never forget the panic and regret, nor the family's pain at the loss.

Meg rubbed Edyth's back. "Trust Ada, Edyth. She's delivered hundreds of bairns. You cannot ask for a better physic."

Edyth looked into the drink, seeing out the corner of her eye Gelis' worried hovering. She did not know what to do. If she refused the drink, she could die, and the baby along with her. At least, according to this woman. This experienced, knowledgeable woman who she'd seen tend to the ailing right beside her. Ada was skilled and knew her herbs. But this was dangerous, wasn't it?

This was not so easy as mending flesh and giving comfort to the dying, this was forcing a child into the world. Her child, for whom she'd earnestly prayed. Ada lifted white brows. "The choice is yers o'course, mistress. Ye can wait and see, wait for the locking o' yer joints and the tremors tae begin, but by then it'll be far too late."

"But what of the bairn," asked Edyth, her breath stolen away. "Will the babe survive?"

Ada frowned slightly. "I cannae say, mistress. But I ken well enough that if we dinnae urge the babe tae come soon, ye'll both likely die."

Edyth wanted to weep. She stared hard into the cooling mixture, black and swirling with herb debris. She wanted to live—and for her child to live of course—but it felt like a gamble. She thought of Ewan, of his fears of her dying, of his plea to her ere he left, to promise she would not die.

It was with these thoughts that she lifted the cup and took the potion in three long gulps. She gagged after, but kept it down by breathing deeply through her nose, her throat clenched tight.

"That's a good lass," said Ada approvingly, taking the cup from her. "Rest ye here awhile and I'll come back later for the next dose."

Meg helped Ada to leave, telling Edyth that she would be right back, leaving her alone with her maid.

Gelis, who looked close to tears, busied herself around the room, needlessly wiping off tabletops with her apron.

"Gelis," said Edyth softly. "I'd like to write Ewan a letter. Bring me paper and ink, would you?" The maid readily obeyed and, unable to hide her tears, sniffed loudly and wiped them away with the back of her gnarled hand.

"Himself as made me promise tae keep ye from harm, mistress, afore he left" said Gelis miserably. "But I fear...I dinnae ken how tae...."

Edyth shushed her tears and placed hand to a bony shoulder. "Hush now, sweet Gelis. He may as well have bade you promise to stop the rain from falling." She gave her a soft smile, hoping it conveyed hope. "Pray now, Gelis. For both our souls."

# Chapter Twenty-Five

Edyth woke in the middle of the night, a pain radiating in her lower back; it reached its heated fingers, stretching toward her front, where it gripped her lower abdomen tightly. She'd been achy and uncomfortable for weeks now, but the little aches and twinges of pain were different now. Ada's tea seemed to have increased these pains a hundred-fold.

She forced herself to relax into the wool-stuffed mattress, a thread of equal parts fear and excitement racing through her as the grip on her body subsided. The long ordeal of labor had begun.

Edyth was no stranger to the birthing process. At least objectively. Knowing what to expect and doing the hard work were two very different things, however. One thing she did know from experience, it would be hours yet before any real progress was made.

She'd sent Gelis to her own room hours ago, wishing for sleep. The maid had not liked the command, but she'd grudgingly obeyed. Meg had lain next to her in bed for a time, telling her stories, but they'd both eventually succumbed to slumber. What felt like hours later, a keening cry was heard outside of Edyth's chamber door and a sleepy Meg was pulled away by the nursemaid.

It hadn't been difficult to go back to sleep. The aches and pains of her body, she assumed, were simply a part of advanced pregnancy. But now, hours past and two tonics later, the pains had changed. *Sharpened*. The midwife's tonic had done its work.

She thought of going and fetching Meg, or asking a guard to send Ada, but she'd talked herself out of such a thing. It would not be prudent to wake the household now. Her time was far away, surely, so she stayed abed, her eyes fixed upon the shuttered window, wondering at the hour. It was still dark and no sounds, however small, hinted that people walked the halls. Yes, it best for her to stay in her chamber and not wander in search of some lone man who stood guard in the hope he could find Ada.

Edyth waited for the next pain to come, her mind drifting unerringly to her mother. She'd lost children, as many women did, and had mourned for them. Edyth recalled quite clearly her mother's tearful existence after each loss. It was easy to feel, even now, how her own heart had hurt watching her mother mourn for a lost hope.

Her father's grief had been different. His had been a quiet anguish that grew whenever her mother's tears were given voice. He'd worried mostly for her, of course. Worried for the heartbreak that weighed his wife's heart down so thoroughly. Edyth hadn't considered the cost for him before.

Haps he felt the sting of loss as keenly as her mother had. She'd never asked, for such a thing belonged hidden away, held amongst the tender places in a heart, and not on a tongue. She doubted words could articulate such a grief anyway.

The thought that she, herself, could lose her child, or her own life, was terrifying, but it, like so many unpleasant thoughts, had always seemed far away. Like a bird on the horizon. Untouchable and outside of her immediate concern. Edyth stroked her hard belly, searching for movement. Suddenly, she couldn't recall feeling the baby much all throughout the day and a worry blossomed to life within her mind.

She could have already lost her child.

"Please, Mother," Edyth whispered into the inky dark of her room. "Stay with me."

Another pain began, slowly at first, with a dull ache that quickly spiked into that of a honed blade. She shifted in the bed, hoping that a change of position might be more comfortable. "Mother," whispered Edyth into the dark, her legs pulled up to abut her unborn child. "I'm frightened."

Two more contractions came and went before she moved to her knees, rocking slightly as she caught her breath. The pains earlier that day had not been so intense. Indeed, she's slept through them. Now, though, they came as a sting of ice and flame at once. The last pain had stolen her breath. She consciously relaxed her jaw and unclenched her fists. It would do her no favors to fight it and exhaust herself. She must welcome them, as difficult as it would be.

A thought entered her head then. No, not a thought. A song. One that she'd long forgotten. She could hear her mother humming, as she so often had, here in the quiet of the room. Edyth smiled softly and closed her eyes. Her mother's hymn, so plaintive and beautiful, fell from her own lips: "Little red bird on the lonely moor, the lonely moor, the lonely moor. Little red bird on the lonely moor, where did you sleep in the night? Out on the bare branch, dark and wide, dark and wide, dark and wide. Fast the rain fell on every side. Poor was my sleep in the night."

Edyth blew out a careful breath, the backs of her eyes stinging with emotions she hadn't felt in some time. Of course she always missed her parents, but here, in this moment where she felt so unsure and terribly afraid, the want of her mother's reassuring presence was keenly sharp.

She held the image of her mother in her mind, thinking of her strong hands, stained with the juices of some weed, of the curtain of her auburn hair falling over her face as she worked the pestle, at the plaintive songs that were perpetually falling from her lips.

The feeling came upon her so gradually that she could have overlooked it. She could have dismissed it as her own wishful, desperate hopes, but she knew better. She was no longer alone. She could feel her mother there, unseen and unheard, but felt as surely as she could feel her own heart beating.

"Thank you," whispered Edyth softly, grateful tears leaking from her eyes. "It's only fitting you be here for such an event." Edyth felt herself relax more fully into the mattress, knowing that she was being watched over. Softly, she began her mother's song again, rocking on her knees.

Edyth did not know how long she labored. It felt like it had been long hours since she'd awoken and she was growing weary of the constant pain. Hoping to distract herself from it, she'd started to walk the length of the room. Back and forth she'd gone, her breathing sharp through her nose, resting against the bed when the pains subsided.

Now, though, she could not walk through the discomfort. She would pause in her pacing to grip one of the bed posts or a chair, her knuckles white, panting. A soft moan escaped her as the latest cutting pain wracked through her. She clutched at the bed curtains, half falling to the mattress.

Wiping hair from her face, Edyth glanced to the window and could see the subtle change of light through the crack in the shutters. Dawn was approaching. She'd spent the whole of the night—or nearly at least—desperately trying to hold in her cries as the pains became unbearable. She didn't know how much longer she could go on. "What shall I do?" thought Edyth. There was no way she could walk the distance to Meg's chamber now. She could barely make it two steps together.

Jittery and exhausted, thirsty and growing tired of the pain, Edyth considered the growing light through the slats in the shutters. The pains seemed to be coming faster now. She hardly had any reprieve, no time to rest or gather her thoughts before another spasm overtook her. She ran a shaking hand through her sweaty hair, wishing for Ewan's hands upon her back. Wishing for Meg or Gelis. She'd even take Rory.

The thought of her husband's captain faced with such a challenge as active birth made her laugh. It only escaped her as a soft huff, however. The smile on her face fell away as another pain shook her body. She clenched her jaw in an effort to hold in her cry and sank to the floor. There she stayed, holding herself her hands and knees, breathing as though she'd run a race. "I...I think I might have waited too long," confessed Edyth to the empty room. But it was not empty. Not really.

A sudden spurt of warm liquid gushed down Edyth's legs just as the door opened. She looked up through her stringing hair to see Gelis standing in the door frame. Her expression was, at first, rather blank, but that quickly was replaced with a look of alarm, then aggravation. "Sommat told me tae hurry along this morning. Lucky for you that I listened."

Lucky indeed, thought Edyth. "Th—thank you," she rasped to the room at large, thinking her mother might have had something to do with rousing her maid.

Gelis' familiar, strong hands moved the hair from Edyth's flushed face. "How long have ye been having the pains, then?" she asked in her usual no-nonsense tone.

Edyth waited for the most recent pain to subside, then said, "H—hours ago. My waters have just broken."

"Mmph. As I can see." Gelis left her and went to the door. "I'll be right back, milady. I passed a guard not long ago."

Edyth did not respond but, after a few moments, she could hear Gelis' sharp command to the unseen guard. "You there! Quick, I say. Get my mistress's cousin. And the midwife, mind. My Lady is soon tae deliver."

Edyth spared no thought for the commotion in the hallway and groaned. Gelis reappeared as suddenly as she'd left, her voice softening as one might do at the edge of a sickbed. "Do ye wish tae stay on the floor or do ye want the mattress?"

Edyth considered, moaning through another shot of pain and shook her head. "I can—cannot move just n—now."

"The floor it is," said Gelis as she walked to the bed. She pulled off the coverlet and yanked the sheet from the bed with swift movements. "I'll just lay this doon for ye, mistress, and then I'll get ye a wee sip of sommat tae slake yer thirst."

Gelis moved with a swift efficiency borne of competence that settled Edyth's mind. "Thank you," she muttered. "I hoped you'd come soon."

"And why ye didnae send for me sooner, I'll never know. Here, walk yerself ontae the sheet, mistress. I've got some pillows for ye."

Edyth obeyed, gratefully slumping onto the pillows. She was on her side, panting, and wet through when Meg arrived. Her cousin was only partially dressed, her hair unbound, and red in the face. "Saints above, Edyth!" chided her cousin. "I'm sorry I fell asleep with the bairn!" She looked to Gelis. "Why didn't you come get me as soon as her pains started?"

Gelis scoffed softly, her gimlet eye on Edyth as she offered her a horn cup partially filled with water. "I only just found her meself, milady. She didnae utter a word o' complaint."

Meg grunted, a noise full of displeasure, and moved to open the shutters. "Averin has called for the midwife; she won't be too long. Still, I daresay we can catch a baby as well as she can."

"We've experience enough between us," panted Edyth, trying and failing to smile. She let out a keening moan then that reminded her of a barnyard animal. If she wasn't in so much pain she might've laughed at herself.

"Och, dinnae ye worry yerself, mistress. Moan and greet all ye wish."

Meg, coming to kneel beside Edyth, began to braid her hair. "Do you feel it in your back? Shall I rub it for you?"

"Y—yes." Tears gathered in the corners of her eyes. She was so tired and done with the pain. "I want it to end," she confided. "Tell me it will end soon."

"Do you feel like pushing?"

Edyth nodded vigorously, gasping as another pain shot through her. She hardly registered as her chemise was lifted and hands pulled her knees apart. She did not hear the words spoken between her cousin and her maid. Her vision blurred, either from tears or fatigue, she wasn't sure.

Gentle hands touched her, comforting words were uttered. Edyth panted, unconscious tears streaming from the corners of her eyes.

"Let's try and have a go then, Edyth," said Meg. "The next time the pains come, push as hard as you can."

It was as if everyone held their breath, waiting for the right time. The room was still and quiet save for Edyth's panting as she tried to catch her breath.

"It's coming. My back—" That's all she got out before she clenched her jaw and pushed, a grunt ripping from her throat.

"How did that feel?" asked Meg, her face suddenly looming before Edyth.

But Edyth did not answer, for the door opened at that moment and Ada appeared with a young maid, holding a birthing stool. Ada's commanding voice filled the room and Edyth, unable to focus on any words, only responded to the arms that tugged her up and onto the stool.

She knew this conveyance well. She'd seen it used many times, but this was the first that she'd ever sat upon it. Where the flat bottom of a chair would usually be to support the user, instead there was a hole in which the baby would fall. And instead of rails to support her back, the rails were at her front, so she could lean against them as she needed.

Hands and words, a cloth to her face, an offer of water. She gritted her teeth and pushed until she thought she might faint. But then she heard Ada's voice cut through the haze in her mind. "Shoulders are next. Rest while ye can."

Labor was, in a word, excruciating. She thought she might die from the pain of it. She felt like she was being rent in twain, and then, just as suddenly as the agony had come, it fell away. She felt the child slip free of her body, heard Ada's praise, and beheld her child for the first time.

She was the most beautiful creature she'd ever seen. Tears clouded Edyth's vision as she watched Ada wipe her daughter roughly with a cloth, eliciting a shrill cry. Nothing had ever sounded so sweet to her ears. It was agony and ecstasy in one, this business of life. Edyth laughed tearfully as Ada lifted the baby so she could better see. She waited impatiently for someone to sever the cord, and then the babe was placed into her waiting arms.

She was no longer crying. The baby gazed up at Edyth through puffy, unfocused eyes. "Hello," whispered Edyth, touching a pale cheek with her finger. The baby was like many others, her skin mottled pink and grey as life took its hold. She was small and impossibly light, fitting easily against the length of her forearm. She had a whorl of dark red hair, fine and plastered against her skull, ten fingers and ten toes. But she was not like other children in that Edyth thought her heart might break with loving her.

Soon the afterbirth was delivered and the baby was taken from her arms for the space of time it took for her to be moved to the bed. Her daughter was once again placed in her arms, the women's soft gazes and fond smiles heavy upon the child.

"What will you name her?" asked Meg.

Edyth thought for a moment. Of course she had thought long and hard about the importance of a name for her child. She and Ewan had offered suggestions the whole of her pregnancy, but there was one name now that came to her, that she knew fitted perfectly. "Her name is Cecily," said Edyth softly. She'd known a girl once called Cecily who had changed the very course of Edyth's young life. She'd not known the girl well. In fact, she'd tried her best not to know her at all. But the Cecily of her past had taught Edyth a lesson she'd never forgotten. Cecily Marsilia."

Meg smiled. "An honor for your mother. She would be pleased."

"Yes, I think she is," answered Edyth, deliberately using the present tense.

"Is Cecily a family name on your husband's side, then?"

Edyth shook her head, running a gentle finger over her daughter's cheek. "No. The name belonged to a young girl I hardly knew. She...her family perished in a fire when I was young, and I've carried her with me all these years. It feels right, to have my own daughter share her name."

"It's a beautiful name. Just as she is."

Edyth heartily agreed. Indeed, she'd never seen a more beautiful sight. She thought she might never grow tired of looking at her. Cecily slept, exhausted from the ordeal, but Edyth could not bear to set her down.

# Chapter Twenty-Six

Ewan and Alec spent many days travelling, going from village to village, calling upon their retainers to go north to Nairn, where Cait and her husband, William resided. He commanded that they tarry there and help where they might until he could arrive. They, all of them, did not seem surprised to find him come, and all good men that they were, readily donned their swords and armor, and bid farewell to their families.

It filled Ewan with equal parts pride and regret, to see these men he loved so well accept an unknown fate. His retainers left in groups of four, eight and ten, the sun at their backs and the daunting mountain passes looming before them, grim and stoic.

With only one more village left to visit, it was with gritty eyes and tired limbs that Ewan once again mounted his horse. "Westward, Alec, and soon upon yer own fair lands once ye take the knightly vows."

Alec, who was just as weary, mustered a smile. "I'm glad we come this way," he confided. "I would see once more the heather in full bloom upon the feet of the hills there."

Ewan nodded, urging his steed onto the road. "And so ye shall, Alec."

It was an entire week later that Ewan and Alec finally came into Nairn, heralded by bells. The keep consisted of a four-story tower with east and west wings, lead-lined windows and a curtain wall still in construction. Or haps it was being repaired; Ewan could not tell from his vantage. There was a dry moat that encircled the whole of the structure and a drawbridge, which was currently down, but the portcullis closed.

His heart lifted at seeing Cait upon the gate wall, the wind high in her skirts, her hand pressed to her forehead as she looked out into the sun.

He saw the moment she'd recognized him for who he was. Alec carried the Ruthven sigil as was customary upon approaching a keep, but as Ruthven retainers had been arriving in groups for weeks now, she'd most likely anticipated more retainers, and had only hoped to find her brother come at last.

She was gone from the wall in a rush, her hair blowing in a fan behind her before she ducked out of sight. Going for the stairs, no doubt. Sure enough, a cry sounded for the gate to be lifted and she was there, staring at him through the gaps in the portcullis, with happy tears in her eyes.

She didn't wait for the gate to lift fully before ducking underneath and rushing forward, her skirts bunched in her fist. Ewan dismounted quickly and hurried to meet her, lifting her in a fierce embrace. She cried against his neck, a rare occurrence to be sure. Seeing her so full of emotion pricked at his heart.

"I've missed ye so," she rasped against his neck.

He ran a gloved hand over her head before setting her down on her feet. He held her apart from himself and smiled down at his sister. "Is Nairn really that bad?"

She laughed and knuckled away a stray tear, shaking her head. "Not bad, only different."

She seemed to become aware in that instant that they were not alone. She looked to Alec and curtseyed formally, seeming to suddenly recall that she was the mistress of this household and should at least attempt to act with decorum.

"Alec," she said with a smile. "Will ye no' come and greet me?"

Alec, who watched this entire exchange with shy avidity, dismounted and bowed over her hand. "Mistress Cawdor," he murmured.

She shook off his hand and threw her arms about his neck, a warm smile on her face. "Enough of that," she said with false censure. "We are too good of friends tae hold with such formality."

Alec, who had been quiet and strained since dawn, seemed to relax at her affection, a genuine smile returning to his face. Ewan had wondered at that but hadn't pressed. Cait and Alec had always been good friends, or so he'd thought. Ewan wondered idly if they'd quarreled afore she'd left Perthshire to marry William.

Thinking of the man, Ewan suddenly realized that Cait's husband was absent. "Where is yer lord husband?" He looked about them as if he'd somehow missed him.

Cait beckoned them in, calling for a page to take their horses. "Tell Martha tae prepare the west apartment for my brother and the room beside for our other guest," Cait said to another lad who hovered anxiously for some form of employment.

"William is no' tae home at present," she informed Ewan, "but I expect him in time for supper. Come and refresh yerselves. There is much to speak of." She gave him a significant look and added. "Iain is with him."

Somehow in all that had happened, Ewan had forgotten about the meeting in Inverness that Iain had promised to attend. His mind was pulled in so many directions that he could hardly think straight. He had many questions but he held them in. The bailey was not the place for such a discussion.

Ewan was shown to a well-appointed room on the second floor in the western wing of the estate. From his window he could see the distant shore of the wide firth yawning wide and wished Edyth were there to enjoy the view. Much like a tender injury, he shied away from the pain that came with thinking of her. No matter how hard he tried, however, he couldn't *not* think of his wife. She would be soon to deliver now, no doubt, and was in good hands, but he couldn't help his worry.

He said a quick prayer for her and child and refocused his mind. If he spent all this time worrying over her, he would not be able to do what was required of him. He washed quickly and changed out of his road-weary tunic and surcoat, replacing it with his only other change of clothes he'd brought with him. He left the soiled garments out to be laundered and left his room, not interested in resting.

Ewan couldn't rightly recall the way back to the main portion of the keep, but with only a few wrong turns, he was able to find the correct thoroughfare evidenced by the servants bustling about, preparing for the coming meal.

Spotting a young lady standing at a window, gazing out of the glass into the garden below, he thought to pause and inquire of his sister's whereabouts. "Pardon me," he said politely. "Do ye happen tae ken where I might find yer mistress, Lady Cawdor at present?"

The young girl turned to him, her blue eyes sparking with interest. "Which brother are you?" she asked pointedly. "Ye've got the same look about the eyes as our Cait." At Ewan's lifted brow she hastened to add, "Cait said as how her brothers were soon tae come, but I've yet tae meet either. Ye are her brother, are ye no? She wouldnae give the best rooms tae just retainers."

This must be one of William's sisters, for no servant would speak so informally or ask such pointed questions. Ewan remembered his manners and bowed. "Aye, I'm her eldest brother, Sir Ewan Ruthven."

The girl's eyes crinkled in a smile. "Och, I thought as much. I'm Audrey, Willie's sister," she said with a curtsey. "Do ye wish for me tae show ye the way? She's no doubt in the room off the hall with that big man. I cannae recall his name." She frowned in thought. "The one with the stodgy eye."

"Graham?" Ewan supplied, hoping it to be the case. He missed the man immeasurably.

Her face lit up. "That's the one! Come on, then." Ewan followed after her, listening to her chatter. "I'm no' allowed in the room when guests are present," she said confidentially. "Lately it seems that we always have guests, but mayhap as yer family, I'll be allowed in this time?" She gave him an assessing, hopeful glance that reminded him so well of a younger Cait that he could not help his smile.

"Haps," he said noncommittally.

They rounded a corner and took a flight of steps up to the next level and traversed through a set of double doors before Audrey paused. "That's Willie's study there," she confided, "but this is where Cait comes with Graham." She motioned to the door on the right and knocked softly, her hopeful expression still present.

Ewan could not help but like the girl, who he supposed was only about twelve or thirteen years of age. The door opened to reveal a surprised Cait, her eyes gone wide. "I thought as how ye'd be resting, Ewan. How many days is it now ye've been sleeping in the rough and living off oatcakes?" She opened the door wider and motioned Ewan in but stopped Audrey with a long-suffering look.

"Seeing as how it's yer brother, I thought I might come and hear," wheedled Audrey.

Cait looked down the hallway before piercing the girl with an experienced eye. "Isn't it time for yer lessons with Gilly?" asked Cait. Audrey had the good sense to look contrite. "But it's been ages since he's told us any good stories. Now he keeps going on about right moral action and the soul."

Cait laughed lightly. "Yes, the moral lessons are always the worst o' the lot," she said forlornly. "Alight. In ye get, but only for little while."

Ewan had expected to find a table surrounded by men, or at least a place where a meeting should take place. Instead he found a room lined with shelves holding an array of weapons. And there stood Graham in the center of the room, holding a short sword. For whatever reason, he seemed flustered and set down his weapon upon a shelf before coming to greet his laird.

"Forgive me for no' coming tae greet ye after yer arrival."

Ewan looked between Cait and his tracker, trying to figure out what exactly was going on. Cait let out an exasperated sigh. "He willnae punish ye, Graham. I'm no' a wee bairn, nor am I under his charge." She looked frankly at Ewan and said, "We've been practicing with an assortment o' weapons while William is no' tae home. Not that he disapproves," she hastened to add. "It's only that it passes the time. Waiting can be a heavy burden."

Audrey's gasp of awe at such a declaration was enough to make everyone smile. "Can I learn?" she asked with some level of reverence.

Cait gave the girl some vague response, mentioning William, but Ewan did not endeavor to hear. He was interested in hearing from Graham. He wanted to know all that had transpired since their last meeting.

Graham, who knew his laird as well as he knew himself, anticipated his desires and motioned him toward a door set between to shelves. The attached room was more to what Ewan had anticipated. A table surrounded by chairs took up the center of the space and was covered in maps, drawings, scribbled notes, and an assortment of whittled figurines, very much like those they'd seen in de Warenne's offices.

Pulling back the drapes, Graham allowed more light into the room, which spilled upon the table in a gilded pool. Ewan studied the map carefully as Graham spoke. "The Thane and Iain are presently on their way back from Avoch," he explained, pointing unnecessarily to the Moray holding.

"The meeting called upon by the sheriff of Elgin in Inverness gained us some important information, thanks to yer brother and uncle," started Graham.

Apparently, his Uncle Niael, pretending to hold some secret knowledge borne of spies, shared with the group at large that the Moray planned to lay siege upon the Castle Urquhart. "This wasnae expressly true," said Graham. "He does plan on taking all the English loyalists keeps in time, but his real goal at present is Dundee."

This false information was given in the hope that the sheriff of Elgin would command troops be sent to protect the keep upon the banks of the Loch Ness, leaving the road to Dundee open to Moray's advance.

"We have routed out many already," explained Graham, "and replaced the ministers and bailiffs with our own men."

"And the people within these counties assume their authority? They submit to those appointed by the Moray?"

Graham nodded. "Aye, so far as yet." He continued to explain. "We set our eyes upon Dundee, as it is an important holding upon the Great Glen."

Ewan well understood the significance. The Great Glen was one of the few natural routes through the treacherous passes. If they could control Dundee, then they could invariably keep the English out of the highlands entirely. But Ewan saw a flaw in this plan. "But so too is Urquhart upon the Great Glen."

"Aye," nodded Graham, motioning toward the figures set upon the map. "All in good time." He then explained that after the meeting, William and Iain and Niael, all supposed supporters of King Edward, tarried in the city thereafter, so as to be sure to be seen.

With their alibi secured, others of their company had laid in wait upon the southern road and had ambushed the lord of Urquhart, a Sir William Fitz Warin. "Unfortunately," said Graham with some regret, "the scunner escaped back tae his keep. Moray doesnae wish tae lay siege until he kens the mind o' the Lady Ross." Graham pointed at the map, where the Countess of Ross' holdings—or those of her imprisoned husband—were located. They were neighbors, Lady Ross and Fitz Warin.

"Mmph," grunted Ewan in understanding. "So they set their sights on Dundee. When will it happen?"

Graham clicked his tongue softly, his gaze upon the map. "For that, we await news from Avoch." Now that the Moray was openly fighting, there was no reason for him to stay hidden away in William and Cait's home. "Iain and William are expected tonight."

They stood in silence, staring at the map, both engrossed in their thoughts. The only sound came from the adjacent room where Cait had apparently given in to Audrey's pestering. The steely hiss of slow-moving blades and muffled instruction could be heard through the closed door.

# Chapter Twenty-Seven

T he sound of clanking armor, the ringing of chausses and hauberk alike sang with each step as the men marched upon the road. They couldn't go quickly. It was impossible to move such a large body of men and weapons with real efficiency. Nor would it prove fruitful to tire their horses when they would be needed for the oncoming fray.

Ewan and Iain, along with William's men, were to meet the larger body of the combined allies outside of Dundee in the forests of Belgay. When all were assembled, they would then move as one body, into Dundee proper, where they would lay siege to the keep and take a portion of the Great Glen for Scotland.

With Cawdor and Ruthven retainers together, they were a company of two hundred men at arms, fifty of which were calvary. A formidable enemy to be sure, and only a fraction of the other men Moray had gathered. Wagons pulled by mules and horses carted tents, pikes and halberds, swords and bows and all manner of other weapons the men could not keep on their persons and walk or ride. They'd also packed crocks of oil for flaming arrows and for lobbing over walls, should it come to that.

The procession had, as yet, not been hindered in any way, as they'd taken friendly roads and kept to the trees at night, not bothering with setting up tents for sleep. Already they were only hours away from their meeting place, having walked for three days at a smart pace. Still, despite Ewan's tiredness and his preoccupied thoughts, he kept this mind focused on his surroundings.

Ewan rolled his bad shoulder, which was perpetually tight and prone to aching of late, thinking of Edyth's reoccurring dreams. Was Castle Dundee the brownstone keep she'd described? Was this the fruitless march she'd envisioned so many times, where an entire army turned away without a fight? It would fit well with her descriptions, set against the Firth of Tay, but how could they be sure?

He could not help but wish she were here with him, as impossible such a thing could be. Even had she not been soon to deliver, he would not bring her into battle. Still, he could not deny that Edyth's presence would bring him much needed peace. Thinking of the whole of Moray's army abandoning their pursuit of Dundee for another unknown plot of land could mean that the siege was easily won. Haps the lord of the estate would simply give it up in deference to certain destruction.

"The scout returns," informed Iain, who rode beside him, uncharacteristically quiet. They watched as William's scout raced towards the long procession that was their company. William was ahead of them, toward the front of the line. Lifting his hand and calling for a halt, which came to a slow stop.

"Bugger this," muttered Iain, apparently unwilling to wait. He pushed his horse around the wagon in front of them and, circumventing the procession, rode toward where William was speaking with the scout. Ewan followed suit, coming upon the Thane and the messenger, who had ridden hard and fast. This horse's flanks were heaving, its legs and belly covered in mud. The rider didn't look much better.

"The army is arrived and makes camp," informed the scout, "but Moray bids ye come quickly, milord, for Bran has come at last, with a message from Wallace."

William, looking alarmed, asked, "Bran? Yer certain?"

The scout, still slightly out of breath nodded fervently. "Aye. I saw him meself, milord. He's been unable to get back due to Wallace's own

demand. He said as how Bran had discovered his place among the trees in
Selkirk, that he mun not leave until he proved himself a man of honor."

William looked between Ewan and Iain, his eyes alight with relief. "I
sent Bran tae entreat Wallace into joining forces months ago but hadn't
heard back as yet. I worried the worst had happened."

"Will Wallace join us in Dundee?" asked Ewan of the scout.

The man, who had been taking a drink from his waterskin swallowed
heavily and said, "I cannae say. I was bid come and tell my master tae
make all haste and join them in Dundee, for the siege begins at dawn."

They wasted no time. "Send calvary ahead," suggested William. "I will
stay behind with the wagons and infantry."

It was a mere four hours later that Ewan and William's infantry found
Moray's army, encamped in the hills amid the Belgay forest. Castle
Dundee was aware of their presence, as a priest from within the keep had
been sent with an entreaty to desist their plans. "There be no need for
bloodshed. Pray, lift the gate and surrender the keys," Moray had replied
evenly. The gate, as yet, was still closed, however.

Iain and Ewan had left their steeds with their men to be rubbed down
and fed and sought out Moray's tent, which was presently filled with
nobles. They were in deep discussion on the best plan of action. "The war
engines are no' yet come," said a gruff man from the corner, his grey eyes
glinting with candlelight. "We have no hope of overcoming the estate
without them."

"We mun only climb the walls at night as has been done between Banff
and Inverness," suggested another man.

Moray, coming to realize that the Ruthven brothers had arrived, bid
them report.

"We bring fifty calvary with the Thane of Cawdor close at hand. He brings two hundred well-armed infantry men, but no war engine," Ewan informed the group.

Moray welcomed them and bade them sit and discuss, leading with William's messenger that had apparently returned from the dead. "Yer brother-in-law's messenger returned early this morning with a message, saying that Wallace is eager to join forces. He informs us that Surrey and Cressingham converge their forces together to route him out of Stirling."

Ewan saw the issue at once. Wallace needed aid in the south against the considerable might of the English calvary, but here was Moray, on the cusp of taking the Great Glen. "We argue the point now," said Moray needlessly. "Some say that the best way to help Wallace is to help ourselves, here and now. Others say that we must leave at once and join forces with Wallace to ensure that the routed English dinnae take hold of the northern counties once more."

Ewan's mind was spinning. This was Edyth's dream come to reality. Dundee was, indeed, the castle left to a smaller body of the army. They would march south and meet Surrey and Cressingham in Stirling. It was there that swords would clash and blood would pour. He glanced at his brother, whose face was surely as white as his own.

"What say you, Sir Ruthven? Where would ye make use of yer men?"

Ewan swallowed and carefully chose his words. "Wallace cannae win with so little men at his charge against such a force. We must go and offer our swords, but why must we choose between the Great Glen and Stirling? Let us leave a portion of men here, and take the remainder south. Let us win our freedom swiftly and in both places at once."

This seemed to appeal to many of the gathered nobles. Debate broke out once more about the probability of Dundee's surrender with a smaller portion of the army left behind. Ewan half listened to the arguments around him, his mind full racing as he tried to recall everything Edyth had imparted to him.

She'd said there had been a swift river, snaking through a marshland, intersected with a narrow bridge. She'd said she could see no faces of men she knew nor ensign declaring a house soon to fall. Did that mean he would be safe? Could it mean they would be victorious?

"Then it is decided," declared Moray. "Let us leave a portion here. Once Sir Cawdor arrives, we will begin the siege on Dundee and take our leave with the larger portion for Stirling. God see us fruitful."

# Chapter Twenty-Eight

T he last two weeks had been glorious for Edyth, save that Ewan was not with her. Cecily had already changed so much since she was born and Ewan knew nothing of it. She drew Cecily for him, again and again, but it was not enough. It was not the same. She could not depict how Cecily's eyes seemed to speak a silent language, how the sound of her breathing made Edyth's spirits light, nor how the curve of her cheek and the purse of her lips in slumber filled her heart so full of love that she thought it might break.

She'd asked—begged—Rory to bring him news of his daughter's birth and that of her own wellbeing, but he had refused, stating that his place was now by her side until further notice. It was not until these two weeks had passed that Edyth finally was able to convince Rory otherwise. She'd had a dream. The first since Cecily's birth.

It was the same dream, as always, but with one small difference. There had been dozens of emblems, pikes holding aloft clan ensigns had swayed as the shadows had fought.

The fighters looked to Edyth as a roiling bed of vipers; she could not discern one body from the next. They'd churned and fought and died with screams that had pierced through her. Thunder had boomed through her, shaking her very bones. And when the lightening flashed once more, there in the middle distance, she'd seen her husband's ensign: two rams, horns curled, battling on a field of white.

She'd watched its slow descent, as sure as a tree felled in the forest, as it was swallowed up into the dark mist. The horror that had struck her in that moment was beyond description. She'd searched, frantic and unbreathing, for a familiar face, her eyes focused upon the place where the ensign had fallen.

And as if God himself and parted the clouds so the moon could shine down upon this obscure shape, she saw there a body. Was it Ewan? Iain? She'd wished to move, to run and see, but her feet had remained planted, no matter how hard she'd thrashed or how terribly she'd screamed.

She'd awoken in the dark of night, weeping, with a biting anguish filling her breast. It weighed her down, as heavy as a stone around her neck. She'd paced her room, praying, holding her daughter, making plans.

The choice before her was difficult. She could not stay, of that, she was sure. But could she travel to Perthshire and warn Ewan so soon after birth? The haste she would need to use in getting home would be difficult for her physically, but what of Cecily? To travel with her child meant she would have to go slower. She could leave Cecily behind, but.... Grief gripped her, an ache inside her chest as if someone had ahold of her heart. She could not leave Cecily but nor could she stay here with such a warning in her heart for her husband.

But what warning could she give? "Be careful? Don't go?" He would not heed her counsel. She knew him far too well to think he would forgo battle. But could she let him go to his potential death not ever beholding their child? Of knowing that they were both safe?

She stared, transfixed at the subtle curve of Cecily's lashes on rounded cheek. Edyth soaked in her daughter's bowlike mouth, pink and shining with moisture as the moonlight fell upon her. She thought of the long distance between Balgowan and Perthshire and wanted to cry.

How could she choose? How could she possibly choose between her husband and their daughter? Tears filled her eyes and she bit her lip lest she wake Cecily with the cry that clawed at her throat. "I cannot choose," she whispered to the night. "Do not ask it of me."

No answer came, however. No secret thoughts that did not belong to her. No feelings save for the desperation coursing through her. She paced, her feet shuffling through the dried rushes and lavender littering the floor. If she went to Ewan, he would be angry with her. He'd said as much long before Moray had ever been a part of their lives. He'd warned her that he could not trust her to do as he asked...to stay where he'd put her.

But what of her own heart? What of Cecily?

Moving to the trunk at the end of the bed, Edyth pulled out a long swath of swaddling that Meg had given her, a few changes of clothes, and her satchel. Come morning, she would gather her daughter and wrap her tightly to her chest, secured by Meg's swaddling cloth. She would stuff as much as she could in Harris's saddle bags, and she would go.

The next morning, feeling exhausted from her sleepless night, she sought out her husband's captain. He wasn't difficult to find. She joined him at one of the tables in the great hall where he was breaking his fast.

"Mistress," he said, standing with alacrity upon noticing her. She waved his politeness away with a hand and sat opposite him. Sitting, he filled a cup of cider for her then offered her solicitations as he waved for a serving wench.

She waited for the servant to deposit a bowl of congealed parritch in front of her before she spoke. She did not know what she might say but the truth. "I dreamed last night," she announced, watching for Rory's reaction.

He blinked at her a few times, his mouth pulled into a frown but he said nothing.

She pressed on, "I dreamt of a battle and...and I saw the Ruthven ensign fall. I am leaving at once for Perthshire."

Rory's mouth fell open slightly, his eyebrows raised. "That's a long journey for a new mother."

"And Cecily," she informed him.

Rory's alarm grew. "Ye'd risk—"

Edyth cut him off, grasping his hand. "Yes, I risk! I would have my husband see his daughter before he...goes to war." She was about to say, "before he dies," but refused to put words to her fear. "Of course I know the journey will be difficult, but my comforts matter little to me. I think only of Ewan and Cecily."

His disapproval was clear but still he asked, "Can ye tell me, Mistress, what it was ye saw?

Edyth paused, looking into her cup. She could easily see the roiling clouds and the falling men. She could still hear the screams from men and beasts alike. She shivered and took a sip. "I've seen a gruesome battle and a bridge over a swelling river. There...there are many ensigns, most of which I cannot discern, but I saw...I saw our standard fall. I saw it disappear into the mists of fighting men to be swallowed up."

Rory looked white to the lips at her words. "Is that all? Did ye see Himself fall, as ye did before?"

Edyth gripped her cup very tightly, her throat dry. "No," she said, meeting his gaze. "I saw no faces I knew. I only know that if Ewan falls, I would have him know we are safe and hale. That we live still."

Rory, looking rather ashen faced, said "I cannae...Forgive me mistress, but I cannae say as if he is in Perthshire." At Edyth's alarmed look he added, "There was some question as to whether or not the sheriff would believe Ewan's innocence. When I left, Iain was preparing to fight. I dinnae ken whom he was planning to strike down. The Moray or the English."

Edyth's heart sank to her knees. She felt gutted, her mind racing. "Where would he go?" she asked, her lips numb.

"Himself as said how, if the worst should happen, he would gather his men scattered in the clan lands and go north, tae meet Moray."

"Dear God," Edyth muttered. She felt many things all at once. Betrayal, for Ewan's silence on this matter, grief for the potential loss of his lands, anger that she must chase after him.

That thought brought her up short. She *couldn't* chase after him. If he had gone north, she could not follow him with any speed. The mountain passes were difficult to climb, nor would she put Cecily through that long of a journey. But, as Rory had said, there was no way of him knowing fer certain what had transpired in Perth. Ewan could be traveling north or he could still be in Perthshire.

She glanced at Rory and could see his distress. The hall was nearly empty now, with bustling servants carrying trays of empty platters back out to the kitchens. "If there is a chance that Ewan is in Perthshire, then I will go," she stated. "And haps I can help convince the sheriff of his innocence."

Rory made a noise in the back of his throat, opening his mouth to protest, but she stayed him with a hand. "I go with or without you, Captain. It's you that must choose."

Rory stared at her for several long seconds. She wondered what he might be thinking, if he, like her, recalled the last time she had been in his charge. Soon after Ewan had left for the battle at Dunbar, Edyth had waylaid Rory, steeping broom into his tea, causing him great discomfort so she could slip away unnoticed. If Rory was thinking about it, he did not let on.

The worry in his eyes give way to reluctant acquiesce after a long moment. Inclining his head he muttered, "I cannae let ye go alone, mistress."

# Chapter Twenty-Nine

The way to Perthshire was not as arduous as Edyth had anticipated. The showers of early spring had given way to warmer weather, leafy trees, and even flowers. The streams had lowered to a more respectable depth, allowing easy crossings as well.

Meg had shown Edyth how to wrap Cecily in a long cloth, binding mother and daughter together, so she was held close against Edyth's chest. They had gone as quickly as they could, stopping every few hours to feed Cecily, and then they were off once more. Edyth was terribly sore, but Rory had laid down a thick blanket, to help with the long hours that were required in the saddle.

Geils, for her part, had borne the long distance without complaint, though Edyth could see her weariness. Part of her regretted pulling Rory and Gelis away from Balgowan, where they had been welcome and comfortable, but the other part of Edyth regretted only that they could not sprout wings and fly there.

The first view they'd taken in of Perthshire from across the river had been jarring. The dark scar of the ruined garrison was as formidable as when it had been being built. But where the promise of English menace had lived, now there was only a hulking shell of spent violence, reminding Edyth of the burnt crofter's huts of days gone by. And while she well knew that the violence paid upon the English might be deserved, seeing the evidence of suffering was never easy.

The keep, to her relief, was intact. Indeed, as they neared, the familiar bells tolled, signaling their arrival, but no English soldiers greeted them at the gates. Alefred was there, a look of shock on his bearded face at seeing their arrival.

The gate had been immediately closed behind them, Alefred wasting no time in reporting to his captain. "There are only men left that did not perish in the fight against the English," he explained. "Himself and Sir Iain have left to join the Moray."

Rory stopped in his tracks, grabbing hold of Alefred's sleeve. "Iain has gone as well?"

"Aye," said Alefred, his surprise giving way to shared concern. They would be poorly defended should anyone come upon them and wish to take their home. Alefred explained that after Iain came with Lady Alice and had battled the English—killing all—he'd left with Ewan, leaving his wife alone to command the fortress.

Edyth could not believe it herself. "But where is Moray? To where have they all gone?" she asked, thinking of her dreams. Upon which battlefield were they congregating. Indeed, she might even be too late.

Alefred's concerned look only deepened as he motioned them toward the keep. "Sir Iain sent his lady wife news only yesterday. A wee pigeon arrived holding a message just for her. She said as how they move south from Dundee to Stirling. William Wallace calls for aid. That was a week ago."

Edyth grasped onto Rory's arm, feeling the familiar surge of panic take over. "It is begun," she said, her other hand cradling the baby against her chest.

They did not linger long in the bailey. They ate and changed their clothes and packed again for the necessary journey to Stirling, which, according to Rory, was three days ride southwest. "And that's if we can ride a full eleven miles each day."

Edyth knew going slowly was not ideal, but going much faster would be painful and difficult with a newborn baby. Rory, of course, had tried to talk her out of going altogether. "We are tae home now, mistress, safe and well. Tarry here with yer new sister and dinnae trouble yerself with a long journey. Only let me go in yer stead and deliver the news."

Edyth had only glared at him, reminding him of her willingness to go alone should he refuse to take her. Of course he had relented in the end, and had agreed to leave at first light the following morning.

Once prepared, Edyth had sought out Alice, who had been shocked but gratified at finding Edyth there. She'd readily produced the message from Iain when Edyth had asked for it, her worried expression hovering over the top of the page.

"I do not linger long," said Edyth. "I must impart some important news to my lord husband. And...and I would have him see his daughter," she added. Alice, for her part, did not attempt to dissuade her, but only stared at Edyth, her face gone pale.

Edyth did not sleep well, and no wonder. Cecily cried most of the night and so Edyth had walked the length of the floor with her, speaking to her incessantly of her own fears, of Ewan, and of her dreams. So it was with little vigor that Edyth rose at dawn, Cecily finally asleep, and dressed herself. After tying Cecily once more against her breast, she made her way down the stairs, both of them wrapped in her arisaid.

Rory met her at the front entrance, taking Edyth's satchel from her shoulder, which was filled with dried herbs, cloth for binding, catgut thread and a few needles. If she was going to Stirling, she might as well help where she could.

Just as Rory left, Edyth heard a sound coming from the stairs behind her. Edyth felt the surprise show on her face at seeing Alice there, a bag packed, her travelling cloak fastened around her neck.

Alice stopped at the bottom of the stairs, staring at Edyth with her dark eyes, daring her to say something.

Edyth's estimation of Alice grew, seeing her so willing to ride toward danger. "Who then will hold the keep, Lady Alice?" she asked, her voice echoing slightly in the cavernous space. "It is with confidence that I leave the charge of my home and my people into your capable hands."

Alice studied Edyth for a long moment, her dark eyes glinting softly as the light from the torches flickered. "I heard tell that ye're a great sorceress," said Alice, the color on her cheeks the only indication that she held any emotion at all. "That ye can tell some people's futures."

Sighing softly, Edyth closed the distance between them. "I have no power save what is granted to me through dreams, and those I cannot control. Rest easy, Lady Alice, I have not seen Iain's death."

"But still ye go with all haste tae yer husband's side and forbid me join."

Her hands went to cradle Cecily's body without thought. "I must go," she said, "for I have a work to do. Your work must be here, in the keeping of Ruthven. Knowing you are left to care for the clan lends me the strength. I will not fear, knowing you stand at the gates and command my husband's men."

With a slight curtsey, Alice bowed her head, looking dejected. "As ye say, Mistress Ruthven."

As Edyth turned to leave, Alice called after her. "Pray, tell my husband—tell Iain—that I bid him take heed tae no' be injured. And...and give him this, if ye would."

Edyth took the proffered gift, held aloft in Alice's hand. It was a kerchief, embroidered with thistles and vines smelling strongly of roses.

"Of course," said Edyth, pocketing it, and then she hastened out of the great doors and into the cold, predawn.

# Chapter Thirty

E dyth's first view of Stirling was just as she remembered it, save that there was a stoney abbey set atop the hill above the winding river. The forest above the sloping marshland was alight with a hundred fires, turning the bark of the oaks and pines a bright orange, interrupted by shadows of men and tents. It wasn't as loud as Edyth would have guessed, with hundreds of men gathered together.

Relief surged through her. They were not too late.

They passed a paddock of horses and row upon row of tents. It was as a small village, complete with aisles for streets; animals bleated, tied to stakes. Rory and Edyth traversed on horseback through what seemed to be the main throughfare.

Men looked up at them with solemn eyes as they passed, vacant of expression. The people, ranging in ages from young pages to grey-bearded elders, all mingled one with another. Some gathered around fires, eating, while others sharpened weapons. They passed a raucous group of younger men playing games of fortune, laughing and apparently unworried over what was to come.

Rory dismounted and asked a man stirring a pot over a fire a short way off for directions to his master. The man must not have known for Rory quickly moved on from him, pausing only momentarily to motion to Edyth to wait. Her body hurt. Every muscle twinged with pain and her backside was the worst of the lot. She would need help dismounting. She only hoped her legs did not give way once she was made to stand.

She patted Harris' neck as she gazed around them. Cecily squirmed against her, no doubt ready to be fed. "Wait just a little longer, dearest," she whispered to what was exposed of Cecily's downy head. Rory returned, looking confident and said, "This way. Follow me."

They wound their way through the wider spaces but eventually they had to dismount. Rory was careful to help her slide out of the saddle and hold her steady until she was ready. "I think I can walk. Slowly," she added.

Rory took hold of Harris' reins and they walked the remainder of the distance to a round tent, set near what seemed to be the center of the encampment. Edyth's legs felt like water and she wanted to cry with the sting of her injuries from childbirth, but she held herself upright through sheer will of force.

Cecily was huffing now, not having been given what she wanted, and Edyth did her best to console her by cooing and patting her through the layers of fabric. She felt lightheaded herself, having not eaten for what felt like many, many hours, and what they'd had was poor indeed. She'd had her fill for five days of salted meat and stale bread. Even the suspicious odor of what might've been burnt rabbit stew made her mouth fill with saliva.

Rory asked her to wait outside of the tent, which she was happy to do. Not moving was preferred to walking just then. He left the horses next to a rather large tree and entered the tent, his muffled voice indiscernible. Edyth waited impatiently, eager to see Ewan. She craned her neck, as if looking from a different angle, she might spy him through the small opening in the tent.

She didn't have to wait long. The flap of the tent was thrown wide and out came Ewan, wide eyed with alarm and dark with anger. He spotted her quickly and hastened toward her, his mouth set in a grim line.

She'd known he would not be pleased. She'd counted on it, but she was not in the mood at present to argue. Part of her understood his anger with what was on the horizon. She knew how bad it would be quite soon. She'd been seeing it for months on end. He did not wish such things for her. Or for their daughter.

Ewan stopped just short of her, his brows knitted together, his mouth already forming the words of censure, but he stopped short as he spotted the squirming, rootling babe wrapped against her chest. The anger in his eyes softened and he raised a hesitant hand as if he were afraid to touch her.

"The babe," said Ewan, "what—"

Edyth pulled on the knot just under the baby's body and loosed it, careful to hold her body as she unwound the wrapping. It fell away from the baby's face, exposing her perfect little frown.

"She is hungry, but she is whole and hale." Edyth's eyes misted with tears and seeing Ewan's reverent astonishment. He gazed upon Cecily with such adoring hunger in his eyes that she rather thought he might cry, too.

"She...a daughter. What is her name?" he asked, taking her into his arms. Cecily stuffed a chubby fist into her mouth and produced a voluble sucking sound that made both of them laugh.

"I named her Cecily Marsilia."

Ewan lifted the baby closer to his face, cradling her in his large hands. Indeed, she looked impossibly small against Ewan's body. "Cecily," he whispered, and then he kissed her cheek. "Hello, wee one," he said. "I've been waitin' tae meet you."

And then she realized that he *was* crying. Firelight glistened in the unshed tears filling his eyes. "She is verra bonny, Edie."

Cecily broke the spell of his trance with a hearty wail. "We are both very weary and hungry."

Ewan nodded and, taking her hand, led her, not into the large round tent, but a smaller shelter a short distance away. "While I'm verra glad tae meet our daughter and glad tae see ye both well, I'm no' happy at all tae find ye in the hell brewing 'ere. What were ye thinking?"

Edyth squeezed his hand. "Do you honestly believe I would come here if it were not of the upmost importance?"

Ewan glanced at her, the baby cradled in the crook of his left arm. "Mmph." He let go of her hand just long enough to lift the flap so Edyth could enter. The tent was dark but she could see shapes of furnishings outlined within. She waited for Ewan to light some candles from the brazier and was surprised at what she saw. The tent was spacious and far better appointed than she had anticipated. A rich carpet in hues of red and blue covered the ground near a cot. The other side of the tent held a small desk and chair.

Edyth immediately sat on the cot and began to open the neck of her gown, pulling on the ties at her shoulder. She motioned for the baby and Ewan settled her into her arms. He watched with interest as Cecily latched onto Edyth breast and fed with a sort of ferocity one might expect from a wild cat.

"She's a good eater," boasted Edyth, "and she sleeps most of the days and nights away. At least for now." She met Ewan's eyes, emotion suddenly coloring her voice. "I could not leave her with Meg. I had to bring her with me. I couldn't leave her." She begged for him to understand.

Ewan sighed and ran a hand through his hair. He moved the chair from the table closer to where she sat. "What have you dreamed, Edie? As ye say, if yer here, then I know it cannae be good, but I...it's just that war is imminent. Surrey has been sending his priests tae us, demanding we depart, for twa days now. This is the worst possible place for ye."

Edyth frowned. "Do not forget that I have seen it...have been for some time, Ewan. Only the dreams have changed. You'll recall the bridge and the winding river?" At his nod she continued. "It will fill with bodies and...and they river will swallow many men as well." She looked at Ewan's face, taking in his troubled eyes. "I saw...I saw the Ruthven ensign fall."

Ewan did not speak for a long moment. Indeed, he did not seem to even breathe. Finally, he took a long breath and asked, "Is it my death ye've seen, then? Is that why we've come?"

She shook her head, her eyes stinging. She hoped it wasn't Ewan's death she was seeing. "I did not see a face. I only felt heavy with sorrow. I cannot say who it was...but the ensign, Ewan. What can it mean?"

He leaned forward, resting his elbows on his knees, his fingers steepled at his lips. He was deep in thought, she knew. She could practically see him turning thoughts over, examining all possibilities, and unable to dismiss any. "Before when ye dreamed—at Dunbar, I mean—it was my face ye saw. Again and again. Aye?"

She nodded, her throat tight. "Yes."

"But this time it's no' faces ye see, but my ensign. It...it can only mean one thing," he said, his face starkly white in the candlelight. "My house will fall. We will lose this battle. Even if I survive this fight, my house must fall."

"Can you...will you leave, Ewan?" she asked, her voice breaking on his name.

His dark eyes pinned her to the spot. "Ye ken well enough I am up to my neck in this. First was my presence at Dunbar, then Graham caught by the English at Chester, then the garrison burnt tae the ground, and now I am here. Surrey and Cressingham's priests have seen me and all my men." He paused long enough to scowl down his long nose at her. "And now my lady wife joins Moray and Wallace's forces." His scowl softened into one of exasperation. "No, Edie. There is no way out for me, nor would I wish tae leave. I am here and here I intend tae stay. This is our fight for freedom; I willnae run nor hide, nor lick the boots of men who would rule o'er me."

He stood and looked outside the tent. "I think ye'll be safe enough in the village a few miles north o' here. I'll take ye there in the morning and beg the people tae give ye and the babe a place until...until this is done."

Edyth took in a shaking breath, her hands clutched around Cecily's small body. "I won't go, Ewan. Let me stay in the abbey. I will be safe there," she pressed at the dark look he shot her. "We will be better protected in the abbey than in the village, Ewan."

At least he considered her words. After a pause he said, "Haps yer right."

"When will it happen? When will the battle start?" she asked.

Ewan gazed down upon them, his eyes taking them in as if memorizing their features. It made Edyth's heart stutter. "Two friars have requested us meet with them in a cottage near the abbey. They've already met with us twice, bringing word from the English commanders. They wish us tae leave in peace, and if we do so, we go with favor." He scoffed, looking at the wall of the tent.

Ewan continued, "They ken that with us controlling Inverness, Elgin, Banff and Aberdeen, that we cannae be easily conquered, even with their mighty calvary. Stirling is the key into Scotland. If they lose this fight, they will have lost control of Scotland altogether. Sae they send their churchmen and beg us leave all the while threatening us with our destruction."

"Can they win, do you think?"

Ewan bit his lower lip and seemed to consider her question. Finally, he nodded. "Aye, they can win. It all depends on how they go about engaging with us." He shook his head and said, "If only I had eyes and ears in their camp. If I knew what they planned, then we could prepare and be ready."

Edyth looked down at Cecily, who had had her fill and lay sleeping, her milky mouth slack. "I will go," she said, her voice small. "I will go into their camp."

Ewan's head whipped around to level a glare upon her that would have made a guardsman shrink. "Are ye mad, woman? And you with our child in yer very arms committing yerself tae death."

"No one would suspect me. I am a woman," she said needlessly. "I would be ignored."

"No, Edyth. I willnae allow such."

Edyth made a noise of complaint in her throat but changed tactics. "If not me, then send Alec. Take him upriver and cross. Let him walk into camp and see what he can find."

Ewan pinched the bridge of his nose but she could see him considering it.

"No one will know him," she pressed. "He is still young enough that he could disguise himself as a camp worker or...or a squire to some obscure knight who is loyal to the English. It could work, Ewan."

He looked as if he'd like nothing better than to pace but the tent did not allow for such. After what felt like a long time, he nodded. "I'll ask it o' him, but I'll let the choice be his."

# Chapter Thirty-One

Alec waded through the shallows of the river two miles upstream from the English encampment, holding his clothes well above his head. While the moon was bright enough to gleam off his pale skin and draw unwanted eyes, he hoped no one who mattered was around to take notice of him. His feet slipped and skittered across slimy rocks, but the water was slow enough that he was able to catch himself before he fell in.

With only a little effort, he emerged, dripping wet from the chest down onto the opposite side of the river, his ears attuned to the slightest sound. The breeze rustled the tall grasses that lined the bank, but he heard nothing else.

He hastily threw on his sark and yanked on his woolen breeks, grunting softly with the effort to pull them over his wet thighs and hips. He donned his boots as quickly as possible then gave the signal: two low hoots using his cupped hands. The sound seemed to fill the night air and he waited, breathless, for the returning call from his lord. He didn't have to wait long. As soon as the low signal sounded, he was off, keeping to the shadows as he'd been instructed.

Alec's bold infiltration into the English camp filled him with both pride and trepidation. He could not—would not—fail his laird.

It didn't take long to reach the encampment. His mind had been preoccupied as his feet had eaten up the distance, but he could see the orange glow of a hundred fires now, tinting the space between shadows in a deep umber red. It appeared very much like how he imagined the maw of hell might look. Or at least purgatory.

He shook his head, scattering his thoughts, and crouched down near a tree and surveyed the area. It would be easy, he told himself, urging courage. He eyed the dark shapes of tents and men and trees, all unaware of his presence.

*Men do not take notice of people who act as if they belong, and they notice even less if they were busy gaming, eating and drinking.* Alec saw a sentry ahead, speaking to a camp follower, who offered him a trencher of food. He denied the food, but stooped to kiss the woman's neck, drawing a gasp and a giggle. A perfect distraction.

Alec moved to the left, emerging from the trees with an easy stride, his heart in his throat. He felt awkward, loud. He was exposed now, in full view to the enemy, but he tamped down his fears and focused on his next target: the shadowy confines between two tents. He forced his feet to slow and eased the stiffness in his shoulders. He refused his body's desire to look over his shoulder and became as a shadow. Irrelevant. Fluid. Ignored.

He waited, listening between the tents as two men walked past, speaking in low tones to each other. Not far away, he saw a boy younger than himself struggling to carry tack. His arms full, leather straps, reins, and harness dangled well past his knees. A bridle drug on the ground behind him.

Licking the dryness from his lips, Alec let out a shaky breath and said a prayer for courage. And luck.

With a quick scan of the wood, he slipped from obscurity and fell into step behind the boy. "Here, let me help you," he offered, picking up a trailing length of rein.

The boy jumped slightly at Alec's abrupt appearance, but his face smoothed into a grateful acquiescence as he allowed Alec to take part of his burden. "Thank you," said the boy. "I've got to take it just there." He pointed with his chin to a place Alec did not see, as there were dozens and dozens of tents scattered throughout and he'd pointed into the thick of them.

Alec said nothing as he followed the boy, who walked industriously toward a tent bearing a green banner emblazoned with a scarlet boar somewhere in the midst of the shelters.

"Here we are. You can just set them there," said the boy, depositing his own load onto a barrel set just outside the tent door. "Thanks again." He turned to Alec with a smile and a nod. "I'm Bram, page to Sir Devlyn. Are you a squire?"

Alec shook his head. "My mam is a cook and I've come along to help."

The boy nodded, taking what Alec said for fact. Armies were large, moving machines, the wheels of which were oiled by the daily requirements of living. Food, laundry, care of animals, the careful and precise art of packing and unpacking quickly...these essentials kept the army engaged and ready to act and required the use of many hands. It would not be unusual for a boy to accompany his mother in such a task.

Alec dropped the tack atop the barrel and said, in as offhand a voice as he could muster, "I've n'er seen so great a camp. How many men does yer master command?"

Bram nodded importantly, moving inside the tent, saying, "Sir Devlyn is a great lord, commanding nigh onto two hundred men." He invited Alec forward with a tilt of his head to a disordered heap of weapons that had been carelessly laid upon a cot. "Do ye mind helping me again? I've got to bring these down the way for sharpening."

Alec did as he was bade, holding his arms out in front of him as Bram loaded him down with as much as he could carry. Bram carefully hefted a few pieces himself and backed out of the enclosed space, Alec following in his wake.

Bram led him through a tangle of tents and fires, past a large area of hobbled horses, and stopped in front of a large, open tent wherein a gathering of men sat over grinding stones, sparks flying as they sharpened their dirks and swords.

Alec's arms were aching by the time they arrived, and he had to try very hard not to just dump the lot of his load onto the ground. A large, bearded man stood from his work at the wheel and took the load from Alec, grunting his salutation.

"There's a stone just there, ye can use, boy. Start with this," said the man, choosing a long dirk from the small pile and pointing to a whetstone set upon a stump in the corner. Bram smiled widely at Alec, nodding at him encouragingly, as though he was giving him a real treat.

Alec hesitated, thinking he should excuse himself to find Surrey's or Cressingham's tents, but did not feel he could decline. Besides, it might prove useful, sitting forgotten amongst fighting men.

It didn't take long before the rhythmic *shush shush* of the blade on the stone eased his nerves. Perhaps it was the muscle-memory of such a task, but he found the menial task put him at ease. He ignored Bram's nod of approval as he peered over his shoulder to inspect his work.

"I can see you've done this before," he said cheerily, sitting in an adjacent seat and setting to work on his own blade.

A rather rotund man stood and tottered over to retrieve another sword, his bowed legs making him more suited for a horse than a grinding stone. "Not sure if Surrey will need all of these sharpened. Most of them are sharp enough as it is."

"It pays tae be well ready," said a man with remarkably crooked teeth who sat opposite Alec. He held a short sword up in the weak light, his eyes squinting to slits as he inspected its edge. "Though," he continued, standing up to return the weapon to the table, "I would be surprised if half o' the blades see blood."

"Och, aye," said the bow-legged man, "Surrey is none too worried. We out-man Wallace and Moray's army by the thousands. Thousands! And they with no more than three 'undred calvary." He made a rude sound with his lips, bending over the wheel once more, shaking his head in scorn.

"Mmph," agreed the man with crooked teeth, raising his voice over the whirring wheel and the scrape of metal on stone. "He's in a hurry tae see the end o' Wallace and Moray, that's for certain."

Bram leaned to the side so that his mouth was near enough to Alec ear to be heard. "My master said that King Edward is none too pleased with how much money and resources he's poured into fighting the rebels. He's putting a lot of pressure on the great men to see it ended, and quick."

Alec didn't even try and hide his interest. "Your master told you this?"

Bram's face colored slightly and shrugged. "Not exactly. I...I was waiting outside the tent in case he needed me. They were all arguing and shouting and, well...it was hard *not* to hear them."

"What else did he say?"

Bram's mouth puckered as he thought, looking down his nose at the weapon in his hands. "Let's see. Lord Lundie bid the council tae let him take a portion of the calvary upriver to outflank the rebels, but Cressingham thought it a waste of resources."

"Why would that be a waste of resources?" asked Alec, thinking it would be a smart strategy. Indeed, it would put them in a difficult position were Surrey to follow through.

Bram shrugged. "Some were for it, some against, but in the end it was determined that the bridge would be the quickest and surest way to victory."

Alec returned his eyes to the blade he was to be sharpening, his brows furrowed in thought. "Do ye think it will happen soon, then?" he asked, sounding timid. "Should my mam and I take our leave soon?"

*Abbey Craig*

All speech ended abruptly as two friars entered their midst, their shoulders steaming from the cold rain in the heated confines of the tent.

The stout friar bowed, his nervous disposition evident in his small, shifting eyes that never seemed to settle on one place. The taller of the two—clearly the man in charge to Ewan's way of thinking—did not bow from the waist as his companion. Instead, he inclined his head slightly, waiting with a blank expression to be acknowledged as an emissary from the English.

Wallace's eye twitched as he viewed the two men, his arms crossed. His surly expression seemed to unsettle the fat friar further, for he hastily made the sign of the cross and sidled closer to his companion.

"Lord de Warenne bids us come and command your surrender of these lands in peace," said the taller friar. His bushy eyebrows twitched as he spoke, like little antenna. "He wishes to remind you and many of your noblemen here—who have treasonously gathered—" he continued, his pale eyes roving over the faces in the room as if merely his gaze could compel them, "of their pledge of fealty to the English throne."

"I have sworn no such fealty," grunted Moray. "It is yer King and his Lords de Warenne and Cressingham who trespasses upon my freedoms. If they wish for peace, then let them return to their own lands."

Undeterred, the friar pressed on. "You cannot hope to win," he said boldly. "You stand against the might of the English calvary as well as gathered Welsh and, might I add, your very own countrymen. God will not favor you." He let his voice drop, as one would confiding advice to a friend. "Let this end peacefully."

"We are not here to make peace," said Wallace. His voice held a warning, like a low, rumbling growl of a great wolf before it strikes. "We are here to do battle, to defend ourselves and liberate our kingdom. Hear me now: let them come and we shall prove this to their very beards."

The friar's feathery brows rose slightly, perhaps in disbelief. Ewan couldn't blame him. The force of the English calvary against their smaller infantry would have cowed lesser men. But the men among him were no cowards.

"Your lords have their answers. Go and tell them to make ready for war," said Moray, all but pushing them from the room. They left, the taller of the friars looking disapproving while the fat one looked only relieved to be leaving.

"Cressingham, de Warenne and Surrey have camped across the river for two days now, sending us messages as frequently as a discontented lover," explained Moray. "What does your squire say?" he asked, looking to Ewan.

"Alec heard tale of Lundie's offer to outflank us by crossing the river upstream."

"Did he?" asked Wallace, a look of frank approval on his face. "That's smart."

Sir Richard Lundie, Ewan knew, was a Scot's knight who had pledged fealty to England and, unlike himself, had apparently meant it.

"Sixty horsemen could cross upriver abreast," warned Moray, his eyes roving over the map on the table. "Here," he said, pointing with his middle finger, "or here," he added, his finger sliding farther north along the line denoting the river. "The water isnae so swift in these parts."

"That's good work, Ewan. Tell Alec so," muttered Wallace, rubbing his chin in thought as he viewed the map. "We must plan for it, whatever they decide."

"Aye," agreed Ewan, nodding in thought. "Let us hope that Cressingham's persuasion to reject that plan is heeded," he added, telling them how Edward's appointed treasurer had disliked the suggestion, preferring instead for a direct attack across the bridge.

Moray's eyes seemed to light up, and he pulled the map closer to himself, peering down upon it and muttering to himself. "Quill and ink," he commanded, snapping his fingers impatiently, eyes fixed on the map.

"If what Alec heard is true," said Moray, taking the writing implements from an attendant, "and Cressingham gets his way, then not all hope is lost. There is much that can be done to ensure our victory. How many men do we command between us?" he asked, dipping his quill into the inkpot.

"Between us, three hundred cavalrymen to the English's two thousand," answered Wallace.

"Mmph," grunted Moray, scribbling figures on a bit of parchment. "And infantry?"

"Six thousand among us," grunted Wallace, moving to peer over Moray's shoulder.

"And the English?"

"Scouts believe more than seven thousand," offered Ewan.

"Aye, that is my estimation as well," said Wallace, his mouth pulled into a frown as he puzzled over Moray's drawing of army positions.

"I would think," said Moray, tossing the quill to the side and moving to better show his drawing, "that if Cressingham has his way, then our infantry will have the advantage. The bridge will accommodate no more than two horsemen abreast at a time."

"An effective stopper," muttered Wallace. "We could save the bulk of our calvary for the possibility of outflanking from Lundie, should he be allowed to try."

"Aye, those are my thoughts as well," said Moray, tapping a finger on the table. "Let us hope that we see no more of Surrey's emissaries."

"Aye," agreed Wallace, clapping Moray on the shoulder. "It's time for our swords to speak for us."

The morning came far too soon for Edyth's liking, who had slept fitfully, dreaming once again of the battlefield. This time, however, there was noticeable difference. She had stood in dark stone walls of the abbey on the hill, surrounded by the dead and dying. She knew it was the abbey only because of the silent, obscure nuns that tended beside her.

It had been dark and dank, and the smell of blood had clung to her nostrils as thick as dew on a field of grass. There were no faces that she knew. Only the shadow of rent limb and torn muscle. Only the stench of blood, vomit, and loosed bowels. She had awoken, as always, with her heart beating a wild tattoo within the cage of her ribs and her blood coursing.

Not able to go back to sleep, Edyth had instead carefully extricated herself from the cot she shared with Ewan and fed Cecily in the little chair opposite, covered in Ewan's plaid. Her dream had changed. She'd seen herself *here*, in the midst of the battle or at least in the aftermath, tending to the ailing.

She knew in her very bones that she was meant to stay, but she could not—would not—keep Cecily here in the very heart of the battle. What was she to do? Ewan would balk at her desire to stay. He would demand she leave; he'd take them both away himself. But she could not leave. What if it was Ewan she needed to save? Or Iain? Or Alec?

She waited for the sounds of the waking camp, of a fire being stoked, of the shuffle of feet, and hushed conversation before she returned Cecily to her fur pallet on the floor near the brazier. She'd barely touched Ewan's shoulder and he jerked awake, bounding up as if there were some emergency, but once his eyes registered that it was Edyth, and not some page brining orders, he calmed.

He wiped his sleepy face with his hand. "What's wrong?" he asked. "Didnae ye sleep at all?"

She must have looked sorry, indeed, but she ignored his question. "I'm not leaving."

His shoulders stiffened. "The hell ye are," he rasped, his voice still laced with sleep.

Edyth sat down on the edge of the cot and took his hands. "I dreamt last night, Ewan. I've seen myself here. I'm meant to work in the abbey with the nuns. I...I saw myself here. There is work for me to do. I *must* stay."

Ewan opened his mouth to retort but she cut him off, squeezing his hands. "No, Ewan. You once told me that you would never doubt me again. Honor that promise now."

He stared at her for several seconds, his face betraying his emotions. "I do trust ye, Edie, but this is...this is war."

She wanted to laugh. As if she didn't know. As if she didn't see the grotesque slaughter that lay ahead. But she did not get a chance to speak. He pressed on. "And what of Cecily? Ye would put her life at risk as well as yer own?"

"She will be safe in the abbey with the nuns."

"You would abandon her in the care of the abbey?"

"Abandon!" She did her best to swallow her choler and failed. "I would see her safe, as you wish for me. Why is you leaving us alone in an unknown village not abandonment?"

"Edyth, you are her mother—"

"Yes, and you are her father! And you are my husband!" She forced her voice lower, glancing to the spot where the baby slept. "You expect me to leave you, when I've seen that my place is here?" She shook her head. "No, Ewan. Do not break your promise to me."

Ewan ran a hand through his disheveled hair, swearing softly under his breath. "Aye, but this is madness."

"Cecily and I will be safe in the abbey. Far more so than in a village, for none would lay waste to such a place."

Ewan knew she was right. She could see his reluctant acceptance in the fall of his shoulders. After a long moment, with Ewan's stern mouth pressed tightly into a frown, he said, "Ye'll no leave the grounds, Edie. D'ye hear? Not one foot o'er the threshold."

The next day Ewan had been fully engaged in his duties, usually holed away in the great tent with Wallace and Moray, making plans, but still no fighting had started. Edyth hadn't seen him all day and so she was relieved when he entered their tent at last.

"I didn't mean to wake you," he whispered, pausing in undressing to kiss her brow.

She smiled up at him, catching his fingers briefly before he pulled away to finish unbuckling his boots.

She watched him disrobe in the low light the fire afforded through the walls of their tent, painting his body in dancing, flickering shadows.

"Wallace and Moray are pleased with Alec's work," he whispered, sliding into the furs with a slight shiver. "You were right to suggest it."

His body was cool from the night air, but she welcomed the stark contrast of their temperatures, pressing herself against him. He wrapped his arms around her, and she breathed in the scent of him. Fire and leather, sweat and green fields.

"I'm not a man afraid to say when I'm wrong," Ewan said, the low thrum of his voice making her blood sing.

"Oh? "she prodded, pulling him into a kiss.

He smiled against her mouth as her hand found his backside.

"What is it you're wrong about this time?" she asked.

He returned her kiss and ran a hand up her leg, drawing her chemise with the path of his hand. "As much as I dislike ye coming here, I was wrong to suggest you should have stayed in Balgowan," he muttered, punctuating his statement with a kiss to her neck.

"That was a suggestion?" she asked, half laughing.

Ewan paused in his ministrations, his shadowed face looming over hers. She could see his eyes, intent and full of love in the dim. She could feel his heart beating against her own breast. "I am a coward, Edie," he whispered, sobering quickly. "I could not bear any harm coming to you, but likewise, I cannot abide being parted from you."

Edyth kissed his chin, his mouth, speaking a language that needed no words.

He pulled away slightly, his eyes dark and solemn. "I commanded ye tae live...before, when I left ye in Balgowan. Ye and the babe, both, for ye wouldnae give me such a promise. But I ask ye now, Edie. Promise me ye'll be safe."

Edyth, knowing what lived in his heart held his face in her hands. "I will do as you ask," she said, unable to vow more.

"I knew that I had to leave ye then," he continued, his dark eyes intent, "it tore at me; I've thought of little else since. Even so I was angry at seeing ye follow me here, into Stirling." Ewan paused, a hand stroking her hair, searching for words. "I cannae abide the thought of ye in danger, but I am glad ye've come, for yer presence is a comfort to me. If this should be our last, then I am grateful for it."

Edyth could not promise her safety no more than he could promise his own. There were no guarantees, no matter how earnest their wishes, so she did only what she could. She breathed him in and joined with him, praying it would not be the last.

"My heart has grown soft in your care," whispered Ewan sometime later. "I cannae say...I dinnae ken how I could live, should ye be taken from me."

Edyth placed a hand over his heart, beating so sure. "And you think it would be so easy for me? You told me once that it was half your heart I held within my breast. If I have half of yours, then surely you have the whole of mine."

The morning came swiftly. Edyth had slept only a little, and what sleep that had come had been punctuated with dreams that she could not recall in detail. She could only remember the feel of them, heavy and clinging, imprinted upon her like a stain.

Ewan was dressing for battle; she could hear the sounds of metal chiming and their soft speech as Alec prepared his lord in the next tent over. Despite being exhausted, Edyth rose with an anxious energy and dressed herself in the cool predawn, a perpetual prayer in her heart. *Lord, keep him safe. Return him to me.*

While she hadn't *seen* Ewan fall, it didn't mean it wouldn't happen. She did not need dreams to envision such horrors.

The village of tents surrounding Abbey Craig were like stiff, white waves on the Firth, foaming and plentiful, but they were nothing compared to the numbers below the hill. She could see them, winking at her from across the river in the dark. *Not waves. Teeth*, she thought. *A great maw of teeth waiting to spring closed and devour us all.*

Edyth shook herself and pulled the plaid more tightly around her shoulders, thinking of Cecily. They must survive this, she and Ewan together. They must survive for her.

She coaxed the blackened, smoking coals outside their dwelling into life once more and fed it, watching the flames lick to life. Cait had told her that some cunning folk could read flames as one might read the sky for rain, but Edyth saw nothing. Warnings, so far, had only come to her in dreams, unbidden and usually terrifying.

She turned from her brewing tea at the approach of a jangling Ewan, laden down with pounds of thick, burdensome chainmail. He looked different with it on. Changed. "It will be today," he said simply. She could feel his constrained emotion held in check on a short leash. She reached a blue-white hand to touch his own, drawing his eyes. He didn't have his head covered yet, so the violent curl of his hair blew in the wind. He hid his feelings from her and she did not press him. She knew what he felt, for she felt it too.

Alec was close behind him, searching for food, no doubt.

"I'm brewing tea now," she said in way of greeting. "It will calm your nerves."

Alec's mouth tightened and he nodded. He could not hide his feelings as well as his master could. He was not so inexperienced as to have that youthful exuberance for war, where one who had never seen such destruction was blind to the possibility of loss. He had been in the thick of it in France, where master and squire had saved each other's lives.

Iain joined them, nodding his greeting. There was little to say and much to think on.

"What news?" croaked Iain, breaking the silence. He cleared his throat and took a sip. His eyes darted to Edyth, a question written there. *Have you seen what is to come?*

She shook her head and looked away, wishing she had something more to offer them than tea.

Moray's squire ran through their camp just then, his eyes alight and his breath short. "Make haste," he called, excited. "Assemble yourselves on the field! The time has come!"

The boy was gone, just as quickly as he had arrived, like a summer gale, to stir up the remainder of the clans.

Alec dropped his cup, all color draining from his face. Offering a quick apology, he darted to their supply tent, Ewan following in his wake.

It didn't take long to complete his ensemble. Only ten minutes later he was walking toward the fire and toward Edyth. He clinked and chinked as he moved, the weight of his armor seeming nothing, but when he stood before her, perhaps for the last time, the window to his thoughts were shuttered closed.

"Give me your blessing, *boireannach glic*." he said, his voice strong, hiding any fears he may have.

Edyth stuttered, her mind reeling, but she nodded and swallowed with difficulty.

Ewan knelt before her, his curling mass of hair hidden under chainmail. She wished she could touch it now, to run her fingers through it once more but pushed the thought aside just as quickly as it surfaced in her mind.

She placed a trembling hand on his crown and closed her eyes, searching for the words. "Oh God," she started, her voice wavering only slightly, "who grants strength and constancy, I beseech Thee to preserve, this, Thy servant, who has a sincere and faithful heart unto d-death. Amen."

When she opened her eyes and withdrew her trembling hand, she saw a line forming behind her husband. Iain, Rory, Johnne, even Alec...they all wanted her blessing. She fought the tide of emotion that rose within her and beckoned Iain forward, her eyes prickling painfully as she placed her hands upon his head.

When the war drums started, beating a slow tattoo that reverberated through the trees, the men began to disperse. But before her men, Ewan, Iain and Alec left, their swords sheathed and their eyes distant, they drew close to her.

Ewan's mouth was a hard line as he gazed at her, his eyes speaking words that made her heart flutter and tear with emotion. Tears threatened, pricking at the backs of her eyes but she forced them away, swallowing hard. She would not cry now, as he left her. She would have his last image of her be one of courage. A courage she did not feel.

Ewan's gauntleted hand touched the side of her face, cold and unfeeling, the worn leather on the palms soft against her heated skin. "*Tillidh mi thugad, a ghaoil, mo chridhe. Na cuir teagamh ann,*" he said softly. *I will return to you, my love, my heart. Do not doubt it.*

Edyth closed her eyes lest the building emotion spill from her eyes and pressed her cheek more firmly to his palm. She turned and kissed his covered hand, inhaling his scent.

When she felt she could speak, she said, "I will hold you to it, beloved."

He leaned in and kissed her, full of love and suppressed emotion. It was quick, but felt too much like a goodbye so, when he pulled away, she had to repress the urge to cling to him, to fall to pieces at his feet.

Iain filled her view then, Ewan having stepped away to don his helm. So focused on her husband, she didn't realize Iain's blackened fingers, covered in charcoal from the fire, as he brought them to her face, marking her.

"In days of old," he said, the low timbre of his voice vibrating in her chest as he ran two fingers across her eyes, "warriors painted their bodies with woad. They covered themselves with symbols of protection and with the promise of blood." He ran the fingers of his other hand down the side of her face, a wide band of black that ran from her temple to her jaw. "While you will not stand on the field with us this day, you are our equal. You are a warrior, *piuthar*. Do no' forget it." He leaned in and kissed her cheek, coloring his lips grey.

She pressed his hands, sniffing, her eyes filled with tears that she begged away. "Be well, Iain. Be safe."

Iain smiled softly at her words, his eyes filling with affection. It was an idiotic thing to say, she knew. How could he be safe? He was leaving to hack and cleave his way through a mass of men, the number of which far exceeded their own.

Alec was last. His wan face full of determination and conviction, determined not to show weakness. Resolved to his fate, whatever it might be, she knew he only wished to do his master's bidding. To prove faithful once again. He bowed over her cold hand and kissed her fingers. "My Lady," he muttered. His voice had grown deeper these last months. His long, muscled frame had yet to fully fill out. The roundness of his face was a testament to just how young he still was.

He looked away, uncertain, and she squeezed his hand, urging him to speak. He did. "It is an honor to fight for such a lady," he said. Edyth wanted to say that he wasn't fighting for *her*, but for Scotland, but she held her tongue. To him, to such a boy—a squire who followed his lord almost worshipfully—to Alec, he was fighting for her. He was fighting so that his master would return to them, hale and in once piece. He was fighting so Edyth and Cecily could live free.

"Be well," said Edyth, wishing there were better words. "Stay near to him as well as you can, Alec." A sadness overcame her, a flash of some despondency that was more than nerves. She clutched tighter to his fingers, worry filling her heart.

Alec registered her sudden feelings and nodded. "Please, if ye would, mistress, tell Ceana—" He licked dry lips, his eyes straying from her face as if embarrassed. "Tell her that I will build us home amongst the heather, when my lord sees fit tae bequeath the lands tae me."

Edyth wanted to clutch him to her breast, so tender were her feelings for the squire but she only squeezed his shoulder and said, "You will tell her yourself. When this is done, we'll return to Perthshire and you can tell her yourself."

Alec's eyes searched her face, his mouth slightly agape as if there were words keeping it open, filling his mouth. But his lips closed after a moment, his eyes shuttered, and he bowed away from her. "As ye wish, my lady."

"It's time," announced Ewan. "We've tarried too long as it is. My men are in need o' me. Come," he said to Iain and Alec as he turned to the paddock where their horses waited. "Go to the abbey, Edyth," commanded Ewan. "Do no' tarry here."

She nodded, her heart in her throat and watched as they disappeared through the trees to where his men awaited him.

Waiting was the worst part of it. Complete torture. And it was made worse by being a witness to the achingly slow-moving machine of a vast army. She watched from atop the abbey's wall as the English calvary mounted in neat rows and columns, their thorn-like lances and pikes pointing skyward, waiting for the call to begin. Cecily was held tightly in her arms, her mouth slack with sleep.

The Scottish army was smaller, missing many of the great men one usually saw on a battlefield, but not because Scottish noblemen did not align themselves with Wallace and Moray. No, the majority of them were now being held against their will in England, captured at the battle of Dunbar and made to be punished.

*Imprisonment is better than death*, she told herself. It had been her doing, so many months ago, that had saved their lives. She had seen the slaughter that was to come in a dream and had acted, changing everyone's fortunes. But there was no dream foretelling Ewan's death this time. Only that they must come.

There was movement starting now, along the wide flood plain of the River Forth, where the English pushed a two-person column along the dirt road to the mouth of the wooden bridge spanning it. Only wide enough to allow two horsemen side by side at a time, Edyth watched, barely breathing, as the English calvary started to cross. The thundering of so many hoofbeats reverberated up the sloping hillside to where she stood, her heart in her throat.

She watched as the English who had crossed the bridge reassembled themselves in the sandy loop of the river. More poured forth, filling the space as the whine of the bagpipe wound up, carried to her on the wind.

Then the drums started, beating a slow and steady pace. Something in her ribs threaded and knotted tightly, making it difficult for her to draw breath. She placed a trembling hand over her heart, as though she could ease the tightness therein, but knew only seeing Ewan and his men hale at the end of this could ease that ache.

"Please, Milady," said the soft, plaintive voice of a nun from behind. Edyth started at the intrusion and turned, unblinking, to the hand beckoning her into the safety of the abbey. The woman's lips rolled together in worry at Edyth's negation, but she did not linger and left her alone in her deathwatch.

Edyth could not force herself to retreat behind darkened walls of the abbey, even knowing it was what Ewan would demand of her. How could she? Witnessing such hell seemed the only support she could offer and the only way in which she could take part. Perhaps they could feel her eyes, even now, willing them strength.

*Please*, she prayed. *Do not let him fall*. She knew that if he did, she would never recover.

# Chapter Thirty-Two

The war drums matched Ewan's heartbeat, reverberating through him. His blood stirred, pulsing through him at a fever pitch. Even as his body ached to move, to surge forward, sword in hand, and plant it, to divide bone from sinew, his wame curdled, nauseated. He would be a fool not to fear the coming tide of bloodshed, for with dread came a careful alertness that gave purpose to his sword strokes. Fear kept him in possession of himself. He welcomed both feelings like old friends, two sides to the same coin that came with battle.

He squeezed his hands into fists, the leather of his gauntlets protesting tightly across the expanse of knuckles. Even the beast between his legs pawed the ground, no doubt equally affected by the energy permeating the very air. They breathed it in, all, giddy, sick, fearful for the fight. Ewan absently patted the horse's neck, his eyes drawn to the man to whom he had treasonously aligned himself. Wallace rode in front of the gathered army on the marshy upland from the river, his back straight as a lance. His eyes piercing souls.

"This day, brothers!" he shouted over the noise of pipe and drum, his horse canting to one side. "This is the day we stand together as free men. We are outnumbered in body, but never in heart, for we are *Scotsmen* and we shall die as free men!" He pulled his sword from his back, his heavily muscled forearms flexing taught with the weight of it. He held it over his head with one arm, his gaze half mad with the fury of injustice forced upon them. "We choose to die free, rather than suffer to live under any other name. *For Scotia!*" He screamed, his heels urging his beast forward. As the horse ran, he stretched forth his sword to touch pike and halberd, sword and mace.

A cry erupted from the men around him, vibrating through Ewan's body with such force that he felt it sing in his bones. He raised his own sword, thinking of another battlefield in faraway France. He rotated his shoulder, more out of habit than out of pain.

"You will wait until the pipes sound your advance," cried Wallace, his sword now at his side. Still his horse moved, restless. Back and forth, back and forth. "And then you will unleash hell upon them, these men who would rule you!"

The pipes ceased then, but the drums continued, their cadence increasing feverishly. "Upon the pipes, brothers, claim your lives! Claim your freedom!"

There were at least a thousand or more of the enemy gathered there, in the sandy nook nearest the bridge. Ewan watched, his mouth dry and his fingers itching as a force of men—calvary—broke free from their ranks on the opposite side of the river to cross.

Ewan looked to Alec on his right, whose face was white beneath his helm. He held the Ruthven coat of arms aloft, red and black. Two rams in battle. "Here is our duty," Ewan said, motioning with a jerk of his chin toward the line of calvary entering the Firth.

Alec nodded but did not speak. Ewan doubted the lad could speak even had he wanted to. "You have proven your worth already to me, Alec," said Ewan, watching the young man's throat flex as he swallowed in nervousness. "You are as brave as any man and I owe ye my life for your service tae me. Stay close tae me now and let us pray ye'll have no need tae do so again."

There came a sound of quiet, honored acknowledgement from Alec and then he waved the banner, his eyes bright and full of barely concealed fear. The sight of it moved Ewan better than any rousing speech.

Once Ewan's men were signaled to ready themselves, he tightened the bracers on his arms with his teeth, his visor open to better observe his men. "Prove here this day your skill and bravery, and tomorrow I will call you Sir Alec."

Alec's shoulders straightened, looking pleased yet determined. "I will no' fail you, Laird."

Ewan only nodded and looked down the line, at his retainers who sat grim faced, eyes narrowed across the expanse of moorland that sloped toward the winding river. At the enemy. At Scotsman and Englishman alike.

The pipes droned into life, signaling the archers behind them. Ewan's heartrate increased tenfold. Arrows were nocked, bows angled toward the sky, arms strained against the pull of the bowstring, then the pipes ceased.

There was a desperate moment of silence, as if the world held its breath, and then the whoosh of hundreds of arrows filled his ears.

A war cry sounded and the line of calvary moved forward, Alec waving the banner high above them.

"Sons of Perth! Come and sink your swords into tyrants!" cried Ewan, urging his horse faster. His men followed him, the hooves of their steeds thundering and quaking the ground.

The two hundred or so English that had crossed were trapped up against the bend of river and the water too wide and too deep to retreat. A poor choice, to cross here, but all the better for them. Their leaders screamed commands to keep their feet and be unmoved, even so Ewan saw some men falter.

It is a great test of will, to stand rooted in place when hell is unleashed upon you; Ewan knew the feeling well, but he could not give place to those thoughts as he barreled toward the advancing adversary.

His war cry ripped from his throat, burning with the force of it, as he lifted his sword, eyes narrowing on his prey. He ignored the evident dread in some of the eyes of their front lines, ignored the rank perfume of sweat and fear as he lowered the visor on his helm and took aim.

The collision of their swords was merciless. The opposing man's sword arm was strong, but Ewan had the advantage of speed, and he knocked the weapon from his hands with the force of his blow. Ewan's horse cried and reared at the man's counterattack, but he kept his seat, planting his sword neatly into the weak junction of shoulder and neck. The man fell in a heap onto the pebbled ground. He might have cried out, but Ewan could not hear him for the sound of his own breathing within his helm, his heart beating a staccato in his ears.

Ewan drove forward into the line of awaiting enemy calvary, cutting through helm and bone with powerful swipes of his sword. His horse turned at the slightest of directives from his thighs and heels, helping him both avoid and dole out blows. His horse kicked its back legs, connecting with something Ewan did not have the capacity to take notice of.

The movement jarred him, however, making him miss his intended target: a man with a jessed falcon upon his surcoat, a great grey plume of feathers swaying from the dome of his helm. Ewan leaned heavily backward and to the right, narrowly avoiding getting a blade through his visor. Thankfully he was able to right himself fast enough to counterattack.

His sword arm was growing weary, the muscles straining, aching, but he could not falter. Suddenly his horse screamed and missed a step. It took several desperate seconds for Ewan to realize that its armor had been pierced by a crossbow bolt. It canted heavily to the side, tripped, then fell. Ewan tumbled from the saddle, using all his strength to roll away from the great beast, lest he be crushed by it. *Up, up,* he commanded himself, feeling stunned but unwilling to wait for the barest of seconds lest he be impaled, or stepped on by a horse.

He regretted the loss of his beast. He also lost his helm and already a man was upon him, long sword in full swing. Ewan ducked, the woosh of the heavy blade cutting through the air so terrifying close his bowels turned to water.

Ewan had been using his short sword, easier to handle atop his horse. But to fight this man and win, he needed to pull the great sword from his back. Ewan jumped away from the long reach of the sword as it cut toward his middle. His chainmail could protect him from most blows, but the tapered edge of the blade and weight of it was capable of piercing through.

Dropping his short sword—he would have to pick it back up once he dispatched this man—he pulled the heavier, longer great sword from his back and set his feet just in time for the next blow. The force of the swing sang in his bones. His fingers and wrists ached fiercely, but he gritted his teeth and absorbed the shock, quickly resetting his feet.

He'd aimed for the weakest part of the armor where neck met shoulder, but the man raised his arm, shying away; Ewan's sword merely glanced off, but the blow made the man stagger backward.

Ewan took advantage of the loss of balance and pressed forward, sword clashing, and pushed with all his might. The man fell heavily atop a prone soldier, his helm falling off and rolling in the muddy, blood-soaked earth. Ewan met the man's eyes, which widened with alarm and with the acknowledgement of his imminent death.

Ewan changed the grip on his great sword, allowing the tip to fall toward the ground, toward the man's heart, which lay beneath chainmail and gambeson, beating as sure and fast as a bird's wing. He did not look away as he thrust downward with all his strength, piercing through layers of would-be protection. He kept the man's gaze, for he would wish the same. I acknowledge your sacrifice, it said. And I honor you with a warrior's death.

He did not have time to gather his wits, for as soon as he pulled the blade free, he was knocked sideways by a grappling pair. A mace hitting home splattered blood and brains across his face. He nearly lost what little was in his stomach, but he gritted his teeth, his breathing fast, and found his short sword.

His shoulder was in agony. The tendons popped and ached, but he could not falter here, where minds were numbed to butchery. His own mind was dulled, his body moving as if in a well-rehearsed dance, automatic and emotionless. It had to be this way. The alternative was to go mad. Some men did. Their own souls lost and sick with killing.

Iain's face was wet with sweat and splattered blood. He jerked his sword free of armor and bone and reset himself just in time for a coming blow. He'd lost his horse to a pike, and a damn shame too, but at least he was unharmed. He'd lost count of how many men his sword had claimed; it was better this way. At this point, he did not wish to know.

At least two more, he promised. This man now grappling with him and then Cressingham. He'd spotted the bastard not but a minute ago but had been waylaid with the current inconvenience now swinging a sword at him.

But Iain would find his quarry again and he would fulfill his promise to Alice. Of that he was sure. He pushed the man in front of him with a grunt, whose sword was locked with his, nearly losing his own footing in the churned field. It smelt of blood and the pungency of loosed bowels. He would hate to die in such a place.

Iain pursued his attacker, who had tripped over a fallen comrade in his haste to find his balance after Iain's shove. Iain, long past feeling, did not falter in his strike. His sword found the man's neck with such speed that his helm flew off; it rolled a few feet and settled against the side of a dead man, covered in so much mud that Iain could not discern to which side he belonged.

He paused, surveying the landscape, his chest heaving and his bowels griping, looking—praying—to find Cressingham's ensign. There. There he was, still atop his steed, the mud and blood on his great surcoat not enough to completely hide the three black swans adorning it.

Iain staggered toward him, his sword dragging, bumping over fallen men and debris, his eyes locked on his target. Cressingham was standing in his stirrups, leaning forward to drive his sword into a nearby Scotsman presently fighting with another.

"Cressingham!" shouted Iain, his throat tearing with the force of his shout. "*Thig, blais mo chlaidheamh!*" *Come taste my sword.*

He'd heard him. Their eyes locked across the field of broken and fighting men, only fifty yards away. Hugh Cressingham smiled or grimaced; it was impossible to tell. The man's helm covered most of his face, but it did not matter. Iain would shove his sword through his teeth and then it would not matter if he smiled or sneered.

Hugh's horse picked up speed as the man leaned forward to pluck a broken pike sticking out of the mud. The thunder of the beast's footfalls went through Iain, but Iain did not move his feet. He planted them in the churned earth and prayed. "Dinnae make me a liar." He'd promised his wife.

Cressingham was naught but seconds away, but the horse faltered, its right foreleg catching on a fallen soldier. Hugh rolled forward but kept his seat, the pike dipping toward the ground and missing Iain by an inch; he rolled his shoulder away from the pike and the horse and swung his sword as hard as he could at the passing man.

The clang of Iain's sword hitting Cressingham's plate armor rang in his ears. The blow hadn't been deadly, but it had been forceful enough to unseat him at the very least. He fell face-first into the muck, one shoulder plowing through the wet ground with a loud clang of plate armor. The horse blew and ran away, its tail high and its eyes rolling.

"Ruthven is it?" asked Cressingham, righting himself quickly and spitting muck out of his mouth. His helm and exposed flesh was painted with filth, one side of his visor stuffed with black turf. Hugh removed his helm, exposing black, sweat-drenched hair matted to his skull. "I'll be sure to include your name in my report to the king."

Iain smiled with far too many teeth. "We shall see. Come," Iain commanded, "and meet yer undoing."

Cressingham hissed through his teeth, a quick intake a breath and a shrug. He rolled his shoulder and lifted his sword.

Iain did not wait. He attacked with such force it surprised even him. He was tired; his sword arm near to being finished, but he had the strength for this. His blow was blocked solidly, however, making Iain's bones judder with righteous agony. His muscles quivered but he stepped into the parry, his teeth bared in a grimace.

Cressingham stepped back, too smart to be caught in such a game of wills and reset himself. "Such eagerness," chided Hugh. "Take heed, man. It will make it easier for me to kill you."

Iain raised his sword, ignoring the taunt. "It is not for my own purpose that I take your life, but in the name o' my wife, Lady Alice Stewart."

Recognition lighted upon Cressingham's face. "Ah, so it *was* a wedding feast. I should have known better than take the word of that scut, Robert. Are all Scotsmen such liars?"

Iain smiled and gripped the hilt of his sword more tightly, the muscles in his forearm bunched and tense. "We only lie tae the de'il. And the English." Done with talking, Iain charged, a war cry ripping from this throat.

Hugh's eyes widened in involuntary fear. Iain swung his sword into the man's collar; felt the bone give way, felt muscle rend and tear. Blood sputtered from Hugh's open mouth; his eyes fixed resolutely upon Iain. Hugh's hands grappled for purchase, pulling on Iain's shoulders in an attempt to stay upright.

"The dead are avenged," said Iain into the air. He did not know if Alexander could hear him, but he knew that, somehow, the man would know and be now at peace.

Cressingham's eyes lost their focus as the light left them. He slumped to the ground, Iain's sword coming away with only a slight tug. He let it dangle toward the ground, his arm spent. It was done. He'd fulfilled his promise to Alice. It was done.

He wanted to sink into the mud and muck but he forced his feet forward. It would be easy to be overcome by the steely clangs of swords and the cries of battle all around him, to succumb to the desire to walk from the field with his life, but he could not. Honor was not won in such a way. So it was with great effort that Iain hefted his weapon and met the next soldier.

Ewan hacked his way to the water, faltering over fallen men. He watched dazedly as some of the English, choosing to risk the water rather than be slaughtered, drown under the weight of their armor. Cries echoed around him, chaos reigned as he slashed and pushed and cut down men.

One cannot account for the passage of time in battle, so Ewan did not know how long he had been fighting, but quite suddenly, his sword met no more resistance.

He turned then, surprised that his sword was not met with enemy steel. Bodies were heaped upon the beach and floating in the water, the bridge stoppered with the fallen, pierced through with arrows, bodies split open. Somewhere, seemingly far away, a horn sounded retreat. A horse trotted by, blowing and shaking it great head.

Ewan's eyes turned from the water's edge to the sloping hillside he'd fought his way down, searching for his scattered men amidst the churning bodies still on the slope. He looked for his standard, but he could not see it. Frantic, his eyes searched again, touching briefly upon pike and shield, upon helm and body, but it was nowhere to be found. What's more, he could not see Alec.

Terror seized him. It was easy enough to be separated on a battlefield. The focus one must have amid the chaos is paramount, yet Ewan felt sick with sudden worry. He'd told Alec to remain near him, yet he'd been so distracted with keeping his own head that he'd failed to keep an eye on his squire.

Ewan called Alec's name. Who would dare pause to hear, to help? It was madness, the battlefield. Perhaps Alec was simply temporarily out of sight. Well and alive, but only hidden from his view.

He called Alec's name again, his eyes searching for the familiar helm, his recognizable surcoat. For one heart-stopping moment, Ewan thought he saw him, the back of his dark head caved in by a mace, but when he turned the body over, he saw that he did not know the man.

He scrambled over bodies, both living and dead, passed fallen horses and broken weapons, turning bodies over, dismissing them. After he had moved halfway up the slope, he recognized the Ruthven flag, draped over bodies, the pole broken by some foreign blade.

He moved swiftly, avoiding blows and stumbling men, pushing any from his path with a ferocity borne of panic. He passed his brother, who was presently running his sword through someone, but Ewan only had eyes for the body half concealed under the Ruthven ensign. He was lying quite still, but hunched as if in pain, an arm thrown over his middle. Alec.

Ewan fell to his knees at Alec's side and pulled off the lad's helm. He was alive at least, his pained eyes meeting Ewan's in a daze. "Can ye stand, man?" asked Ewan searching with his eyes for sign of injury. All was hidden from him, save for the creeping blood staining the white surcoat under Alec's arm. Ewan reached for Alec's wrist and tried to lift his arm, but Alec resisted, grunting in panicked refusal.

"Let me see, lad. Let me help." Alec, either too tired to resist or unwilling, even now, to disobey his lord, relented and Ewan lifted his arm, exposing the grisly gash across this abdomen. Ewan stared, breathless for a heartbeat, then sprang into action.

Ripping the Ruthven ensign from the end of the fallen pike, Ewan wrapped it tightly around his squire's middle, ignoring his mewling gasp, and tying it tightly to staunch the flow of blood. "Yer Mistress will see ye well again, Alec," vowed Ewan, readying himself for lifting Alec bodily, but he quickly realized that his course of action would take up too much precious time.

Carrying him to the abbey where Edyth waited would take too long and be far too painful for him. Ewan scanned his immediate surroundings and spotted a riderless horse, trotting toward them with wild, frightened eyes. Licking his lips, Ewan made for the horse, only slowing when he got near enough so as not to scare it off.

With luck, he was able to grab the horse's reins with little trouble, speaking softly and stroking its nose. He pulled it toward Alec, stepping over fallen bodies, and then knelt at his squire's side. "Ye mun get atop the horse, lad. Do ye hear?"

But Alec shook his head weakly, his eyes fluttering closed. Ewan grasped Alec's shoulder and shook him, hard. "Dinnae ye sleep. Ye stay with me, lad."

Ewan pulled the horse closer, calling for his brother, a desperate sound even to his own ears. "Iain, *dhomhsa! Iain!*" There weren't many fighting now, only a few left from the English side still living. Ewan scanned the group of men and spotted his brother once more. He waved his arms, catching his brother's attention. He must have seen the panic written on Ewan's face, for Iain immediately moved in his direction, shouting at people to move aside.

Ewan turned back to Alec, whose eyes were closed. Panic raced through his veins, choking him. "No, Alec. Ye willnae sleep now, laddie. I forbid it! Do y'hear? Alec!"

To his relief, Alec's eyes roved under his eyelids, his lashes trembling with the effort it took to open them. "I'm weary, *maighstir*. Let me sleep."

"Nay, Alec. I'm taking ye tae yer mistress. Dinnae close yer eyes, man."

Iain was there, then, and helped to drape a weak Alec over Ewan's acquired horse, but in his eyes, Ewan saw his brother's disbelief. The white field of the ensign wrapped around Alec's middle was quickly changing to crimson. It didn't matter that Iain doubted that the boy could live; Iain did not know his wife as he did. Iain did not know what desperate hope lived within his breast that Alec would survive. He *must* live. Such hope would see him through. God would not let the lad fall.

*Abbey Craig*

The dead and dying were lined up along the dimly lit walls of the abbey's cloister, the soft voiced comforts of the nuns drowned out amid the cries for water, for bandages, for a hand to hold as the soldier's bodies failed them. They'd been brought steadily in after the English's signal for retreat. Edyth did her best not to feel overwhelmed by the sheer volume of those needing attention, setting her mind to the task. One by one while a nun cared for Cecily in a far off chamber.

Edyth was holding one such hand, marred with blood and vomit, smoothing back dark curls from a pale forehead. It wouldn't be long now; the youthful body was draining of its strength between each shallow breath. She'd done her best to staunch his wound, a gaping slash the length of her forearm along his left thigh, but his eyes were glazing, the warmth leaving his skin as quickly as her own breath left her breast.

"Tell me your name," she said, squeezing his cold hand. She watched as he struggled to focus on her face, his hazel eyes dilating irregularly. The torchlight flicked above them, sputtering loud enough to mask his muttered reply. Edyth leaned closer, her ear to his cracked lips. "Again," she prodded. "Tell me your name."

"Ed—gar."

"A strong name," she said against his ear, to ensure that he would hear her, but when she opened her mouth to ask him about his home, or his family, or some other distracting subject, she felt rather than saw that his chest failed to rise.

She looked to his face, her own chest unmoving as she held her breath, and she saw that where there had been life in his eyes, there was now only a vacant stare. She did not know him, but she mourned for him all the same. In him, she saw her father's empty eyes, as he laid upon the scrubbed wooden table of the cold storage room of her childhood home.

She saw in him her fear. He could be Ewan. Or Iain. Or any of the men she so loved.

Despite her experience with death, and of her express knowledge that life did not end when the body failed, sorrow tugged at her heart, insistent and unrelenting. She placed his hands atop his abdomen and moved to the next man, propped up against the wall only a few steps away, his head bleeding freely.

Head wounds always looked especially grievous for the amount of blood they produced, but she knew it must be serious if he were here, in the abbey, and not lined up outside or being pulled to camp by his comrades, where they would all stoically drink away their pain. She knelt next to the man, touching his shoulder lightly as she surveyed the damage. He was missing an ear and had a rather deep gash in the muscle where shoulder met neck, but he was otherwise unhurt, from what she could see.

She stood, searching her pocket for the roll of linen she had stuffed there, when a cry stilled her. The room was full of pained shouts, so many, in fact, that they had begun to be as the buzzing of bees, indistinct and unobtrusive, but this cry sent a bolt of icy fear into her heart.

"*Dhòmhsa, Edyth!*"

Never had she heard such a sound come from her husband. Not in all the time she had known him. Was it pain or fear that fueled his bellowing?

"Edyth! Where are ye, lass? *Bring me my wife,*" he barked to some unseen person. "*To me, Edyth!*" The man at her feet forgotten, she rushed toward the door, her heart in her throat. She prepared for the worst in her mind, even as a part of herself reasoned that if he could shout like that, he wasn't too badly hurt. But when she rounded the corner of the hallway and the light of open doors spilled around him, she understood his pain.

Alec was draped in his arms, his armor rent and bloodied. Ewan had lost his helm and his sword at some point, his sweat-drenched curls clinging to his scalp. Ewan's eyes were wild as he struggled to hold his brother in all but blood.

But the boy was no longer the skinny lad he had been even a year ago. He was a now man grown and was slipping from Ewan's battle-weary arms. Ewan fell to his knees and let go of Alec long enough to gesture Edyth forward.

"Save him," Ewan demanded, his voice rich with emotion. "Help him."

Edyth quickly surveyed Alec, seeing the rent surcoat and chainmail, both saturated with blood. Ewan's hand fumbled for the knot holding the blood-soaked cloth he'd tied around Alec and let it fall to the floor wetly. The grisly wound exposed, Edyth felt the color drain from her face. He'd lost far too much blood. What was more, the rent in his abdomen was a promise of death.

Ewan, fingers stained red, put a hand to Alec's pale face. "Hear me," he said. "Wake, Alec."

Edyth could not speak. There was no way to help Alec. There were no herbs that grew upon the earth that could save him from this. No tincture or poultice, no matter how potent, could save Alec now. She shook her head, mute, her eyes stinging. He was still alive. By some miracle, he'd obeyed his lord, his drooping eyelids fluttering open.

*Oh, Alec. Not Alec.* He had so much life ahead of him. So much to look forward to. A wife. A title. A parcel of land on which to raise a family. A life filled with love. It was fading as quickly as the light from his eyes. *Not Alec.*

Hot, sticky fingers wrapped around her wrist. "Edie," pleaded Ewan, his voice breaking. "Why do ye no' save him? Why do ye no' h—help?" The frantic look in his eyes gave way to something else, something that broke Edyth's heart to witness. "Why," he said on a whisper, his eyes dropping to his friend's pale face.

Edyth fell to her knees and, cradling Alec's bloodless face in her hands, leaned in closely and whispered, "You will not be alone, Alec. Life goes on, for I've seen it. You will have a place and be loved."

Alec's glazed eyes turned to Ewan. "Din—dinnae weep, *mo charaid*." His breaths were shallow, his chest barely moving.

A sob escaped Ewan at the words, his face pulled tightly in a rictus of pain. "Never have I had a more worthy friend," said Ewan, squeezing Alec's pale fingers, tears falling unchecked down his face.

Alec's eyes moved from Ewan's face to some unseen place in the middle distance before he closed them and his hand grew heavy with slack. Ewan shook with quiet emotion while Edyth's heart, so raw and tender, broke open anew.

Edyth stood and laid a hand on her husband's damp head, as she had only hours before, her own heart breaking. Tears fell freely from her eyes as she watched her husband mourn. She'd never before seen such emotion from him, though she knew the intensity of his feelings were strong and ran deep.

She touched his stricken face, whispering his name. He let go of Alec and rose to his knees, his arms wrapping around Edyth's middle. He cried against her breast, his great shoulders shaking with the effort to control his suffering.

"He is whole and at peace," she said to his hair. "Come, Ewan, let us wash and care for him. Let us honor him as he deserves and bring him home."

# Chapter Thirty-Three

"Sharpen the shears and make all else ready, but do no' begin as yet. Not until yer master returns," advised Alice to a village shepherd. He'd come to her, saying the men and the beasts had come down from the high places, ready for the shearing season, but she was not familiar enough with the Ruthven's management of the process to command much more.

The bells tolled loudly, interrupting their discourse, her heart flying to her mouth. The villager and Alice both raced to the window, eager to see who had come, but nothing could be discerned from this vantage point. "What means this tolling?" asked Alice.

The shepherd crumpled his hat in his hands. "It means someone has come. Someone friendly, mistress, else there wouldnae be both pealing together."

Alice left him, not bothering to dismiss him or even take her leave. She lifted her skirts high as she maneuvered down the winding steps to the lower level, then ran the distance of the gallery into the great hall, skidding as she rounded the corner toward the great doors.

A servant hastened to open them for her as she neared, the light from the afternoon spilling across the stones. She could hear the portcullis lifting, the heavy chains jangling as men worked the winch. Slowing, she made her way across the bailey to the milling group of men and women crowding the entrance.

Seeing her, they made a place for her, and when she saw who was come, her heart lurched with joy. It was Iain, seated atop is black destrier, sitting straight and hale. Relief loosened the very joints of her body; she felt the invisible weight she'd been carrying for so long lift. He was well. He lived. Where were the rest of them?

She ignored the murmurs of those around her and left the shadowy place under the gate to meet Iain and the line of men following him upon the road.

Upon seeing her, he dismounted a few yards from her, sending dust into the air. She faltered. She'd run out to meet him, in view of all the household, and now did not know what she should do. "I'm glad ye're come home," she said, raising her voice to be heard above the gusting wind.

The veil covering her head caught in the wind and pulled from its pins. It flew away as if it were a bird escaping its cage. Iain knelt before her, his armor chiming, and bowed his dirty head in deference. "I am come home, Alice, and with the news that I have kept my vow. Yer father is avenged...Cressingham died at my hand."

Alice's breath stuttered, her heart feeling as it never had before. She didn't know this emotion. It was foreign to her and so she could not name it, but it was warm and grateful, and so very relieved to hear Iain's voice once more. Little did she care for vengeance. At this moment, all she cared about was that he was here, and that he hadn't taken her into his arms yet.

She knelt before him and took his besmirched face into her hands. His eyelashes were heavy with dust from the road, his wavy hair come loose from its thong. "I worried—" She swallowed her words, remembering that others might hear them, but then pressed onward, forcing her reticence away. "I feared ye'd no' come back tae me, Iain." Her voiced wavered slightly as she spoke.

His grey eyes searched her own for a moment, a fierce determination filling them, before his mouth found hers. His kiss was jubilant and possessive all at once. She kissed him eagerly back her hand going to his shoulders to brace herself lest she fall over.

He pulled away, laughing softly, and helped her to rise with him, a hand on her elbow. "I'm in want of a bath, wife," he informed her unnecessarily. "Will ye no' take me above stairs and see tae my comforts?"

Alice felt the flush of her skin but she nodded, turning and calling out to one of the page boys watching the spectacle. "Bring my lord husband the bath and hot water to fill it. And after, see that our supper is brought to our rooms. I daresay we will not be joining the rest in the hall."

The roads home had been slow and choked with wagons. Iain was gone, having left before Ewan and Edyth, with those of their clan well enough to walk or ride. Edyth had chosen to stay behind and tend to those who were ailing, careful to bind their wounds and make space for them in wagons.

Ewan had helped her wash and wrap Alec, binding his body in a shroud they'd procured from the abbey. Ewan could not bear to leave him behind in Stirling, even with a promised grave in the shadow of the abbey.

Though Alec was not an official knight, Ewan had bade Iain command an elaborate coffin carved for him, complete with his likeness in full armor. Little did it matter to Ewan that he'd yet to take the vows and doff the vestments. Alec was as knightly as any man he knew at heart, and Ewan would make it known to all.

They'd lain Alec, along with their other dead, in the back of a wagon, shoulder to shoulder. All the long way home, the anguish that had filled Ewan's heart and mind doubled and redoubled as he thought of their wives at home, of their children who would grieve their losses for all their days. Death was a steep and weighty price for their freedom.

And now they were home, greeted with both sorrow and joy. Looking at the bodies after their Mass had been said, ready to be laid in the earth upon their own lands, their veiled, unseeing faces upturned toward the watery sun, filled him equal parts pride and anguish. Their families cried around him, some volubly and with great lamentations that stung his eyes. The priest was saying the proper words, sprinkling each man at rest in an open grave with a portion of holy water.

When Father Thale was done, he turned to Ewan, inviting him to speak.

Swallowing his own emotions, he looked at each tearful face. "They dinnae die for glory, nor wealth, nor honor, but for freedom, which no great man surrenders except with his life," he said, his voice gruff with unspent tears. "These great men we praise, who have sacrificed breath and heart and mind, sae that we can live in peace. We vow tae live with their sacrifice fresh in our minds, and live with honor all our days, sae we willnae lose what they, with their deaths, have gained us. We willnae forget. N'er will we forget. *Tha iad a' dol gu Dia le urram sgrìobhte air an anaman.*" *They go to God with honor written upon their souls.*

Lids to their coffins were affixed amid more cries from parent and child alike, punctuating his goodbye with heart-rending weeping. And then the sharp blade of a shovel was thrust into black soil, falling upon their coffins with a sound like rain upon the battlements.

There were others not buried here, others who had been brought home to their families throughout their clan lands with the news that their deaths had not been in vain. The English had been routed. They'd fled back to England, with Wallace and a wounded Moray following after.

Edyth's hand found his, soft and cold, but welcome. He looked at her through clouded eyes, seeing her own sorrow plainly, Cecily held in the crook of an arm. She was beautiful to him in all the ways that mattered;

his heart, so full of grief, somehow still had room to swell with love for her and their daughter.

He bent and kissed her forehead. At last, finally, they were home safe. They were free and had the whole of their lives together.

But they were not done here. Next came Alec, who he could not bring himself to bury in the kirkyard. The squire would be laid to rest in the family's tomb, beneath the kirk, where Ewan hoped he could more easily ease the pain in his heart with visitation. They'd laid him out in the kirk for the vigil and said their prayers, commending him to heaven.

The effigy had been well constructed. Beathan had carved Alec's form and likeness well, with one hand curled tightly around the hilt of a long sword, the pointed tip reaching his feet, and his other arm holding the Ruthven shield with all its heraldry. Beathan had then carefully painted and gilded portions of Alec's likeness, so that he truly seemed in peaceful repose, yet ready for duty at any moment.

Ewan caught Ceana's eye, who was weeping silently, holding tightly against her breast sprigs of heather. The white, purple and pink flowers called to his mind Alec's eagerness to look upon the fields that kissed the mountain's feet as they mustered the Ruthven men. He'd spoken of how he'd planned to make a home there, upon his newly-gifted lands, amongst the bonny heather. The vise around Ewan heart tightened at the remembrance.

A squeeze of his hand from Edyth told him it was time to go into the kirk and walk down the long steps and into the coolness below the earth. To at last lay his beloved squire to rest. He cleared his throat of the knot of emotion that had taken up residence there and nodded to the priest, signaling that he was ready.

Not everyone would attend, but those that knew and loved him best were there. Rory, Graham, Fingal and Iain, among others. Their eyes were rimmed in red just as Ewan knew his were. Together they slid the heavy lid over Alec's shrouded body and fastened it closed.

As one, they hefted the weight of the coffin onto their shoulders and carried him carefully to the tomb's entrance, following slowly in Father Thale's wake.

The burden of carrying Alec down the narrow steps was a welcome penance for Ewan, one he did not fully comprehend. He just knew that doing so, taking the sharp edge of the wood onto his bad shoulder, felt right. As if the pain of this last service rendered to his squire could make up for his not being at his side all through the battle.

The air was stale and heavy under the kirk. The sputtering torchlight made the solemn faces on the effigies come to life. They laid Alec near their great uncle who was laid against the far wall and waited as Father Thale said the words and made the sign of cross. "Here we lay Alec Ban Marshall of Pembrooke, in the hope of peace as he is made ready for heaven."

Ceana stepped forward and placed the bouquet of flowers she'd gathered upon the coffin, her face streaked with tears. Edyth went to her, holding her against her side, speaking softly into her ear.

Ewan and Iain found their father's coffin, each looking down upon his stern face in silence. Ewan's heart swelled with further emotion, wishing for the hundredth time that he could speak to his father in truth.

"It is done," said Iain, his eyes focused on the likeness of their father. "You continued the work he set out to do, Ewan. Ye've kept our lands and our people free."

Ewan had to swallow twice before he could respond. "I hope he is proud...that he approves—"

"He has always been proud of you," said Iain emphatically. He met Ewan's eyes, misted with emotion. "He has always approved of you."

Ewan considered his brother for a moment. "D'ye ken he told me once that I should strive tae adopt your penchant for levity. He said as how I should take more risks, like you, and with a smile upon my face, lest I be too burdened with grief when life took from me what I valued most. He said that life's burdens would ne'r steal awa' yer peace, for ye were resolved to always find happiness, even if ye were condemned tae the dark places of the world."

Iain's surprise showed on his face. "He preached only vigilance and prudence to me." He laughed softly and said, "Looks like ye followed his counsel, bringing home an English bride from the battle of Dunbar and forsaking yer plans tae keep me here while you ventured off tae fight."

Ewan clapped a hand on Iain's shoulder. "I would do well if I endeavored tae be more like you in all ways, brother."

# Epilogue

The kirk was bright in the early morning, shafts of silver light pouring into the cavernous space. Cecily was dressed in white, held tightly in the arms of her uncle, Iain, sucking on a fist. The red down of her hair sparked like embers in the light, drawing Ewan's eye. Just looking at her filled him with such pride.

"Bring the child," instructed Father Thale, a soft smile gracing his features. Iain handed off Cecily to her mother, who smiled brightly into the babe's face before handing her to the priest, who stood behind the baptismal font.

"The water is a sign of life," said Father Thale to the audience at large. "Without water, naught can grow. And so it is, that we wash away the sins o' the parents and impart upon us all the symbol of new life into which we all must enter."

Carefully cradling Cecily's head in one hand, her body laid along his forearm, the priest held her over the font and poured holy water over her head, saying, "I baptize ye, in the name o' the Father, and o' the Son, and o' the Holy Spirit."

Cecily, who didn't care for being doused with cold water, squawked ungraciously, drawing smiles and light laugher from the witnesses. Ewan took Cecily, wiping her head with a cloth, and breathed in the scent of her, indescribably sweet and fresh, despite the slight odor of sour milk. The soft skin of her cheek brushed his nose, his heart full of love.

He turned to the villagers that had come to their christening and lifted Cecily in two hands, careful to cradle her head.

"She's a right bonny lassie," said Roslyn, who had come home at last. Her blue eyes were soft with affection as she gazed into Cecily's face. "She takes after her mam, but I'm proud tae see that she's a fair likeness of you, too. She has yer chin, I think," she said. "And haps a bit o' her temper."

Ewan laughed and handed Cecily to her grandmother. "Aye, she might at that." Cecily had squalled off and on all evening yesterday, which had amused Roslyn. When she'd taken her granddaughter into her arms, Cecily had quietened and had gazed up at Roslyn as if making a study of her.

"We made friends," explained Roslyn, bringing Cecily over to Alice, who, like aways, surveyed the room in quiet.

Iain came and shook Ewan's hand. "Congratulations, brother. Ye'll be sure tae keep me well apprised of my goddaughter."

"Will ye no' stay a bit longer," asked Ewan, though he knew Iain was anxious to get Alice to *Goal Ghlinn Amain*.

Iain shook his head. "Och, I've yet tae bring Alice anywhere but through danger. She's just as eager as I am tae settle into routine and make a home."

Ewan could not help his smile. He well understood the need to move forward, to build a life they dreamt of. For too long they'd been living with one foot in a world of violence and potential danger. "We will come and visit after ye've had a chance tae settle."

Iain slapped his brother on the back in response. "Come, let us celebrate yer daughter. I cannae begin to understand how it is ye're the faither o' that bonny wee lass."

Ewan privately agreed. As he followed the procession down the long aisle of the kirk and out into the sunlight, he couldn't account for the abundance of blessings that had been bestowed upon him. Edyth's hair glinted as brightly as freshly-forged steel in the sun and, with his daughter in her arms, he thought his heart might burst with feeling, so full it was.

Her vibrant green eyes found his, a smile on her lips. "Come, husband. Take us home."

He could not help himself; he bent and kissed her. "Aye. Home."

The End.

# Afterword

While I did my best to stay true to real history, I found that, in the end, I had to take some liberties otherwise this book could be used as a doorstop. Real history tells us that many more events took place (little skirmished here and there) that were spread over a longer period of time.

The English loyalist's meeting in Inverness, for instance, occurred in May of 1297, where, immediately following this event, Fitz Warin was attacked on the road. Fitz Warin was not lord of Castle Dundee, but of Urquhart. Moray did attack Urquhart but was unsuccessful, having no siege engines.

Because I needed my timeline to move a little faster and because I wished to use the Sheriff of Elgin's meeting with the English loyalist in Inverness, I made the choice to change real history to fit my needs.

Real history also tells us that Moray died from wounds he sustained at the battle of Stirling, leaving William Wallace to shoulder the fight against the English alone, so to speak. The Scots were later defeated at the battle of Falkirk, which resulted in Wallace's capture and ultimate death. It was not until 1306 that Robert the Bruce became King of Scotland, winning freedom from English rule.

Ewan's words at the burial ceremony are partially taken from the Bruce: "We fight not for glory, nor for wealth, nor honor, but only and alone for freedom which no good man surrenders but with his life." I found they perfectly fit Ewan's own feelings and were so eloquent that I had to include them.

In an effort to draw this story to a neat close, I left the story as if they won their freedom after the battle of Stirling, which was, in truth, a turning point for the Scots. Winning against the vastly superior English army drew many more nobles to the side of Wallace and Moray. Moray's role in the fight for Scottish freedom is often forgotten in popular culture. I hope this series helps shed light on his efforts and sacrifice.

After the battle of Stirling, Cressingham was flayed and his skin divided amongst the victors as a token of their conquest. It's said that Wallace used his portion to make a belt for his sword, though I'm not entirely sure if this is mere legend or true history.

The remaining English fled back to Berwick thereafter, leaving Stirling isolated. They altogether abandoned the lowlands to the Scots. At least until King Edward defeated William Wallace at Falkirk in 1298.

The song Edyth sings whilst in labor is an old Celtic song that I do not own the rights to. "Ushag veg ruy" as it's called in the language of Manx, is one of the names for "robin". For inquiring minds, Manx is a Gaelic language closely related to both Irish and Scottish Gaelic. This lullaby was collected and translated by Arthur W. Moore in 1896. There are slightly different versions of the song, but I highly recommend you listen to this, my favored version, performed by Meg O'Dell Chittenden. You won't be disappointed. https://www.youtube.com/watch?v=Y-BZEk_8RD4

I hope that, through this series, you were entertained as well as educated on the rich history of Scotland during this time period.

# Acknowledgments

No one can write a book, let alone a trilogy, by themselves. Thanks, of course, must be given to Bryce, my supportive husband. Thank you for cheering me on. Thank you to my sons, who bring me such joy. Thank you to Kristal Winsor who has been there for me through every book idea, plot hole, writing slump and more. Thank you for lending your ear so often. I think with my mouth, much like Alexander Stewart, and Kristal is patient and willing to hear me.

Thank you to my beta readers, Debbie Calderwood, Tresha Beard, and Neil Calderwood, who diligently read and reported all my mistakes. I'm so grateful for you. So, so grateful.

I must also thank my editor, Kelly Horn, who gave this book much needed attention. I appreciate your insight and expertise. Thank you for making me laugh at myself and for your quippy responses to my mistakes.

Last, thank you to my readers. Your response to my work have been a happy surprise and I appreciate every message and comment I get on my social pages.

# About Author

Jalyn C. Wade is an American author who currently lives in northern Virginia with her husband and three sons. Married to a military man, she has had the great opportunity to move often and fall in love with people of all walks of life. Her works merge multiple genres, featuring elements of historical fiction, romance, and adventure. She has been a public educator -specifically a teacher of the deaf and hard of hearing- for most of her career but has dabbled in creative writing her entire life. Outside of writing, Jalyn also enjoys gardening, painting, and spending quality time with her family. If you enjoyed reading A Storm Summoned, please consider leaving a review. If you'd like to receive updates on upcoming works, you can visit https://jcwade-originals.mailchimpsites.com to be added to the newsletter mailing list.

# *Also By*

**The Fate of Our Sorrows: a prequel novella**

Carlisle, England

-1287-

Join Edyth in this prequel novella to its companion piece, <u>The White Witch's Daughter</u>, as she navigates the complexities of self-discovery, only nine short years before her life takes a most devastating turn.

Nine-year-old Edyth DeVries does not know she's different. She does not yet understand what fate has in store for her. But after a terrifying nightmare becomes a reality, she questions who she is, and what her visions could mean.

**The White Witch's Daughter, Book One**
**There is no such thing as a secret kept, so long as the bearers live and breathe.**
—England 1296—

Losing her mother to the witch's noose—and her father to those who placed her there—Lady Edyth DeVries flees for her life into the wilds of Scotland. With all her hopes pinned upon reuniting with the only family left to her, Edyth is tormented as a keeper of a dangerous secret—one that she is only just beginning to unravel. As King Edward I of England dismantles loyalties and spills innocent blood, Edyth traverses the deadly landscape with little hope of success. On all sides bitter conflict looms yet help comes from an unlikely source. But can Edyth trust Ewan, the heroic, young Scots knight with her secret -or with her heart?

## A Conjuring of Valor,  Book Two
### *1296 Scotland:*

In the village of Perthshire, Edyth Ruthven finds that life as the new mistress of the household is not as comfortable as she'd hoped. Rejected by her husband's people as an outsider with a dangerous reputation, Edyth struggles to make a place for herself amid the rampant rumors of her past.

What's more, Edyth struggles to make sense of her nightmares, forewarning of a deadly event fast approaching. When her only friend and good sister Caitriona is forced into an arranged marriage, the full weight of a divided and prejudiced people falls upon her shoulders. Ewan, meanwhile, walks along the edge of a twin blade, forced to choose between loyalty to his own people or to embrace the English King. When a nefarious sheriff is appointed to their lands, the life the Ruthvens had hoped for unravels before their very eyes, leaving them in a tangle of wicked machinations set forth by the wicked sheriff.

Made in the USA
Middletown, DE
27 August 2023